LEVIATHAN'S FEAR
©2022 CRAIG MARTELLE

This book is protected under the copyright laws of the United States of America. No part of this publication may be reproduced, stored in a retrieval system, or transmitted, in any form or by any means, without the prior permission in writing of the publisher, nor be otherwise circulated in any form of binding or cover other than that in which it is published and without a similar condition including this condition being imposed on the subsequent purchaser. Any reproduction or unauthorized use of the material or artwork contained herein is prohibited without the express written permission of the authors.

Aethon Books supports the right to free expression and the value of copyright. The purpose of copyright is to encourage writers and artists to produce the creative works that enrich our culture.

The scanning, uploading, and distribution of this book without permission is a theft of the author's intellectual property. If you would like to use material from the book (other than for review purposes), please contact editor@aethonbooks.com. Thank you for your support of the author's rights.

Aethon Books
www.aethonbooks.com

Print and eBook formatting by Steve Beaulieu. Artwork provided by Vivid Covers.

Published by Aethon Books LLC.

Aethon Books is not responsible for websites (or their content) that are not owned by the publisher.

This book is a work of fiction. Names, characters, places, and incidents are the product of the author's imagination or are used fictitiously. Any resemblance to actual events, locales, or persons, living or dead is coincidental.

All rights reserved.

To those who support any author by buying and reading their books, I salute you. I couldn't keep telling these stories if it weren't for you and for the support team surrounding me. No one works alone in this business.

SOCIAL MEDIA

Craig Martelle Social
Website & Newsletter:
https://www.craigmartelle.com

**Facebook:
https://www.facebook.com/
AuthorCraigMartelle/**

BATTLESHIP: LEVIATHAN TEAM INCLUDES

Beta Readers and Proofreaders—with my deepest gratitude!

Micky Cocker
James Caplan
Kelly O'Donnell
John Ashmore

The Main Players Within
Ambassador/Major Declan Payne
Executive Officer/Major Virgil Dank
Mrs. Ambassador/Lieutenant Mary "Dog" Morris/Payne
CEO Tech Inc/Tech Specialist 7 Katello Mateus "Blinky" Andfen
Tech Specialist 6 Laura "Sparky" Walker
Tech Specialist 6 Augry Byle
Tech Specialist 4 Salem "Shaolin" Shao
Tech Specialist 4 Huberta "Joker" Hobbes
Combat Specialist 7 Cointreau "Heckler" Koch
Combat Specialist 5 Marsha "Turbo" Skellig
COO Tech Inc/Combat Specialist 3 Alphonse "Buzz" Periq

[1]

"Space is vast, but nothing compared to what one person can accomplish in the company of friends." –From the memoirs of Ambassador Declan Payne

"They'll hit us as soon as we enter normal space." Leader of the Seven Races Declan Payne studied the tactical board. By using the neural net sensing system Lev had developed, he was able to see the Ga'ee ships searching for him but was able to avoid their detection using the masking technology they employed on their own ships.

It was the only reason *Leviathan* was still alive.

"I need to stop in normal space for an extended period of time if I am to fix the fold drive." Leviathan used telepathy to communicate with the crew, but they always perceived it as if he were speaking aloud.

"Therein lies the problem," Admiral Harry Wesson replied. "Once we enter normal space, they seem to be able to see us."

Lev was painfully aware of the challenges. He was afraid, not that he would die, but that he would fail, and humanity would be obliterated by the silicon-based beings. Built for war to protect the peace. He couldn't stay neutral, and he couldn't make war on ten thousand planets.

"I think that's only because of their extensive network since this is their space." Payne pointed at the board, which showed a seemingly infinite number of red icons scattered around them. "They are everywhere. Once we enter normal space, we tend to block neural transmissions. Instead of seeing us, they see an empty spot that shouldn't be empty. They've correctly interpolated that to mean God 1," Lev replied. The sentience that ran the most powerful warship in the galaxy was the ship itself. He was also a pacifist.

Until the Ga'ee showed up in the seven races' sectors of the galaxy and attempted to eradicate all carbon-based sentient life. They could not be negotiated with. They could not even be fought except by a fleet of ships. Their capabilities far surpassed any of the seven races' ships but not that of *Leviathan*, a ship of Godilkinmore design.

"If we can change course while in a sensor shadow, then they might lose track of us. We can hide behind a black hole or in a quasar."

"A nebula, maybe," Lev replied, "but trying to hide near a black hole where the strain would possibly destroy me isn't something I'm willing to do. A quasar is a greater threat to the ship by orders of magnitude. We won't be hiding in there. You used to be smart."

"I'm fighting not to be the smartest guy. You know what they say, Lev. If you're the smartest in the room, time to find a better room." Payne gave Lev two thumbs-ups. During the process of inserting the Ebren language into his brain, Lev had added the entirety of human knowledge. Payne's mind was active and contained the information, but he had yet to find a way to access it. He had subconsciously partitioned it away from himself.

He knew it was there, and it frustrated him. Lev's efforts to help him discipline his mind had fallen short, probably because of the stress of fighting an intergalactic war in which all humanity would die if they lost. It made it hard to focus on anything else. He had no hope of clearing his mind to let the knowledge flow.

"Okay, not a quasar," Payne admitted. "There has to be something that affects the neural waves they use to communicate. That's where we have to go."

"Inside a planet."

Payne and the admiral looked at each other. "Tell me he's joking."

Major Payne shook his head. "I don't think he is. What do you know that we don't know, Lev?"

"That list is quite long, but I expect you mean as it relates to my suggestion." Lev waited until Payne rolled his finger to continue. "Since I have the entirety of the Ga'ee's star surveys in my database, I've discovered that four hundred light-years closer to the heart of Ga'ee space is a planet the Ga'ee cannot use because it is a hollow shell—almost a Dyson sphere. It has no atmosphere, which will ease our entry inside unless we re-enter normal space within the planet itself."

Payne blinked quickly, then tilted his head back and stared at the ceiling. For a brief moment, the calculations necessary to fly with such precision raced through his mind. He embraced and massaged them, and still the task seemed impossible. More variables. He needed to account for more variables, which would add to the complexity of the equation.

The admiral was more straightforward. "Can you do that?"

"That is the question, is it not?" Lev replied. "Can I re-enter normal space at the right place and right time to hit a target four hundred light-years distant? I believe *we* can. We have three of the brightest minds in the entire galaxy right here.

Putting them all together, we should be able to. I'll cross my fingers, too."

The admiral studied the tactical screen. There was no place to go. They'd be harried for months if they didn't get the fold drive fixed. The chain of tragedy was filled with heavy links that could not be broken if *Leviathan* continued its journey while limited to FTL speed. When they finally arrived in friendly space, they'd be followed by an armada filled with the latest Ga'ee technology. Drones that didn't go ballistic when their carrier died. Overwhelming numbers of carriers that dwarfed the survey ships.

"We have to risk it. Find a place to change course without being too obvious." That was the admiral's code for "make sure the enemy couldn't track them as they headed into the maelstrom at the heart of Ga'ee space." Ten thousand conquered worlds. "Have we picked a battle we can't win?"

"Did you pick the war?" Lev countered.

"We did not. The Ga'ee came to us."

"Then you can only do your best when it comes to selecting where to fight the battles because if you do not, the Ga'ee surely will."

"Lev, no one has to worry about being the smartest guy when you're around. Sometimes, you have to feel like you're saddled with us. Like we're nothing more than an infestation since we are so far below you on the evolutionary scale."

"Don't sell yourself short, Harry. I enjoy the company of those on board. Very much so."

Payne refocused and fixed the admiral with clear eyes. "Lev, I've sent you the calculations to target the planet in question. All you have to include is the target planet's current location, orbital velocity and trajectory, stellar drift, intergalactic rotation, stellar body gravitic influences, and point of origin."

"Is that all? I thought there would be more," the admiral quipped.

"There is, but those are already well in hand," Payne replied seriously.

The admiral shrugged.

"I'll run these past Davida, and we'll work on them. Thank you for doing the core work, Declan. How many decimal places should our calculations be made to?"

A setup question. "All of them, of course. If we can't, then we may end up in the middle of a star a full system away. Over the course of four hundred light-years, we cannot be off more than a few hundred kilometers. The math is simple, Admiral. Two hundred divided by nine point four six one times ten to the twelfth power times four hundred. That is our margin of error. To express it as a percent, move two decimal places to the right."

The admiral had expected that the probability of error was massive. He waved a hand as if the margin was inconsequential. "I expect that also means flying through the access to get inside the planet, so is the margin of error still two hundred kilometers, or is it something less? No matter. Don't make any mistakes."

Payne didn't acknowledge the madness. They needed more data to make the calculations. Were they up for the challenge? They had to be.

There were all kinds of ways to die in space. Almost all of them were fast. If they hit the entrance, it would be at the speed of light, assuming the entrance was facing their approach vector.

"Are you sure you want to shoot for all the way inside the planet?" the admiral wondered.

"Or we get swarmed by the Ga'ee," Payne replied. "It's the risk we assumed when we took the fight to the enemy. Everything we did from that point was life or death, but the goal is worthy. We fight for all humanity and every other living creature from our sectors." He shook his head and chuckled. "That's the do-it-for-all-mankind speech. None of us needs that. We're all volunteers. We knew the risk. Lev, take your best shot. Here's hoping that we don't hit anything. I think I'm going to have a beer. Well, after we pivot."

"Distance calculated. Ten minutes until we drop into normal space. I'll let everyone know."

"Mosquitoes, assume ready-launch status but remain on board unless I give the order to depart. Payne, you too. Lev, prepare to fight. All defensive weapons active. Ga'ee shields up."

Payne ran from the bridge to a cart waiting in the corridor.

"I'll be ready, Harry. The second we drop out of FTL, everything will be live. May the good grace of all the gods bless us on this sacred journey."

"Since when did you find religion, Lev?" the admiral asked.

"I thought I'd give it a try to make you feel more comfortable."

"You know what I'm thinking, so what's your estimate of how it's working?"

"It seems it has had the opposite of the intended effect."

"There you are. You got it in one guess."

"I didn't have to guess, Harry. My apologies. I shall marshal the incredible intellect and resources at my command to protect the ship and everyone within by dominating the enemy and bending him to my will."

"That has to be counter to your guiding principles, but I'll take it over praying for luck."

"It is within my programming to fight an enemy that is a threat to all otherwise there will be nothing left to save. At some point, maybe even the Ga'ee will give up."

"If you ever have an idea of what it will take to make the Ga'ee give up, let me know and we'll do it. It'd be better if we didn't have to die, but that's not a limiting factor."

"I have been on the lookout for the "golden bullet" as you would say since we arrived in Ga'ee space, but I have not yet found it."

Admiral Wesson sat down. He knew that he'd be standing soon enough.

Payne's cart raced through the doors to the starboard side hangar bay and straight up to the nearby team area where twelve powered combat suits waited. They doubled as environmental suits, too, but their main purpose was for combat. They were cleaned and ready to go, as they always were. They looked new even though they had survived a great number of encounters, combat, and harsh conditions. One of the suits was much larger than the others, a complete suit for Kal'faxx versus the helmet only that the Ebren champion had been using.

The burning Ga'ee ship had prevented him from deploying. His body could withstand the cold of space but had no ability to manage the intense heat of plasma fire. Even the team's suits had suffered, but they escaped before anyone was injured.

The others were already getting dressed. The combat specialists, Cointreau "Heckler" Koch and his better half, Marsha "Turbo" Skellig tossed their clothes aside and were first into their suits. Others, like Augry Byle, Salem "Shaolin" Shao, and Huberta "Joker" Hobbes folded their jumpsuits neatly, spending more time in the buff than the rest of the team.

Major Virgil Dank, the team's executive officer, its XO, was happy tossing his jumpsuit on the deck. He ran his suit through its paces quickly. Laura "Sparky" Walker was the team engineer. She worked on big systems, like ship-sized weapons and power plants. The cyber-engineering specialists, Katello "Blinky" Andfen and Alphonse "Buzz" Periq, weren't present.

Lev needed them to continue to work on breaking the neural net code of the Ga'ee. They'd deciphered the language, but the new conversations they'd found in this part of space were encrypted in some way. They had to break the code. Nothing was more important than that. The two were plugged directly into Lev's processing power.

That left Mary Payne. She'd joined as Payne's XO, but with Virgil's return, she'd accepted a role as combat specialist and was almost killed. She'd then left the team to be a logistics specialist but returned when she discovered it was easier to be at risk than to wait on board *Leviathan* while her husband was missing. She returned to the team in her combat specialist role. She had bulked up for it but had a long way to go to be close to what Turbo was capable of doing.

Kal struggled to get his suit on. It was the first time he'd deployed. The others dressed, grabbed their helmets, and moved to *Ugly 6*, the newest iteration in the long line of uglymobiles that were getting progressively bigger with added combat capability.

By flying at FTL speed, Lev maintained his production capability. Otherwise, there would have been no new combat suits or uglymobiles.

It was a positive tradeoff in a bad situation.

"Hurry up, Kal." Payne started to get into his suit but thought he'd be more help outside of it. Kal had twisted his legs about when climbing in.

"A warrior fights naked!" he argued.

"For Pete's sake, get in the suit, you big baby. You have to get out first and then climb back in."

"Are you trying to motivate me, Declan?" Kal asked.

"I'm trying not to leave you behind." Payne pointed at the right leg hole.

"Four minutes," Lev announced.

Kal shoved his leg in, then teetered precariously. Payne steadied him, using both hands and bracing himself to do so. "Your balance is better than that, Kal. Come on. Take it like a man."

"I'm not a man. And men take sound beatings. I've seen it for myself. Hell, I've done it myself. To you!" Kal drawled.

"Only one of us walked out of that ring, Kal. Don't make me relive the pain of my victory."

"That you did." Kal worked his left foot in and stood. With a command, the suit secured itself up the back. He flexed his fingers within the gloves and took a halting step.

Payne jumped into his suit, and it buttoned up while he walked away. He had to return for his railgun. He jogged to *Ugly 6* and climbed in with less than two minutes remaining until *Leviathan* re-entered normal space.

"Hang on to your butts! This is going to be the wildest ride yet!" Payne shouted. The team stared at him as if he'd grown a second head.

"Excuse me, sir?" Heckler waved a hand to get Payne's attention. The major ignored him.

"Anyone else have any questions?" Payne asked.

"Sir?" Heckler pressed.

Payne pointed at him. "Yes, Specialist Koch?"

"Are we going to leave the ship this time? We seem to have a perfect record of boarding the uglymobile and remaining within the uglymobile without moving, only to return to the equipment area to change back into our clothes. I move that we declare a motion of hope since it's about time we do something."

The outer doors rotated down, and the screens lit up. Forty seconds to transition.

"Heckler, I'd like to point out that leaving the security of the ship when there's nothing we can do to make a difference in the battle outside would be sheer folly. I must be the first to admit, we've done some massive folly on this team, but all of us dying for no reason will never happen on my watch. It would be the folliest of follies."

Heckler raised his hand.

Payne closed his eyes. When he opened them, there were still twenty seconds. He tipped his chin toward the combat specialist.

"You don't wear a watch."

Payne picked up his helmet. "Helmets on." He led the way; his was the first to snap into place. The heads-up display brightened. The team's suits changed from red to green as their helmets locked and their environmental controls took over. Pulses ranged from sixty to seventy for the human members. Kal's was a solid thirty beats per minute, normal for him.

Three...two...one.

A short wave of nausea passed as they transitioned to normal space. The tactical screen populated with a huge bright spot of the star they were too close to. Initially, nearby space showed clear, but within two seconds, red icons populated.

Leviathan was surrounded.

[2]

"First to fire isn't necessarily the first to win a fight, but it sure does help." –From the memoirs of Ambassador Declan Payne

Commander Yeldon of the *Levant* watched the screen for the Ga'ee ship. They had received a communique transferred via a ship traveling at phased FTL speed that had registered using the energy vibration technology Lev had provided to the Fleet. It meant they could send messages across vast distances instantaneously, but they were one-way. Only a ship that executed a series of FTL moves for precise times down to hundredths of a second could reply using a code initially developed by the crew of *Cleophas*.

The Ga'ee carrier was coming to BD23, one of three surviving Berantz worlds.

Hunter-Killer Squadron Two, HK2, was ready for them. Only four Payne-class battlewagons strong, but that was more than enough to mass fire and destroy a carrier. They'd been tested once before, and it had cost them a ship.

Yeldon didn't feel a difference this time, just like he thought they were ready last time.

"Give me the squadron, please," he requested.

"Broadcast is open," the communications officer replied.

"Hunter-Killer Squadron Two. Prepare to fire your main weapon. Target data as soon as we have it."

The countdown clock ticked past the estimated arrival by five seconds, then ten.

"Be ready. He's going to come out right on top of us. Prepare to fire Rapiers!"

The Ga'ee ship finally appeared in normal space right on top of them.

Ship-to-ship missiles with ten-megaton warheads jumped out of the battlewagons, which were little more than massive weapons platforms, and raced across the void. Time to target was only one second.

Not enough time for the Ga'ee to raise their shields. *Levant* transmitted the code to keep the shields down.

But there *was* time, and despite the golden key, the shields rose. The first missiles out of the tubes splashed against the energy barrier. More pounded helplessly against the energy shield as the kilometers-long hangar bay doors opened.

Yeldon growled.

"We do it the hard way. Fire the mains. Three, two, one. *Now!*"

The four battlewagons fired, though not quite simultaneously since they were at different distances and different levels of adrenaline-fired response times. The shields shuddered under the first two shots but stayed in place. The third and fourth shots took it down and penetrated, the beam weapons doing little damage after being dispersed by the remainder of the shield.

"Recover to a secondary firing position," Yeldon ordered.

Drones flooded into the void.

"Defensive weapons on automatic."

The weapons systems officers frantically tapped the settings at their terminals while trying not to look at the image filling the screen.

The stark gray Ga'ee ship filled the screen. Utilitarian design meant no aesthetics. It didn't need to intimidate through sharp lines or prominent weapons pods. It performed its function. The drones within performed their duties as well. The cloud of three-pointed craft accelerated out of the hangar bay and toward the battlewagons. The speartips of the three arms extending from the outside of a small, central core pointed at *Levant*, their intended target.

"Rapiers, fire!" Yeldon ordered even though defensive missiles and projectiles and energy weapons streamed across the short distance to be intercepted by the drones. Massive explosions filled the screen.

As *Levant* accelerated backward from the Ga'ee carrier, it maintained its orientation to keep the primary weapon trained on the target so it could fire the instant it was reenergized.

It was a race against time.

BW08, *Africa*, accelerated toward the enemy, flushing all tubes in a mad rush.

"No suicide runs!" Yeldon shouted at the screen, but it was too late to change anything.

However, it wasn't a suicide run but a calculated risk. The ship accelerated faster, moving forward rather than back. The drones wouldn't be able to accelerate to maximum before impacting the ship, which would result in less if any damage. If the Ga'ee ship was destroyed, the drones would become inconsequential. *Africa* veered over the top of the Ga'ee, clearing it by hundreds of meters. The closer, the better.

Thousands of drones bounced harmlessly off *Africa's* keel while the void filled with the fury of secondary blast effects, concussion, and radioactivity. Missiles flashed from launch tubes arriving instantly at the desired target. Drones attacked the open hatches before they could close and forced their way inside. There would be no second wave.

Levant continued to accelerate away.

Too slowly. Drones smashed into it, ripping and tearing at the outer hull and attacking the launch tubes and weapons ports. The defensive systems cleared a massive swath, but it wasn't enough. As Major Payne's after-action report on fighting the battlewagons had stated, the beam weapon was vulnerable to attack from within the firing tube, which was easily breachable by something as small as a Ga'ee drone or as large as a stealthy insertion craft.

The focus of their defensive weapons fire was to protect the main weapon.

"Twenty seconds," the weapons officer reported, the countdown until the beam weapon could fire again.

More Rapiers launched into the void.

They were intercepted by drones.

Explosions temporarily blew holes in the drone swarm between the battlewagons and the Ga'ee carrier, but the gaps refilled too quickly for the Hunter-Killer squadron to exploit the opportunities. The human force only needed to buy a little more time. The main weapons would do what needed to be done.

Drone clouds flooded into positions between the battlewagons and the carrier.

"The Ga'ee are going to intercept the mains," Weapons reported evenly.

"One more salvo of Rapiers, please. Indirect course around the swarms. All ships. Fire."

Africa was only able to launch twenty-one of the huge ship-to-ship missiles. They arced away, and the launch tubes were immediately attacked. The drones ripped off the outer hatches and foiled the interior guidance rails, twisting the metal to prevent the tube from reloading.

"Only one tube remains viable."

One shot. It was all they had left.

Systems status board flashed pips of red when the first wave of drones hit more than just the launch tubes. "Keep the beam weapon clear," Yeldon ordered unnecessarily.

By splitting the drone swarm, the Ga'ee weakened their attacks on the battlewagons, which were hardened to defend against the drones. They had been built with one enemy in mind.

Chain guns, lasers, railguns, plasma, and short-range missiles filled the space in front of the battlewagon. At the cyclic rate, the weapons would burn out. One minute was the maximum time they could engage.

That was twenty seconds longer than they needed.

The main weapon's status flashed from red to green.

"Fire the main!" Yeldon roared loud enough for the Ga'ee to hear. He surged out of the captain's chair. Two beam weapons lit the void, splashing thousands of drones on its way to the carrier.

Too many drones.

The beam hammered the carrier, ripping away the hangar bay doors and torching the inside of the hangar, but they were too weak to penetrate farther.

Two more beams from the outlying battlewagons raged from the huge swirling vortices in their prows into the drones to lay waste. They filled the void with even more debris, adding to the bits and pieces of the battlewagon that was already out there, parts of the ships ripped away by the force of the energy beam.

On the Ga'ee's part, that energy came from kinetic strikes. The Hunter-Killer squadron delivered energy from power plants surged to maximum for the engagement. Both forces hoped the physics of the attack would overwhelm the defensive abilities of their enemy.

The Ga'ee carrier briefly glowed under the energy delivered before returning to a cooled state. It would launch no more drones, but it didn't need to. It only needed to control the drones filling the space surrounding it.

The clouds accelerated toward their individual targets. *Levant. Russia. Africa. Australia.* Four remaining battlewagons from an initial deployment of five ships.

Yeldon remained standing. The air seemed to disappear from the bridge. The weapons officer closed his eyes.

"Transition to FTL, all ships. Rally at BD27."

"Wait!"

In the silence of a defeated crew, an incessant tone signaled a missile on final approach. The weapons officer checked his screen. Rapiers had gotten through. Not all, only a fraction, but fifteen megatons of explosive force zeroed in on the spine of the Ga'ee carrier. Missiles from each battlewagon had arced past the drone clouds.

They accelerated to maximum, burning the last of their fuel to deliver the greatest impact for maximum penetration before exploding inside the hull to punch into the ship's vulnerable guts.

The first explosion amidships shook the entire carrier. It lurched, and metal rippled like a wave of water racing outboard from the point of impact. The next two hit aft and delivered devastating results, tearing off two kilometers of the ship, multiple power plants, and the engines. A mini sun appeared within the resulting rupture as the Ga'ee's energy sources unleashed their explosive fury.

The next missile hit forward and traveled through the bay to the reactor. The resulting blast broke what was left of the carrier's back. The ship came apart in an expanding fireball of released gases, energy, and debris.

The drones lost their drives, assumed ballistic courses, and started bouncing off the hulls of the four remaining ships of Hunter-Killer Squadron Two.

"Begin repairs. Recover metal as necessary to support the process."

Yeldon slouched in his seat.

"Comm, give me the fleet."

"Channel is open, sir."

"All hands, your diligence saved us today. *Levant* is down to a single Rapier tube. Our priority is to repair our launch tubes. After that, we'll repair other systems. Since the coding to take down the Ga'ee shields no longer works, we'll have to do it the hard way. As soon as our missile launch status is higher than ninety percent, we will execute a series of FTL burns to send that message to all sectors. Five-ship squadrons to engage the Ga'ee or risk losing the battle. Yeldon out."

[3]

"A better mousetrap achieves the same thing as the original, much to the mouse's dismay." –From the memoirs of Ambassador Declan Payne

"Defensive systems at maximum," Lev reported in a cheerful voice. The tactical board showed ten thousand drones scattered across the space—not too much of a threat—but there were new ships, too.

Spherical and a kilometer in diameter.

"What are those, Lev?" Admiral Wesson asked.

As the drones neared the ship, even at their fantastic rate of acceleration, lasers and plasma fired by railguns sniped them from the sky. It was nothing more than target practice for *Leviathan*. Had the numbers been ten times that count, as they'd seen before, *Leviathan* would have been destroyed.

"Mines."

Payne's mouth fell open. He was still in *Ugly 6*. The team watched the tactical board intently.

The admiral said what they were all thinking. "Why would

someone make mines that are a kilometer in size and then deploy them within their own territory?"

"Suggests that we might not be the first to come to Ga'ee space," Lev replied.

"It also suggests that whoever came before us needed to be blown up with a mine the size of a small moon," Payne added.

"It's nowhere near the size of a small moon, Declan," Lev clarified.

"It's more than a billion times the size of a usual mine." Payne used his hands to show the size of a large dog.

"We might have erred." The admiral shook his head while continuing to stare at the board. "When can you get us out of here, Lev?"

The two closest spheres started accelerating without an obvious means of propulsion.

"Momentarily," Lev replied.

The drones massed away from *Leviathan*, grouping to make their attack more effective and overwhelm the point defense systems.

"Who's controlling the drones?" Payne asked.

"Faster-than-light drive is down," Lev reported.

"How in the fuck does that happen?"

"Breach," Lev announced. "Drones have accessed the hangar bay and penetrated into the interior of the ship."

Payne gestured toward the side doors of *Ugly* 6. "Dismount!" The doors swung upward. Payne snapped his helmet into place and was the second one off the ship, right after Major Dank. The team members followed them out.

The team's HUDs populated. The breach was on the other side, where most of the space fighters were located. The drones were flying down the corridors but were trapped on this deck. Eight drones.

Sixteen.

"Mosquitoes, point defense, port hangar bay. Stop the intrusion!" the admiral ordered.

Commander Woody Malone had seen the drones break through the hangar bay door moments before. The pilots had been in their ships, ready to launch, but they had been told not to leave *Leviathan*.

They had been caught by surprise because the Ga'ee shield was supposed to protect them, for a short time at least. Yet, it did not. It hadn't even slowed the drones down.

"Face the hangar bay doors and light 'em up," Woody ordered, bringing his ship to a hover so he could more quickly change his firing angle. He lined up on the breach as the starting point of his sector of fire to overlap with the fighter next to his. With a thought, his cannon barked and splashed a drone coming through, then two more. The next fighter over blasted intermittently. With two ships firing, it reduced the intrusions through the single penetration to zero.

The drones stopped coming.

Impacts on the hangar doors let the Tricky Spinsters know they were coming along a wide front.

The space fighters taxied through the hangar bay to create a defensive force, aiming outboard.

"Better watch our six. Fourteen and nineteen, watch inboard. The bastards are behind us, too."

Two "Rogers" followed, and the fighters pulled out of line and moved into position facing the two main exit corridors leading into *Leviathan*.

A flurry of drones ripped a new opening with the violent fury of multiple and simultaneous high-speed impacts. The door split, and more drones expanded the breach. "Ace" Barton and "Deli" Sennich fired individual shots, but the rent was too large. They took turns with timed fire, ten shots a second up and down the breach. A single plasma impact was good for a kill if it struck home.

If in doubt, cycle the guns. Saved ammunition doesn't help if it gets you killed.

More breaches appeared as the relentless drone attack continued. Space Fighter Squadron 317, the Tricky Spinsters, addressed each new breach with firepower, maintaining steady rates of fire without overdoing it. After thirty seconds, they stopped overlapping fire as the number of breaches grew. One ship per breach until the number of breaches outgrew the number of Mosquitoes.

"Hey, Lev, we probably need to get out of here, or we're going to have some problems."

"FTL is still down," Lev replied.

"Virge, take four starboard side aft. I'm going to port." Payne accelerated down the corridor leading from one hangar bay to the other.

"Sparky, Turbo, Byle, and Dog, with me," Major Dank ordered. They took an immediate left and ran toward the engine space.

Lev had shut down the inter-deck ramps to keep the Ga'ee from using them, but the vertical shafts in the engine space were subject to breach.

The Ga'ee were searching and incrementally destroying equipment.

A drone on guard accelerated toward Major Dank as soon as he came into view. The XO fired, and the two SOFTies on his flanks fired as well. The three railguns unerringly took the drone and its partner out.

The HUD flashed fourteen.

Dank slowed as he approached the hatches leading to the engine room. They'd been shredded by the piercing tines of the drones, ripping the metal and peeling the hatches out of the way.

Inside, they found two drones in the vicinity of an electrical switching station, jabbing it repeatedly.

Dank killed them with three well-aimed rounds. The drones tumbled to the deck, looking intact but for the holes through their brain centers.

The HUD showed twelve, but where? Four more were supposed to be in this space, but they couldn't see them. "Spread out." Virgil gestured to his right, flashing two fingers, and to his left with two more fingers. He hatcheted down the middle for himself, then walked slowly, looking down the barrel of his rifle, ready to fire wherever he looked. The HUD showed movement.

They were in there.

"Why can't we see them?" Turbo growled. Fear rose in their throats.

Invisible drones.

"They're not invisible," Dank groused. Movement. He zeroed in. "There he is!" Dank fired before he ran to get a better angle.

Turbo lit up an access tube using fully automatic fire when she found a drone shredding the walls to get at the cabling beneath.

Dog fired into the overhead, and a second later, Sparky joined her. They dodged out of the way as the drone made a kamikaze run at them. It was dead by the time it impacted the deck, gouging the metal deeply when it crashed. The drone slid across the deck and slammed into the bulkhead, where it came to a rest.

The HUD showed one more. Dank ran ahead, and Dog and Sparky ran after him. Turbo and Byle took firing positions near the corridor in case the last drone got past their teammates.

A vertical access hatch had been breached. Dank dipped his head in and back out. He had seen nothing, but sensors showed the drone was somewhere below. He activated his lights and took a longer look down. The shaft was clear.

"Going down," he told Dog and Sparky. He hung into the shaft until he caught the ladder attached to the side and hurried down. Dog leaned over and forwarded her visual feed to Dank's HUD. He could see himself descending while looking straight ahead at the handholds.

Sensors showed movement below. He caught a silver flash.

"Look out!" Dog shouted. Dank swung sideways off the ladder to hang on with one hand and stand on one foot while he tried not to shoot through his boots. The drone accelerated upward. Dank's aim was all over the place until the drone was so close he couldn't miss.

Dank thought he hit it in the sweet spot, but it rammed him and peeled him off the ladder. He started to fall and grabbed one of the drone's three forward-facing sword-like blades. The Ga'ee device started to fall.

The count on Payne's HUD dropped quickly, then stopped at eleven. He didn't have time to think about it since he had his own challenges coming up.

Two drones met them as they rounded the corner into the longitudinal corridor. Payne snap-fired wildly, missing both. The drones were too close to accelerate quickly, but their armor-shredding tines didn't need much speed to tear through a combat suit.

Payne dove out of the way. Behind him, Heckler fired. Kal fired, too; he carried a plasma cannon. Both drones blasted backward after the plasma eruption, then bounced down the corridor and settled on the deck, their wreckage still smoking from the plasma impact.

Joker fired two rounds, one for each drone, as added insurance.

The HUD count dropped to nine. Payne climbed to his feet. "Lev, why are the internal sensors not showing us exactly where those are? We should have known a drone was mere feet away from us."

"The ships are bouncing my signal, which is yet another new development in this part of space."

Payne couldn't be angry with the AI. He was doing the best he could. The Ga'ee kept throwing curveballs.

"Keep your heads on a swivel," Payne told his team. He hoisted his railgun and headed down the corridor. The HUD showed eight drones remaining.

Dank must have killed one more.

Payne didn't need a report. He only needed to know where the final eight were.

Straight ahead.

Kind of.

Maybe.

"Two by two, people." Major Dank had taken the center, but Payne held down the point position. Heckler moved left with Joker. Kal moved right with Shaolin. "Take it easy with the cannon, Kal. This is our engine room, and we don't want to blow it up. Are you ready with maintenance bots, Lev?"

"I am. They are. We will make the repairs as quickly as possible, with the bots from six decks ready to move in the second it's safe to do so," Lev replied.

Payne acknowledged the information. He moved quickly

into the engine space with the team close behind. They flared out to cover the flanks and begin the search. "Looking for eight drones." The order was unnecessary, but he was anxious. Every second they wasted was one second closer to the drones and mines destroying *Leviathan*. The sounds of metal rending echoed throughout the space. "Hurry."

The first pair of drones was easy to find. They were attempting to penetrate one of the reactors located at the front of the engine. Heckler moved quickly to the side so an errant round wouldn't penetrate the power plant and sniped the first drone. The second pulled back to race away, but the combat specialist was too quick and too good. He knocked it down with one shot and killed it with the second.

Kal ran past an equipment complex that had been torn loose from its mounts and rammed against the bulkhead to get to the next area. When he got there, the sounds of a sledgehammer hitting an anvil reverberated through the soles of his boots.

Beside the engine were two drones in a confined space, hammering on a restraining support that held the engine in place—a delicate balance that needed not to be upset. Kal lined up the two drones and fired a single round from the plasma cannon. It blasted the first one into the second and sent the resulting piles of scrap into the bulkhead beyond. They crashed to the deck.

Shaolin moved next to him and added a point-blank-range railgun shot into the nerve center of each to make sure.

[4]

"Fear slows you down. It makes you incapable of doing what you need to do so you won't be afraid. It's a dichotomy the warrior must master." –From the memoirs of Ambassador Declan Payne

Admiral Wesson shook his fist at the tactical screen. "We have to kill those mines."

Lev launched another salvo of forty-eight Rapier-class missiles at each mine. The drones swirled like a flock of birds, then accelerated to intercept the missiles. The attack lessened but didn't stop.

There were enough drones to destroy everything Lev had brought to this sector of space.

"How did they know we were coming?" the admiral wondered.

"The Ga'ee are so numerous that they could be everywhere in this part of space in these numbers."

"That would be disturbing." Harry watched the missiles, feeling helpless to affect the battle. Lev was fighting the enemy. His very survival was at stake. "Maybe another salvo while the first is still on its way?"

"That would be optimal. I'm ready to launch as soon as the tubes are ready. I'm trying not to expose my launch tubes to an attack."

Commodore Nyota Freeman hurried onto the bridge and headed for the admiral.

"Limited raw materials for repair or manufacture," she reported.

"I could have told you that, Harry," Lev interjected.

"I wanted an eyeballs-on account. Plus, you were busy," the admiral replied.

Nyota shook her head. "Plenty of biomass. Moving nearly a thousand bodies off the ship cut our usage rate when Lev already had enough to last us a hundred years. The Fleet's last resupply of fresh is already running low. They hadn't shared very much, as you suspected."

"I think LeClerc gave us food off his table. I'm not sure we received a full supply, no matter what the president said."

"That would track with what Cookie reported. I also have to say that what we received was good. If LeClerc did give us that load from his own stores, he gave us the best of what he had."

"I'm oddly intrigued by that. He was a company man, a team player for the bureaucrats until Payne got a hold of him. Warped him to think like a Fleetie and put the front-line troops first."

"Maybe he wants to be on the right side of history."

"Or maybe he just wants to do the right thing. Ease his conscience. Taking care of us came with a risk, but he knew the mission we were on."

The first salvo of Rapiers was intercepted by drones one by one until none remained. Lev rolled and fired from the opposite side, sending half a salvo at one mine and half at the other. The missiles arced wide and spread out to frustrate the drones.

More peeled off from the attack on *Leviathan*. Lev cycled

through his defensive systems to kill outbound drones to keep them from reaching the attacking salvo.

With a thought from the admiral, Lev brought up the visual from inside the port hangar bay. The Mosquitoes were arrayed facing the doors, which were peppered with holes and tears.

The space fighters were holding their own but barely. They fired constantly, adjusting but maintaining a rhythmic hammering. Lev included the sounds of the combat that hadn't extended beyond the hangar bay except for the desperate battle Team Payne was fighting to clear out the drones that had penetrated *Leviathan*'s engine and power plants.

"Fire the worldkillers," the admiral requested.

"That might be the only way," Lev agreed.

The second salvo drew the drones away from a direct line of fire to the mines.

Lev aimed at the closest one. The way was clear. "Firing one."

The worldkiller flashed from the massive tube near Lev's keel, immediately transitioned to faster-than-light, and returned to normal space a tenth of a second later. It crashed into the mine and kept going. It exploded at the same time as the mine detonated. The blast washed away from *Leviathan*, taking hundreds of drones with it.

The second mine continued its relentless march toward *Leviathan*.

"Prepare to fire our last worldkiller."

―――

Only four remained. Heckler vaulted to a catwalk and ran like a madman toward the signal on the HUD, even though it was iffy at best.

A steady vibration had followed them down the corridor and into the engine room: the cyclic and periodic fire of a squadron of Mosquitoes fighting to keep more drones from breaching the ship.

Maintenance bots streamed into the space. Payne jerked around and took aim, but the mindless units immediately turned to repairing the most critical systems, fixing the damage at the speed of thought. Payne smiled.

"Nothing gets past us. We need those bots to work without issue. Shaolin, you have bot overwatch. Kal, with me." Payne scaled a ladder to get to a higher catwalk. Kal jumped up, caught the decking, and pulled himself up. He climbed over the rail and stood behind Payne.

Without a word, Payne bolted aft to look for the last pair.

Railgun shots resonated from the other side of the port engine. Payne hesitated to listen. The HUD updated. Only two drones remained.

"Keep jamming, Lev, and get us out of here soon as you can," Payne transmitted.

"That is my plan," the AI replied.

But the drones weren't in the space. A shaft just like the one Major Dank had run across headed down.

"Virgil, heading down the vertical transfer shaft. Any words of wisdom?" Payne slipped past the torn hatch and over the threshold. He opted to use his suit's jets to manage his descent. He kept his legs shoulder-width apart but still couldn't see what was directly below him. It was a physical shortcoming of the suit. "Virge?"

Payne pulled up the other group's vitals. Dank's system showed that he'd been injured and was currently unconscious. "Sparky, what the hell happened to Major Dank?"

"Drone took him down the shaft. Surprise attack from below. We're working our way down there to recover him." The tech specialist sounded businesslike, which was exactly what Payne expected from his team.

"Keep a lookout for the last two drones. They're somewhere around you. Kal and I are headed down. Heckler, secure the access point. Let the bots do their work on the FTL."

"Roger," Sparky and Heckler both replied.

Payne maneuvered to grab the ladder and climb down. He'd save his jets since he could look down every couple rungs without upsetting his balance and flying into the wall.

Kal started to climb down above him, but the Ebren's abilities with the suit were restricted. "Take off your suit, Kal. We're not in space."

Kal leapt up, caught the edge of the access, and pulled himself out. The bots were working to restore the FTL. There was less sense of urgency to destroy the last drones. They only needed to corner them and keep them away from important equipment.

Which was where they were cornering them. Payne wanted to slow down instead of rushing headlong into a death trap.

He continued to descend instead of waiting for Kal. The Ebren would be out of his suit in a moment.

The sensor systems showed the drones were one deck down in an area where they could access the keel side of the engine complex. The engines worked in all orientations by manipulating gravity. They didn't push against a bearing or pressure plate to propel the ship forward, yet the engine had to be held in place and deliver energy in a consistent form.

The drones were attempting to rip the guts out of *Leviathan*.

"Fuck it," Payne growled. He stepped off the ladder and descended at breakneck speed, using his jets to keep himself marginally under control.

He caught the movement on his HUD before he could look —a drone coming toward the shaft.

He turned off his jets and let himself drop. He bent at the waist and put his arms out to keep from tumbling.

A drone appeared below him from a side shaft.

Closing speed was his friend. He needed to hit it before the deadly tines pointed upward.

He tried to spin to hit the side of it when he reached the bottom of the shaft, but he was moving too fast. He crashed down, the force generated by gravity accelerating him downward. The momentum created by the masses of Payne and his suit hit like a train wreck.

The deadly saber points hadn't made it upright. Payne had been in time, but the impact was so violent that it rocked his world. Although his suit and body were not torn in half by the drone, he felt as if they had been. The drone was fazed, but not for long. Payne struggled to get his railgun around so where he could shoot the thing, but his limbs felt like dead weight.

The weight of the major and his suit kept the drone from pulling free, so it started to jerk back and forth. Payne's only option was to hang on. He seized two of its forward-facing points and braced his legs against the side of the shaft, but even with the suit's augmented strength, Payne didn't feel strong enough to hold the drone in place.

His HUD showed movement beyond the access through which the drone had come. Payne couldn't move. "Need a little help," he called softly.

An instant later, a body slammed into him and the drone. He grunted from the impact. Kal's big hand pulled his railgun out from between the suit and the drone. He held on while firing through the access hatch in short, controlled bursts.

He stopped shooting and turned his attention to Payne. Kal pinned the drone with one foot and fired through its brain center. It stopped trying to jerk free. Payne slumped over top of it. He hadn't realized how much energy he had been expending to hold the drone in place.

Kal pulled Payne to his feet. "Life is better when you're upright, pardner," Kal drawled as he handed Payne's railgun back to him.

HUD now showed zero drones inside *Leviathan*. The rhythmic pounding through the hull continued.

Payne held out a gloved hand. "Although our respite may be brief, at least we made it this far."

Kal wrapped his big fingers around the armored hand and shook.

A wave passed over them as the ship transitioned to faster-than-light speed.

Payne almost collapsed in relief. Kal continued to support him.

"Maybe you should lose the suit." Kal helped Payne through the access hatch into a lower engine room. Payne parked the suit and climbed out. That was when it hit him.

"That's gonna leave a bruise. My whole body hurts."

"Off to Medical with you." Kal gave Payne a once-over with a critical eye. "Humans. The galaxy's crystalline marshmallows."

Payne snorted. "How long have you been waiting to use that one?"

"It's been a while."

Virgil has been recovered. He'll join you in Medical, Lev announced in Payne's mind. *Wait where you are. A cart will arrive momentarily.*

"Looks like I get a ride, good buddy." Payne winked at Kal.

The Ebren helped Payne to the cart after it arrived and loaded him in. "Bye, darling. Miss you already."

"I don't know what to say to that, Kal. You keep me on my

toes except for times like now, when I think I'll be happy on my back."

"You better give orders to the team," Kal suggested without a drawl.

"Lev, please pass the following. Heckler, take charge and recover all suits to the team cage. Store the weapons, and give us a countdown until we're going to get where we're going."

"It is done, Declan."

The cart sped away. Payne lounged within, feeling the same way he had felt following the beating Kal had given him.

The cart used the medical lab on that level since it was closer for both majors. Dank groaned at Payne when he arrived.

"Hey, Virge," Payne croaked. He laid back while the equipment worked on him. In the end, he was dumped into an ice bath. He found his voice. "You suck, Lev!"

"Yes, yes, you're welcome. I aim to please," Lev replied in good spirits, then explained the battle that had taken place in and around the ship. The loss of one irreplaceable worldkiller missile.

At least the damage to the FTL engine was reparable.

"It's a sealed system," Lev explained. "Only the power feed to it was disrupted."

The ice's bite dulled the pain. It almost made Declan feel human again. After taking a handful of pills, Payne was able to stand on his own and step out of the tub.

Mary handed him a towel. "Where'd you come from?" Payne asked, looking around. He expected to see others from the team too.

"I was here the whole time," Mary replied easily. "You were in your usual post-combat stupor. I came to see Virgil, but he'll be fine, too. He took a tumble."

"Is everyone heartless today? I jumped down a long shaft to defeat the bad guys." Receiving no sympathy, he continued, "It was farther than I thought. I couldn't use the jets because the drone would have had time to face me, and you know what that would have meant. Why does everyone seem so lackadaisical?"

Mary kissed him and stepped back. "We have thirteen days before we come out of FTL. We're on mandatory downtime, admiral's orders. We need to be ready for next time in case we get more of the same. So, we'll get up close and personal with ship's systems and try to figure out how to keep drones from causing us grief."

Payne nodded. He understood only too well.

"Lots of work to do."

[5]

"Battered and bruised is when it's time to do your best thinking since you can't do a whole lot of doing." –From the memoirs of Ambassador Declan Payne

Leviathan sped onward, deeper and deeper into Ga'ee territory.

Payne limped slightly while Dank used a crutch. Neither was participating in the training Heckler had scheduled—hand-to-hand combat with an eye toward disabling a drone.

Using a mockup of the Ga'ee drone, he pushed and pulled it around their training room. They ran through the paces in slow motion: how to grip one of the three sword-like arms, how to hold it so a teammate could finish it. They maneuvered around it, but it was too slow.

Payne kept shaking his head. "Those things move fast. You have milliseconds to figure it out before you have to act."

"What do you suggest?" Heckler asked.

"Give me a boarding axe." He gimped forward. With the axe in hand, he assumed the spear thrust stance and shoved the point of the axe back and forth as fast as he could. "Practice grabbing that!"

Kal strode forward, crouching as he closed. He tried to time the thrusts, but Payne delivered a staccato in syncopation. Kal lowered his hands, and when there was a new jab, he whipped his hand around to knock the axe aside and spun past the blade to come face to face with the major.

"Nicely done, Kal." Payne put the axe down. "The key is to stay outside the tines. If the damn thing pins you, you're done."

"Even with your suit, you were having a hard time controlling it."

"I was battered and bruised, but yeah. Those things don't want to be held down. Their little engine can accelerate them to fantastic speeds, but that's counting on the minimal friction of space and not having a body pinning it down. Even so, it's stronger than we are, even with a suit."

"Close-in weapons," Heckler said. "We can't fight those things hand to hand. When we were in the corridor, Kal blasted one with the plasma cannon. What if we had a small grenade launcher for close-quarters combat of the explosive kind."

"I like how you think, Heckler. We'll do speed drills over the next twelve days to heighten our hand-eye coordination. Otherwise, it's weapons training. Being able to hit a target approaching you with a short-barreled grenade thrower. Heaven help us if drones penetrate the ship again," Payne lamented.

"I shall harden all the access points using the metal from the drones. With the wreckage you left behind, along with the number of drones littering the hangar bay, we'll put covers on the key systems and lock out spaces. They'll not have as easy a time should they get aboard again," Lev announced.

"How about those hangar doors?"

"Can't fix those until we're stopped and I can send the maintenance bots outside."

"We're vulnerable until we get that repair time," Payne

paraphrased. "Thanks, Lev. I'm sorry you got so beat up out here. We can't seem to catch a break. Bad luck is our only luck."

"I believe we're about to make our own luck, Declan. Then we'll make a difference."

"That's what I like to hear. We'll talk about it later on the bridge. I look forward to your thoughts."

"Firing range!" Heckler shouted. He and Turbo ran out the door without waiting for anyone else.

Payne walked gingerly toward the wall storage, where he stowed the axe. Dank tottered to the hatch and waited. The others were gone by the time he got there, except for Declan and Mary.

"You should probably stay off those." Mary pointed at his heavily bandaged ankles. Not broken was the good news. Sprained to the verge of ligament tears would keep him out of action until the next stop.

"Yes, Mom," Dank replied, earning himself a punch in the chest that almost toppled him.

"It's common sense. Don't be a dillweed."

Dank straightened, giving Mary the hairy eyeball throughout.

"She's right, Virge. You need to heal. Limping around isn't going to make it better any more quickly. Why don't you go to the bridge and keep the admiral company? Send him for a health walk while you hold down the fort."

"He won't leave the bridge. I think he's sleeping in there."

"Lev projects a great view, three hundred and sixty degrees, from twelve o'clock low to twelve o'clock high. It's not a bad place to hang out," Payne replied.

"If you insist, Mr. and Mrs. Ambassador."

Payne held out his hand, and the two men shook. "We took on the drones in CQB, and we won. That's nothing to take lightly. Those things could have killed half the team."

"We interjected our bodies to keep that from happening." Virgil climbed into the waiting cart and rested his feet on top of the dash to reduce the throbbing. The cart left, knowing Declan and Mary wouldn't be going to the bridge. They were heading to the range, even though Payne needed to stay off his legs, too.

The cart took them not to the range but to the Paynes' suite. "What happened? I was thinking firing range with my very best thoughts."

"You've been overruled. I don't want you to be a cripple at the grand old age of thirty-five."

"Is that how old you think I am?" Payne quipped.

"I know you're that old," Mary replied. "It was on the marriage license."

"We have a marriage license?"

"No."

Payne stared at her with a blank expression, his IQ of six million nowhere to be found.

"Lev told me because I strongarmed him."

"He doesn't have arms."

"I think you have a bruised brain, too," Mary offered. "You're in for a long, hot shower, followed by rack time. Sleep. And take this bag of pills Lev gave me for you."

"What did I do to deserve this?" Payne complained.

"Deserve someone who cares about you? I honestly don't know. I need you to clean up and lay down. After that, you can argue with Lev all you want. I'm going to the range to learn how to shoot one of those blasters Heckler was talking about."

Mary waved and tossed her hair over a shoulder before leaving the room. The door quietly closed behind her.

Payne continued his grousing. "I want to go shoot the cool gun, too."

"Mary had parting words for you," Lev announced. Payne

sat on the bed and gestured for Lev to continue. "Take it like a man."

"I'm going to stop using that since it's being misused by the uninitiated."

"Sleep well, Declan," Lev warned.

"Dammit, Lev, don't you dare knock me out!"

Payne didn't remember anything else.

Commander Yeldon read the status reports. There was never a status report that didn't need to be read.

He put them aside. "Weapons, report."

"Seventy percent of missile stock replaced through internal manufacturing. There were no Fleet resupply ships in Berantz space."

Not yet, anyway.

They'd make do.

"Helm, report."

"Engines are at one hundred percent. We can maneuver as needed. FTL is online."

"I like hearing that. Comm, report." Yeldon liked the verbal reports. It engaged the crew rather than the captain performing his sacred duty of reading the almighty status reports. He decided he wouldn't do that. Critical systems could be verbalized in an executive overview. All he had to do was ask.

He relaxed into his seat.

Comm's report wasn't as rosy. "Short range, voice-only channel is operational. Other systems are hard down. Sensor systems are down."

"Priority of repair was to weapons and engines. Be patient. Your time will come. Get me the other ships with that short-range comm if you would be so kind."

It took two minutes before Comm reported that the other three commanders of Hunter-Killer Squadron Two were on.

"Are your ships combat-capable?" Yeldon asked without preamble.

"*Africa* is fifty percent operational. FTL is possible. Weapons systems are shot. We need more construction materials, which we are attempting to collect at present. Blowing the hell out of the carrier scattered the debris to the four winds."

"The alternative was far less savory," Yeldon replied. "Do what you need. I believe we have time. The Ga'ee have already hit this area three times. Is that not enough?"

"*Russia* is at fifty percent as well. We lost a number of personnel and are below minimal staffing. Fifty percent on weapons, and FTL is down."

"I guess we'll see how low we can go and remain nominal," Yeldon replied. There was no extra crew, not without returning to the shipyard and poaching from those waiting for their ships. They couldn't do that until the portal was built.

Which was ongoing at BD23, the system's gas giant. Had the HK squadron not been there, the portal would have been destroyed and the planet infested.

"Good thing we're not going anywhere," Yeldon added. "Priority is to weapons and then engines."

"*Australia* here, and we are at one hundred percent across the board."

"Picket duty for you. No good deed goes unpunished." Yeldon replied. "Weren't you in the same fight as the rest of us?"

"We were, but farther out. We took some hits, but all non-critical systems. Weapons, engines, and sensors are all operational."

"You'll send the FTL message, then. Copy this to send. Destroyed, one carrier, BD23. Minimal losses. Remaining on station. Portal construction at forty percent."

"Got it. Will work up the coding, and we'll be off," the captain of *Australia* replied before signing off. BW09 maneuvered away from the others and the debris, then transitioned through a series of small FTL jumps as a message to those with code books to decrypt them.

"Thanks for attending my meeting. Our visual is down. Otherwise, I would have regaled you with my ninety-seven slides of the most mundane crap you can imagine." The others chuckled. "But no. You've been saved. This time. Tend to your ships and then to your people."

Yeldon motioned for his communications officer to close the channel.

Once free of his squadron command duties, he rose from his seat. "I'll be touring the ship. Call if you need anything."

The commander strode off the bridge, walking like he had a sense of purpose because he did: crew morale. He'd catch them where they were working and let them know that once more, the Hunter-Killer squadron had saved a system from a Ga'ee incursion. There'd be more battles since the Ga'ee seemed to have limitless resources.

That bothered the commander more than anything. At what point would the Ga'ee throw more resources at the system than could be defeated?

Yeldon hoped not to find out while being terrified that he would learn.

[6]

"Nothing like a punch in the mouth to wake you up." –From the memoirs of Ambassador Declan Payne

The tactical screen showed an unexceptional stretch of interstellar space. The Ga'ee were nowhere near, according to the neural network they'd tapped into.

They didn't dare stop. That would show the Ga'ee what God 1 was up to, complete with course and probable destination, along with reinforcing where the ship had gone. They'd be swarmed, although maybe not before they could adjust their course to reduce the margin of error.

The risk wasn't worth it.

"You're confident we'll hit that target?"

"I am nearly one hundred percent certain that we will end up somewhere, Declan," Lev replied.

"With that kind of confidence, how can we miss?" Payne joked. "What do you think, Mary?"

"We stick with the original plan." She was unequivocal.

"That cut and dry?"

"You asked what I thought. It's a good plan. If we stop, the risks are too great. We torpedo our chances of fixing the fold drive. If anything needs to happen, we have to have the ability to get the hell out of Ga'ee space. Otherwise, we'll fight the whole way until they wear us down."

"We're already seeing that. Look at those hangar doors and the hardening of the vulnerable access hatches. And the fact that we're flying at FTL for days on end. I can't imagine what Lev looks like from the outside."

Mary nodded knowingly. *Leviathan* had withstood a great deal and was still flying, but there was only one of him, unfortunately. There were millions of drones. If he died, there would be no more superdreadnoughts.

There would be no one to tell the Ga'ee to stay out of the carbon-based lifeforms' sectors.

"You know, I've been thinking," Mary started.

"Did it hurt?" Payne interrupted.

She gave him her best mean look, which made him laugh. She didn't do a good mean look. "If the Ga'ee destroy plant life on the planets they invade, they are destined to die out when they've killed it all. They need oxygen to live, and plants are the greatest source of oxygen on every planet we've ever been to. How can they survive?

"By taking over new planets, but the Ga'ee can't grow once they've destroyed all the carbon-based life because they need oxygen. They can't do anything with water, so electrolysis to break the oxygen out of water wouldn't be successful once carbon dioxide was too prevalent in the atmosphere, or hydrogen. It would violently recombine with the oxygen with a small spark."

"Are you sure it works that way?" Payne asked. "It would take a lot of hydrogen."

"The Ga'ee will destroy a whole planet. Look what they accomplished at the Berantz homeworld in a month. Half the planet is a wasteland, and it was only half because the Berantz were fighting tooth and nail to keep them from going farther until they lost everything."

"They have to colonize to stay alive because they are so invasive." Payne stared into the distance. Something tickled the back of his mind, but he couldn't solidify the thought. He tried to focus on it, but it slipped away from him.

Mary watched her husband. His ideas didn't come to him in the shower. They came to him when they were talking about something else, creating a catalyst, a cascade of connected thoughts leading to innovation.

"How fragile are we?" Payne asked. "We never thought we were the highest form of life in the galaxy, but we could hold our own. We proved that by fighting the Blaze Collective to a stalemate. Then Lev came along and believed in us. Let us think we were the future—and we were, for our small part of the galaxy. Reality suggests we're little more than a speck of dust."

Payne clasped his hands behind his back and started pacing.

"A speck of dust that is wedged into the eye of the Ga'ee. They can try to root us out, but they're going to hurt themselves doing it. If their resources are limited, then they won't be able to replace their losses. We are killing tens of thousands of drones with each engagement. I think it's time to revisit the beam weapon, too. We need everything at our command. Is there any hope of restoring the worldkiller that we had to use?"

"I can find the necessary components within a Ga'ee carrier, but we'd have to kill it first and then have a few hours to recover the right materials."

"Let's say the answer is no. Makes the beam weapon even more vital. If you can turn their shields off, we can use the beam to cut them in half. We may have to link the Ga'ee power plants into more of the ship."

"That is a great deal to ask. We've fought them off so far

and sent helix worms into their midst to destroy more malevolent code, but I cannot be certain we've got it all since we need the Ga'ee digital instructions to operate their power plants. That's not something I'm able to take over. Not yet, anyway."

"Maybe that can be a priority, although I know you're still trying to decrypt the wealth of signals out there to find a silver bullet or a golden egg or a platinum ring."

Mary wondered, "A platinum ring?"

"Since we were tossing out precious metal metaphors, I thought I'd add one and see if anyone was paying attention."

"Of course, we're paying attention." She shook her head. Payne was always testing the water to see if it was warm enough to dive in.

This time, he was on a different tack. He was trying to talk through ideas to recover the elusive thought until it came to him. Humor was Payne's defense mechanism when things weren't working.

Lev couldn't help. Although he used telepathy, if Payne didn't crystallize the thought in his mind, Lev didn't "hear" it.

"How much time before we return to normal space?" Payne asked.

"One day, Declan. Your trepidations will either be allayed or realized on the morrow."

"I'm not sure if that was meant to be comforting or not, but it wasn't," Payne replied.

"It was my way of counseling patience. There is no value in worrying and keeping your mind from reaching its full potential."

"My mind is a chromatic miasma painted on a fractal landscape," Payne replied. "One day. I hope the rest of the galaxy is getting along without us. I'm not exactly feeling great about what we left behind since the Ga'ee had an invasion fleet poised to swoop in. Waves. They're coming in waves, and we're not ready."

"Why do you say that?" Mary asked.

"Because the Ga'ee must expand to survive. You pointed that out. I bet the number of Ga'ee in this part of space is static, even though it's a really big number. There's nowhere for them to go but into the neighboring sectors of the Milky Way."

"You said we weren't ready. The battlewagons aren't sufficient?"

"They are, but we don't have enough of them, and without the portals in place, we can't move quickly or easily between the Blaze systems. We need a year to be ready. Twenty Hunter-Killer squadrons in place, ready to attack, ready to swarm an unsuspecting Ga'ee fleet..." Payne let his words drift off.

There were three Hunter-Killer squadrons whose crews were barely trained to move the ships around, let alone to fight a determined enemy, but they would make do. Payne expected it would come at a high cost.

"FTL relay registering on the energy vibration system," the sensor operator reported. She quickly decoded the message. "HK2 has destroyed a Ga'ee carrier at BD23. Three ships sustained heavy damage that can be repaired."

Lieutenant Commander Barry Cummins nodded and pressed a button on his console, "Commander, did you see the FTL message?"

"I did," a disembodied voice answered. "I'll be right in."

Commander Jimmy Josephs strolled onto the bridge, exuding the confidence of someone who is comfortable with himself and his decisions, like putting Barry Cummins in the captain's chair. It suited the young man.

"What was the time stamp on the original engagement?" he asked.

The sensor operator answered, "Twelve days ago."

"Does that mean they're not coming to Earth?" Barry wondered, taking a new interest in the tactical display as if a Ga'ee carrier had been there all long and he'd somehow missed it.

Jimmy shook his head. "We need to always assume they're coming."

The portal activated on a link with Vestrall space. "Fresh meat," the weapons officer announced.

"Send the standard welcome message. They are to stage here until a second battlewagon arrives. Then the two will head to Ebren space to fill out HK3 by joining the first three battlewagons currently on their way."

"Roger," the communications officer confirmed while transmitting the message, including the latest information, like that regarding the engagement in Berantz space.

"Captain Trey'gidor of the battle beast *Ebren Champion*. We look forward to returning in triumph to our home planet." The Ebren had gone to Vestrall with the human volunteers to crew the new battlewagons.

Cummins and Josephs looked at each other. Jimmy smiled and shrugged. "Does it matter what they call their ship?"

"I guess not," Barry replied.

Commander Josephs gestured at the communications officer. Once the pickups were live, he nodded at the commander. "Captain Trey'gidor, welcome to Earth. As soon as the second Ebren-crewed ship arrives, we'll send you both. We realized it was better to have two ships traveling together in case of trouble. The Ga'ee are doing what they can to cause us grief."

"The second ship is right behind me, Commander. We are ready to go."

"Set your course, and once the ship is here, get underway. The Ga'ee wait for no one."

"I like your attitude. We are ready to strike first and strike hard."

"Keep training your crew, Captain. The Ga'ee won't give you a second chance."

"We are ready now but will sharpen our skills during the journey to Ebren with the *Ebren Warrior*."

"*Champion* and *Warrior*. Roger. I'll register those names with the directorate. Good hunting, Captain."

The instant the communications channel closed, the tactical display flashed red. A Ga'ee carrier entered normal space near the portal, within five hundred kilometers of the *Ebren Champion*.

Commander Josephs was galvanized into action. "HK1, target and prepare to fire." It was a long-range shot but would keep the Ga'ee engaged for the Ebren battle beast, as they called it, to turn and fire from point-blank range.

The Ga'ee's hangar doors started to open.

Four battlewagons maneuvered into a firing position. The fifth ship, *European Union*, was too far back.

They couldn't wait. "Activate the code and fire," Commander Josephs ordered.

The system transmitted the coding they'd been given to takedown the Ga'ee's shields. They trusted it would work.

It didn't, but they were already committed to firing.

Four battlewagons sent streams of energy toward the Ga'ee carrier. The shields held against the long-range shots, but four at once, even at that range, blasted and sparked, energy overwhelming energy. The Ga'ee's shield collapsed.

The ship was unfazed.

"Recycle and fire the main weapon when ready. Launch a full salvo of Rapiers, all ships. Target aft reactor spaces." Jimmy

Josephs held onto the back of the captain's chair. His previous confidence was shattered by the failure of four battlewagons to damage the Ga'ee vessel.

The *Ebren Champion* accelerated away from the Ga'ee ship, only to roll over and corkscrew into a firing position.

Drones streamed from the Ga'ee ship and targeted the closest craft.

The second Ebren battlewagon.

The Ebren-crewed ship slid through the portal to a position between the Ga'ee and the *Ebren Champion*. The drones found the target too easy; they slammed into the unprotected battlewagon with relentless fury. The void filled with debris, pieces of the *Warrior* ripped away by the hundreds and then thousands of impacts.

The Ebren ship fired its defensive systems, sending lasers flashing across space along with chain gun projectiles and short-range missiles. The Ebren fought with everything they had, knowing it would not be enough.

With each penetration, more cracks were opened and exploited. More drones swarmed into the expanding vulnerabilities.

It took seconds before the first bit of atmosphere vented to space, followed by a fountain of fire from an explosion inside the ship. The running lights flashed as the *Warrior's* power fluctuated.

More drones attacked the helpless ship, and tens of thousands impacted it. The engines flared as the *Warrior* attempted to get clear of the portal.

Champion cleared a firing lane and unleashed its beam weapon into the vulnerable midship spine. It penetrated the hull, throwing melted metal and debris into the void. The ship bucked and twisted with the explosion, but the drones continued to come. The cloud shifted and reshaped as it moved to get between the Ga'ee ship and the inbound missiles.

The Rapiers arced through the void on two hundred and fifty different trajectories, each looking for an opening without letting the Ga'ee mass their defense.

Hunter-Killer Squadron One watched and hoped.

Twenty seconds to a four-shot salvo that would destroy the Ga'ee carrier as long as its shield was still down.

It was too late for the *Ebren Warrior*. The ship's momentum carried it away from the portal before it came apart. Five-hundred-meter-long sections broke off and spun into the sun's gravity well to assume a course for their ultimate demise.

The Rapiers sliced toward the carrier. The first ones died far short of the ship by taking out a cluster of drones. The missile exploded, and ten megatons radiated a blast wave that quickly dissipated.

The *European Union* raced ahead of the other four battlewagons and cleared its firing lane. The ship's beam weapon lanced through the void and slammed into the Ga'ee carrier like a battering ram. It caught the midship chasm carved by *Champion's* beam, and the carrier slowed to a stop.

The drones lost their guidance and floundered. Rapiers raced past the unformed clouds and hammered the Ga'ee carrier. From stem to stern, ten-megaton warheads shattered the enemy ship. Explosion after explosion split it along dozens of seams. The first of its three plants went critical nearly simultaneously. The ship erupted in a single fireball of molten metal and shards.

Ebren Champion put itself between the explosion and the portal, blocking the worst of the debris from damaging their only path to Vestrall space and reinforcements. Its defensive systems cycled to blast the debris before it impacted the battlewagon, splitting the remnants into smaller pieces.

"Weapons free. Destroy those drones," Josephs ordered.

Four ships from Hunter-Killer Squadron One moved forward together, their close-in weapons systems spun up. Tracers, lasers, and plasma lanced outward and picked off the drones one by one. They rapidly fell to the massed weapons fire. The ships continued through the cloud, hitting each of the tens of thousands at least once. Some of the drones spun into the void. The rest died, never to be resurrected.

The materiel from the remainder would be used to repair the damage on the battlewagons. It could be towed to the shipyard, too, to help in the building of future ships.

"Captain Trey'gidor, please accept my condolences on the loss of your countrymen."

"They died well, fighting to their last breath. There is no shame for the crew of the *Ebren Warrior*. They lived up to their name," the Ebren captain declared boldly.

"Then we shall celebrate the battle they were unjustly thrust into. Your course is set. Make sure any repairs you need are completed, and then continue alone to Ebren. Waiting here for a week for the next battlewagon will be a waste of time. I suspect Ebren is under siege once more."

"Then we will fly without further delay. Good hunting," Captain Trey'gidor replied. The ship maneuvered to a new heading and disappeared into faster-than-light speed.

The energy vibration sensor tracked the Ebren-crewed battlewagon on a direct course toward Ebren. Estimated arrival in twenty-one days.

"We need a second Hunter-Killer squadron," Jimmy stated. "One to protect the portal and one to protect Earth. Same for every portal distant from the system's primary planet. The Ga'ee dropped out of FTL right on top of the portal. Next time, it might be right on top of Earth. We were lucky this time, being out here to meet the Ebren *battle beasts*. A fluke on our part, but the Ga'ee had to know we were here. That means they didn't bother stopping to change course, but our trick to eliminate their shields didn't work."

Commander Josephs spoke in a stream of consciousness to no one in particular. Lieutenant Commander Cummins listened but didn't interrupt to add his thoughts. He didn't see anything unique except that the commander had stepped in to captain the ship during the brief but vicious battle. It was his privilege as the squadron commander.

"Comm, get me President Sinkhaus and channel the line to my quarters." Jimmy Josephs strode off the bridge as quickly as he had arrived mere minutes earlier. In between, they'd lost the newest addition to their fleet of Payne-class battlewagons, and the Ga'ee had lost their carrier and all the drones—more than a hundred thousand on the ship and in space. He stopped and leaned back through the hatch. "Send a status update via FTL to the Fleet. Destroyed one Ga'ee carrier, Earth. BW15 destroyed."

Jimmy hung his head and continued to his quarters. After he sat down, the communications link on his terminal flashed. He tapped the screen to find the president looking at him.

"We lost one battlewagon in another Ga'ee attack on Earth's portal, but the portal remains intact." He preferred reporting facts, the good and the bad, without the speculation the president loved. He expected her to ask about future incursions.

"How many more battlewagons can you lose, Commander, before Earth becomes vulnerable?"

"The ship we lost was caught while transiting the portal from the Vestrall shipyard. We are still one hundred percent combat-effective to protect Earth, but I'm going to bolster our defenses with future ships. We need to station a Hunter-Killer squadron both at the portal and by Earth. The Ga'ee came out of FTL right on top of the portal. We cannot leave it undefended, but they could have just as easily appeared at the moon base, destroyed our shipyard and staging area, and then attacked Earth directly with overwhelming force."

"You don't paint a rosy picture, Commander. I approve of your plan. As many ships as you can put on station. Earth is the key planet in this alliance and must be protected at all costs."

"I agree, President Sinkhaus. Until we have sufficient forces, I will protect the portal because we will never increase our firepower if we lose the link to Vestrall space. I encourage the BEP to withdraw to a low orbit to keep drones from getting inside the atmosphere until we can get close enough to destroy the carrier. And for the record, the Ga'ee have already modified their systems, so we can't spoof them with digital coding. We have to batter their shields, and that is taking all the firepower we have and a second-round salvo. We will need a resupply of Rapiers as soon as possible."

"Rapiers aren't cheap," the president replied.

"Cheaper than the complete destruction of all humanity. Is cost the conversation you want to have? Ambassador Payne made sure humanity incurred no costs in building the new battle fleet, but that doesn't seem to be enough. I'm done here. Get our fucking Rapiers. Josephs out."

Jimmy angrily stabbed the button on the terminal to close the connection.

"Why do I let your dumb ass get under my skin?" he grumbled, then answered himself. "Because I care about the things you don't, and you don't care about the things that I do. You take us for granted, up to and including the deaths of more than a hundred Ebren warriors and the destruction of a nearly irreplaceable ship."

He contacted the bridge. "Barry, send an FTL message expressing our condolences on the loss of the *Ebren Warrior* and all hands on board. Use Captain Trey'gidor's language that they died well, fighting to their last and ensuring the destruction of the Ga'ee carrier. Captain Trey'gidor's actions were equally heroic in ensuring no damage to the Earth portal."

"Is it okay if I ask *European Union* to send that message? They are one hundred percent combat operational, and we have a couple little things to clean up."

"As you need, Barry, with my full support." Josephs closed the link and stared at the darkened terminal, replaying all that had transpired in the past ten minutes. A lost ship. A destroyed Ga'ee carrier. An unsupportive hierarchy. He suddenly felt all alone.

Then he smiled.

"I dropped an F-bomb on the president's head."

He suspected it wouldn't be the last. He also knew he had no desire to go back to Earth despite his willingness to die in its defense.

[7]

"When life gives you lemons, you better wake up because you're dreaming. We don't get lemons in the Fleet, just sour looks."
–From the memoirs of Ambassador Declan Payne

Payne paced the corridor outside the starboard hangar bay, where his team was dressing and checking their weapons.

Mary stayed with him, leaning against the bulkhead. "Time's running down. We should get ready."

"We could also die in the next two minutes."

"That never stopped you before. Isn't that how it is every time? That's why I'm back on the team—since I couldn't deal with it out here. It's so much easier in there. Everything I love is in there." She pointed at the hangar bay. "I suggest everything you love is in there too."

"The heart and soul of what we do, our closest friends and family," Payne replied. His face went slack, and he stared. "The Ga'ee must have the same. They are intelligent, but the drive through other systems with the complete elimination of everything that supports life, theirs included, doesn't pass the logic test. Why? We have to know why if we're going to stop them.

We can't defeat them with military power alone. How do we turn off their instincts and turn on their ability to think?"

"That's a little deep, Dec, especially since we're under two minutes to arrival. We can discuss it later if we're still alive."

"The future is now, Mary. The tide cannot turn until the moon is driven from orbit. The upheaval will tear the planet apart." Payne continued to stare down the corridor.

Mary took Declan by the arm. "We need to go." He didn't resist but wasn't fully compliant, either. She hurried as much as she could to the team area. Payne stripped mechanically as if he were an automaton.

"What's wrong with the major?" Heckler asked while making a face.

"He's exercising that sixty billion IQ of his, and it's hurting his brain."

Heckler nodded while he shared a knowing look with Turbo. They bit their lips. Mary frowned.

"When he comes back, he'll be better than ever," Mary suggested.

"Sure thing, Dog," Heckler replied with zero conviction.

Payne lightened up. "Crap! How much time?"

"One minute!" Major Dank shouted from *Ugly* 6.

"Why didn't someone tell me?" He looked at Mary.

"Are you serious? Do you remember how you got here? Forget it. Get dressed. We got places to go, people to see."

"I don't," Payne admitted, scrunching his face before hurrying through the suit's startup procedure. He grabbed the railgun that Mary held out for him, and they ran to the nearby insertion craft. They were the last two to board. Lev had just started the ten-second countdown. "Button us up. Helmets."

The team put on their helmets and snapped them into place. When the countdown hit zero, the ship transitioned from FTL to normal space. Instantly, the head-twisting sound of metal scraping on rock reverberated through the ship. *Leviathan* jerked sideways. The passengers usually didn't feel due that to the inertial dampening ability of artificial gravity, but not this time.

The movements were so pronounced that the gravity field couldn't keep up. The sound died, and the ship stopped moving.

"Bullseye!" Lev declared.

Heckler and Turbo high-fived.

The tactical screen populated, showing Leviathan within the hollowed-out planet. However, the ship wasn't alone. Hulks and other debris filled the cavernous space.

"Threats?" Payne asked. The icons on the screen showed yellow, not red or blue.

"No power. Infrared shows the cold of space. We are here and lost in the clutter that is the interior of the destroyed moon's shell, which is ninety-four percent ferrite, with quartz accounting for the next five percent. Trace amounts of gold and silver, along with other exotic metals, make up the remainder," Lev replied.

"Can we dismantle those ships?"

"They appear to have already been scavenged for key components necessary to build another worldkiller missile. I'm sorry, Declan, but all of my other repair needs will be met."

"I'd like to take *Ugly 6* and explore our new digs. I want to see the limits of our realm. Where we need to stay to keep from being seen."

"I think that's prudent," Lev agreed.

"I think that's a good idea, too," Admiral Wesson interjected. "We'll keep the Mosquitoes where they are. The insertion craft is better at not being seen, even though the Ga'ee saw it on BD18."

"We were danger-close. That probably made the difference." Payne adjusted in his seat. "Open it up, Lev. Let's see what we've got."

Ugly 6 lifted gently off the deck and maneuvered to the hangar bay door. It drifted out as soon as the opening was wide enough and accelerated slowly.

The external cameras showed the scene on the screens of both doors as if the team was looking out both sides of the ship. Hulks, some unrecognizable as ships. Others were stained and battle-scarred.

"These are the Ga'ee's victims," Payne posited.

"That's what I think, too," Major Dank replied. "Sparky?"

The team engineer, who dealt with ship design, had an opinion. "Sub-light, light speed, and fantastic. These ships represent everything from newly spacefaring races to ancients like the Progenitors. Still, none of them could stand up to the Ga'ee. I'd like to board a ship or two and take a closer look. Even though they seem to have been salvaged, I'm sure there's still something to be learned."

"Me, too," Joker added. The rest of the team followed suit.

"When Team Payne was initially put together, our mission was to explore ships left behind by the Progenitors, in addition to being a tactical strike team. Exploring is fully half of our mission, and over these past couple years, we haven't done any of that. Back to the beginning. This is the easiest decision I've made all day. Lev, deposit us on whatever ship Sparky chooses after we've run the perimeter."

"That one," Sparky pointed at a ship shaped like an amoeba with mottled green and blue coloring. Compared to the more staid metal monsters, it stood out in stark contrast.

Ugly 6 veered away from the selected ship and accelerated toward the starscape visible beyond the graveyard.

"How did you not hit anything?" Payne marveled. "We should be dead."

"Sometimes luck is a factor that cannot be discounted or ignored. Plus, we did hit something—the wall of the cavern and two ships. The hulks didn't fare as well as I did," Lev replied.

Payne chuckled. "We thought we heard something, but it wasn't too bad," he lied. "Staying off the Ga'ee's radar was critical. The next question is, where do we go from here?"

"We don't have that answer, but once the fold drive is operational, we'll have a lot more options," Admiral Wesson answered.

"Sorry, sir. I forgot you were still online."

"Where else would I be?"

Payne shrugged and shook his head. Neither movement translated into anything the admiral could hear. "You could have come with us."

"Why ruin my perfect record of never leaving the ship?" The admiral waited for two seconds before signing off.

Payne gestured at the team to take off their helmets. It would take an hour to get to the outer edge of the interior at the slow speed optimized for stealth.

"We *thought* we heard something." Mary shook her head. "It sounded like the ship was coming apart."

"Considering that we were only off ninety-nine kilometers after flying a distance of four hundred light-years, I have to agree with Lev. Bullseye. A little scrape on the side of the ship is like a sexy scar," Payne replied.

"It's not," Turbo countered. "It's like a big ugly scrape from a new driver hitting everything in their way."

"Make your jokes, but that was the greatest FTL transit of all time!" Payne raised his arms and gave a hearty cheer.

"You're a psycho," Mary remarked. Payne winked at her.

The insertion craft continued toward the inner boundary, an opening two hundred kilometers across that was protected on all sides by what was left of the shell of the planet. They were inside an iron ball with a great view of space beyond.

"Thoughts on how to defeat the Ga'ee?" Payne asked, looking from face to face. He nodded at Kal.

"Me? What do I know?" the Ebren drawled.

"You watch and listen. I think you're the smartest out of all of us, in addition to being the strongest."

"Y'all are gonna make me blush," Kal replied. The Ebren's fibrous skin didn't have capillaries, so they weren't capable of blushing.

Payne didn't call him on it. They had more important things to discuss than Lev teaching Kal how to speak. The Ebren scanned the team. All eyes were on him.

"To be the champion, being big and strong is important, but the real power is in how that's used to exploit an enemy's weakness," Kal began without his accent. "The Ga'ee's weakness is in their centralized control. When we destroy a nerve center, the carrier and the drones become nothing more than debris."

"We killed a carrier, and the drones still came. I'm not sure that's always the case," Payne replied.

Kal smiled easily. "We didn't kill the control center for *those* drones. I suggest all of the ships are under one master in this sector. The neural net is everywhere." Kal gestured at the space around them. "That's why we're hiding inside this thing. That's why the derelicts are here. They won't interfere with the net. Find the central point of the net. Kill that."

"In our space, the ships operated autonomously..." Payne stopped and stared at the deck.

Blinky tried to snap his fingers, but his gloves prevented it. "If the central control is dead, there's no one to tell the ships to go to our space. What if we recalled all Ga'ee ships to the core planet?"

"You assume there are no backups or secondary nodes," Payne countered.

"That's why the recall. We plant the seed to obviate any backup leadership sources."

"Can we hack their system to insert a virus of that magnitude?" Payne wondered.

"Not yet," Blinky admitted. He pointed at *Leviathan*. "That's why we should be back there, working on it. We have enough data, but their system is so different, we have to relearn everything we know."

"Look at yourselves. You need to make sure your bodies don't quit on you. Sixteen hours a day is all I'll allow you to work with Lev on the Ga'ee's language and coding. Two hours to work out and six hours to sleep."

"We can do with four hours of sleep," Buzz suggested.

"Sixteen hours plugged in, and that's non-negotiable." Payne pointed at the two techies. "Eight hours separated from Lev and the mental grind. Look at yourselves!"

Blinky didn't break eye contact with the major. He knew what they looked like. "We'll do our best." He turned to Buzz, and they nodded at each other.

"I know you will, just like you have from the first days you were on the team. We owe our lives to you. Humanity owes its fighting chance to you two and Lev. I want you both in shape to survive what we're going to have to do."

"We don't quite know what that is, do we?" Virgil Dank asked.

Payne shook his head. "I had a thought but lost it. This damn brain of mine is working against itself." No one made a joke as Payne drilled a finger against his temple, scowling. "I think Blinky is on the right track. Who else?"

Virgil cleared his throat. "It's also important to note what we can*not* do, and that's fold space unless it's to go *all the way* back to where we came from. We can't be sure we'll have two minutes, let alone two hours. They have *mines* that are a kilometer across. Who does that and why?"

"Someone who's afraid of being invaded," Joker offered. Everyone turned toward her since she usually didn't speak. "Maybe they are projecting because they so readily invade everywhere else. They might think they're vulnerable. So what weakness does a big-ass mine cover up?"

Payne smiled. Mary caught that and gave him a questioning look.

"You are the smartest people I know," Payne stated.

Virgil raised a finger. "In ground warfare, mines were used as an area denial weapon. When covered by something like artillery, they created a dilemma for an encroaching enemy. Two ways to die, and neither good. It's like putting the enemy between a hammer and an anvil."

"Area denial? They were in the middle of nowhere, just a place we chose to change heading." Payne blew out his cheeks, trying to work through the possibilities.

"That's all we used it for, but what were the Ga'ee using it for?" Major Dank continued.

"It's thirteen days away from here," Payne noted. "Blinky, what signals did we collect in that area?"

Blinky shrugged within his combat suit. "All of them?"

"What the hell was different there than in the previous place? That's the question we need answered."

"I'll work on that immediately," Lev interjected. Blinky tried to stand, but he was buckled in and didn't make it very far.

"Where are you going?" Mary asked.

"We need to help Lev!" Buzz nodded.

"We're probably two hours from getting back to *Leviathan*. Relax." Mary gestured, but Blinky and Buzz were still agitated.

"Easy for you to say. You need answers, and we're the right people to dig into the questions."

Payne gesticulated randomly. "Then put on your helmets and commune with the big dog. You don't need to be over there. You can do it from here."

"But it would be better..." Blinky started but stopped when Payne drew a finger across his throat.

"You're here, not there. Do the best you can." Payne pointed at their helmets. The two clicked them into place and leaned back to relax and let their minds engage with Lev and the data.

The insertion craft slowed as it approached the outer barrier. The sensors on board listened intently to make sure the craft didn't penetrate the neural network active beyond the barrier.

The tactical screen blinked as faint signals registered. *Ugly 6* backed away. "I can calculate where the barrier is effective," Lev stated. The insertion craft continued across the opening to slow once more and ease forward until the sensors picked up a faint signal.

"Any way we can collect data from the signals?" Gridlines appeared on the screen with go and no-go areas highlighted. Payne looked at his team for more information.

"I don't think so," Lev replied. "If we get in the way of the signals, there will be the slightest blip. We risk revealing ourselves."

"Don't want to expose ourselves. That would be unseemly," Payne suggested.

Mary gave him the Look. He felt bad for about a millisecond.

"Who's giving the direction to the Ga'ee? They are highly centralized," Payne continued.

Shaolin raised an armored hand. "If the neural net is representative of how they communicate, could it all be one big brain, and they are all connected? The decisions are made by the Ga'ee race as a single thinking mind."

Payne tipped his head back. The team watched him carefully as a smile spread across his face.

"I know what we need to do," he began. "But I need to talk with Lev first while I can pace because that helps me think. In the interim, I'm going to get some shuteye. Let me know when we've reached the ship we're going to board."

Without waiting for an answer, Payne clasped his hands before him and closed his eyes. His breathing slowed almost instantly since, for the moment, he was at peace.

[8]

"The time to act is now, but the time to think never ends." –From the memoirs of Ambassador Declan Payne

Ugly 6 moved close and hovered just outside a blown access hatch. The sides of the insertion craft rotated upward to allow the team to egress.

Sparky was the first one out, with Shaolin and Byle by her side.

Kal, who was wearing his suit, was shifting uncomfortably. Blinky and Buzz were also there, having been released by Lev for the near term. Behind their face shields, they were gaunt, their cheeks sunken and their skin sallow. They looked unhealthy, despite Lev's reassurances. It was good that Payne didn't have to see them through their mirrored face shields; otherwise, he would have been displeased with Lev all over again.

They'd been through that once.

Payne couldn't disagree since the fate of humanity rested on them solving the Ga'ee problem. He thought they needed healthier bodies to approach the problem, but Lev knew more about Blinky and Buzz than Payne did, so he was forced to accept that they were the right amount of physically healthy.

He still didn't want to look at them.

They entered the craft one by one. Payne would have spread the team out to cover more territory, but the ship was a kilometer long.

They had the time.

"Separate by deck. Sparky, where do you think the engines and power plant are on this big bastard?"

"On the central axis, middle of the ship. I suspect it has an exotic form of locomotion. I don't see anything that looks like weapons ports, but Byle can go forward, looking for anything weapons-related there. Shaolin can head to the keel and look for systems there, even though the ship is stripped. We still might find something."

"Roger," the two weapons specialists replied. They pulled their way in zero gravity through the wreckage and deeper into the ship. It was nothing more than a superstructure and decks. Any wiring, transistors, circuits, boards, and silicon were gone. Gaskets or other soft materials had deteriorated in the harsh conditions of space if they'd ever been there.

The ship had been gutted.

"Look familiar?" Payne asked. "Remember all those Progenitor ships we boarded looking for ancient technology? This looks just like those."

"Exactly like those," Dank agreed. "What's it mean, Dec?"

"It means we've got a serious fight on our hands, but we already knew that. If the Ga'ee were in the system before humanity took hold, why didn't the Ga'ee stay?"

Shaolin raised her hand, "What if the Progenitors engineered the Ga'ee, and they left this system once the Ga'ee started to expand? Maybe they thought they could control them."

The air seemed to leave their combat suits.

Payne didn't believe it. He refused. "Lev, did you know of the existence of the Ga'ee?"

"I did not. The other ships you explored were stripped by the Godilkinmore. There is no doubt about that."

"Back to the logic train. Did the Godilkinmore strip this ship?"

"They did, or someone who was trained by them. The systematic dismantlement that stops at certain components while being more thorough with others is too much of a coincidence to discount."

Payne scanned the bulkheads as he moved deeper into the ship. He was following Sparky toward the center, looking for the bridge or the main power supply center. He didn't expect to find anything, but he had to be sure.

They had time. They also had many questions.

Because the ship had been gutted, there were no barriers to movement. They continued unopposed to their respective areas.

"It had weapons," Byle reported from the forward section. "Standard configuration for a railgun, plasma, particle beam, or laser. Judging by the size of the space for the power conduits, they were relatively low power. Maybe a railgun or ion cannon, but not a laser or beam weapon. It would have fired something. External port is too small for a missile. Continuing to the upper deck to see if there are any missile ports."

"Shaolin here. Keel is barren. Limited access. If there were weapons protecting this section, they were extremely small, like chain guns or point-blank lasers. I don't see how they could have had missiles down here, at least not in this section. Will continue aft."

In the center of the ship was a "bathtub" to protect a central core. It was similar to the one on *Leviathan*, but this encompassed only a deck and a half and a thousand square meters of deck space. Nothing remained except that shell.

"Lev, this looks like good metal. I suggest you send a bot over here to evaluate it," Payne stated. The others added their observations.

"Advanced ship, or one that just looks advanced?" Payne asked.

"Looks like a run-of-the-mill ship," Sparky replied. "The external configuration gives the appearance of something nearly bio-mechanical, but it is not. This ship is a metal framework with conduits to feed power to the ship's systems. It had both offensive and defensive weapons. I suggest it was capable of intra-atmospheric flight, based on the lifting body design. I'm heading aft to take a look."

"What I hear you saying is that this ship was nowhere near as advanced as *Leviathan*," Payne confirmed. Sparky agreed.

They finished their survey, finding nothing of renown besides the high-quality bathtub made from a titanium alloy. Even if all the materials to build a missile weren't present, Lev could fabricate some components, leaving the other elements of the systems for when he acquired the right raw materials.

"Recover to the uglymobile, then on to the next ship," Payne ordered.

They went on and investigated the fully scavenged hulks of six more vessels to determine that they had nothing to exploit except for limited but varied metals.

Lev's maintenance and construction bots were hard at work, slicing and dicing to bring as much as he needed into his storage bays and feed the fabrication equipment.

Ugly 6 parked in the hangar bay, and the side doors levered up. The team disembarked, walking slowly after a full day. Declan, Mary, and Virgil were the last ones off the craft after tapping Blinky and Buzz on their helmets to root them out of their seats. That galvanized them into action. They ran to the team area, where they changed and bolted before anyone else was finished.

The others were still dressing by the time the final three reached the team area.

"Penny for your thoughts," Mary said softly.

Dank chuckled. "I'll double that. Two cents!"

"I'm contemplating life on the tree of woe," Payne replied mysteriously. He disappeared into his thoughts and changed into his jumpsuit almost mechanically. Mary hurried to catch him as he sauntered toward a waiting cart and jumped in with him, to his surprise.

Dank remained behind to go through the weapons locker to see what Heckler and Turbo were hiding.

"What's up, Dec?" Mary asked. The cart moved slowly into the corridor because Kal and the Cabrizi were playing fetch.

"What can I say? They missed me!" the warrior shouted as he ran down the corridor.

Payne nodded. "What the team said when we were flying around. The missing pieces. I've been doing some calculations. I need to talk with Lev to confirm."

"You can talk to Lev whenever you want. You don't need to be on the bridge," Mary replied.

"Captain's chair. Words are too slow." Payne stared down the semi-darkened corridor.

"You were always the smart one, but now you're the geeky one, too. Can't wait to geek out with your friends, Declan?"

Payne smiled. "Geeking out with a thousand-year-old AI and his human girlfriend. I can think of no better way to invest my time."

"Probably Blinky and Buzz, too. Did you see how they shot out of the hangar bay?"

"They must be on to something."

The cart accelerated down the ramps to get to the bridge level, where it pulled up at the massive hatch that opened onto the bridge. It almost always stood open, as it did now.

Mary and Declan walked through at a pace that screamed a sense of urgency. The admiral and the commodore were there, studying the main screen, where repair statuses and salvage operations competed for attention.

Payne climbed the dais on which the captain's chair was mounted and slumped into it. The admiral noticed the movement and turned around. By the time he opened his mouth to ask what Payne was doing, Declan was fully immersed.

Mary answered the unasked question. "He said he had calculations he needed to run through with Lev and words were too slow."

"That doesn't sound like the Major Payne I've known for the last twelve years. Then again, this is a whole new campaign. The rules are different."

"Do you think he has a plan to get us out of this?" the commodore wondered.

"I don't think he's looking at getting us out of this as much as going deeper. You know him. He took us to Vestrall Prime," Mary replied.

"Look who the cat dragged in," a heavily muscled avatar said from behind a massive computer terminal.

Payne had never had to share the digital space before. "Is that you, Buzz?"

"Sir, that cuts me deep. I'll probably be scarred for life." Another avatar appeared. This one looked like a stuffed toy, a teddy bear.

"You guys. Is this how you act while treading Lev's digital hallways?"

"It is," Blinky replied. "But harassing us isn't why you're here. Lev said you had some calculations you needed to run through. Well, bring 'em on, bitch."

"Upstarts! Look at you, being the playground bully," Payne laughed. He looked down. He was overwhelmingly unimpressive in digital form. He appeared as a stick version of himself. "Lev?"

"Yes, Declan." Lev did not have an avatar, just a voice that seemed to come from everywhere at once.

"The neural network acts like what we would think of as a brain but on a vast scale. It's more than just speed-of-light synapses firing; it's a vibration through the energy field, like the system you use to see movements at faster-than-light speeds across hundreds of light-years. The neural network is a blending of those two systems—synapses vibrating across the cosmos at nearly instantaneous speeds. We need to calculate how long it would take a message to cross the entire distance of the ten thousand Ga'ee planets."

"That's thirty-three-point-two seconds," Lev replied.

"That's how long it will take to dismantle the Ga'ee empire," Payne claimed.

"I don't understand," Blinky said.

Buzz agreed. He didn't understand either.

"Ten to the fifth power, just to be safe. That's how many ships and planets we need to subvert. It starts with one ship. That one influences ten, which impact ten more ships, and so on. By the end, every ship will have new instructions."

"If only it worked that way," Buzz replied. "How do we get the Ga'ee to transmit a message of our choosing in the first place, and why would that influence the rest?"

"One brain. We only need to convince it of the efficacy of the message."

"Please don't attack the humans?" Blinky asked incredulously. "I don't see it working."

Payne's avatar shook its oversized head. "To grow, the Ga'ee must shrink."

The Blinky's and Buzz's avatars looked at each other.

Lev spoke up. "That level of thought is something I could never achieve. It makes no sense while being completely logical. Change the parameters of the conversation by changing the nature of it. Tell us more."

"We only have to convince one ship's brain. Plant the seed."

"And that one neuron has to convince the other million. I'm not seeing how this is going to work." Buzz remained skeptical. Blinky shook his head.

"We show them the math, and that is why I needed to come in here. Neuron density and the loss during transmission. They are weakening their race for eventual demise by spreading too far from the core. What is the transmission loss?"

"Miniscule," Blinky replied.

"But miniscule transferred through thousands of light-years, even tens of thousands, and all of a sudden, you have a breakaway group that is doing its own thing. The incursion into our space was supposedly only a scouting effort, although they completely took over the planets. Nothing was left to share with greater numbers of settlers. This is antithetical to an expansion plan. Their scout ships are leaving nothing to be colonized, and the homeworlds get nothing. Resources. Expanded brainpower. None of it. Instead, they cower here, ready to attack anyone who invades, defending a dying race."

"They're invading. They don't think of themselves as a dying race."

"They do, but they don't know why. They are furiously

trying to expand despite the fact that their scout ships have all been destroyed and their second invasion fleet ran up against our battlewagons. The second wave has been destroyed. Looks like Ga'ee population control. It's making them dumber. We'll add the math to show them they will grow by consolidating to their central planets. All we need to do is take over one active Ga'ee ship."

Blinky laughed. "What are the other active Ga'ee ships going to be doing while we're having tea and crumpets with the beasties on board one of their ships?"

"Trying to kill God1 while rallying every available ship to the effort."

"It took us two weeks to say the first words to the Ga'ee, and they were like a three-year-old babbling to an adult. But we're going to convince them before they kill Lev?"

"We are," Payne stated with a great deal of confidence. "We'll soften them up by sharing our calculations while planting the seeds that they are losing control of the ships that have journeyed to the far reaches of space."

"How will that help the Berantz, Earth, the Ebren, or the Rang'Kor?"

"The forward ships will pull back to fight on that side of the civil war. They are connected enough to not want to cut all ties with the home front."

"How do you know this?" Blinky pressed.

"It's an educated guess," Payne replied.

"It's fucking bullshit." Blinky stepped away from the panel his avatar was working in to face Payne's representation. He was much bigger than Payne in the digital world. "You're going to get us all killed."

"We will all die. That is true. *When* is the question. Do you see any other way?"

"Not yet." Blinky loomed over Payne's avatar. With a single

thought, Declan's caricature grew and filled out until it loomed over Blinky.

"Digital posturing at its finest. Are we going to waste time seeing who can grow a bigger make-believe body? I prefer that we work on the calculations. The unknown factor is how many nodes exist in Ga'ee space. Ten thousand worlds, but how many ships that consolidate the local consciousness? That is our target number to work with."

Blinky backed down and returned to his station.

Payne used his digital finger to scrawl calculations in the air. Blinky and Buzz worked with Lev to parse the data from the neural net to determine the number of unique signatures.

It only took Payne a few minutes to fill the space around him with a formula. He only needed the number of individual nodes to complete the calculation. He started a new series of formulae. With the current expansion, how long until the existing brainpower collapsed from a failure to be refreshed? Intellectual flight. It was like an alcoholic killing their brain cells a little at a time, changing what they were into something less.

[9]

"Our smart people are smarter than your smart people. We got that going for us." –From the memoirs of Ambassador Declan Payne

"Got it all figured out?" Mary asked. Payne blinked and took in his surroundings. The captain's seat on the bridge. He was sitting higher than everyone else. It was a good seat. Comfortable.

"Got what figured out?" Payne was confused. It was like he'd woken up from a long nap. He had a nagging feeling that he'd missed something.

"How to defeat the Ga'ee." Mary looked closer to see if he was kidding.

He wasn't.

She continued. "You jumped into the chair to connect with Lev because words were too slow, according to a version of you from an hour ago."

"Indubitably," Payne replied. "Lev, do you have it figured out?"

"We are much farther along than when we started. Thanks for your insight," Lev replied.

"You still don't remember any of it, do you?"

"Not a bit. Last thing I remember was being on the uglymobile and encouraging the team to go see their girlfriends, boyfriends, make-believe friends, or whoever."

"You're not turning schizo on us, are you? Lev, is he okay?" Mary pounded her fist into her hand. She scowled at the front screen.

"He is working through the reconciliation between his conscious and subconscious. When he is able to bridge the gap, he shuts off one side or the other. Currently, his subconscious is blocked. I don't know if he'll ever be able to actively manage both states of consciousness simultaneously because he doesn't want to."

"Damn, Lev! You make it sound like I'm not the star pupil."

"You are not."

Mary snickered and turned away. She composed herself before facing back, offering Payne her arm to help him down off the dais. "Declan Payne. Not invincible, but still the leader of the seven races."

"Husband of Mary Payne," he added with a smile.

"How delightfully sugary but correct," Admiral Wesson quipped. "Lev, what did Major Payne propose?"

"To convince the Ga'ee to contract instead of expand, based on the justification that they are losing control and their thought capacity diminishes the farther apart they grow. Density of neuron mass through close proximity optimizes the thought process. The calculations have confirmed Declan's postulation."

"How are we going to convince the Ga'ee to listen to us when every single one of their ships in this sector has orders to kill us?"

"Declan proposes to take over one of their carriers," Lev offered.

"Oh." The admiral nodded, crossed his arms, and nodded again. "Is that all? I thought you were going to propose one of your usual insane plans."

"My *usual*? I feel like I should be offended."

"Probably," the admiral agreed. "We'll have to refine how we're going to take over the Ga'ee carrier. We don't have a great track record in that department."

Payne tapped his nose. "Blinky and Buzz will figure it out."

The admiral winced. "That doesn't instill a lot of confidence, Major. Nothing against your people, but the fate of humanity is at stake. By the way, what are we supposed to be doing while you're trying to talk with the Ga'ee ship?"

"Trying not to get killed?" Payne suggested.

The admiral wasn't buying it. "What's the backup plan?"

"Backup?" Payne turned serious. "We're out of options, Admiral. We know we can't fight all the Ga'ee. They outnumber us a hundred thousand to one. The odds are not in our favor."

"Level the playing field by taking on one ship." Mary took Payne by the arm and steered him toward the hatch.

"High risk, high reward," Commodore Freeman noted. "A hundred thousand to one. I don't like those odds."

"Me neither," the admiral agreed. "Where do we find this lone ship, vulnerable to your tender ministrations?"

"Don't know," Payne called over his shoulder. "Not yet, anyway. Let me know when we can fold space."

"You'll be the second to know," Lev promised. The admiral stared at the screen. It didn't show anything outside the shell of the world within which they were hiding. They were blind and had a plan that made little sense.

Commander Yeldon scowled. The portal was taking too long. With limited support ships and delays with the supply chain, he had a tough decision to make. If the battlewagons helped fabricate the pieces using materials from the destroyed Ga'ee ship, they could expedite the schedule. As it was, they were two months from finishing when they should have only been one.

With the battlewagons one hundred percent committed, they could compress the schedule to three weeks.

"Should we do it?" Yeldon wondered.

"That means we have to spin down the mains. We'll be defensive weapons only while working," the weapons station reported.

"How fast can we dump the fabrication and go on the offensive?" Yeldon asked.

"Estimate is two minutes,"

"That's too long, just like two more months to build that portal. Two ships on watch and two ships actively participating in the construction process. A compromise that will hopefully buy us the two minutes should the Ga'ee rear their ugly heads."

"I'm not sure they have heads," the executive officer replied, "but they're ugly all the same and hell-bent on destroying us."

"They were just here, so I calculate the risk as acceptable at this point in time. *Levant* and *Russia* will assume overwatch. *Africa* and *Australia*, reconfigure yourselves as the Vestrall need to help them build that damn portal."

Yeldon frowned. The ships maneuvered into position.

"If the Ga'ee enter normal space at the portal, we're screwed. Anywhere else, and we have time. Do we know if they got off a message during that last encounter?"

"No idea," the sensor operator replied. "We're not sure exactly how they communicate with each other. Leviathan's notes spoke of some kind of neural interface they had difficulty isolating. We have a massive range of frequencies to look at, and from what we saw, the Ga'ee constantly radiate in all of them."

"That isn't helpful at all." Yeldon drew acceleration arcs along the gravity wells within the system in the air with his finger. Planetary and stellar confluences, but speed of movement wasn't anywhere near as important as speed of action. "Battle station drills. We need to reduce our response time to being able to fire the main weapon to within five seconds. If we can get a shot off before the Ga'ee raise their screens and before the drones launch, we might buy ourselves a second shot."

"Do you expect them to come in right on top of us?" the XO asked.

"Train for the worst case," the commander replied, "but I also expect the worst case. Next time, they'll come in so close to the portal that they'll have drones trying to rip it apart before your heart realizes it skipped a beat."

"I don't know what you said, Commander, but the BEP just transferred some righteous chow. Fresh eggs, sir!" the chief of the boat, Chief Tremayne, said.

"And a lot more," Jimmy Josephs observed. "Crates of food. Enough for a couple weeks. This could be the best Fleet resupply ever!"

He looked around to find everyone staring at him.

"COB, make sure the other ships received something comparable. If not, we'll share."

"Already done. Looks like all five ships been blessed by Earth's largesse," the chief replied. "I'm sending the stuff that will spoil the quickest to the galley for preparation tonight. We'll get a few days out of it. Made-to-order omelets. Fresh pork ribs with Joe's barbecue sauce. Prime rib with fresh horseradish.

I don't know where to start. My stomach has shrunk so much out here, I don't think I can do it justice."

"Spread it out, Chief. It'll last. The eggs will last longer than you think. Weeks, if need be. Cook up the pork ribs first. Get the prime ribs marinating with salt and a vinegar and oil glaze. They'll be ready tomorrow."

"How do you know that stuff? Fleeties don't know how to cook."

"My parents own a restaurant. I know; it's hard to believe that I have parents, but down there is a little dive called Dubuque. Best food in the galaxy. Every single day of my Fleet existence, I pray for when I can return home and eat myself silly. This will be the next best thing."

The chief brightened. "Sir, if I might suggest, to keep the abuse to a minimum, you assist the ship's cook with the preparation of the meals over the next few days." He looked around to make sure no one was listening and found that everyone in the work party was focused on him and the commander. He whispered, "Our cook isn't good. He needs a lot of help."

Jimmy Josephs smiled. "I can do that. I noticed but am jaded because of the time I've spent in space. I think we lose our sense of taste, and that, Chief, is a horrible thing. The greatest sacrifice one can make is losing the joy of eating."

"Bring us joy, sir. Lots of joy."

"Would you look at that? The duty roster has you on it, and you'll miss dinner. I feel horrible about that." Jimmy walked off to snickers and snorts before the chief could reply.

Two people walked hand in hand in the garden on Deck Thirty-seven. "Virgil, be honest. Are we going to get out of this?" Anneliese asked.

He didn't answer right away.

"That tells me what I want to know," she added quickly.

"If anyone can get through this, it's us. It won't be easy, but we've gotten through all kinds of rough scrapes before. Major Payne has a perfect track record. Still, I'd hate to waste the time we have." He pulled her close.

"Why, Major Dank, I believe you're trying to proposition me."

"Is it that obvious?"

"Please, send me to my death with a smile on my face," Anneliese deadpanned.

"I didn't say that." The look on her face suggested she wasn't making it up. "No way. Someone actually tried that line on you?"

She touched her nose with her pointer finger. "I didn't fall for it, and that guy was gone. Clearly not the right person for me."

"You asked me to be honest, so I will. I'd love to get sweaty with you, but our relationship isn't contingent on that." Rich black dirt was mounded around each plant. Virgil dipped his fingers in and let the dirt fall through. His eyes glistened. "I don't want to be alone. I don't want to die alone."

"Oof," Anneliese exclaimed. "That's deep but true. I don't want to be alone either, Virgil. We're in the middle of enemy territory, but once the fold drive is repaired, we can jump all the way back to Earth. But we won't, will we?"

Dank shook his head. "We're here to save all humanity, along with the survivors of the seven races. We're here to end the Ga'ee threat to our sectors once and for all."

"Then what?"

"Then we revel in what we did. I don't know what comes next, Annie. I just want to see the other side of the Ga'ee. We can figure what we'll do then if there is a then." He brushed his dirty fingers off on his jumpsuit.

Anneliese faced him but kept her distance. He wondered why until she unzipped her jumpsuit and let it fall to the ground.

―――

Federico, Alex, Wysteria, and Digitus waited in the dining area as they'd been asked by Mary Payne. They hadn't questioned it.

She walked in with Major Payne by her side. When she spotted the four, she made a beeline toward them. They straightened and stiffened.

"What are you doing?" Mary asked.

"Are we in trouble?" Alex asked.

"No. Why would you think that?"

"We don't get called to the boss's office for no reason."

"I'm not the boss, and this isn't an office." She looked sideways at them. "I'm here to talk about Sparky, Byle, Joker, and Buzz."

"We're up for talking about them. Why? What's happened?" Wysteria demanded.

"We're going on a hazardous mission. I want your support."

"Do we have a choice?" Wysteria asked.

Alex tapped her on the arm. "Do we need a choice? I volunteered my body for science and look at us." He gestured to take in the entirety of the universe, but to the casual observer, it appeared like he was pointing at the food counter. "Here we are. Showing the universe who's boss."

"Is that what we're doing? I thought we were hiding inside a planet," Federico offered.

"We're repairing and rearming," Mary corrected him. "But

I've asked you here to reiterate that life is too short to waste time."

The four looked at her, not understanding what she was talking about.

She only had moments before the rest of Team Payne arrived. She needed to change her approach to one that was less philosophical.

"You are good for our people. We can only tolerate each other so much, and the team is not the sum total of life. We saw that during our year on Vestrall. We need more. Some of us have each other, but then there are those who don't. They need a reason to come home. They need something more than saving all of humanity."

"That's a pretty good reason," Alex replied.

"But it's not what makes the difference when we're knee-deep in it. We fight for each other, but we fight to come home to something. Fighting for a higher ideal is why we are in the war, why we get sent to fight, but once there, it comes down to a very simple premise of what we want to live for. The answer is a time beyond war, a time to celebrate the victory with people who matter to us, not politicians, not the media. Only us." She pointed at the four.

"So, you're saying we're not in trouble?" Alex joked.

"I don't know what Byle sees in you," Mary replied.

"Devilishly good looks, a sharp wit, and I'm willing to massage her feet."

"It was you!" Federico pushed Alex. "No wonder Laura asked if I'd rub her feet. Stop doing crap that makes me look bad."

"How about you make *yourself* look good?" The two men stood.

Mary stepped between them. "Sit your dumb asses down." She poked Federico in the chest. "It goes both ways. You rub her feet, she rubs yours. And you can talk about anything and everything. Be a better man, for Pete's sake. Our people need your support. *Humanity* needs them."

Federico looked angry for a moment but lightened up. "Foot rubs..."

Team Payne strolled in and stopped when they saw Mary Payne with their boyfriends and girlfriends.

Sparky went on alert when she saw Federico staring at the table. Kal had no idea what was going on and didn't seem to care. He headed for the food counter. He'd been working out harder and needed massive amounts of food.

Blinky and Buzz were with the team. Buzz smiled weakly when he saw Digitus. She jumped up from the table and took his arm to guide him to a seat. She made him stay there while she went to the counter to get him something to eat.

Sparky was first to the table. "What's going on?"

Before Mary could answer, Federico spoke. "She's being mean to me."

Sparky didn't look at Mary. She put her hands on her hips and looked down at Federico. "So?"

"Do you really want me to rub your feet?" he blurted.

She took a step back and glanced at Mary before returning her attention to Federico. "I do."

"Prophetic words," Mary mumbled.

"Hey!" Sparky shot her a look.

"Okay. And then sex." He thought he was embarrassing her.

"Of course. Goes without saying."

"Hungry?" he asked.

"That also goes without saying, too." He stood, and they headed for the counter. Heckler and Turbo were already there, ignoring the verbal scrum.

The individuals paired off while Shaolin pulled up the rear.

She tipped her chin to the side. Mary stepped away from the others.

"They need this," Shaolin said softly.

"There's no time to let things progress normally. Lev helped in the initial matchmaking, but they needed a more profound nudge." Mary felt obligated to explain. The conversation had not gone as she wanted.

"Profound is the right word. There is no time. We exist until the Ga'ee trap us, then it's another race against time. We know this is going to suck." She pointed at the team members filling their trays. "And that makes it hard to get too excited about the future."

"No time like the present. I'm trying to make the most of it for everyone."

"Somebody has to," Shaolin replied. She gripped Mary's shoulder. "I like that Payne calls you Dog."

"I'm pretty sure I don't." Mary smiled.

"You're one of the team. Shaolin? Wouldn't be my first choice, but we all get nicknames. There's no way I'm carrying a cauldron of glowing coals with my forearms to brand myself with dragons. No Shaolin for me. I prefer turtles, and if I must fight, I'd rather shoot the enemy with a railgun."

Mary chuckled. "Me, too. I saw plenty of up close and personal when Declan fought Kal on Ebren. It was brutal. But we can't do that out here. The Ga'ee don't care how hard we can kick."

"You and the major are good?" Shaolin asked.

Mary nodded while continuing to smile. "I've never felt more comfortable with someone. I can't imagine my life without that nutcase."

Payne bellowed from the corridor, "You fucking demons from the deepest pits of hell!"

Kal immediately put his tray down and crouched. The

Cabrizi raced through the door and straight for him. He caught them both as they leapt and hugged them to his chest. "How did I know he was talking about my babies?" Kal cooed.

Payne walked in. His jumpsuit was torn, and he bled from a scratch that went from his left collarbone to the right side of his chest. He looked at Mary for sympathy. When she maintained her blank expression, he pointed. "Look what they did?"

Mary whispered to Shaolin, "Duty calls."

Payne waited while Mary joined him, examined the injury, and then kissed it.

He made a face.

"Hungry?" she asked.

"I told you not to throw the chew bone," Kal called, still hugging the Cabrizi. When he put them down, they stayed close to him. Cookie tossed a couple pieces of faux jerky over the counter. Kal caught them and carried them with his tray to the side of the dining area, close to the others but far enough away so the dogs wouldn't be annoying.

The team started to sit but apart from each other. Payne hugged Mary to him before leaving the chow line to stroll among those who had already gotten their food and made their way to the tables.

He pointed at Heckler and Turbo. "Bullshit." He faced Kal and pointed once more. "Bullshit." He waved his finger at everyone sitting down. "Bullshit and more bullshit. We're a team. We sit together. And we're not any team; we're Team Fucking Payne. We bent the Vestrall to our will after defeating the five races of the Blaze Collective. We're the only people who have ever been on a Ga'ee ship. They don't take kindly to the non-silicon types. Team Payne! We have a line of battlewagons named after us. You thought it was me? Bullshit! I am nothing without you." He pulled Mary to him and spoke softly to her. "I am nothing without you."

"You were plenty without me," she whispered. "But you're even better now."

"Gag!" Turbo called loud enough for everyone to hear.

"It's like a syrup-fest over here. Somebody save us from drowning." Heckler raised his clenched hand, and Turbo fist-bumped him.

"Weren't you two supposed to blow up a planet?" Payne retorted. He took Mary's hand and headed for the counter. The others were filling in around Kal and the Cabrizi. Heckler and Turbo slide their trays closer to the others.

"We're biding our time. When you least expect it, *blammo*!" Heckler slammed his hand on the table. The Cabrizi snarled and growled.

"Easy." Kal worked to calm them, then drawled, "I'd be obliged if you didn't rile the critters."

"Sorry, man," Heckler mumbled.

The Paynes picked up their trays without having to order. Cookie had delivered four slices of his best pepperoni pizza on each tray, along with buffalo chicken pieces. None of the food had real meat. It was all biomass creations, but it tasted like the real thing to the humans' tastebuds. They knew it wasn't real but ignored the truth to embrace their version of reality.

It worked for them and Lev, too.

"Way to go, Cookie! Adult chicken nuggets and pizza pie gooey with cheese and sauce." Payne beamed. He saw the same thing on Mary's tray. "Didn't you want a salad or something?"

"What are you trying to say?"

Payne clenched his mouth shut. He knew when he'd entered a minefield. The only possible tactical decision was to get the hell out of the minefield.

"The team's waiting. We can't disappoint them. If I walk funny, it's because I have a salad shoved up my ass. Pizza good. Mmm." He sniffed and smiled.

"You are too ridiculous for words." She gestured with her chin toward the tables. "Live for the moment. Tomorrow will come soon enough."

"Twenty-four hours of liberty," Payne announced before sitting down. "Starting now. Enjoy yourselves."

No one moved.

"We just got settled, and you're already trying to chase us off?" Sparky wondered. "Honestly, getting laid has messed with your brain."

"Hang on," Mary protested.

Payne bowed his head and tried not to laugh out loud. When he looked up, he was biting his lip. "Just wait until I use that line on you. Turnabout is fair play."

"Also, 'mother' is only half the word," Heckler mumbled. He and Turbo shoulder-bumped.

Payne saw an opportunity to get on his soapbox. He pushed away from the table and stood.

"I like this. We've trained hard. We've deployed into the worst shit anyone has seen and come back in one piece. We've got one more big fight, then God willing, we'll be able to put all this behind us. Live our lives without staring into the abyss. We've earned that."

"Don't wreck our home," Virgil stated from the doorway, where he stood with one arm draped around Anneliese's shoulders. She smiled shyly.

"I think he's talking to you, Lev. I've never wrecked you."

"I shall endeavor not to be wrecked," Lev responded, "but no guarantees."

[10]

"We fight because someone has to. Better that it be us." –From the memoirs of Ambassador Declan Payne

"One week until the portal is completed. Construction is progressing normally," the Vestrall engineer reported.

Yeldon acknowledged the report. "*Levant*, continue on Patrol Route Four."

The battlewagon shifted course into a lazy S around the portal. *Russia* assumed a mirror course within range to provide supporting fire as necessary. The other two battlewagons were connected by energy tethers to the portal, to which they supplied a constant stream of newly manufactured parts.

"Firing Drill Seven. Defensive weapons, offensive missiles, and then main beam. Execute in five, four..."

Two Ga'ee carriers appeared simultaneously, both danger-close to the portal.

"Fire the main weapon!" Yeldon ordered.

The beam had been kept hot on ready standby for the past two weeks, cycling through firing phases to keep it fresh. The beam weapon erupted from the opening in the bow of *Levant*.

The quick response delivered the energy on target before the Ga'ee screens rose.

The weapon sliced a rent into the side of the ship that ripped the hangar's doors away and eviscerated tens of thousands of drones.

Russia accelerated toward the Ga'ee from the far side of the portal.

"Missiles away," Yeldon ordered calmly. He needed to buy two minutes for *Africa* and *Australia* to clear the portal and bring their weapons to bear on the enemy.

But two carriers?

Levant fired on the ship it had just attacked, the complete spread.

Yeldon watched helplessly as the second Ga'ee carrier unleashed its drones. They streamed from both sides into the void.

Endlessly.

Yeldon's stomach turned, and bile scorched the back of his throat.

We've failed, he thought.

Russia brought its main weapon to bear on the second ship and fired, but the energy screen absorbed it. Hundreds of drones streaming through were torched and destroyed, but thousands more continued unhindered. *Russia* continued to a position between the Ga'ee and the portal. Its defensive systems lit up the darkness of space as it cycled every weapon in its arsenal.

Tracer rounds streamed from the ship beside flashes of laser beams and plasma sent at high speed down the railgun mounts. Rapiers jumped from their launch tubes and began their circuitous journeys to the Ga'ee carrier. It wouldn't take long since the ships were within knife-fighting range of each other.

"Pull back to a position in front of the portal," Yeldon ordered. The ship had been slowing. It reversed course almost immediately with no appreciable change for the crew since the artificial gravity removed everything but the most significant inertia.

Africa and *Australia* fired their defensive arsenals while they shut down their tethers. Parts and materials floated into space. With a victory in the battle, they could recover them. With a Ga'ee victory, those parts wouldn't matter. More firepower flooded into the void like two tidal waves angling toward each other.

The drones soldiered on relentlessly. They didn't try to avoid the incoming fire. They would absorb it as they always had, fill the gaps left by their dead, and continue accelerating toward their targets with merciless fury.

A fury born of their collective minds, but not the fury of emotion. They had none as far as anyone knew. They acted as an advanced race, building starships, but for their singular focus on expanding into the galaxy using the scorched planet approach, destroying all in their wake.

The firestorm that erupted from the four battlewagons filled the void with an impenetrable barrier into which the Ga'ee drones stormed.

The titanic struggle started with the first impacts, plasma hammering into the lead drones, then more and more. Drones streamed past the first ones to die. Debris packed tighter and tighter into the space between the two ships.

The battlewagons continued to pour fire into the void.

"Drone count," Yeldon requested.

The sensor operator had been keeping track through the system Lev had developed for the Payne-class ships.

"One hundred and forty thousand drones launched, and ninety-seven thousand drones remain."

The countdown clock for a recharge of the beam weapon showed fifteen seconds.

The first drones impacted *Levant*. Clouds of drones angled toward the other battlewagons. The Ga'ee carriers followed the clouds until they were less than five kilometers from the portal.

When the countdown reached zero, Levant fired. From that range, none of the power bled off; it impacted the screens and tore them away. The residual energy continued through to the ship, melting the external panels and armor and ripping at the Ga'ee.

The ship continued. Scarred and damaged, its energy signatures spiked as its power plants flared to provide more energy to the failing screen.

The second Ga'ee carrier slowed to a stop. The fistfight was underway, with the two goliaths already doing battle.

Russia fired her main weapon from point-blank range. It burned through the shield, rocking the carrier and twisting the ship off its axis.

The drones continued to come. *Africa* and *Australia* maintained their defensive fire. After a full minute at the maximum cyclic rate, they only had another two minutes before their ammunition would be exhausted.

Two minutes was forever in space battle fought within spitting distance of each other. Like two sailing ships of old Earth, lined with cannons and linked by grapples, fighting for primacy. The one who could load and fire the quickest would sail away. The other would be introduced to the bottom of the ocean, burned and crushed.

More drones left the carrier and were only seconds from the battlewagons. They flew in a condensed cloud until they could spread out.

That helped the defenders, but not for long. The Ga'ee changed their tactics. A second and then a third wave of drones arced away from the field of fire.

The battlewagons were maxed out. Time was on the Ga'ee's side.

Yeldon watched the countdown for the other ships. "*Africa* and *Australia*, fire on the target marked G2 two hundred meters forward of the aft end. Match bearings..." the countdown timer read two when *Australia* hit zero. Yeldon waited. The instant *Africa* hit zero, he ordered, "And shoot."

The two battlewagons fired their main weapons. The proximity pounded the Ga'ee screens, and they came down. The beams continued through to the aiming point. The energy tore into the upper decks of the Ga'ee ship, gouging deeply, but the angle was too acute. The thirty-degree angle deflected too much of the energy, and it skipped harmlessly into space. Best would have been a ninety-degree shot to deliver the full power.

That was not what they had. The enemy wasn't congenial when it came to giving a good angle on target.

But the battlewagons were nose-on to the incoming, limiting their exposure. The Ga'ee weren't a normal enemy.

Drones started impacting the battlewagons. The first targets were the Rapier launch tubes. They hit and ripped into the tubes. The drones were shattered by a second and third wave impacting them and the same area. They streamed in, accelerating to increase their momentum and the damage they would cause. The longer the final approach, the greater the speed.

The drones were capable of achieving close to the speed of light if given enough space. They destroyed each other in their sacrifice to destroy their enemy.

The vastness of space, but the two fleets were squeezed into an area no bigger than a major city to determine who would keep the BD18 system.

Damage reports flashed across the screen. *Levant* was taking damage faster than the main weapon could cycle.

Helm gasped and continued to stare. Mortality was a vicious beast, raising its ugly head at the worst possible times.

"Target G2 and flush the tubes. Get those Rapiers out of here before we lose the capability," Yeldon said calmly, feeling the need to explain to his crew. Recognize the angst they felt, but keep them from ratcheting up their anxiety to the point where they could no longer do their jobs.

They would have to.

"Angle on the bow is zero," Yeldon said. "Prepare to accelerate to maximum."

"Sir?" Helm wondered.

Mortality, that ugly bastard.

"We can die in place, or we can take them with us. Which will help us succeed in protecting this portal?" The words raced from Yeldon's lips. He had no time to explain but explain he must. The crew needed to buy in.

They were all going to die.

"No one will know what we've done if no one survives." Yeldon jumped to his feet. "*Russia, Levant.* You have the squadron now. Do us proud." Commander Yeldon gave the finger to the larger-than-life image on the screen, the Ga'ee carrier. It was damaged and streaming debris but very much alive. "Full ahead!"

A computer voice reported, "Collision. Collision."

"Yes, sir," the pilot shouted in reply. With a tap and a slide, the ship's engines fired. The distance between the two ships started to disappear.

"Head-on, Mister Simms. Cut her in half."

The pilot made one minor adjustment. There was no time for more. The drones swarmed into *Levant,* tearing and clanging in their relentless attack.

"Collision. Collision," the voice repeated in a calm but urgent tone.

The ship started to break apart. Structural integrity had lost its fight, but its momentum carried it forward.

"Reactor to critical," Yeldon ordered, still on his feet despite the bucking and jerking of the deck.

The engineering section replied, "She'll blow." They understood clearly what the captain wanted.

"Collision…"

Levant twisted at the last instant to impact the more vulnerable hangar bay. The prow cut its way toward the interior.

The reactor didn't go critical. Engineering had a better plan. The ship shifted for a nanosecond as it sought to transition to faster-than-light speed. The energy expanded outward and through the Ga'ee ship.

With the light of a supernova, *Levant* and the target designated G1 became a single entity before blasting away from the portal as a funnel of superheated plasma.

The drones hugging *Levant* went with it, caught in the warped space bubble. Tens of thousands of drones and a ten-kilometer-long ship, gone in a flash.

"Launch Rapiers! All ships," Commander Rusty Blighe ordered from *Russia's* bridge. The flash of light that had been *Levant* and the first Ga'ee carrier was still burned into his retinas. He blinked quickly to regain his vision.

The launch tubes had been under a heavy drone assault. Like the final launch from *Levant*, any missiles that cleared the tubes would be the last. Thirty-one missiles answered the call. The tactical board cleared the icon of the first Ga'ee ship. There would be no more threat from it or its drones.

But *Levant's* missiles hadn't been wasted. They flew toward

G2 from the flank. No drones were in position to intercept them.

The screens were still down.

"Three chain guns are down. Six. Eight," the weapons operator reported.

"I understand," Blighe replied. "Focus on what *can* fire. Don't waste time on what can't." He checked the main screen. Eighteen seconds to recycle the beam weapon, but with the forward defensive systems going down, the drones could strike deep and take the weapon out.

There would be nothing he could do about it.

Fifteen seconds was all he needed.

Africa filled an inset of his screen with its vitals. Structural integrity started flashing red. The ship was breaking apart. Engines flashed a red zero. The ship was dead in space. Weapons systems flashed, and then life support. The image onscreen showed a ship going dark. Flashes of light indicated the drones that were continuing to attack.

There were more flashes as drones broke off and headed for the portal.

Eleven seconds.

"Prepare to accelerate," the captain ordered, taking a cue from *Levant*. They needed to kill G2 before the drones took out the portal.

Helm didn't hesitate. He didn't prepare. He kicked the ship in the guts, and it lurched forward.

Engine status flashed from yellow to red, and *Russia* started to drift.

Levant's Rapiers accelerated with the last of their fuel, which was substantial because the ships were so close. With a bright flash of light, the missiles disappeared and reappeared an instant later, then ripped into the carrier before exploding. Each warhead was ten megatons.

G2's central superstructure lifted, leaving the forward and aft sections behind. Now bent in half, the carrier belched a massive cloud of atmosphere-fueled flame.

The drones lost guidance but only for a moment—a moment that the Rapiers took advantage of. Those final thirty-one raced through the drone cloud.

When the drones came back to life, it was too late.

Three, two, one.

"Fire the main!" Blighe screamed, nearly unhinged with the revelation that survival was within reach.

The weapons officer's finger had been hovering. At zero, he planted it on the fire button. Even with drones heading into the cavity from which the beam came, the weapon was unhindered. With the carrier buckled, the aiming point had changed. The aft-end power plants were no longer available, but the entire front end was looking at them with only a ten-degree offset angle.

The beam slammed into the armored hull and tore its way inside. The front reactor blew, shearing off the front half of the ship.

Ten-megaton explosions rippled across the spine as the remaining anti-ship missiles delivered their payloads.

The ship twisted and turned as the impacts drove it back. It continued on a slow ballistic course away from the portal. Unguided drones bounced off *Russia's* hull.

"*Australia*, are you there?" Blighe called.

"Comm is down," the communications station reported.

"Restore comm, pri one, and restart construction. Get those work ships back here. Last I saw, we were a week from completion."

The XO sidled up next to the commander. "Maybe we can bury our dead first?" he whispered.

"When reinforcements arrive, we'll take a moment to celebrate the lives of those we lost. Until then, there is nothing more important than finishing this portal. Nothing. These people died for that. We can't squander their sacrifice."

Blighe stood and stepped away from the captain's chair.

"If you don't have a job that can be done, get somewhere and make yourself useful. I'll be in Engineering." He headed off the bridge but stopped at the hatch. "Good job, people. You saved BD23, this whole system, and once the portal is active, we will reinforce our position and make it so the Ga'ee will never take it. Never!"

[11]

"Passion is more than just heat. It's a love for what you're doing. Well, it's heat, too. Have you seen my wife?" –From the memoirs of Ambassador Declan Payne

The team spread out around the one conference room they used, despite all the decks of space. Admiral Wesson and Commodore Freeman were there, as was Commander Woody Malone.

Kal stood while the others sat. The Cabrizi wanted to run, but they'd closed the door. The ship was secure. Anyone who wanted to listen in could. The remaining crew was trustworthy. The dogs would distract them by running in and out, even though they were well-exercised. Almost as well as Team Payne.

"How are we going to isolate a Ga'ee ship so you can board it?" the admiral asked.

"We send a message to tell one to come here and check this place out," Payne replied confidently.

"What's the chance that only one ship will come?" Nyota asked.

"There's always a chance something will happen that we

don't intend. That shouldn't stop us from trying. The worst thing we can do is expose ourselves. That would ruin our hiding spot. If we pop out, they'll see us and move to high alert. If we send a small probe, we can replicate the neural transmission and send a signal through the net," Payne explained. "We've done the calculations. We think it's viable without giving ourselves away."

The admiral scowled. He looked from Payne to Dank and then at the commodore. "Lev, tell me this isn't the only plan you have."

"It's not the only plan we have," Lev replied.

The admiral sighed and relaxed. "Okay. Tell me the other options."

"It is the only plan we have."

The admiral leaned forward, put his elbows on the table, rested his chin on his hands, and glared at Payne.

"He's just doing what you asked him to do." Payne nodded emphatically. The admiral held his head in his hands.

"An alternative is we fold space back to a friendlier location and fight the Ga'ee there," the admiral finally offered.

Payne nodded. "That is an alternative. It's probably the most viable, but also one that doesn't resolve the problem. They said the ships that wreaked havoc were only scout ships. What the hell do they have that we don't know about?"

"The kilometer-wide mines are one thing that comes to mind," Heckler mumbled.

"Ten-kilometer-long ships with a hundred thousand drones each and a nearly infinite number of ships. Eventually, they'll all make it to our space. Eventually, they'll wear us down and take everything we have. Maybe we can stall them long enough for us to survive for a while, but all we'd do is delay the inevitable. They're coming, Admiral, unless we can stop them here."

"I know," the admiral admitted in a voice barely above a whisper. "Your plan is a go. Send a beacon out to infiltrate the neural network and issue the request for a physical inspection of this place. They have to know it exists because they had to be the ones to stash this junk in here."

"There isn't enough left of any of these ships for Lev to kluge together a working model with additional firepower. Not enough of the key components. It's just us," Payne commented. "We'll be in *Ugly 6*, ready to deploy, but we'll need the ship to get close, inside the interior where we won't interrupt the neural network."

"Right where they'll see and block *Leviathan*." The admiral shook his head. "You're going to have to be out there, invisible to everything. Lev will disappear behind the wrecks, as far away from the opening as he can get. We can fold space if need be."

No one mentioned that they'd have to leave Team Payne behind.

It wouldn't be the first time.

"We'll make do. As long as we can get on board the carrier, we can talk to it, can't we?" He looked at Blinky and Buzz. "Can't we?"

"We can. It'll help if we can link to Lev while we're trying it."

"*Trying*." Payne emphasized the word.

"We have a great number of processes we will run through, but we'll do it in a very short amount of time. We will try them until we find one that works, and then we'll exploit the hell out of that one to get what we want," Blinky explained in a tired voice.

"I need you two at the top of your game. Report to Medical as soon as we're done so Lev can knock you out for a solid eight hours. Then feast, then rest. Then we're pulling the trigger."

Payne looked at the admiral to confirm his order. Admiral Wesson nodded.

"We have a couple loose ends to tie up," Buzz started.

Payne pointed at him. "Not with burned-out brains, you don't. Get sleep, and then a good meal. After that, you can sharpen your digital knives."

Blinky and Buzz looked at each other for support but conceded. They didn't have enough energy to argue, which was Payne's point.

"The fate of the many in the hands of the few," the admiral added. "When you first boarded *Leviathan*, I saw the ship as a weapon to use against the Blaze Collective. A tool to exploit, nothing more. But I learned that in our way, we're all tools working together to build something greater. Lev, my friend, you have given us a chance to survive. Well, not necessarily us, but our race and the races who have allied with us."

"You are very kind, Harry. I was built to keep a war from happening. When I couldn't do that, I buried my head and watched that genocide didn't happen, consoling myself with the parity of the forces and the survival of all species, though war was taking its toll. Humanity advanced their knowledge. Then the Vestrall, the remnants of the Godilkinmore, appeared behind the curtain.

"The Godilkinmore interfered with the natural development of races on dozens of worlds. The Vestrall interfered with them after they established themselves as viable. Finally, the Ga'ee appeared. I wanted to believe they could be negotiated with. That their purpose wasn't the complete destruction of all the worlds that could support life.

"Now we are in a struggle that is truly life or death. I cannot carry out my initial programming, which was to be a deterrent. The Ga'ee absolutely don't care. They want to destroy me because they know where I came from. God1, they call me. I never believed pure evil existed, but the Ga'ee have a self-destructive purpose that will take the whole galaxy with them. It makes no sense, but destruction is the only thing they know. I only have one worldkiller remaining, but I long to use it on the original home planet of the Ga'ee. Take away something they hold dear, as they have done to thousands of worlds and countless races."

"Vengeance, Lev?" the admiral wondered.

"It's not pretty that a doomsday weapon seeks to make war, but it is logical. The Ga'ee must die. They cannot be allowed to remain in our galaxy or anywhere in the universe. Their purpose is antithetical to all carbon-based life forms."

"Lev, buddy, cool the jets. We only want them to stay out of our sectors. We can't have the goal of destroying them. We need a thousand ships like you, up-gunned and battle-ready." Payne leaned back and shook his head. "We don't have any of that. It's just us. An achievable goal is to sell them on the logic of pulling back. Reducing their numbers to what can be supported. Improve their ability to think as a collective by reducing the distance between the nodes."

"If we can get them to withdraw, we can get them to fly into the nearest star. All of them."

"We'll take it one step at a time, Lev, but I'm not up for genocide, and you shouldn't be either," the admiral replied.

Payne looked patently uncomfortable. "We need you to support our efforts, Lev. We have to stay together. We hang together, or we shall surely hang alone, as some smart guy from history said."

"I understand, Declan, Harry. I want to eliminate the threat, but to do that, I have to become that which must be despised. How could I reach such a conclusion? I need to think about what has happened."

Lev removed himself from their minds as thoroughly as if he'd physically walked out of the room.

"That worries me," Payne remarked. "We need to end the war, not win it. I don't think we *can* win. The Ga'ee's numbers are far too great. The carriers can operate independently, even if we cut the link to the central brain, whatever that is, wherever that is. Maybe we'll find out, but I'm pretty sure we don't want to go there."

The admiral scowled, then his face transformed, showing extreme worry. "Can you do it?"

"We're counting on it. We will. If we fail, fold back to Earth and tell people to start packing their bags. We need colonists to go where the Ga'ee won't find them for a thousand years if we're to save humanity or any of the other races. Can Lev fold space to another galaxy?"

"Who's to say worse isn't out there?" The commodore pointed at the ceiling.

Payne shrugged. No one knew. "Is the unknown worse than reality? How can it be? The Ga'ee are hell-bent on killing us all. They've already destroyed two races. Why haven't they attacked Vestrall Prime? Lev?"

Lev didn't answer because he hadn't heard the question. He was gone from their minds and the minds of everyone on board.

"What if the Progs created the Ga'ee?" Blinky asked.

"That's the most fucked-up thing you could ask," Payne shot back. "I wouldn't put it past them. A failed experiment, abandoned. They don't attack the Vestrall because they are Godilkinmore, but the Ga'ee have a death warrant out for *Leviathan*. How come one and not the other?"

Payne looked at Blinky and Buzz for answers. They held up their hands in surrender.

The admiral stood. "We're getting nowhere. The original plan: send a probe out to send a message on the neural network, summoning a ship to investigate the junkyard. Team Payne will be deployed in *Ugly 6*, ready to board the Ga'ee carrier once the digital penetration team gets in."

Payne snickered. "Someday, I may be mature enough not to laugh at something like 'the digital penetration team gets in,' but that's not today."

The admiral looked down his nose at the unrepentant and unapologetic major.

He needed to joke about something. They all needed it.

The next stop would be more than just *Ugly 6*. When they sent the probe into space, it would be for all the marbles. For the survival of the seven races.

[12]

"Sometimes you just have to laugh at the absurdity of it all."
—From the memoirs of Ambassador Declan Payne

"That's it, Barry. Bring her around." Command Josephs encouraged the team as they decreased their response times. He was working with Hunter-Killer Squadron One to tighten the team and deliver better performance.

Five Payne-class battlewagons maneuvered as a single entity, wheeling through space to reorient their main weapons through three hundred and sixty degrees to lay waste to any Ga'ee carrier that dared enter Earth's space.

The lead battlewagon from HK4, BW16, named *Japan*, waited near the portal. It was protecting the gateway to prevent another tragedy like the one that befell BW15, *Ebren Warrior*. Japan ran through its own drills as the crew familiarized themselves with the ship's operations. They were human volunteers, desk jockeys from the last Fleet base on Earth who had one last chance at serving in space, fighting a battle that mattered.

Admiral Ross remained at the shipyard, preparing the crews before they moved to their new ships while simultaneously managing the logistics to keep the shipyard operating at peak efficiency.

"HK1, lazy S. *President* as the anchor," Jimmy ordered. BW1 came to a full stop and started to rotate as if it were on a platen. The other ships fell into line, with the fifth accelerating through an arc.

In front of them, just outside the moon's orbit, space crackled. Then a Ga'ee carrier appeared.

Jimmy growled. "Continue rotation. Bring mains online, match bearings, and on my mark, shoot."

The battlewagons continued the maneuver. The Ga'ee's screens came up. A second Ga'ee carrier appeared on the hip of the first.

When the battlewagons aligned, the squadron fired five shots as one.

The beams hammered the shields and kept going, licking deep into the first carrier. Each beam had enough energy to melt the outer armor and dig deep into the interior when it reached the carrier, shredding the ship. It came apart in six sections. Three of the reactors went critical, radiating beams of light and energy. Not a single drone escaped before they all died.

"Fire Rapiers, full spread, corkscrew approach," Josephs ordered. The battlewagons lined up on the second ship but held their positions to maintain their distance until their main weapons recharged.

Nearly two hundred and fifty Rapier anti-ship missiles flushed from their tubes and raced into space, immediately assuming radical and varied courses so they wouldn't arrive simultaneously from a single vector but from different directions over the course of five seconds.

The countdown clock showed thirty-five seconds. The second carrier's hangar doors rotated open, and drones streamed out. They formed a massive cloud accelerating toward the battlewagons. The carrier accelerated on a collision course for the center ship, BWo3, *European Union*.

"Defensive weapons, all ships. Fill the sky, people." The defensive systems cycled, instantly sending lasers, projectiles, and plasma into the space between the ships.

Twenty-five seconds.

The alarm from BWo3 sounded through *The President's* speakers. "Collision. Collision."

"Retrograde to moon base. Maintain defensive fire," Jimmy called. The clock wasn't his friend. The drones were going to arrive before the weapons recycled.

Five seconds was a big overlap. The drones could do a great deal of damage in that amount of time.

The first wave of Rapiers hammered into the second carrier's screens. They detonated on the outside, raining nuclear fire along the shield. Explosion after explosion lit the sky and highlighted the bathtub of energy surrounding the carrier. Two hundred and fifty missiles equaled twenty-five hundred megatons.

None of them penetrated the shield.

Drones veered toward the battlewagons, an equal number toward each. Defensive fire wreaked havoc on the leading edge of the wave, but still they came.

Then they hesitated and turned back toward their carrier.

Jimmy was surprised but pleased. That was all it took to change the dynamic. The battlewagons would be able to fire before the first drone impacted a ship.

Japan re-entered normal space just beyond the Ga'ee ship and fired its main weapon into the weakened shield. It penetrated and kicked the ship in the aft end. The carrier started to tumble, exposing its spine to Hunter-Killer Squadron One.

The countdown clock hit zero.

"Fire!" Josephs punched a fist at the tactical screen.

The five battlewagons once again unleashed their main beam weapons as one at five targets on the spine. The angle of attack was nearly ninety degrees, a perfect broadside. The beams blasted the ship apart in a single, immense explosion that sent debris toward Japan, which tried to turn away from the molten metal and shards.

Japan took the brunt of the expanding cloud. It lost its attitude thrusters and started to spin on the longitudinal access, then the power flashed and went out.

"All hands, rally to *Japan*. Take it under tow, and let's get it repaired," Jimmy ordered. HK1 broke formation.

"Sir," the communication officer interrupted. "It's the office of the president with an urgent request."

A new contact appeared. A third Ga'ee carrier entered normal space near the portal.

"Ignore her. All ships, FTL to the portal now!" The coordinates were transferred, and the five ships entered faster-than-light speed before they completed their maneuver, leaving the drifting *Japan* behind.

Drones launched and attacked. By the time HK1 re-entered normal space, the portal was getting hammered.

The five ships fired again, but there was a new twist. The carrier had launched a salvo of missiles. Nearly two hundred Rapier-size birds were in the void, targeting the Payne-class battlewagons.

The beam weapons headed for the carrier, tore the shield down, and ripped into the massive ship. It died without coming apart. The drones continued on ballistic trajectories, mostly harmless.

But not the missiles. They continued on deadly courses, independent of guidance from the carrier.

"Defensive weapons, fire!" Barry shouted at the weapons station. Space lit up with tracers, lasers, and plasma.

The sensor operator jumped out of his seat. "Ga'ee carrier, right behind us!"

Only visual sensors had picked up the ship's entry into normal space, but the sensor operator had been watching closely. He was still unnerved.

A fourth carrier. One ship was drifting, but the five original ships of Hunter-Killer Squadron One remained.

"Flush all tubes and rotate on *President*'s longitudinal axis," Jimmy ordered. The ships complied with the order, and one hundred and fifty Rapiers darted into the darkness of space. The reload had not yet finished. The ships were arrayed around inside a shooting gallery. The beam weapons would take time to recharge, but the aft end was the least well-defended. The battlewagons needed to attain a bow-on orientation for maximum defensive weapon effectiveness.

Drones streamed from both sides of the carrier. Anti-ship missiles followed them into the void. The drones accelerated at five hundred gees, closing the gap in seconds.

The attack had been well-planned. The fourth carrier brought the punch and equaled the odds. Its arrival had been perfectly timed.

The first drones impacted all five battlewagons simultaneously. The impacts caused torn metal to screech from the blunt-force attack. The sounds of the attack radiated throughout the ships. Hammering. The rending of metal. The shrieks of ships in pain.

"Come around, damn you!" Barry exclaimed, more excited than he should have been. He sounded desperate.

The maneuver had exposed the launch tubes, and they were getting savaged. The status board showed the Rapiers going offline and quickly.

If we survive, we'll show the enemy the keel, Jimmy vowed.

"Continue your maneuver," Jimmy directed calmly. "Begin firing forward defensive weapons at ninety degrees to target."

He crossed his legs while sitting casually in the captain's chair, trying to exude confidence. The crew winced with each new clang and screech and ducked their heads in unison as if the overhead would come down on them.

They were located away from the outer hull for higher survivability. They needed it.

"Venting atmosphere from dorsal vertical shafts three, seven, and nine. Bulkhead doors breached to Deck Fifteen," the environmental control station reported.

The Ga'ee drones had penetrated into the interior of the ship and were only three decks from the bridge.

Barry needed everyone on the bridge to do their jobs. There was no spare crew to put in the corridors with railguns as a last line of defense, but there were…

"All hands not at stations, into the corridors with railguns or blasters. Whatever you can get your hands on. You see a drone, kill it. We need to buy all the time you can give us."

Sixteen seconds.

It looked like it would be too much. Drones ripped the spine apart, and weapons stations floated into space. The bow came around faster and faster.

The aft end moved away, saving the engines, but they too were being attacked on all five ships.

China sparked, and its central reactor exploded. At first, it was constrained to a fountain of fire, but the ship slowly separated on the lateral center line. The lights went out and it continued its spin, but it would never fire.

Ten seconds.

There was chaos in the passages. Railgun fire echoed through the secured hatch, but the fire stopped all of a sudden.

Barry clenched his teeth and watched the countdown clock.

He knew his people had died an ugly death. A massive body rammed the hatch, bowing it inward.

Eight seconds. A second and third impact signaled that the drones had arrived.

Commander Jimmy Josephs counted the seconds remaining in his life. The carrier would survive, and six battlewagons would be dead. The portal would be destroyed. Without reinforcements, Earth would fall to the Ga'ee.

He didn't think about a battle well-fought. They had killed three carriers. He only thought of the ultimate failure.

HK1 had been overwhelmed.

"Impacts on the Ga'ee," the sensor operator reported.

From where? Jimmy didn't say the words aloud because there was no time, but on the main screen, fountains of flame erupted from the ship as if its shield were down.

The countdown reached zero. Weapons didn't wait. "Firing the mains!" he cheered after he hammered the button. The beam weapon sliced deeply into the carrier. *Germany*, *China*, and *European Union* followed suit. A cloud of drones filling the void was incinerated as the energy tore into the enemy.

The drones lost their guidance as the beams ripped the ship apart.

Jimmy took a deep breath, having stopped inhaling for the final salvo.

"Get that hatch open," Barry pointed at the sensor operator, who was only too happy to comply.

Despite the convex shape, it swung open. Dead drones lay in the corridor beyond. Chief Tremayne stalked toward them while putting his railgun on his shoulder. "You might want to shut that."

The sensor operator closed the hatch while the COB put the drones out of his misery. He opened the hatch from outside while yelling over his shoulder. "Get these things off my ship!"

Commander Josephs stood on shaky legs and held onto the captain's chair until he was steadier. "COB, how about using those things to repair our ship?"

"Belay that!" Chief Tremayne shouted at an unseen crew member. "Cargo Bay Four. Load 'em up and fix my ship!"

Jimmy walked up to the sensor operator, who was still standing by the hatch. "What happened to the Ga'ee shield?"

"*Japan*, sir. They hit it with all the jamming frequencies, and one of them worked."

"*Japan*'s not dead?"

The sensor operator shrugged and shook his head. It seemed obvious that the ship was very much alive. Jimmy checked the main board. *Japan* steamed toward the debris field, looking fresh and fully capable.

Jimmy pointed at the communication officer. "Give me fleetwide." Comm signaled. "*Japan*, I don't know how you did it, but you saved us twice. All ships, we killed four Ga'ee carriers. What will they send next time? We don't know, but we defeated them and only lost one ship. We should have all died, but we didn't. Human perseverance and Godilkinmore technology. We delivered quality weapons fire on target. That made the difference. Tend to your ships. There's plenty of excellent debris floating around. Help yourselves to seventy-five percent, and then get on the repairs for the portal. We need that thing active. Earth needs it active."

Jimmy drew a line across his throat to cut the comm.

The communication officer pointed at the panel. "There's a delayed message from the president's office."

"I'll take it in my quarters. None of you needs to hear what nonsense she has to say."

They nodded knowingly.

Jimmy worked his way around the drones to the door to his

room. Inside, he helped himself to a long drink of water before pulling up the message.

"Whatever you need, Commander, let us know, and we'll make it happen. This threat is not transitory, as was initially estimated. Earth is at risk. There are no two ways about it. Sinkhaus, out."

"Well, now, that was unexpected. Fleet is the good guys again. How about that?" Jimmy smiled at her sincerity. The message had been sent before the fourth Ga'ee carrier appeared, and it was even more applicable now. But, four carriers? If the Ga'ee hit Ebren or Berantz or the Rang'Kor with four ships, those systems would fall. "What about the Vestrall?"

Why weren't they being attacked?

[13]

"When the time for talking is over, you have to go to work. No sense giving it anything less than your all." –From the memoirs of Ambassador Declan Payne

Ugly 6 hovered at the edge of the hangar bay. The buoy passed them and flew into space.

Blinky and Buzz were heads-down in their computer systems. Payne felt like it was time for a speech, although the team could do without it.

Still, Payne had to do what he was compelled to do. He unbuckled and stood. The team had their helmets off and would remain that way until the buoy penetrated the neural net.

"Nooo," Heckler whined.

Payne called for calm. "We have set events in motion that cannot be undone. They can only be managed. No matter how hard we train, the real battle will be fought on the neuroscape."

Dank leaned over to Buzz. "Is that a word?"

Buzz shook his head without looking up from his computer.

"We will do what we have to. Our goal is to take over an intact Ga'ee carrier. We have a high-power plasma rope to burn through the central bulkhead in seconds." Self-ignited plasma, five times hotter than thermite, contained on a sticky ribbon that could be attached and fired up. It had served them well to get into the last carrier. "We get in and hold off the little demons while Blinky, Buzz, and Lev work their magic, then we send the message. Quick in, quick out."

"We'll probably have to fight a few drones to get in there," Major Dank clarified.

Kal lifted the plasma cannon. "I'll clear the corridor. Y'all do the rest," he drawled.

"Your confidence in our abilities exceeds even our own," Blinky replied.

The team waited, but Payne didn't have anything else. He waved and sat down.

Mary gazed at him, wearing a half-smile.

"What? Heckler would be rolling his eyes and making faces if I said any more."

"I would," Heckler confirmed. He high-fived Turbo.

"We may have a planet for you to blow up," Payne replied. "Be flexible."

"Now you're talking. Next time, start with that." Heckler gave him a thumbs-up.

"These are the people who are going to save the universe or die trying," Payne whispered to Mary.

"They are the very best people," Mary replied. "If anyone can do it, it's them."

"Us," Payne corrected. "We all have a role to play on this, the galactic stage. Every action matters. Every action, if executed with sufficient violence, will move us forward one step at a time until we are staring into the abyss. We'll toss in grenades and explosives while yelling, '*Eat me!*' It is what we must do."

"So profound." Mary took his armored hand, and they sat

that way while *Ugly 6* maneuvered into the space with the derelict ships and hulks. Lev had salvaged very little from them, but the fold drive had been repaired. They could escape to their own space if they needed to. The drone bodies reinforced the area outside the ship that led to the external fold components.

The coordinates were locked in. Lev was ready.

Using energy tethers to repulse the hulks, Lev worked his way farther inside the shell until he was no longer visible from the space outside the serenity of their hiding spot.

Ugly 6 took its time going to the edge. It stopped and waited.

The buoy accelerated out of the shadow and protection of the shell and maneuvered into the neural network using the inertia from its final surge. Once inside, it sent a pre-programmed message, planting a seed that the boneyard might be worth checking out.

"Passive seed planted," Blinky announced. "Now we listen and wait."

Blinky's and Buzz's computers started receiving feeds from the neural network, forwarded from the buoy. The data streamed down the screen, being translated as it went.

Logistics and more logistics. Expansions and replacements.

"I'll feed your HUDs if you want to follow along," Blinky offered.

The team put on their helmets. First in line was Payne.

"Boring as shit," Major Payne observed. "Look what happens when you become an advanced race. You devolve into bureaucratic nonsense. Is there anything useful in there, like a search for us?"

"Nothing like that. Not yet, anyway, but we've been listening for a grand total of ten seconds."

"Speed of thought, Blinky! They have to be looking for us."

"I concur, but nothing is still nothing, no matter how important we think we are. What if they think of us as nothing more than a pimple on their ass, annoying but not all-consuming? They probably have more important things to discuss, like moving limited supplies around."

Dank tapped his finger as the thought came to him. "Damn! You guys were right. They *do* need to contract. They're robbing Peter to pay Paul."

"In a big way. They need to expand for resources, or they die in place," Sparky replied.

"Unless they contract to reduce their demand for resources," Payne argued. "Even though I expect the closest planets to their central core are barren wastelands, devoid of anything worth having." Payne watched the information stream until it filtered through the chaff. A response. A ship was on its way to take a look. Investigate the anomaly identified within the lunar shell.

"We have a bite," Payne announced.

"More chatter about the issue." Buzz twirled his finger.

Payne's lip twitched. "Who delivered the order? That's where we ultimately want to go."

"It's a neural network," Blinky explained. "It's circular and interconnected. The synapses fire, and information gets transferred in all directions."

"You know you wanna know, and I think you're already working on backtracking where that order came from."

Blinky half-smiled. He and Buzz hadn't bothered to put on their helmets. Their information was coming through their computers, with additional feed sent to their minds via Lev using telepathy.

"Subtle stab to the heart of our cyber warriors," Dank intoned.

Heckler removed his helmet and spoke loudly. "Weapons

review." He tapped the mid-size weapon, which was the size and shape of a submachine gun, right down to the drum-like magazine. "I bring you the Heckler Koch anti-Ga'ee plasma torch weapon. Pull the trigger, and you get a laser-thin line of plasma to shred a Ga'ee to a range of about two meters. Hold down the thumb button and then pull the trigger when you want to share the love across a broader front. One meter wide to two meters, but that will also drain your main vein in about two seconds. Use it sparingly."

The team looked at their torch weapons to identify the thumb button, which was conveniently located slightly above where their thumbs would naturally be placed on the weapon. They would feel it while firing normally and could readily shift if they needed the full spread.

"Nice piece of gear, Heckler." Payne bowed his head. He had hoped for something with a little more range, but the Ga'ee were hard to kill. This improved their odds without shooting their railguns at point-blank range within a ricochet-producing metal box.

"Who has the rope?" Payne asked.

Joker raised her hand. Sparky and Dank also raised their hands.

"Redundancy is good." Payne gave them the thumbs-up. "Once more, the plan." He removed his helmet and stood. "The second the ship gets close enough, we jam all frequencies. We cut a hole in the hangar door opposite the central corridor. We'll enter the land of fifty thousand drones, with the uglymobile jamming the neural net from inside the hangar bay to keep the drones from activating.

"When we reach the central corridor, Kal leads the way, using the plasma cannon to clear it out. Sparky sets the rope, which burns an access through the bulkhead. We secure the corridor while Blinky and Buzz work their magic with a direct access to the ship's brain, and ultimately to the entire network. We sit back and watch the magic happen."

"Any bets on it actually going like that?" Heckler wondered.

No one took him up on it, although the team members looked like they wanted to.

Payne looked put out until Mary nudged him and leaned close. "You don't have a great track record." Her suit's speakers blasted her whisper. She quickly removed her helmet.

Payne looked nonplussed but couldn't maintain the expression. "We train to adapt and overcome. What's our goal? Get Blinky and Buzz to where they can seize control of the ship and bend it to their will. Everything we do goes toward that single purpose. If one of them falls, then we get the other there. We fight until there's no one left. Only then can we say we gave our all."

"Morbid much?" Shaolin asked softly.

Payne expected that from Heckler but not their soft-spoken monk in training. He had to smile. "I want us all to come out of this alive." They had time to kill, so he changed the topic. "Did everyone enjoy their break? Get some private time worth having?"

"What did Lev do?" Sparky asked.

"I don't understand," Payne replied.

"Federico is so head over heels in love with me. I know better. I'm singularly unlovable. Look at me. It's ridiculous. Did Lev brainwash him?"

Payne's mouth fell open, and he stared. "I'm pretty sure not. I always look at you, but I don't *look* at you. Brainwashing? Turbo got a proposition on Earth that one time. Heckler, too."

"We don't talk about that," Heckler said, quickly turning away from his wife.

"Ga'ee carrier," Buzz announced.

"Thank God!" Payne exclaimed softly. "Helmets, people. It's showtime."

Between the data feeds on their HUDs and the tactical screens on the side doors of *Ugly 6*, they had all the information they could handle. Payne kicked himself for the distraction. He needed his team focused.

"One carrier, standard class we're used to. Ten kilometers in length. Distance from the opening, one thousand kilometers and closing." Payne spoke like an announcer, stating the facts without editorializing. He let the team members build their own frame of reference. They had experience with these ships—one empty, one heavily damaged. They'd never been on board one with a full hangar bay.

That was about to change.

"Jam the fuck out of them, Blinky," Payne growled into his helmet. No one else heard. They weren't meant to hear, only to do their jobs. He could feel the adrenaline surge. His anger seethed below the surface. Why did the Ga'ee have to come? Why did they even have to exist?

They'd carve a path through the drones and take over the ship. They'd taken over one before, but they were far better now. Payne trusted his people. Blinky, Buzz, Lev, and Davida were the best in the universe.

Even if Payne was the only one who thought that.

They'd bring the Ga'ee to their figurative knees, then take over their entire society through a single dominant brain cell. He didn't think they'd be able to become the one. He suspected they would have to go to the source, the one that had ordered the carrier to investigate them. That cell needed to die. The rest would fall in line with the new dominant voice.

Payne was counting on the Ga'ee doing what he'd seen them do. Follow the leader, even if the leader was just another neuron of equal standing.

"Fifty kilometers. It's actively scanning the interior," Virgil reported. "Can you guys do something about that?"

Blinky didn't mince words. "No."

Payne shook his head, but his helmet didn't move. "We can't interfere with what they normally do. We'd summon the whole Ga'ee fleet. Let them scan. *Leviathan* has gone dark, radiating no more energy than we are."

"That's hard to believe," Dank blurted.

"Shielding and dampening. Lev is active," Payne countered. "He just doesn't look that way."

"Roger," Virgil confirmed, feeling stupid since he knew that. He closed his eyes for a moment to regather his wits. Now was not the time to relearn old lessons.

Tension filled the air. The team *acted*. Sitting and waiting wasn't their forte. Heckler and Turbo tapped their armored feet in unison. Even with their external audio pickups at maximum, they couldn't tell how loud it was.

Payne waved to get their attention. When Heckler gave the thumbs-up, Payne pointed at his boots.

The tapping stopped. The major tried to focus on the mission but found his mind wandering. They wouldn't know until they were there, and they'd have to flex to the situation. Every step they took would be determined on the spot.

"They're closing and increasing their scanner power," Blinky stated. "We're invisible to them."

"What about *Leviathan*?" Payne asked.

"He is a drifting hulk, just like these other ships. We are invisible because we have successfully told them to ignore us."

Payne had missed the part where he was supposed to ask why they were invisible. He took Blinky and Buzz for granted, and that wasn't going to stop anytime soon.

"Top-notch work, guys. On your order, we'll head in."

"It'll get much closer. Inside the outer barrier," Buzz replied confidently. The two tapped furiously on their keyboards.

The view outside the insertion craft showed the massive ship approaching. It slowed rapidly and neared until it could have rammed them if Lev hadn't drifted slowly inward as if he were riding a bow wave from an approaching seagoing vessel.

Ugly 6 accelerated along the port side of the carrier, following the closed hangar bay doors until it reached where the central transverse corridor was located. The craft bumped against the Ga'ee carrier and remained in contact. Two high-intensity plasma torches started cutting a hole in the doors.

They knew exactly how thick the doors were and the material from which they were made. The plasma cutters had been adapted for exactly this purpose. Lev, in lock-step with the team, had improved their chances for success. Payne's initial plan had called for blowing the opening with a torpedo.

He had been overruled by everyone.

Blinky and Buzz continued to tap on their keyboards while Lev managed the initial access. The carrier stopped advancing into the moon's shell, a third of the way in and two-thirds out—exactly where Payne wanted it to be to stay away from the neural network.

"Are they going to ignore us when we get inside?" Payne wondered.

"Working on it," Blinky replied.

Payne's eye twitched. He checked his railgun—full load at full power and two spare magazines with integrated power packs. He carried the plasma cutter in case they needed to manually address a wriggler infestation.

An entire ship filled with Ga'ee.

His mind raced with what it might look like inside. A cavern filled with bugs climbing the walls, ready to drop on them from the ceiling? Come at them from holes near the floor?

How would the Ga'ee ignore them after they cut the first hole in the ship? What about the second one, and after they started playing with the ship's programming?

Ugly 6 pushed gently on the cutout and it fell inside the ship, bouncing off a drone and taking it to the deck. *Ugly* 6 assumed the spot the drone had filled, but the insertion craft was much bigger. It ran into drones on five sides. The only respite was behind the craft, the part that was open to the interior of the graveyard. *Ugly* 6 filled that with a small forcefield to retain the atmosphere within the hangar bay.

The insertion craft tried pushing forward, but the drones were packed in too tightly. Payne checked the team on his HUD. They were all green, but pulses were starting to climb in anticipation of what they knew had to happen.

"Open the side doors, Lev. Looks like we're walking. Heckler and Turbo up front. I'm next with Kal, Shaolin and Joker, Blinky and Buzz and Sparky and Byle, and Virgil, you and Dog bring up the rear."

The outer doors rotated up and out of the way. The drones were packed tightly, but not so tightly that they couldn't get out. They dropped past a drone to the deck. By turning sideways, Heckler found they could get between the drones, take two steps and then turn sideways once more.

They had over a kilometer to cover. "This is going to take a while." Heckler stated the obvious. He moved as quickly as he could, counting on Blinky and Buzz to hold the drones in place however they were managing it.

The team spread out. Instead of two by two, they went single file. Virgil and Mary had to wait, standing there with drones hovering centimeters from them. They wanted to move, but there was nowhere to go.

Kal barely fit in his new powered combat armor. It made him the biggest target, too. He had to push past the hovering drones, shoving them out of the way. They swung back to where they started immediately after being released like they were held in place by tethers and not under their own power.

"Why are they so solidly in place?" Payne wondered.

Blinky and Buzz were on the move and couldn't check their systems, but Lev maintained a low-power comm channel with *Ugly 6* and was reading the data. "There is a high-energy power grid in the hangar bay. You'll want to avoid that."

"How in the hell do we avoid that? We're *in* the hangar bay, trying to squeeze between the drones. These things are jam-packed in here! They're stacked four high and to infinity deep and wide," Payne replied. "Any estimate on numbers?"

"Sixty-two thousand." Lev's answer wasn't surprising. They knew a Ga'ee carrier was able to launch over one hundred thousand drones total from both hangar bays. Sixty-two thousand was half the total, less any in production.

"The good news is if they try to attack us, they can't move either. It's so bad in here that we have to go outside to change our minds."

"Groan." Mary snorted. "How long do we have before they take action against us?"

"They'll remain in place for the time being," Blinky replied ambiguously.

Heckler grunted as he worked his way forward, disturbing the drones as little as possible. Turbo's suit was small and she had less trouble, but Heckler remained in the lead. She would get too far ahead. His pace was more in line with the rest of the team's.

The mission timer showed they had been outside of *Ugly 6* for exactly fifteen minutes when Heckler reported the central transverse corridor was in sight.

"Good news. Keep jamming," Payne replied.

"Bad news is it's filled with drones." Heckler closed with it and stepped aside. The drones filled the space like sentinels.

You shall not pass. Payne could hear the deep voice in his mind, but to accomplish the mission, they had to move into and through the corridor.

"Kal, set up here and be ready to blast these things out of the way."

The Ebren braced himself and aimed.

"Blinky, if you can't get them to move, we'll have to fire them up." The team bunched into the space around the opening to the corridor. The drones were not pressed against the bulkhead, which gave the team a respite from the stifling crush of machines.

Blinky and Buzz sat down and broke out their computers. They immediately started tapping away, not bothering to remove their helmets even with the atmosphere maintained in the hangar bay. The temperature was still too cool for comfort. Despite the hole they had cut in the door, the atmosphere was still contained.

If Kal had to start blasting, things would quickly heat up.

"Plasma rope?" Payne asked. Joker held one out. Sparky held out the other one. Dog waved the wand on the backup to the backup. She was stuck carrying the plasma torch, but she had volunteered. It made her a wide load, and Dank had been pushing her through the narrow gaps between the drones.

"Kal first," Payne continued, much to Heckler's and Turbo's chagrin. "Then you two." Payne pointed down the corridor. "We need as much of that clear as we can get to give us space to work and standoff distance for when they start coming after us. Sparky, fall in behind Turbo. Then Blinky and Buzz right behind me. Follow closely, and Dog and Virge, you cover our six. It would be a rough spot if these birds turned around and started storming down the corridor."

The big problem was that there was no hatch to close off the corridor. This ship had a wide-open feed so the drones could enter the hangar bay directly.

"I know what you're thinking, Dec," Virgil commented. "It would be nice if we could block it with the uglymobile, but there's no way to get it over here."

"A heavy-duty door would work since the drones can't build up any ramming speed unless a few thousand of them deploy outside the carrier to open up an attack lane. Let's make sure they don't deploy. Keep those outer doors closed, Blinky."

"Easier said than done, boss." Blinky didn't interrupt his tapping.

Payne was getting nervous. He had hoped they would be ripping into the guts of the ship by now. A half-hour in, and they were still standing there looking at each other. Blinky had warned him, but Payne hadn't listened.

Then it hit him…

The sensation as the Ga'ee ship transitioned to faster-than-light speed.

[14]

"Sometimes you roll a one, and as a reward, you get kicked right in the dice bag." –From the memoirs of Ambassador Declan Payne

"The Ga'ee carrier has departed," Lev reported. The mission clock read thirty-one minutes and fifteen seconds.

The admiral hung his head. "Team Payne was still on board. How long do they have?"

"With full access to *Ugly 6*, they can survive for three weeks before they run out of water. They'll be out of food in two weeks."

Commodore Freeman hugged him. "There's time for them to do what they went over there to do. What do we do in between?"

"Pray, and see if Lev can decipher the signals our carrier friend sent and received. Lev? You are deciphering the signals, aren't you?"

"Nothing to decipher, Harry. I have tapped into their neural network. I understand what they're saying."

"It's what they're not saying that you need to understand," the admiral replied.

"The carrier reported null findings before leaving with Team Payne."

"Did it say where it was going?"

"It did not, but Alphonse and Katello will send me a message over the neural network when they return to normal space."

"They can do that without being discovered?" The admiral was skeptical despite the evidence before his eyes. Team Payne had boarded the Ga'ee carrier and departed without an alarm being raised. "Did they take over the ship?"

"No. Last report, they were still attempting to clear the transverse corridor."

Admiral Wesson crossed his arms and glowered, wondering why he hadn't received the report.

Lev heard his thoughts, as he always did. "I was in contact with Alphonse and Katello. We were attempting to get the drones filling the corridor recalled to the manufacturing area, which would have cleared the corridor. There was no room in the hangar. It's jam-packed."

The admiral understood. There was no report. "Your buoy is still in the void, listening?"

"My buoy sending me all the chatter. It's back to business as usual. No alarms have been raised."

"What if they're hiding it?"

"Then they will have the upper hand. I have been working to extricate myself from the wreckage and gain a clear line of sight out of here."

"For FTL travel," the admiral realized. "You're not prepared to fold space?"

"Are you prepared to abandon Team Payne?"

"No," the admiral answered simply. "It's nice to have all the options available, just in case. Returning to our space would give you the ability to fabricate another worldkiller but come back to Ga'ee space. There isn't a spot out here that's two hours away by FTL from anywhere, is there?"

"There is not. The neural network is a lattice within which their ships see and hear everything that takes place. Ships are scattered strategically throughout their systems as well as interstellar space. Intergalactic space is too far away by faster-than-light speed to be of any use for a rescue mission to collect Team Payne. There is no safe space in Ga'ee space to which we can fold."

The admiral nodded and looked at the tactical board as if magical information had appeared since Team Payne left. There was nothing besides the subtle movement of the hulks around *Leviathan* as maintenance bots helped shift the dead and drifting ships out of the way.

"I'm sorry, Major Payne," the admiral murmured. "Once again, you are on your own."

"The portal is online," the Vestrall engineer announced. "We will be taking the rest of the week off." He closed the channel without waiting for a reply.

Commander Rusty Blighe pumped his fist. "Get me *Australia,* then prepare the information packet to transfer to Earth."

The communications station flashed green. "Lieutenant Aramas, *Australia.* Does that mean what I think it means?"

"The portal is live," Blighe answered. "We're going to transmit a message to the forces on the other side, requesting reinforcements. I don't know what they'll be able to provide, but if it's anything, they can get here right freaking now."

"Roger. We're still at seventy percent. We need time and downtime to bring our wagon to one hundred percent combat-effective."

"Understand. We're hanging together by duct tape over here. Maybe they can send a freighter with supplies. It'd be nice to get fresh food." Rusty Blighe signaled for the comm officer to close that channel and open a new one. "Activate the portal to Earth's space, and Comm, transmit our message to anyone with ears to hear."

The portal shimmered into existence. Then it cleared to show the sun as the brightest star in the sky beyond Earth, which was little more than a dot as seen from the portal near Jupiter.

"Message sent," the communications officer confirmed.

"How long does this thing stay open?" Blighe wondered.

"I'd ask the Vestrall, but they said not to bother them. You know how they are," the XO, a lieutenant, said.

"We all know. Feeling good about yourself? Talk to a Vestrall for a minute or two. They'll knock you off your pedestal. How did Ambassador Payne win them over?"

"I think he tossed their leader out the window of their command center. They were on the hundred and twenty-fifth floor," Blighe replied.

"Really?"

The commander shrugged. "I don't know. That's the rumor, anyway. I choose to believe it because if I could, I'd send those arrogant little pricks out an airlock. I believe the ambassador does not suffer fools gladly. They might know more than us, but they aren't better."

"As evidenced by the fact that Ambassador Payne is the leader of the Vestrall. The leader of all seven races. And he's Fleet!" The lieutenant smiled proudly.

"He's Fleet, but not like us. He's a SOFTie, Special Ops Fleet, but what you've seen here is Fleet at her finest."

"Receiving a transmission," Comm reported.

Blighe motioned at the main screen, but the image was already there.

"Commander Jimmy Josephs, Hunter-Killer Squadron One. It's good to see the portal is finally active. We've received your info dump, but I haven't looked at it yet. What's your status?"

"Commander Rusty Blighe of what's left of HK2. Down to two battlewagons, *Russia* and *Australia*, and we're only about seventy-five percent combat-ready. Any way we could get some reinforcements to help us hold this portal?"

"I'd love to say yes, Rusty, but we were attacked by four carriers at once. We lost one of ours and took a great deal of damage, but the portal survived. President Sinkhaus will have a cow if we leave the system. When were you last attacked?"

Rusty gritted his teeth before answering. "Nine days. The Vestrall worked like fiends to finish the portal. Those bristly little fuckers came through."

Jimmy chuckled lightly. "They have that effect on everybody, but they're good at what they do. We can't spare anything, but we will rally the freighter fleet to deliver supplies. Maybe a few extra Rapiers, too. Those have worked well for us."

"And us. We're running low. They'll be greatly appreciated as soon as you can possibly get them to us."

Jimmy gestured for an officer to transmit the request. "You caught us on a training run out by the portal; otherwise, there'd be a comm delay. We try to keep moving to catch the Ga'ee off balance." He looked away to see if the comm officer had transmitted his request. When he faced the screen again, he found Rusty waving frantically.

"They're back." His eyes focused elsewhere. "Fire the main!" The comm channel dropped.

"These portals are two-way, aren't they?" Jimmy asked although he knew the answer. Two points in space connected using the same principle as the fold drive. "HK1, follow *The President* through. Bring your mains online and prepare to fire a full spread of Rapiers. Targets TBD."

Three "Rogers" were the stalwart replies. *President* accelerated through the portal, knowing the others would be right behind him.

The Ga'ee had launched their drones, which were closing rapidly on the portal.

"Pick up the pace, HK1. Portal could go down any second now. Weapons, full defensive spread. Hold them off until the squadron is through."

He maintained a laser-like focus on the tactical situation. The two remaining battlewagons of HK2 had already fired their beam weapons at two Ga'ee carriers who were close to the portal.

A second ship from HK1 cleared the event horizon, and a third entered. *President* dodged to avoid being rammed from behind by the rapidly accelerating *America*.

"Bring the beam to bear on target designated GC2," Jimmy ordered.

Barry Cummins hovered near the weapons station, directing the repair teams to pre-stage themselves.

The ships were going to get hit and hard.

A third and a fourth Ga'ee carrier appeared closer to the planet. The standoff distance gave the Hunter-Killer squadrons space to work but left the Berantz to fend for themselves.

GC3 changed course toward the portal.

Germany cleared the portal, allowing *European Union* to enter right behind it.

A drone cloud hit the portal after a full acceleration. The effect was instantaneous. A section of the portal ripped clear, and the energy driving the link fountained from the gas giant through the portal. Earth's space disappeared. The battlewagon that was halfway through was cut cleanly across its mid-section, part of it caught in each sector of space.

The forward half of *European Union* tumbled as it flashed and sparked. Six Rapiers erupted from the dying ship's launch tubes before the vessel went dark.

Jimmy tore his eyes away from the dying ship. The bow was aligned. "HK1, fire the mains."

Three beam weapons lanced through the void and tore into the Ga'ee carrier, ripping past its flickering shields and hammering the ship into oblivion. Its drones died a quick death, condemned to guideless trajectories through the void.

A voice came over the squadron comm channel. "*America* here. *Japan's* code-break worked on this bad boy. Will transmit the jamming spectrum as the Rapiers close with target GC1."

"Rock on, *America*," Jimmy replied. Drones from the first carrier were hounding the remaining two ships from HK2. "Launch a full salvo of Rapiers. Transmit the codes now."

The Rapiers from *European Union* were closing. The paltry number of Rapiers from *Russia* and *Australia* had already been intercepted. The battlewagons cycled their defensive weapons as their mains recharged.

Countdown clocks showed on the screen for each ship, along with an operational status stoplight. Both HK2 ships flashed yellow.

Barry Cummins called from the weapons station, "Close on GC1. Knife-fighting distance, please."

President lurched forward. Defensive weapons cleared the path directly in front of the bow. Explosions rippled across the view.

Twenty-five seconds.

The alarm blared. "Collision imminent."

"Slow us down," Barry ordered. "No sense beating our face with their fists. Keep the beam weapon clear and prepare to fire from danger-close."

That translated to "Brace for the impact from debris." With the shield down and a bow-on shot, the big ship would rip down its centerline, possibly losing containment on six power plants simultaneously.

The shields flickered out of existence, and the dead battlewagon's last gasp of six Rapiers fired their remaining fuel through the engines to accelerate on terminal approach. The missiles dove into the outer hull, penetrated, and continued into the Ga'ee ship's interior before exploding. Sixty megatons of destructive force tore into the guts of the ship. Its groan of pain vibrated through space as the carrier twisted and flames shot from the open hangar bays.

It didn't die, though. The drones kept coming. The screens were down for good. Drones reformed and accelerated back to their carrier in an effort to form a physical defensive shield around the ship.

Many would make it, but others wouldn't.

"Full stop. Back us away," Barry ordered. His initial impulse to close the distance was no longer the right tactic. They needed to stand off to reduce the damage. There were two more carriers to fight after the imminent demise of GC1.

Rapiers corkscrewed through space. Some arced wide. Others raced straight in. Drones flooded the space before them.

The attacks on the battlewagons stopped.

Australia stopped firing and turned away from the engagement, heading toward deep space at a crawl. Its only goal was to save the crew by eliminating taking more damage.

"Rusty, after we kill this bastard, form up with us. We'll take out GC3 and then move to BD23 to deal with target GC4."

In the back of Jimmy's mind, the loss of the portal nagged

him. He'd brought the four battlewagons of HK1 to Berantz space. Earth was unprotected except for *Japan*, which had recently been repaired and was waiting for the next ship for Hunter-Killer Squadron Four.

If they left immediately, they could make it back to Earth in a little over two weeks.

A lot could happen in two weeks. They'd have to see how long it would take to repair the portal. The loss of a section wasn't as bad as the explosive force from the catastrophic disconnection.

Jimmy couldn't shake the thought that he had condemned Earth. He felt a pain in his stomach, the physical anguish of regret burning a hole into his gut.

The clock reached zero before the surviving Rapiers cleared the drone cloud. "HK1, only *President* will fire. Save your beams for GC3." Jimmy pointed at the screen. "Fire the main." They didn't need the other ships. With the shield down and the ship already damaged, *President*'s shot split the Ga'ee carrier from stem to stern. The power plants erupted one after another, sending shockwaves out laterally. Five rings expanded outward.

The drones lost their guidance.

HK1 left the Ga'ee's weapons behind. They could clean them up later. "New course, head-on with GC3," Barry ordered without waiting for Commander Josephs.

Recycle time for the main weapon was longer than it would take to intercept the third Ga'ee carrier.

Three other battlewagons were bearing down on the enemy. Without shields, two were sufficient.

"*Germany* and *America*, prepare to fire your main weapons. We'll save *Russia* and us for the grand finale."

"Slow your acceleration," Barry ordered to keep the drones from reaching the battlewagons before the beam weapons were ready.

"Full spread of Rapiers on arcing approaches. Launch." Jimmy pointed at the board as if he were directing a video game.

"I'm out," Rusty Blighe replied. The heavily damaged *Russia* was barely able to maintain its forward speed. Its defensive weapons were trashed, but it had its main weapon.

"We're not." The tactical screen counted the outbound missiles: one hundred and thirty-four. With unrepaired tubes, that was a one hundred percent launch. "*Russia*, you and *Germany* fire your mains on my mark. *America*, prepare to transition to FTL. Clear the debris field and target your arrival at danger-close to GC4."

The Rapiers took circuitous routes toward the Ga'ee carrier. Germany sent the signal across the targeted jamming spectrum, and the enemy's shields flickered out of existence. The drones instantly changed course to return to the carrier.

"Prepare to fire," Jimmy directed calmly. The drone clouds moved toward the carrier's vulnerable flanks, leaving a minimal presence in front of the ship. "Fire."

Two beams lanced through the void and blasted the Ga'ee carrier. A quarter of the ship was ripped away while the rest struggled to turn the ship. The drones jockeyed to intercept the Rapiers.

The Ga'ee carrier tried to run. It activated its FTL drive and exploded, tearing the ship apart as the energy released through the ship and into space.

"Call off those missiles and recover them. We'll be back. FTL in three, two, one."

President and *America* transitioned into faster-than-light speed for just a few seconds to close the gap to the fourth Ga'ee carrier. When they arrived, it had already changed its heading.

"Fire," Jimmy ordered. In the milliseconds between the order and the weapons officers pressing their buttons, the Ga'ee carrier transitioned to FTL speed and disappeared. The beam weapons skipped harmlessly off BD23's upper atmosphere and dissipated into space. "Ain't that some shit."

"Three ships intact, a fourth damaged, and a fifth heavily damaged that might not be recoverable," Lieutenant Commander Barry Cummins reported.

"And a portal we can't use," Jimmy added. "Comm, get me Commander Blighe."

When the link was live, Jimmy spoke. "Better get those Vestrall repairing the portal."

Rusty Blighe shook his head. "Two were on *Levant*. There were three on a freighter-turned-repair vessel, but that ship was hit about the time you came through to Berantz space. We have not been able to reach them."

"Then we better go looking. Otherwise, we're transitioning to FTL the moment we're able to and returning to Earth space. We've left Earth vulnerable. It's been nine days since the last attack. The next could come any day now. Saving the Berantz might have cost us humanity."

[15]

"If I said what I thought, they would have kicked me out a long time ago." –From the memoirs of Ambassador Declan Payne

"We're going to start blasting our way in if you goofy fuckers don't do something," Payne threatened. "The good news is that the drones can't clear a lane by leaving the ship, so we should be able to handle them. Only the ones in the corridor are facing us. The others can bump us with their backsides. If they can't get their sword points facing us, they're not dangerous."

Heckler looked at the rows of Ga'ee drones behind them and the two-wide queue facing them from the corridor. "If we can kill them fast enough, they won't know what hit them."

"Agreed. The time for fucking off is over," Turbo interjected.

"You all know the plan. Line up, and Kal, if you would be so kind? Clear us a path."

Heckler and Turbo prepared to run into the corridor on Kal's flanks. Sparky was ready to jump in behind them with Payne beside her. The others would go where they were needed. Dank and Dog aimed at the closest drones in the hangar bay.

"You guys ready?" Payne asked, pointing at Blinky and Buzz.

They closed their computers and stood. "All things being equal, no drones should move in response to the plasma cannon. We've told them repairs are underway in the transverse corridor," Buzz explained.

"Then why the hell didn't they move out of the way?"

"I don't think there's anywhere for them to go. I think they are ass-jammed in there. Blasting them to clear the corridor could be standard practice." Buzz was the first to give the thumbs-up.

Kal nodded his helmeted head. He took aim and pressed the trigger, intending to hold it down for as long as he had ammunition. The first drones shattered under the point-blank assault from the plasma cannon. Heckler and Turbo had to dodge back to avoid the molten wreckage splattering in an arc around the drones.

The first two died and crashed to the deck, broken, then the next and the next. Kal eased forward, stepping carefully until he had the rate of destruction timed. Then he marched steadily forward. Heckler and Turbo picked their way behind him. Sparky remained singularly focused on keeping her footing. She had no idea how far they'd gone, but Payne knew.

They met up with the longitudinal corridor leading aft. Kal checked his fire momentarily to allow Heckler and Turbo to pass him and keep moving into the empty section that crossed the ship's centerline. Kal fired into the first two rows of drones and stopped firing.

He finally changed magazines. "Nice piece o' gear," he drawled into his microphone.

He kept track on his HUD as they covered the three

hundred meters. Virgil and Mary were last into the corridor and stayed close to the hangar bay, just like last time they had been trapped in a carrier while it traveled at FTL speed. With all three approaches to the access covered, all that remained was for Sparky to use the rope to access the computer area.

Payne followed the corridor until he reached the section that led into the computer banks. He pointed at the bulkhead.

Sparky slapped the rope on the wall in the shape of a doorway and pulled the activation cord. It started melting a line along the bulkhead. After twenty seconds, Sparky kicked the section of the wall, and it fell inside. She lit up the inside to confirm it was the same.

"It's all you," she said as she ducked out and motioned for Blinky and Buzz to take over. They rushed inside and removed a panel to gain access to the main data lines, then they clipped wires and hooked up their computers.

They removed their helmets and their exhalations fogged the cold air, quickly dissipating with each new breath. It was minus ten Celsius. If they got too cold, they'd put their helmets back on and seal themselves inside their environmentally-controlled suits.

Payne was good with whatever they needed to be comfortable. He watched them until they looked up. "This is probably going to take a while," Blinky said and returned to his work.

"Where are we going?" Payne asked.

"I think I can answer that," Buzz replied. He tapped a few keys and smiled triumphantly. "One-angle-one-set-one."

Payne held his hands up, looking for more of an explanation.

Buzz shook his head. "That's all I've got, but it sounds like the center of the Ga'ee universe."

"We're headed to Ga'ee Central. Pleasant. Twelve of us and *Ugly 6*. Any way we can get that information to Lev?"

"Once we stop, we'll be able to piggyback a message on the neural network. Lev will be looking for that. We figured we'd be a little closer, but it's all the same. The efficiency of the Ga'ee communication network is incomparable."

Payne stabbed a finger at the computer. "Back at it, gentlemen. I need time to think." They needed no additional urging to bury themselves in their work.

The major leaned against a piece of equipment that hummed with power. Sparky surveyed the room as if she'd never seen the one identical to it. Payne gave her the thumbs-up. They had time. What they needed were ideas and a firm plan besides the belief that Blinky and Buzz would crack the ship's systems and flood the void with a compelling order to retract.

If the Ga'ee followed that order, what would happen to Team Payne and *Leviathan*?

He couldn't see the future possibilities. He had no idea how the Ga'ee would respond to the order. Would there be a civil war? How could a brain fight itself?

Schizophrenia? By introducing a new player, would they break the bonds of the one mind?

Payne had questions but no answers. He jammed his armored fingers into his faceplate since he had forgotten he was in his suit and wanted to rub the dull ache from his temples. He checked the corridor before taking his helmet off.

The crisp air helped him focus. It tasted cleaner than it should have since there were no green plants producing oxygen. It was all mechanically generated and filtered. No matter how much destruction the Ga'ee did to a planet, they needed the oxygen atmosphere and a reasonable amount of warmth. Liquid water made sense, even though they kept this ship colder than freezing.

Or did they?

Payne put his helmet back on to contact the team. "Sparky, are the lower and upper decks warmer? Like, above freezing?"

"I'll try to figure it out," the engineer replied. "Why is that important?"

"It'll confirm to me that the Ga'ee don't operate on this level. We won't casually run across one. We can dupe the drones but not an in-real-life Ga'ee. They'll freak if they see us."

"Probably would have seen us already had they been able to," Sparky suggested. She continued her thorough inspection of the technical equipment space. "I suggest the lower decks are warmer, based on readings taken through cabling penetrations in the deck. Can't see anything from the overhead, so can only fathom a guess that if Ga'ee are up there, it'll be warmer, too."

Payne acknowledged the report, then moved into the corridor and leaned against the bulkhead. Heckler and Turbo were prone, their weapons aimed at the back of the drones lined up to enter the starboard hangar bay.

"Maybe you can set charges to help you secure the corridor if those things turn on us."

"We don't have directional explosives, just the big boom kind," Heckler replied, making no move to adjust his position.

"Roger." Payne shook the cobwebs from his head. He needed to be doing something since he wasn't good at waiting. "Kernel of Lev residing in *Ugly 6*. How long will it take to get from where we are to the central planet of the Ga'ee sector?"

"Since we do not know where the central planet is, the calculation is impossible."

"How about the general center of Ga'ee-controlled space?" Payne clarified.

"Twenty-four days."

Payne thumped his helmet against the corridor. Three days longer than their water supply and ten days longer than their food supply.

"That's not going to work for me," Payne replied to the piece of AI embedded in the insertion craft.

"It is a fact, regardless of your acceptance."

"I know. I'm in denial, that's all." Payne returned to the equipment room and opened the team channel. "Bad news. Lev says it's twenty-four days to the center of the Ga'ee sector. That's longer than we have provisions for, so we're going to have to make something happen sooner rather than later."

"No pressure," Blinky grumbled.

Payne didn't reply. The entire plan depended on Blinky and Buzz breaking into the system and sending the message. Those two knew the pressure they were under, but they'd already stymied the drones by convincing them that no one was there even though the team had cut a hole in the hangar bay door and cleared the corridor using a plasma cannon.

That made a racket, yet they didn't respond. The drones waited in neat and orderly rows for the time when they'd be called to action.

Team Payne was nothing to them.

Payne sat down in the corridor, then leaned back and closed his eyes. They would have a lot of time to kill. "Let me know if you're going to trigger anything, Blinky, Buzz. I'll be taking a nap."

"Captain LeClerc, I demand to know where they went, and more importantly, when they'll be back." The president's anger boiled through the video on the acerbic edges of her words.

The BEP captain stalked his bridge slowly, doing his best not to make noise or ruffle more feathers than were already ruffled.

"We received the message that we've since forwarded

regarding the status of Hunter-Killer Squadron Two. It ended with a call for immediate assistance as they were under attack. We have to assume Squadron One transited the active portal to Berantz space to fight the Ga'ee."

"Why haven't they come back?"

"The aft section of *European Union* is hanging in space near the portal. Rescue efforts have been unsuccessful. The portal shut down halfway through transit. Judging by the energy surge, it was a catastrophic shutdown, ma'am," LeClerc replied.

"What the hell does that mean, *Captain*?" The president used LeClerc's rank like a pejorative.

"It means they're not coming back unless they can fix the portal on the Berantz side. Fixing the portal depends on whether they win the fight or not. HK2 only had two partially operational battlewagons remaining. They gained three battlewagons, which left them at parity with the Ga'ee should four carriers show up."

LeClerc wiped the sweat from his brow with his sleeve. He couldn't hide it. The figurative spotlight showed so brightly on him that he was withering under its intensity.

"Get them back!" The president's usually confident voice was shrill.

"There's nothing I can do, ma'am. Everything has to happen from their end. In the interim, we'll clear the area in front of the portal for our next arrival from Vestrall Prime."

The president slashed at her neck while looking at someone off-screen.

Captain LeClerc clasped his hands behind his back.

"A message from the office of the president, Captain," a young Fleetie said.

"Main screen," LeClerc pointed.

"Sir, I think…"

The captain cut him off and stabbed his finger repeatedly at the main screen.

The short text message appeared on the screen.

You're fired. Effective immediately.

LeClerc laughed and gave the comm specialist a thumbs-up. "Who in the fuck wants to have to deal with her?" The crew looked away, smiling and chuckling. "I guess I'll stay in the chair until an even bigger loser than me shows up. Helm, set course for the portal. FTL speed, please."

"Aye aye, sir." The bridge crew of the *Ephesus* went about their jobs with a business-as-usual attitude. A lieutenant sidled up next to him and bumped him. They shared a look and a smile.

"She'll reconsider," the lieutenant assured Captain LeClerc.

"If the Ga'ee show up, who's in charge of this boat is the least of our problems."

"If the Ga'ee show up, what do we do?"

LeClerc shook his head. "We send every ship we can into the atmosphere to kill the drones before they can infect the planet. We rally the people of Earth to fight the Ga'ee with plasma torches, thermite, grenades, excavators, tanks, and anything else they can get their hands on. Time is of the essence. Once a drone hits the ground, we have hours to burn them out. After that, they'll spread, and we'll have to nuke our own planet."

The lieutenant furrowed her brow and frowned. "How did you come up with that plan?"

"I read Ambassador Payne's notes from their first encounter with the Ga'ee and what they had to do to defeat them. Inform the crew that after-action report is mandatory reading."

The lieutenant hurried away to read the report herself before promulgating it.

Ephesus transitioned smoothly into normal space. LeClerc

didn't even feel the change anymore; it had become so commonplace. "Prepare the grapples," he ordered. The *European Union* had been crewed and prepped for battle less than an hour earlier. Now, it was a dead hulk. The small maintenance ships servicing the portal had completed their search and rescue, but no life remained on board.

The captain wondered if they even had time to get their emergency doors in place to seal the ship and prevent the complete loss of life from a catastrophic decompression. The designers, Lev and Admiral Wesson, had not planned on the ship getting cut neatly in two. Even with compartments sealed, there would be no coming back from such damage.

"External repair spacewalk team, suit up, recover survivors from sealed compartments first, and then recover the Rapiers still in *Union's* launch cans."

The supply shortages would continue for the foreseeable future. The battlewagon resupply demands after the last battle with Ga'ee had drained the remaining stocks. There was no sense in letting the anti-ship missiles go to waste. They were the only effective weapon they had against the Ga'ee carriers.

The pneumatic blast that launched the grapples sounded faintly through the cruiser's hull. They never heard the thud of impact. "Grapples in place," Helm reported. He was in control from that point forward. If he accelerated too quickly, he'd yank the hooks free or start the towed ship spinning. The distance between the ships wasn't enough that there was no risk of getting rammed.

It was the opposite. Towing operations in space were fraught with risk.

They had no choice.

"Accelerating at three meters per second squared," Helm reported. That was a little less than one-third gee, enough to get the wreckage clear of the portal. They didn't have far to move it to get to zero gravity, a place where the remains would be pulled to Saturn. A point in space where the parts and pieces of the ship could be recycled, but it would take a Progenitor-designed ship like another battlewagon to make that happen.

Earth's shipyard was too primitive to efficiently recycle the pieces rapidly. They would have to be separated and resmelted. The Progenitors' equipment performed the functions simultaneously, recycling a ship in hours instead of months.

Ephesus adjusted the tethers to start a slow rotation, swinging the hulk around to lead the towing ship. When the remnants of the *Union* were on a trajectory straight away from the cruiser, the towing ship would slow. It was a maneuver the BEP had practiced frequently.

There had been a great deal of debris in space following the final battle with the Blaze Collective.

"Slowing," Helm reported, not taking his eyes off the instruments before him. The portal was clear, and the hulk was in a part of space where it would sit until it could be reused.

The sensor operator gasped. "Two Ga'ee carriers entered normal space inside the lunar orbit."

"Cut the tether. Set course for Earth, best possible speed." LeClerc moved into his seat. "Comm, prepare to broadcast live."

"Two more Ga'ee carriers have arrived beyond the lunar shipyard." The sensor operator flopped back in her seat. She looked at the captain. There was no hope in her expression. She was already defeated. He tipped his chin slightly toward her and motioned for her to sit up straight.

The ship transitioned into faster-than-light speed on course for Earth.

The tactical board populated. The pitiful number of blue icons presented little threat to the Ga'ee...except one.

The battlewagon *Japan* remained in Earth's space, holding

position halfway between Jupiter and Earth to respond to just such an event. BW17 had not yet arrived from Vestrall's space. The speed of delivery had slowed.

LeClerc had been watching from the outside. The Hunter-Killer squadrons had all been controlled and directed by Commander Jimmy Josephs of HK1. LeClerc wished he could be fired so he could return to his quarters, get his stuff, and leave.

There was nowhere for him to go and no one to take the captain's chair. At this point, the captaincy was the booby prize. Who would go down with the ship?

Unless he could make it more.

"Tighten your seatbelts, people. We've got a battle to fight. It's us and *Japan*. That's all that stands between those hogs and Earth."

Ephesus transitioned into normal space beyond the moon, outside the shipyard and danger-close to two Ga'ee carriers. *Japan* was right behind her. The battlewagon transmitted the full spectrum of codes in an effort to take down the carriers' shields.

"Flush all tubes," LeClerc ordered.

Eighteen Rapiers launched into space on an eruption of compressed air. The motors kicked in, and the missiles raced across the short space between Ephesus and the carriers. Forty-eight missiles jumped from *Japan*'s upper hull, half headed for the closest carrier and the other half arcing toward the second carrier.

The screens flickered and disappeared. Missiles accelerated through the space where the shields had been and slammed home, penetrating deep before exploding. The ship's hull rippled and buckled. It would have survived but for the aft shot that detonated too close to the dual power plants that drove the engines. They combined to go critical, and the ship exploded as if it were a bomb.

LeClerc pumped his fist and ended by giving the expanding debris cloud the finger. He scowled at the waste of *Japan*'s Rapiers. Twenty-four of them disappeared with the explosion.

Japan lined up her bow and took the shot as the carrier was turning. Her main beam weapon carved a thirty-degree slice into the enemy vessel. From the port aft corner to midships starboard, the energy melted a wide path through and exited out the far side.

The drones continued to emerge from the hangar bays on both sides of the ship.

"Defensive weapons, fire at the cyclic rate," LeClerc ordered when *Japan* lit up like a fireworks show, energy and tracers outbound to intercept the drones.

The carrier sagged across the middle, an odd action from a ship in space. It started to buckle and continued like a zipper pulling the outer hull toward the central axis.

"Get us out of here!" LeClerc shouted. Helm hammered the controls to spin the ship and accelerate away from the impending implosion. The ship collapsed into itself with a whimper, not the howl of a reactor going critical. The drones lost their guidance as a testament to the final demise of the carrier.

The other two Ga'ee ships had parked themselves in a low orbit. Drones streamed into the atmosphere.

Tens of thousands of drones headed toward Earth's surface.

[16]

"Sometimes, when the chips are down, you just have to kill the bad guys." –From the memoirs of Ambassador Declan Payne

"Byle and Shaolin, spot Kal and guard this corridor." Payne left the equipment room, on his way to the hangar bay.

The two specialists rushed to get in front of him so they could relieve the Ebren. "Sir, can I ask where you're going?" Byle asked the question everyone had on their mind.

"If Blinky and Buzz haven't brought this fucking thing out of FTL by the time Kal and I get to the twin power plants driving the engine, I'm going to blast them into oblivion. We're coming out of FTL one way or another."

Sparky offered her engineering analysis. "That might not be optimal. I suggest we wait; otherwise, a catastrophic transition from FTL would result in the complete destruction of this ship."

"I think you're being a bit sensational," Payne replied. "Are you?"

"No. The shearing forces will tear us apart if the ship

doesn't have a failsafe for transition. In the black and white world of good and bad, this could be really bad."

"We've done it before," Payne argued.

"We haven't, not all at once. Blinky pulled us out of FTL before you blew it up."

"Sweet! Do that, Blinky." Payne knew the answer.

"Dec," Mary offered on a private channel. "Killing all of us won't help you accomplish what you want."

"Blinky and Buzz need proper motivation. Without a deadline, they take forever. With a deadline, they'll come through. It'll take Kal and me a while to reach the aft end. They have about an hour to figure everything out. Once out of FTL, they can get that message sent."

"Do you understand how hard it is to do what they do?"

"I gave them the calculations to help them break the code. I understand what they're going through. I only wish I could maintain focus through that part of my brain so I could just take care of it," Payne grumbled.

Kal joined him, and the two walked toward the hangar bay through the drone wreckage.

"Either kick your brain into gear or lighten up on killing us all," Mary pressed. "I want to get some, and we're not going to do it here."

Payne stopped. Kal took one more step before looking back. "Second thoughts?" the Ebren drawled.

"Kind of," Payne replied over the team channel. "Kal and I are on our way to the aft end of the carrier. We'll look for a way to bring us out of FTL without killing us if Blinky and Buzz haven't already taken care of it. Payne out."

He didn't want to continue the conversation. He needed something to happen well before they were out of range of *Leviathan* and well before they ran out of food and water.

What's next? Payne wondered. When they returned to

normal space, would the message instructing the Ga'ee to consolidate at their homeworld be received and followed? Then what? They would have to expand again...unless they didn't. Would it take a single suggestion to collapse their empire?

No. Another suggestion from a different quarter would extoll the virtues of new worlds and lush minerals that could be extracted. Like a mind, different thoughts could be more compelling at any point in time. What did humanity need to do to ensure the Ga'ee didn't expand farther into the sectors of the seven races?

That was the trillion-credit question that no one had an answer to.

Payne stopped when he reached his wife. They held each other for a wordless moment before Kal moved into the hangar, hugging the bulkhead where there was space to move. He aimed the plasma cannon forward while Payne moved into the opening behind him and headed aft. He was able to walk without his shoulders brushing either the bulkhead or the drones that hovered even with him as well as in rows over his head.

"Come on, Kal. It's not as bad as we thought. It's like a walk on the beach. Sling the cannon and stroll."

Payne kept his railgun in front of him as he moved. He wasn't in a hurry. The team's words had affected him. It wasn't that he'd lost confidence, but the rash version of him was being suppressed by the intellectual Payne. His mind told him they were right. The catastrophic loss of FTL would rip the ship apart. The only way to accomplish the mission was for them to plant the thought for a better and stronger Ga'ee by contracting, not expanding.

He slowed. His thoughts changed as they cleared. He saw the neural network and the way into it. "Buzz, link me in."

Payne studied his HUD as he became fully immersed in it like a virtual reality headset.

"I'm taking control of the link," he told them. They tried to argue, but it was too late. Payne was into the Ga'ee system, becoming one with it. He saw the ship's status: one hundred twenty thousand drones and forty thousand Ga'ee. They were dormant while traveling.

He dug deeper. Twenty-five thousand Ga'ee carriers. Trillions of Ga'ee scattered across ten thousand planets. The expansion fleet was extensive, but Payne focused on the one allocated to the sectors of the seven races.

Forty-two ships. There wasn't an update on success, but they had been sent two by two for initial penetration, then four by four. Any planets that survived would be attacked by whatever ships remained. They would stay connected by the neural network deployed among the forty-two. That was how they worked until they could reconnect to the main network, but the distance was extreme.

It reinforced Payne's initial idea that expanding came at a cost.

But the Vestrall were off-limits. He didn't have time to explore more. The reason was buried. He didn't need to know why yet.

Return to normal space, he ordered the ship.

Inquiry: We are not yet at one-angle-one-set-one.

We will go there when we are finished sending our message of revelation. We have the answer to the Ga'ee's greatest question.

Inquiry: How?

Inspiration. Calculation. Dedication, Payne replied confidently.

Compliance.

The ship *was* alive, as they had postulated over a year

earlier. A living computer, shaped by the silicon-based life forms on board while still being its own entity. The servers on the main axis represented an interface, supplemental storage, a translation device, and more. It could fly the ship without the brain, as they'd found on the empty ship that had appeared in Vestrall space.

"Blinky, prepare to transmit our message. We'll be out of FTL momentarily."

As he spoke, the ship transitioned to normal space.

"Head back, Kal." Payne gestured toward midships.

Kal turned around and stalked back toward the central transverse corridor where the rest of the team waited.

"How did you do that?" Buzz asked.

"Wavelength. Handshake. Recognition. Integration. Shooting you the data stream now." Payne sent the short bit of code he'd used to marry with the ship. It had been intuitive. His knowledge of the Ga'ee languages, both neural and cyber, had come to him as naturally as speaking English. He had simply done what the machine required.

It had been instinctive when it should not have been.

As he worked his way toward the corridor, he started losing the part of his mind that had rallied for him. He stopped once more, but Kal kept walking. When Kal reached Major Dank, he looked back to find Payne two hundred meters behind him. He immediately turned around and rushed aft.

"Message inserted into the network," Blinky reported. "We were close to breaking it, Major, for what that's worth. So close."

"I know. Forgive my impatience. Let *Leviathan* know where we are."

"Already noted that we are out of FTL. Ugly Lev is still working out exactly where we are."

Payne chuckled. "'Ugly Lev.' I like that. 'Kernel Lev.' Lev, the lesser son."

"Dropping the coordinates into the stream," Buzz noted.

"Now we wait some more for our seed to take root. Look for any dissenting voices and find where they are. We'll need to visit them." Payne would have cracked his knuckles had they not been inside armored gloves.

Visit them... Payne saw a clear path to peace with the Ga'ee. Just as quickly, it was gone, but something lurked at the center of the neural network that seemed different from the rest. Lev had felt it, too. Blinky and Buzz had been trying to isolate the voice and learn more about it.

Was it the Ga'ee counterpart to God 1? Payne wanted to talk privately with Blinky and Buzz, but while he was looking them in the face, not over the radio.

"I have their coordinates," Lev announced. "They have dropped out of FTL and are waiting for us. The idea of contracting has been planted."

Admiral Wesson clenched his fist and shook it at the screen with a look of triumph on his face. "Will the forces that have been deployed toward our sectors hear that message?"

"Not for some time," Lev replied.

The big ship moved out of the cover of the moon's shell and into the midst of the neural network. *Leviathan* adjusted its heading and entered faster-than-light speed.

"I'm guessing two hours to get there?" The admiral wasn't guessing. That was how long the Ga'ee carrier had been gone since it had left with Team Payne on board.

Two hours that had felt like two days. The clock on the tactical screen kept the admiral sane and grounded to a linear timeline.

Lev didn't reply. He knew the admiral wasn't guessing.

The tactical board populated with everything Lev had seen during his short time in the network. Within the two-hour flight path to Team Payne were two dozen Ga'ee carriers. He wouldn't find out if they were following them until after they returned to normal space. They wouldn't know what they were up against until shortly before the battle was joined.

They had one worldkiller. They had three salvos of Rapiers and a good stock of defensive missiles but nearly unlimited plasma and projectiles. *Leviathan* was in no condition to fight an extended battle even though the physical damage to the ship had been repaired during their time in the graveyard.

"How many can we fight?" the admiral asked.

"As many as we have to until we can no longer fight," Lev replied.

"That's not a great pronouncement," the admiral said. "Are we set up to fail?"

"Only if Team Payne is unsuccessful, and that, Harry, is my greatest fear. That we die and have made no difference. We lose humanity along with all the races."

"You're not alone, Lev. I fear that, too. Get me Woody. We're going to need his Mosquitoes."

[17]

"The square root of negative two might be an imaginary number, or it might be nothing. I'm really not sure." –From the memoirs of Ambassador Declan Payne

Sirens sounded the alarm across the face of planet Earth. Never in the history of mankind had such an event taken place, not when the first aliens were discovered, not during the Blaze attack on Earth space.

Not ever.

A massive fireball in the upper atmosphere signaled the arrival of *Ephesus,* coming in on a steep angle from space. On the other side of the planet, a second fireball dwarfed the first. Battlewagon *Japan* was on its way to defend the planet by putting itself between the drones and the surface.

The instant the ships cleared into the air, the fireworks started: short-range defensive missiles, railguns, chain guns, and lasers. Everything they had poured into the sky to rip drones from the air.

And still they came.

Air defenses on the ground opened up—everywhere there

was a battery, aged or new. Weapons from wars past were fired by volunteers. Few systems were active. Fleet personnel had abandoned Earth because the leadership had grown too hostile toward them—like Fleet Admiral Wesson and Admiral Ross.

Only veterans and private security remained.

Ephesus started over North America to check on the defenses of the UN, but it would need to head to South America, which had a great amount of unprotected land. *Japan* was to cover Asia.

President Sinkhaus stood atop the UN building, seething. "They left us!" she raged.

Five plasma cannons fired constantly. The cavalcade of noise echoed down the corridors between the tall buildings. It was loud enough that the president couldn't hear herself think, but she had nowhere else to go. The alarm had been sent to the world. She'd check progress in a bit, but for now, the only thing she could do was watch.

The clouds dispersed and the drones descended individually, each looking to establish a foothold. All over the world, ground teams stood ready with plasma cutters and welding torches, pitchforks, shovels, and excavators. They had all been tried and had proven effective against the Ga'ee.

The president continued to wallow in her anger. "I will have Fleet's ass!"

Paragon Virtue shook his head while motioning for calm. "This will be your finest hour. Rallying the entire population of Earth to work as one in defying the Ga'ee. Your legacy will be cemented into the annals of history. You will *be* the history because nothing else matters."

"You might have a point," the president admitted.

She rubbed her chin and watched as the cruiser disappeared over the horizon, firing its close-in weapons systems the entire time.

"The display of firepower is rather impressive, don't you think?" Virtue observed.

Sinkhaus nodded. "We should have never had to see it. Their job was to keep the Ga'ee away from Earth, not fight them over the continents. We have farmers and construction workers, retirees and homemakers, and every level of corporate trader you can imagine out there, forming a human chain putting eyes on every bit of land across the world. Every square meter. Where there are no people, private pilots are flying coverage. So much of North America is frozen, yet still we worry."

"Water isn't their friend. We don't know the verdict on frozen water."

The two stood side by side and watched the display. The cannons laced the sky, creating an intricate and thorough screen over the city. Drones died wherever they tried to get through. The cannons' staccato was oddly calming. It meant patriots were acting in defense of the city and its people.

One thing every human agreed on was that the Ga'ee couldn't be allowed to infiltrate Earth.

There was nowhere for humanity to go and no way to get them there.

"Humanity's last stand," Sinkhaus stated. "Do we have what it takes?"

"You can't doubt that we do, Madam President. You have to exude confidence."

"I know that," she snarled. "This is just us, up here on top of a building. Never mind. Get downstairs and monitor the operations room for me."

"But..." Paragon started. He stopped. He had sealed his fate. The president wouldn't use him as a sounding board or vent to him ever again. He'd lost her trust by trying to counsel her. "Of course."

He moped away, opened the door, and took the steps down.

The cannon fire overhead continued to hammer at his senses. The sights and sounds of the city's defense maintained their intensity.

There was no letting up.

"Fire, damn you! Fire!" LeClerc bellowed. The weapons operator had collapsed. "Move her and take over."

"Sir!" The next operator slid sideways into the main position. The comm officer moved in to drag the unconscious crew member away.

"Medic to the bridge," he requested calmly over the ship-wide comm.

"That's me," a second engineer said from the other side of the bridge. He left his post carrying a small medical kit. He leaned over the weapons officer. The rest of the bridge crew left them alone. They were too busy to be distracted.

The new weapons officer played the console like a piano virtuoso. His fingers flew across the screen as the ship thrummed with the volume of weapons fire it was able to maintain. Warning lights flashed as ammunition and energy levels dropped.

Cyclic rates of fire weren't meant to continue for minutes, only seconds.

"We only get one chance to stop the drones, but we can't stop anything if we melt the barrels. Slow the rate of fire," LeClerc ordered. "Medic, what happened to her?"

The part-time medic looked up and shook his head. He picked her up under her armpits and dragged her backward toward the hatch.

"She's dead?"

"Heart stopped. No sign of trauma," the medic replied

before taking his charge through the hatch and into the corridor beyond.

LeClerc put a hand on his chest to feel his own heart pounding. It didn't get any more intense than this. "Just do your jobs, people. We'll get this through this. Earth will survive."

He wanted to believe, and that would have to be good enough. However, he had to convince the crew that they would get through this. He left the captain's chair to move around the bridge, patting shoulders and nodding at his people while they did their jobs. Tension gripped them. Muscles were tight. Sweat stood out on furrowed brows.

He leaned down beside the engineering officer. "Lower the temp in here by a couple degrees, if you would be so kind," he requested.

The young woman tapped a couple buttons. "Done," she confirmed.

They all looked young. LeClerc was only thirty-two, but that made him the grand old man. Captain by default.

No. Not by default, by connections. He had less ship time than most of the crew. He'd said the right things and done the right things in a plushy job on Earth. He'd only been in space for eighteen total months.

He didn't deserve to be the captain.

That changed nothing.

He had a job to do. "Helm, don't be afraid to use blunt force against these bastards." He stabbed a finger at drones racing downward.

The pilot accelerated the ship on an intercept course.

There were too many of them. Knocking a few out of the sky by ramming them wouldn't change the ratio.

"Punch them right in their smug mouths, Mister Smith," LeClerc ordered.

"My pleasure," the pilot replied. He adjusted their course and accelerated.

Defensive fire slowed to a sustainable rate. Short-range missile stocks were dangerously low. "Save the final missiles in case we have a need."

"We can't get them all," the weapons operator admitted.

"Ground teams will take care of what gets through. Everyone down there is waiting for their turn to strike at the enemy. We'll stop as many as we can, but the ground-pounders have our back, just like we have theirs. Only two Ga'ee carriers instead of four because of what we've done so far. We've already cut the danger in half."

Lurking in the back of his mind was the thought that it only took a single Ga'ee drone to get through and deliver the seed into a mineral-rich deposit. Only one to destroy the whole planet.

No wonder the weapons operator had died. It was too much to think about. Too much worry.

"Focus, people. Kill as many as we can, knowing we're not going to get them all. We'll make it hella easy for those on the ground. Gotta give them something to do, right? Make them feel part of the team, and they will be. We'll call them honorary BEP."

Ephesus crashed into a drone, then a second. The forward arms were ripped away, and the drones tumbled. Defensive weapons sniped at them on the way down. The cruiser carved a wide path on its way south.

"Comm, get me the governments of whoever is below us."

"Standard emergency channel is active." The communications officer pointed at the captain.

"All personnel on the ground. This is *Ephesus*, the ship overhead. We're doing the best we can, but drones are getting through. You must destroy them when they touch down. Five

Ga'ee, silicon-based centipede-like creatures, will emerge and immediately attempt to propagate. You must cut them out of the ground and burn them to death using acid or plasma fire. Show no mercy. Kill them all. It only takes one of those things to destroy our planet since they multiply exponentially. Not even one can get past you. LeClerc out." The captain gestured. "Put that on repeat and keep broadcasting."

Comm tapped the screens at the station and re-sent the message on a continuous loop.

"Where's the leading edge of the wave?" LeClerc asked.

The sensors operator transferred the information to the tactical display. The screen populated with a cloud and a great number of wisps extending from the central mass.

South America wasn't the target of the cloud. It was north, at their six o'clock.

"Bring us about, turn to port, and swing through the greatest concentration. Maintain continuous fire."

Ephesus turned through a wide arc, firing defensive weapons in a display that was startling to anyone watching. Plasma accelerated to hypersonic speeds and projectiles fired from chain guns and lasers, less effective in the air than in space but still useful, lanced toward the oncoming drones.

The invaders exploded from the high-intensity impacts. The lasers sliced through them, but still they came. Too many.

"Accelerate to intra-atmospheric flank speed. Spiral from the outside in, descending with the drone cloud."

The captain should have done that to begin with instead of heading to the deck and working his way up. Follow the enemy to their target to kill more instead of trying to block them where the cruiser had been overwhelmed by the first wave.

The ship fired on the way up and then spiraled down with the drones, finding its fire more effective as it matched descent speeds.

"Now we're cooking with gas!" LeClerc shouted.

The pilot laughed maniacally. "No one cooks with gas anymore, Captain." He didn't take his eyes off his controls or stop tapping. The ship responded like a cutter on an open sea. It banked and turned like it had been made to fly through the air.

"Hang on!" the captain shouted at Comm. "All hands, brace for impact!"

The ship danced on the wind, but it was losing altitude at an extreme rate. LeClerc gripped the captain's chair, grimacing.

The pilot pointed the cruiser's nose toward the sky and kicked the engines to maximum. The ship stopped its precipitous descent, and the massive ionic wash vaporized the drones behind the ship. The pilot banked hard to spread the wash in a circle around the ship.

Artificial gravity couldn't keep up with the radical maneuver. LeClerc strained to stay in his chair. He was plastered against one arm, digging his fingernails into the soft, leather-like pad.

"Helm!" LeClerc managed through gritted teeth.

The pilot shouted, "Wahoo!" The ship continued its vertical flat spin.

"Energy output is one hundred and ten percent. Systems are redlining!" the engineering station reported.

"Helm, dial it back. I said fucking *dial it back*!" LeClerc would have stormed forward if he could have gotten out of his seat.

A few screen-taps later, the ship settled into a lazy spiral. Seconds later, it cleared the last of the drones. Defensive systems stopped firing, and the ship dropped into an uneasy silence.

"Slow to one-third and take us back to the surface. Prepare for ground bombardment."

"Can we do that?" the weapons officer asked.

"We have to wherever a drone has landed and there are no people coming toward it. Sensors, integrate with Weapons. No friendly fire casualties, please."

LeClerc slid out of the sweat puddle he had left in the captain's chair. He straightened his uniform coveralls and strolled casually to the pilot's position.

The captain kneeled next to the helm and waited until the pilot looked at him. "Smith, nice flying."

"I knew she could do it, sir!" he blurted excitedly.

LeClerc shook his head and held up one finger. "Next time, how about we don't take out our pilot fantasies on my ship? We were on the verge of breaking apart and had that happened, we wouldn't have been able to help anyone. There are still two Ga'ee carriers in orbit that we need to deal with, so don't break my ship, Mister Smith."

The pilot deflated. "Aye aye, sir."

LeClerc stood and clapped him on the back. He leaned close to the pilot's ear and whispered, "I bet the designers never figured the ship could do any of that." He faced the bridge crew. "Let's hear it for the pilot of the year!"

[18]

"In the end, the fate of humanity came down to how fast someone could tap keys." –From the memoirs of Ambassador Declan Payne

Clarence Johnson was a heavy equipment mechanic. He drove a tow truck and rescued broken heavy haulers by fixing them wherever they died.

He listened to audiobooks to wile away the hours of boredom when he wasn't elbow-deep in the guts of an aging diesel engine. When he heard the call about defending Earth, he knew he had a new mission.

Nothing else mattered. He rogered the call on his radio and changed from an audiobook to his heavy metal playlist. Metallica shredded the airwaves inside the cab of the heavy tow truck. He rolled down the window and leaned out so he could shake his fist at the sky.

That's when he slowed and pulled off the side of the road. He had to squint to see it, but an aircraft was up there amid a phantasmic display of lights and energy. Dots like small birds streamed toward the ground. The ship's wash cleared an immense section of the sky, but some dots maneuvered away.

The enemy was coming to take Earth away from humanity. Clarence gave the finger to the drones as they came into sharp focus, as they came toward him.

The drones bore curved armatures like cavalry sabers pointing forward—three points to tear apart anything in their way.

The first drone slammed into the ground like a meteor, but it soon wriggled its way free from the impact crater to discharge its living cargo.

Clarence put the truck in gear and jammed the gas pedal to the firewall. He only had a quarter mile to go, but the call to arms had expressed the urgency of dealing with the invasion immediately. No foothold. Not even a toehold. Clarence drove his truck onto a hardpack dirt road and then to the dust cloud that continued to linger.

The enemy drone slowly emerged from the hole, its rounded backside facing the tow truck. Clarence hit second gear with a grind and a screech and the truck lurched forward into the ship, bumper slamming the space vehicle.

His truck straddled the small crater as it continued forward. When it was on the other side, Clarence dropped it into first gear and slammed on the brakes. He kicked it out of gear and brought the truck to a halt. He pulled his personal security pistol from under the seat and jumped out.

Stuck on his bumper and half-wedged under the engine, the drone vibrated as it worked to free itself. He jammed his pistol against the widest part of the backside and fired. He kept pulling the trigger until the slide locked to the rear.

He screamed at the drone as he kept trying to pull the trigger. It took him a moment to realize the magazine was empty.

Clarence rushed back to the truck to reload. When he returned, the drone had stopped moving.

However, the deposit in the crater was just starting to move. The wrigglers were silvery and small, like a mercury spill.

"I know what you are," Clarence snarled. He stuffed his pistol into the back of his jeans and uncoiled the hoses from his welding torch. He checked the system, turned on the gases, and clicked the spark cap, and the torch came to life. He wasn't welding, so he hadn't bothered with the glasses.

He wanted to see the Ga'ee squirm and shrivel. He slid into the small crater with the lit torch and almost lit his sleeve on fire, but he managed to twist away from the flame. He touched the blue point of the flame to the topmost Ga'ee. It curled into itself and quickly charred. He kicked it out of the way and worked his way down through a second, a third, and a fourth.

They come in fives. The words resonated through his mind. He set the torch aside and climbed out of the pit to open the side compartment with his pioneer gear—a shovel, an axe, and a pick. He pulled out the shovel, sending the other tools clattering to the ground. He didn't care about that. He didn't have time to waste.

He hit the bottom of the pit and started to dig. It only took two shovels full before he found the final Ga'ee. He tossed it into the flame before throwing the shovel away from him so he could grab the torch and finish it off.

Clarence flopped back into the crater. His heart pounded in his chest but quickly settled when he realized what he'd done. "Suck my ass," he told the dead Ga'ee. He picked up the torch, turned it off, and leaned on the shovel to help him get out of the hole.

He would have to back out so the drone didn't damage the underside of his truck.

But first, he took the torch to it, cut an opening, and melted the inside of the alien craft. Clarence whistled while he stowed his gear. He looked for more dust from impacts. There were plenty, along with flashing lights and flares where they'd been marked along the open stretch of central Virginia.

"Come on, Betsy, we got work to do," Clarence told his work truck. He slowly backed up over the hole and onto the dirt road, then turned around and headed for the highway. He was an experienced alien-killer. He needed to paint a drone on the side of his truck.

Clarence wondered what the count would be by the end of the day. He better hurry before others beat him to it.

President Sinkhaus watched the cruiser in the distance as it plummeted toward the ground. She assumed it had been killed by the drones when it disappeared over the horizon. She sighed during an extended exhale. No one was around besides her personal security, who stood at a discrete distance, never engaging with her directly. She didn't think highly enough of them to start a conversation.

Hired muscle and nothing more, even though they had passed a background check and been deemed loyal by the security powers that be.

She tapped her watch, which acted as a comm unit, along with everything else she needed. "Virtue, meet me on the roof, please."

The president wasn't one to apologize. *Never show weakness.* But she needed a confidant now more than ever.

Earth was under siege. They couldn't count on Fleet or the BEP or any service she'd poured billions of credits into.

Not her, but she approved all funding. It was her signature on the dotted line.

It only took Paragon Virtue one minute to make it from the command center in the basement to the roof. He didn't look out of breath when he stepped out like he would have been had he taken the stairs and not the elevator.

"Yes, Madam President?"

"I think you might have been right. Rally the world to a single cause, although we've already done that, but we need news crews out there and documenting the victories. The little guy at the pointy end of the spear, living in a place that used to be Nowheresville. And that ship that went down. I want to sing their praises."

"I'm sorry. What ship went down?"

"The big one that was flying over us with all the fireworks." The president tried not to lose her patience.

"That ship did not go down. According to the tactical board, it used its engines to torch massive numbers of drones. It looked like it was going down to us, too, but it didn't. It was simply maneuvering. The Fleet guy said he'd never seen anything like it. I don't think anyone has."

"Good news, then." The president didn't sound like she was pleased. She had used her neutral voice, her default for nearly all things. Being excitable didn't work for her. "We sent exorbitant sums to the military, and they abandoned us in our hour of need."

"One battlewagon and one cruiser destroyed two Ga'ee carriers. They've engaged the final two as well as entered the atmosphere to fight the drones directly. I think they've done us proud. And for the record, the UN has not funded the construction of the Payne-class ships, although the UN has supplied them with biomass and personnel."

"You're shooting holes in all my best arguments to be angry with our military." The president smiled, a rarity in that it was genuine. "Thank you, Paragon. I value your counsel more than you know.

You aren't bringing an agenda besides what you believe the world needs. And what it needs right now is to have faith in its people, those in space and those right here. Today, we're all the good guys."

"That's the message you need to share loud and clear. I'll send the media to get footage of our people fighting the Ga'ee. We'll ask the world to share their stories. It'll be the Great Coming Together. And Madam President, Fleet did us proud. They had a good reason to go to Berantz space. We're all in this together."

Reluctantly, the president nodded. "I want to dislike them as a bunch of knuckle draggers. People who use their brawn and not their brains. But they're flying starships, complex pieces of equipment, far more complex than anything we have on the ground."

Paragon Virtue didn't want to lose his newfound trust, so he simply nodded. That had always been his impression of the military. Bluntly spoken because, in their world, things were simply good or bad. Venting atmosphere to space was bad. Not venting was good. Eating was good. Not eating was bad. The nuances of global politics were lost on them.

Virtue wanted them to be lost on everyone. *Just say what you want!* he screamed inside his head. Too much circumspection. Too much maneuvering where the president was the grand master. She needed the lesson the military provided.

"Make it cut and dry, Madame President," Virtue recommended. "No spin. Not this time. Only kudos to a world fighting for its life and to our defenders in space who saved us. Instead of fighting a quarter of a million of these things, we only have what, fifty thousand? That's a manageable number."

"Is it?" Sinkhaus was not always an optimist, even when she tried.

"The people have to believe it is."

"Let's see what kind of footage we have of people killing these things, shall we?" The president walked slowly across the roof with her hands clasped behind her back. The world's sense of urgency was not hers. Events had already been set in motion that she could not undo.

Despite Paragon's urging, it was all about spin. She needed more than footage.

"Paragon, call up the car. We're going out there."

Clarence rolled up to police firing their shotguns into a crater.

"Welding torch will do 'em up right nice," he called before getting out.

"Shotguns are shit, but the blasts keep the bastards from digging," an overweight deputy replied before firing into the hole again. "What are you waiting for?"

"Waiting not to get shot!" Clarence climbed out, thought for a moment, and returned his pistol to its place under the seat. He didn't know if the police would ding him for it. No need to tempt fate. He had a better weapon anyway.

He quickly uncoiled the hose, twisted the valves, and headed for the crater.

Despite the deputy's claims, only three Ga'ee were visible. "Get the shovel out of my truck. You got two diggers under here."

"What gives? We been blasting 'em soon as they reared their ugly heads, or asses, or whatever they been rearing."

"They come in fives." Clarence used the torch striker to light the fire. He adjusted the flame and slid into the crater, dropping to a knee the second he hit the bottom to fire up the Ga'ee at the bottom of the pile. He efficiently worked his way to the unfortunate alien on the top. "Dig here!" He jabbed at the ground.

The deputy slid into the hole, using the shovel to keep himself from going face-first into the charred Ga'ee remains. He started digging and was five shovels full in before he caught sight of a wriggler going deep. He dug fast.

A sweat stain appeared down the back of his uniform shirt. He ripped into the dirt until he got the shovel's blade beneath the Ga'ee. He flipped it into the growing mound of dirt, where Clarence pounced on it. It shriveled up.

"I'm not seeing another one." The deputy stopped to wipe his brow.

"It's in there." Clarence handed the burning torch to him and gestured for the shovel.

The mechanic dug wide to give himself more room. The second time he stuck the shovel into the dirt, he impacted a wriggling body. He stood on the shovel to drive it deeper. The resistance ended, and the shovel plunged deeper. Clarence removed the dirt to show the two halves of the Ga'ee.

"Gimme that." He took the torch and lit up both sides. When he had five smoking carcasses, he shut down the torch. "Obliged, deputy. I need to be on my way. That's ten of these things down for me. I need to cover my truck in kills. The Ga'ee Slayer. That's me."

He scrambled out of the crater and saw the deputy staring at him. He lowered the shovel down to pull the officer out.

"We make a great team. I'll run blocker for you. How fast will that rig of yours go?"

Clarence only hesitated for a moment. "We're about to find out, aren't we?" He handed the shovel to the deputy and ran back to his tow truck.

And he'd been worried that this was going to be a slow day.

[19]

"The fundamental nature of sentient beings isn't survival. It's that what they do matters." –From the memoirs of Ambassador Declan Payne

Payne loomed over his computer gurus. Blinky and Buzz effectively ignored him until he took off his helmet and thunked it down on the deck next to them.

They both looked up as if in a trance.

"You're smiling on the inside," Payne stated.

"We have to stick with what we're doing, or we're going to lose him. The one voice that is louder than the rest. He's fighting the contraction, but the logic of your argument, complete with the math, is compelling," Blinky replied, his eyes clearing as he talked.

"We think he's on the outer edge of Ga'ee space. Not the center, but we have a lot of outer reaches to explore before we can zero in on his location."

"I love you guys. I've got some faux jerky I've been keeping in my armpit. Should be nice and warm. Take the edge off this chill."

Buzz stared.

Blinky shook his head. "That's a junior enlisted-level joke, sir. You have to up your game."

Payne pulled his arm out of his sleeve and dug inside his suit. He passed a jerky stick in front of his face and took it in his armored hand, freeing it from the confines of his suit. "Fine. I'll eat it myself." Payne worked his arm back into the sleeve before removing the packaging. He took a small bite at first. "Damn. Already cooling off." He stuffed the rest of it in his mouth.

Buzz returned to tapping.

"What they do matters," Payne said, still chewing.

Blinky hadn't returned to his keyboard. He shook his head.

"Making a difference. Separate the followers, which is all of them but one. This isn't a commune where everyone is equal. Almost everyone is equal. We've raised a challenge to the primary voice."

"We're watching the replies. They are overwhelmingly positive. I think the Ga'ee are suffering," Buzz replied.

"What does that look like?" Payne wondered.

"It feels like relief." Buzz scrunched his face as he struggled to find better words but finally gave up. "I can't explain it."

Payne crouched to be closer to the two specialists. "We have a little time before Lev arrives. We'll transfer to *Leviathan* and head to the outer reaches. Just point us in the right direction. We'll stop every few hours to collect more data and then move again. All of this isn't on your shoulders."

"But it is." Blinky smiled. "Remember years ago, when Buzz figured out how to talk with Lev to get us inside the ship and then when he accepted us? It is on our shoulders. All the harm that's befallen him. All the damage. All the people we've lost."

"Fighting for peace." Payne took a knee so he could touch Blinky's shoulder. The one thing the other races didn't do was feel empathy as humans did. Each person was alone in their own body with their thoughts. With Lev, thoughts were open, but he didn't judge anyone for what they thought. He didn't intrude unless the people asked. "We want freedom for all humanity. Then the Ga'ee showed up. We're on the cusp of once again winning humanity's freedom. We only have a little farther to go."

"And the entirety of the Ga'ee is between us and them. Tens of thousands of ships and trillions upon trillions of creatures."

"The good news, Blinky, is that we don't have to fight them all. Just like on Ebren, it looks like we only have to fight their champion. The outer edge? That bastard is the first to feed on a new planet. I guarantee it. Just like the dictators of old, communism for everyone except the one who lives like a king."

Blinky half-smiled. "We'll figure out where that one voice is. You can count on us."

"I have one more piece of jerky," Payne said.

Blinky shook his head, but Buzz held out his hand. Payne went through the contortions to extract it from inside his suit and handed it over.

Buzz used the sensors on his suit to check it. "Nice and warm."

"About thirty-seven degrees Celsius." Payne's body temperature. He picked up his helmet and clicked it into place. He'd had enough of the cold air, but Blinky and Buzz continued helmetless, both tapping. Buzz chewed in rhythm with the staccato clicks from his keyboard.

Payne found Sparky with her own equipment. "What's up?"

"Still trying to figure out the power flow of these things. The one they picked us up in at Vestrall was different."

"We got a lot of good stuff from that one," Payne argued.

"But it was different. It's not like this one at all. It's like the difference between alternating current and direct current. How the machinery is running is different. It's better here. Smoother. That's why they were able to spoof their shields."

"What if the one they sent to collect us was older technology? Are there any signs of a retrofit, or do they just build new?"

Sparky shrugged. "That's a good question. I don't see why they would take a ship out of service. Have we seen anything that suggests a shipyard for things like a retrofit?"

Payne thought through their interactions with the Ga'ee. They fabricated the materials on the planets and launched them into space, where the drones assembled them into the carriers.

"With ten thousand planets, I'm sure they have an R and D facility somewhere." Payne looked around. "Don't they?"

Sparky shrugged once more and returned to her analytical devices.

Payne would have liked to ask Blinky and Buzz, but they needed to focus on finding the dissenting voice.

The more they learned about the Ga'ee, the less they realized they knew.

But they didn't need to know it all to counter the threat. Contraction, not expansion. That was the message. It was finding purchase.

A foothold.

It was what the Ga'ee were trying to gain in the seven races' sectors of space. It was what the Payne-class battlewagons were fighting.

In the corridor, Turbo and Heckler were growing restless. "Drone-butt duty is boring," Heckler said over the team channel.

"If you've seen one drone butt, you've seen them all," Payne replied. "You're safe, Turbo. Heckler isn't going anywhere."

"But he's not." Turbo reached out a fist, and Heckler bumped it.

Payne didn't have a comeback for that. He was still amazed they hadn't blown up a planet in their undying joy of things that exploded.

He returned toward the port side hangar bay and said a few words to Byle, Joker, and Shaolin. They were bored too, but everyone had their eyes on the countdown clock. One hour and forty minutes until *Leviathan* arrived. They'd load into *Ugly 6* and be in space the minute before Lev appeared. They'd board and go on their way before any other Ga'ee showed up to investigate.

Kal leaned against a bulkhead, hanging out by himself but near the three tech specialists.

"How's it hanging, Hoss?" Payne asked.

Kal laughed. "That's more like it, boss man," he drawled in response. "Did we get what we came here for?"

"We did. Even if we do nothing else, we planted the seed of discord in a fertile valley. Ours may become the dominant thought in the neural network."

"May become..." Kal drew the words out. "Which means that they are not yet."

"Our premise is being discussed, but it is the dominant topic. I think we're going to see some movement. There is a dissenting voice that seems stronger than the others."

"What would a civil war between the Ga'ee look like?" Kal asked without an accent.

"I'm not sure it's possible for that to happen. Since it acts like one brain, would a break be their equivalent of schizophrenia? Could two separate and competing Ga'ee personalities exist within one mind?"

"Isn't that what we're doing? Creating that conflict?" Kal pressed.

"Sometimes I forget that you're smarter than the rest of us."

Kal shook his head. "Not at all. I watch, and I learn from y'all. Team Payne asks hard questions. Sometimes, Team Payne even has the answers."

"Sometimes," Payne agreed. He clapped his friend on the shoulder. "Come on, big dog, let's figure out how we can leave our mark on this ship on our way out."

"I heard that," Major Dank called. "I suggest you leave it to Heckler. Just tell him what you want. Nothing left but a burning hulk or not even that. Just give him the end result and save that big brain of yours for more important matters."

"What could be more important than giving our chauffeur a punch in the head?"

"Do we even need to?" Mary suggested.

"Probably not as long as these things aren't shooting at us, but there's nothing to say that the second *Leviathan* arrives, it won't launch drones and/or missiles and try to destroy us."

"Missiles! That's right. Some of those carriers had missiles, but not all of them. New ships, not upgrades." Payne stopped walking and stood facing the bulkhead, losing himself to a new thought.

"Shh," Kal sent over the team channel.

Payne's train of thought went to what they knew about the ships they'd encountered. He cataloged them and came to one conclusion. The upgraded ships didn't matter. They only needed to win one battle.

The battle for the mind.

Payne started walking again.

"A hot meal sounds pretty good right about now, don't you think?" Payne asked.

"And just like that, it's gone," Mary noted. "Did you have any revelations?"

"Only that we're doing everything we can, and more importantly, everything we need to do. You people need to have a little patience. And faith. You should have faith, too. And patience."

"Are you doing that on purpose?" Mary asked.

Payne reached her. They bumped their faceplates together. He held her armored glove for a few seconds, then let go. "Virgil, you know what we should do to this boat on our way out, don't you?"

"We set charges by the aft reactors. Exactly what you planned to do, but since we're not at FTL, we won't have a catastrophic transition. We'll just have a catastrophe."

Payne stepped back. "Since you have the plan, make it so." He handed over his stock of explosives. Kal followed his lead. "You might as well take Heckler and Turbo with you. They'll feel left out if someone starts blowing shit up without them."

The whoop echoed down the corridor without the need to be transmitted on the team channel.

"Come on, Kal. Let's watch some drone butts, just in case they start wiggling."

"You have become a very strange man, Declan Payne," Kal replied. "Downright weird."

"Lev played with my mind. I can't be held responsible."

"It's on you, Dec," Mary added. "You're responsible."

"You want to go with Virgil and set explosives, don't you?" Payne asked.

"I do." Mary waved and started walking aft, following Major Dank. Heckler and Turbo bull-rushed their way through the debris in the corridor.

"You've got drone butts, Kal. I'll stay here." Kal stepped aside to let Heckler and Turbo past. They sped around the corner and down the hangar bay. Kal worked his way down the corridor, leaving Payne alone with his thoughts.

A dangerous place since he didn't know which way his

mind was going to go. An hour and a half remained before *Leviathan* arrived.

Ephesus thundered into the upper atmosphere.

"They've pulled back to the shipyard," the sensor operator announced.

The pilot kept the ship's nose pointed toward the moon. They'd burned an excessive amount of fuel with their intra-atmospheric antics. The pilot wasn't the only one watching what amounted to the fuel gauge.

LeClerc constantly checked the ship's systems. His eyes weren't on the way ahead but on the status. He wanted to know if he could fire Rapiers. He tried to visualize what kind of defense the cruiser could muster against a determined foe, even with few drones. He wanted to know that his people were still alive because the ship's environmental systems provided clean air and water. He wanted to know if the ship could still fight.

It wouldn't take much to overwhelm *Ephesus*.

The ship was low on ammunition and fuel. The biggest punch remaining was its offensive firepower. Two salvos of Rapiers remained. Forty-eight missiles. Would they be enough?

"Take us close, Mr. Smith. We're going to shove a full spread right up their ass."

"Target?"

"Whichever one's closest. Has the battlewagon returned to space?"

"*Japan* is not on my screen," the sensor operator reported.

"Comm, raise that ship. See if they're going to join us. Otherwise, our tactics might have to change."

The communications station tapped, listened, and tapped some more.

The view on the main screen changed to show the deep black of space and the bright reflection of a gibbous moon. *Ephesus* angled toward the dark side of the moon.

The opportunity to pipe the call to arms was lost on him. No one listened to Pink Floyd anymore or any of the masters. The world was different. The galaxy was different.

"I want us nice and close." LeClerc stood, no longer able to maintain the façade of calm. "Did you raise *Japan*?"

The comm officer would have told him if he had, but he should have told him he hadn't to forestall the question. It was not that the captain was impatient, but he had to plan based on everything he knew. He wanted to fill the gaps in his knowledge. Not having *Japan* at *Ephesus'* side greatly reduced his options.

"No, sir," Comm replied.

"Prepare for a half-salvo. Twelve missiles, and I want us close enough that we're inside his shields if we can't take them down."

"What about drones?" the defensive weapons specialist asked.

"Deal with them as best you can. We're plowing ahead. Our best defense against the drones is killing their mothership."

"*Fuck, yeah!*" the weapons officer shouted.

"Decorum, Mr. Blethyn," the captain admonished with a smile. He strolled around the bridge as *Ephesus* raced around the moon. Two Ga'ee carriers loomed large in front of them.

"I have targets GC_3 and GC_4. GC_4 is closest. Targeting solutions locked for twelve Rapiers."

"Thank you, Weapons. Prepare to fire on my command. Helm. In the game of chicken, we better win."

"Roger." The pilot leaned over his console and adjusted the ship's course against the countermoves by the Ga'ee.

"Comm, give me the general broadcast."

The communications officer gave the captain a thumbs-up.

"Ga'ee ships. Leave this system or prepare to be destroyed."

A whistle preceded a reply. "The Ga'ee are at peace with humans," came a mechanical reply.

"How about you go fuck yourself?" Captain LeClerc asked before thinking.

Ephesus bore down on the carrier. Four drones launched.

"Shoot them out of our way. Helm, closer!"

The pilot who had executed the intra-atmospheric maneuvers that had sent all their stomachs into their throats winced at the order. Without the friction of air, he wouldn't be able to turn as tightly, and he was already bearing down on the enemy carrier.

He only touched the controls a hair. He wasn't willing to risk more, no matter what the captain ordered.

"Nice reply," came a new voice, the captain of the Payne-class battlewagon *Japan*. "Give us a minute, and we'll join the fun. Doesn't look like they're able to defend themselves."

"That's what we're seeing. We'll put target GC4 out of our misery and then adjust to GC3 unless a second salvo is called for."

"How much you got?" *Japan* asked.

"Forty-eight Rapiers total. Gotta go." The Ga'ee carrier filled the screen and was getting bigger.

The sensor operator spoke. "Enemy screens are down."

"Fire!"

Twelve missiles raced across the short space between the two ships. The carrier loomed huge next to the cruiser. The Rapiers impacted almost immediately. The side of the carrier erupted in twelve unique explosions. The ship started to turn toward *Ephesus*.

The pilot yanked the cruiser hard over.

"Fire!" the captain ordered.

Twelve more missiles ejected from their tubes and powered into the Ga'ee carrier.

"Over the top, Mr. Smith. Hit it with the full twenty-four when we come back into knife-fighting range. We kill it on the next pass."

Defensive Weapons filled as much of the void as he could with chain gun and laser fire. The impacts on the carrier were minimal, but this was what was known in military parlance as the final protective fire. Fire and launch everything you had until there was nothing left.

The cruiser slid away from the Ga'ee ship and slowed enough to loop back upon its previous course. The pilot accelerated to stay even with the carrier, which was leaving a trail of debris behind it as it tried to escape.

Or was it?

"It's heading for Earth," LeClerc noted.

The pilot added power to improve the acceleration arc. Without screens or drones, they didn't need to be right on top of it.

"Recommend we fire," the weapons officer said in sync with the pilot.

"Fire," LeClerc confirmed. Eighteen missiles ejected into the void. The motors kicked in, and the weapons streamed unerringly into the Ga'ee carrier. They hit it on the spine and unzipped the ship from stern to stem, breaking its back.

And killing it. The reactors lost contact but didn't go critical. It didn't matter. The ship was dead, but it was on a ballistic trajectory past the moon toward Earth.

"Did those last six missiles not reload in time?" LeClerc asked.

"That's correct, sir," Weapons confirmed.

"When they are up, what do you say you hit that ship again? Little pieces will burn up in the atmosphere."

"Roger."

The pilot furiously tapped buttons, trying to get the cruiser to slow down and match speed with the dead Ga'ee ship. "Hit 'em right in the reactors. See if we can break that thing into tiny pieces."

A critical fifteen seconds passed. During that time, the carrier cleared the moon's gravity and continued on a direct course to Earth.

LeClerc could have asked for an estimated time of impact, but letting the Ga'ee crash into Earth would be a failure on his part.

Not when they were at the apex of their victory. A BEP cruiser had killed two Ga'ee carriers. "Not on my watch," the captain said out loud. "Kill that thing now, please."

"Missiles away," the weapons officer said as he activated the launch. The six missiles raced toward their targets, taking three seconds to impact the carrier's hull.

Ephesus banked ninety degrees away from the carrier, the moon, and Earth. Helm punched it into faster-than-light speed the instant two of the six reactors went critical and turned the ten-kilometer-long ship into a mini sun. Debris expanded in a sphere, most of it away from the planet. Five seconds later, Ephesus returned to normal space, sufficiently distant to avoid damage from the explosions.

"Damn," came a voice over the open channel. "Nice work, *Ephesus*. May we realize the same level of success, especially since our boy has decided to run. Align the main and shoot."

Japan's beam weapon hit the fleeing Ga'ee in the aft end and split the ship wide open. The reactor trio erupted, ripping the carrier in half and sending the remaining sections spinning toward deep space.

"That's gonna leave a mark," LeClerc stated. "We're returning to Earth for mop-up operations. Can't let the Ga'ee get a foothold."

"I think we're good, *Ephesus*. Take a well-deserved break. It's up to the people of Earth to kill them on the ground."

[20]

"The thing about karma is that it's a bitch." —From the memoirs of Ambassador Declan Payne

It wasn't safe to stay in the air, so the president's helicopter ride ended in Washington DC, and she transferred to ground transportation. The limousine raced down the road. Smoke trails drifted skyward on both sides.

"There." The president pointed. The driver looked over his shoulder to see where he was being directed, nodded, and returned his attention to the road ahead. They bumped down a rough exit and detoured onto a dirt road toward the flashing lights of a police vehicle and a tow truck.

When they reached the pair of vehicles, they found a deputy in his t-shirt digging at the bottom of a pit while the tow truck operator wielded a welding torch and cheered.

Paragon Virtue tossed a small drone into the air to record the engagement. Two security personnel stepped wide and surveyed the area. One of them pointed into the pit and made a finger pistol, then flashed two fingers.

The president waved him away. He tried to stop her, but she continued into the pit.

"How can I help?" she asked.

"Grab a shovel and dig that wriggly bastard out of there. If you leave them alone too long, they dig almost too fast to catch," the truck driver replied. He dropped onto all fours and stuffed the welding torch into the deputy's latest excavation. "Ha! Got you."

The next shovelful brought out a charred form that looked like a giant centipede.

"Is that a Ga'ee?" the president asked.

"That's what used to be a Ga'ee," the truck driver replied. "How many we got, Bill?"

"That's four. There's still one down there, Clarence."

The president waved at her security. "You can dig a lot faster than I can."

"But ma'am, if we're digging, who is going to watch over you?"

"You want to secure Earth? It starts down there." She motioned at the growing hole at the bottom of the crater.

The security officer holstered his pistol and threw his jacket to the ground. When he hit the bottom of the crater, he took the shovel from the deputy and started to dig like a dog chasing a gopher. The heavily sweating deputy stepped aside. Clarence stared at each shovelful, looking for the enemy.

When it appeared, he dove in.

The deputy grabbed his ankles to keep him from sliding face-first into the enemy. The welding torch did its job. With the help of the president and the deputy, they extricated the driver.

"Twenty-five, Bill!" He tipped his hat to the president. "You look familiar, but we gotta go. Goal is fifty. We got five more of these drones to clean out."

"I'm the president of the UN, President Sinkhaus."

"You're her!" the deputy exclaimed. "Hot damn. But Clarence is right. We gotta go. Giving these things time to dig is not good. We're going to need a backhoe if we waste any more time."

"Backhoes, we can do," the president replied. "Excavators, too."

"Bring 'em on, girlfriend!" Clarence hollered. He scrambled out of the crater, reaching a hand back for the president. They found Paragon lurking up top. "What's wrong with you?"

"Come again?" Paragon asked.

"You let the president come in the hole with the enemy while you cowered out here? What kind of ticklepuss are you?"

"I'm pretty sure I'm not a ticklepuss, whatever that is."

Clarence noticed the drone. "You making one of them challenge videos, hoping to go viral? Buddy, you got messed-up priorities." He tipped his hat. "It's been real, and it's been fun, but it hasn't been real fun."

"Mind if I ride with you?" the president asked the truck driver.

"Climb in." Clarence coiled the hoses and closed the valves. He jumped into the driver's seat.

A brief argument ensued between the president, Paragon Virtue, and her security. In the end, she climbed into the cab by herself, much to the chagrin of her people.

Clarence leaned out the window. "I got me a date, Bill. Get on the horn and find the next drone. Let's go." He turned to his passenger. "If you can get us a backhoe wherever Bill is going, he'd appreciate it. Then again, you brought those strapping young bucks with you. Bill's starting to run out of gas, but you saw that."

The president laughed. She didn't have conversations like

this. People weren't themselves around her. Everyone was guarded. She lost her smile. She had made them that way.

The tow truck spun in the dirt. Clarence leaned hard on the wheel to avoid the limo. The police car's siren wailed as Bill accelerated down the lane. He had a passenger, too—Paragon Virtue.

The video drone darted in through the tow truck's open window. The president caught it and tossed it out, then rolled up the window to keep it from coming back. She wondered for a moment why she had done it. Wasn't she supposed to be collecting fodder for her media campaign?

She reconsidered the campaign. It was exactly what she was trying to sell humanity. Salt of the Earth fighting for them, and it was better than that. They were having fun doing it.

"Why fifty?" she asked.

"Seemed like a good number. We heard there were thousands of those things. There are five in each. If everyone kills fifty, we'll have them cleaned up in no time. That's important. We cannot give them an hour, let alone a day. Good thing I loaded up new tanks for the welder this morning. We got a hundred in us if we can get to them."

"What's stopping you?"

"Time and a fat old man with a shovel." Clarence laughed. "But he's doing the best he can. With your boys driving the steel deep, we'll get more. If you can get us a backhoe, the Ga'ee can kiss their landing goodbye."

"The Ga'ee are not going to get a foothold on Earth," the president promised. "Can I call you Clarence?"

"Just don't call me late for dinner!" He laughed out loud. "You didn't bring any Kentucky Fried or something like that, did you?"

"No. We rushed out as soon as we sent the message to

humanity to fight back. Fight them wherever they landed and kill them before they escaped."

"We got the message. Loud and clear, or as we like to say on the radio, lickin' chicken. Which brings me back to Kentucky Fried. Killing crawly aliens works up an appetite."

"I'm sure we'll find something as soon as we get to fifty, Clarence. Call me Sylvia. Next stop, I'll see if my people can get us something to eat while we drive to the next site."

The radio chirped. "Take the next left, Clarence. Some farmers are fighting one near Old Man Johnson's barn."

Clarence turned serious. "When your number's called, you answer. Today is that day, Sylvia."

"You could be the wisest man I've ever met, Clarence."

"Nah. I'm just at the top of my game, that's all. This is exhilarating. Do you know what my day consists of?"

The president hadn't thought about it. Menial labor. Taxed the body but not the mind, but menial labor enjoyed that.

Didn't they?

"I expect it's about as brain-numbing as mine."

"I don't know what yours consists of. Mine is a lot of audiobooks. I listen to anything I can get my hands on. A couple times a day, I get sent to a broken rig. I have to figure out what's wrong with her and get her back on the road. I guess I'm kind of like a truck doc." The vehicle bounced over a cattle grate, nearly jamming their heads into the roof of the cab. "Hang on," Clarence advised but too late.

The president gripped the door and the dash in a feeble attempt to hold herself in place.

"My day is about the same, but without the audiobooks. I guess it's like having twenty broken vehicles, but only ten of them are really broken."

"That sounds fucked up." Clarence pulled no punches. "I prefer my job."

The police car slid to a stop up ahead, scattering a group surrounding a hole from which a pillar of greasy black smoke rose.

"What do we have going on here?" Clarence squinted through the dust to get a better look, then stopped the tow truck and hopped out. He ran to the crater rather than open the door for the president. She realized that after sitting there for a second and let herself out.

At the crater, the farmer tossed more gasoline on the fire to the cheers of the onlookers.

"Cut that shit out!" Clarence yelled. "That won't kill 'em. We need to torch 'em, and we can't do that if we can't get down there and dig 'em out."

The deputy took over. He rushed to the one with the gas can.

"Just trying to kill aliens who are invading my planet."

"And we appreciate your efforts. All of you," the president interjected.

A drone zipped overhead as Paragon Virtue arrived in the limo and resumed his recording to develop the public's perception of the emergency...and most importantly, the president's part in managing it.

She worked her way around the small crowd. Their looks indicated passing familiarity but not full recognition. The president found she liked the anonymity, but at that moment, she had one job: stop them from adding gasoline to the fire so Clarence could kill the Ga'ee.

"I'm President Sinkhaus, and I need you to step back and let these men do their job. They have already killed twenty-five invaders. They're shooting for fifty." She gestured for them to move back.

"Hey," a younger woman in the group said. "You're *that* person."

"I'm somebody just like you, trying to save the planet from these festering pustules."

"What?" the old farmer asked. He leaned close to an old woman, who repeated what the president had said by shouting at his ear.

The gasoline fire burned quickly. A young man tossed a bucket of water into the hole. It steamed as it hit, and the flames scattered but died. Clarence slid into the hole, along with the security man carrying the shovel. The deputy had been relieved of his duties, and he *looked* relieved. He helped move the people away from the edge.

"Get my torch, Bill!" Clarence shouted. The deputy raced off. The president joined him. He handed her the torch and uncoiled the hose. She hurried to the crater while he turned the valves. She reached over the edge but started to fall. The nearest watcher reached for her, but it was too late. She tumbled into the hole.

Clarence caught her arm and hauled her upright before she face-planted in a small pile of blackened Ga'ee.

She looked surprised, first that she didn't slam into the bottom, and second, that she still had the torch in her hand.

"Thanks for not dropping that," Clarence told her with a crooked smile. He took the torch and sparked it to life, adjusting the flame until it hissed a light blue. He ran it across the already burned bodies. They twisted and contorted before they curled.

"Injured but not dead," Clarence announced. "That's three."

The shovel man knew what to do. He started digging in the small hole left by their passing. He levered around it to widen the hole and see where they went after going straight down. After two shovels full, he found more Ga'ee, blackened and curled. Clarence touched them with the torch and put them out of their misery.

"Thanks, folks!" he called cheerfully, turning off the torch. He waved for the president to climb out. She started teetering backward a third of the way up. Clarence put a shoulder into her backside and pushed until a hand from above pulled her the rest of the way out.

Paragon winced. He'd taken the initiative to live-feed the footage. The president didn't think anything of it. She shook hands with the farmers, thanking them for their interdiction. The deputy returned to his car. After the hose was coiled and stored, Clarence pointed at the cab.

"Gotta go. Can't let these bastards get even a toehold. Not on our planet!" She pumped her fist, and the old farmer threw his arms up.

Sinkhaus climbed in. "Where to?"

"The next one until there aren't any left," Clarence replied. "That's thirty." He pounded the dash of his truck and bounced in his seat. "Bump."

The president turned. "What?" The tow truck was accelerating as it hit the cattle grate, and it bounced. The president hadn't put on her seat belt. She was thrown against the dash, and her head bounced off the windshield.

"You might want to put on that belt. I hear it's the law." He laughed when he saw that she was mostly okay. Blood streamed down the side of her head. "Put some pressure on that. I've got a rag in the glove box."

He didn't slow down. The security guard in the deputy's car was nearly apoplectic when he saw the president through the back window. After a brief wrestling match, the deputy slid sideways onto the highway and screeched the tires on his way to the next impact site.

The president opened the box and pulled out a dirty rag. She looked at it for a moment, then wiped her face and pressed it against her head. She snapped her safety belt in place.

"Are you okay?" he asked with concern once they were racing down the highway. He glanced at her to see the blood-splattered rag.

"I don't feel so good," the president admitted.

Clarence got on the radio. "Pull over, Bill." The squad car's flashing lights eased to the shoulder and stopped. Clarence maneuvered behind him, and the limo rolled in on his tail. Clarence ran around the cab, barely getting there before the security guard arrived. The president fell out the passenger door. Clarence caught her and stumbled backward.

"She hit her head on the windshield," he explained. The guard glared, torn between throwing Clarence into the ditch and beating him senseless. However, he had the president's head cradled in his lap.

Her eyelids fluttered, and she opened her eyes. Her pupils were dilated.

"Looks like you took a nasty bump. Maybe a concussion. These good people will take you where you can get looked at," Clarence said.

"Come with me," she requested after closing her eyes.

"Can't. Gotta fight aliens. You said that was our number one priority."

"Sounds like me, Clarence. Thank you for today. Thank you for everything."

Paragon and the two security guards lifted the president to her feet, and with a shoulder under each arm, they took her to the waiting limo. Virtue waited behind.

He shook the mechanic's dirty hand. "We will see you later. I have all your information. I'm sure the president will have a medal for you or something."

Clarence laughed. "You know I hate politicians, right? I'll pass. I don't mind when people help me do my job, no matter how misguided they are in their daily life." Clarence lightly punched Virtue in the chest before returning to the cab. He leaned out the window. "Come on, Bill. Somebody's gonna get to fifty before us."

"You bastard! I'm back on the shovel, aren't I?" the deputy called before getting in his car.

"Light the fires and kick the tires, Bill. We got bad guys to kill!"

[21]

"May we live to complain about the times when we weren't sure we were going to live." –From the memoirs of Ambassador Declan Payne

Mary was the first one to return because she was running. Virgil was right behind her.

"We still have twenty minutes," Payne told her.

"We may have to leave early," Mary replied.

"What did Heckler and Turbo do? Never mind. Listen up, everyone. Back to *Ugly 6* on the double."

Major Dank took the lead. Mary followed him at a slower pace, taking care not to bump too many of the drones that were stacked and stored, ready to deploy.

The others pounded down the corridor leaving Sparky standing at the hole they'd cut in the bulkhead waiting for Blinky and Buzz.

"There's a hold-up," she reported.

Payne waved Byle, Shaolin, and Joker through. Kal stopped halfway and returned to join Sparky.

Turbo appeared, with Heckler jogging behind.

"What did you do?" Payne demanded.

"Exactly as we were told; set a series of charges to take this ship out. They are set, but somehow, the timing got screwed up. First charge goes off ten minutes before *Leviathan* arrives."

"Fix it!"

Heckler threw up his hands. "That planet you thought we'd blow up accidentally? Well, we're riding on it right now. I stuffed the charge where we couldn't get at it. No one can. We're kind of stuck."

Payne threw his head back and stared into the hangar bay's dark overhead. No revelations appeared. "Get on the boat. We're leaving."

Turbo forced her way through the drones, indifferent to bumping them out of her way. Heckler followed her lead.

"Sparky, drag Blinky and Buzz out of there. We need to go right now." Payne thought for a moment. "Kernel Lev, look for how we can drift with the debris that used to be this ship."

"I think she's going to look like a supernova when she goes. We probably don't want to be too close," Heckler suggested.

"Heckler! You're going to get us killed. We can't just dive into the network and think they aren't going to see us. Any ship within ten minutes is going to show up and kill us."

"Then we should probably try to kill them first," Heckler offered.

"Now's not the time, Cointreau!" Payne was less than amused.

"You know you're in trouble when Dad calls you by your given name," Turbo whispered on the team channel.

"Get those fucking guys out of there!" Payne yelled. Kal and Sparky disappeared through the hole. Ten seconds later, Blinky appeared, then Buzz.

They jogged like their legs had fallen asleep, slowing to a walk to get through the drone debris.

"Hurry up unless you wanna die with this ship," Payne advised.

Kal and Sparky hammered the deck behind them, encouraging them to move faster.

By the time they reached the hangar bay, they had their wits about them. "Sorry, guys. I wanted to give you more time," Payne apologized. "But it's been taken out of my hands. We'll get 'em on a different day."

Blinky pushed forward while he replied, "I think we at least have a vector, and it makes the most sense. It's on a direct line to Rang'Kor space."

Payne reviewed the star charts in his mind. "Which is on a direct line to Earth."

"Seems like they have a hard-on for humans," Buzz remarked.

"What else did you get from the voice?"

"The dissenting voice, as we call it. It's loud and confident. An equal vote but more equal. I think you were right in that this is the target. Remove this voice, and the Ga'ee will step back from their aggressive expansion," Buzz opined. "They'll be susceptible to alternate suggestions."

"All they need is a free-thinking mind, which is strange, considering they have all these ships that are like independent little minds. They die, and all the drones attached to them die, except sometimes when they don't."

"The newest version of the ships. The ones with missiles also have the capability to extend their command and control over any drones in the area."

"But they don't upgrade their ships. They just build new ones."

"From what we've seen, that's correct," Buzz replied. "How is that important?"

Blinky and Buzz sped up as their stiff muscles relaxed. The timer on Payne's HUD suggested they had five more minutes to make it to *Ugly 6* and get into space before the first explosion.

Payne spoke in a stream of consciousness. "That's a good question. I've been fixated on it, but the answer I keep coming back to is that the threat isn't as bad since we're only fighting a small number of ships with supplemental firepower and the ability to control drones from another carrier. Except, with tens of thousands of ships, even the original versions will vastly overwhelm us. That's what the Ga'ee meant when they said the first ships into our sectors were only the scouts. They were old. The new ships would do a number on us if any of those made it as far as our sectors, which I'm not sure they did. I think they simply threw more and more carriers at us. Population control before population explosion. Maybe it's their way to ensure survival of the fittest."

Blinky surged the last hundred meters before using his jets to vault into the floating *Ugly 6*. Buzz jumped in, then Payne. Kal was last. He eschewed using his jets because of his misadventure on BD18, but he was tall enough to grab the deck and pull himself up.

The instant he was on board, the outer doors rotated down and sealed.

"Two minutes!" Payne declared. "We made it in plenty of time."

Ugly 6 backed slowly through the hole it had made.

"Block that hole so there's no emergency decompression," Payne ordered. The insertion craft stopped moving.

"We probably need to put a little distance between us and them," Dank noted.

"If we bail too early, they'll gather their wits and send the drones after us. In two minutes, they'll kill us before their ship blows. Lev arrives in eleven minutes. We have to limit our exposure. You know what they say, exposure kills."

The tactical board wasn't populating with threats. The video showing space beyond the carrier was clear. Nothing but pinpoints of stars in a crowded void.

"The ship has their energy shield in place as if the doors were open," Buzz advised. He and Blinky were already tapping on their computers.

"One minute," Dank reported.

Payne checked the screen one last time. "Push off and accelerate away from this pig."

Ugly 6 moved out of the hole and accelerated beyond stealth speed.

As soon it cleared the ship, a second carrier came into view. It had been lurking on the far side.

Payne snarled at their lack of tactical awareness and being forced into the open too early. It also set *Leviathan* up to be attacked the instant it arrived.

"Not your best move, Heckler. You may have killed us all, and that includes Lev." Payne didn't like being demeaning, but this was a hard truth. Getting the destruction time wrong? That was unforgivable, and they were all going to pay for the mistake.

Heckler didn't reply. He bowed his head and clenched his fists. Turbo tried to wrap her arm around him, but he shrugged her away. He looked like he wanted to space himself.

"Ideas, people. How do we survive this?"

"Which way will the blast be harshest?" Sparky asked.

Turbo answered. "Sideways. It'll probably cut the back half off the ship."

"Then we need to get in front of this thing. Put more metal between us, the shockwave, and the accelerating debris."

"Kernel Lev, put us in front of this ship and keep accelerating," Payne ordered. He gave Sparky the thumbs-up. "Hangar doors remain closed."

"This ship shouldn't launch on us. It thinks everything is okay," Blinky replied.

"What about..." Payne stopped when *Ugly 6* cleared the shadow of the carrier they'd been on, giving them a clear view of the second carrier. Its hangar doors were opening.

"It'd be cool if you guys could tell the second pig not to launch. Really cool." Payne tried not to sound like he was begging, but he couldn't hide it. He was pleading for his life and the lives of his team.

His eyes tracked to Mary Payne, a person with whom he'd not spent enough time.

Time.

Ten seconds.

"Fire a torpedo at the hangar bay closest to us." A second later, the ship shuddered as the large missile left the internal tube and its motor kicked in. "All we have to do is keep the closest drones from reaching us before the rest get caught in the blast. We only need to buy a few seconds."

Payne could feel his butt cheeks clenching as the timer reached zero.

Nothing happened.

"Heckler!" Payne shouted before the delayed effect of the secondary explosion of the power plant coming apart sent a shockwave accelerating at near-light speed into space. *Ugly 6* was buffeted hard but quickly righted itself.

"That was one. The others are coming," Turbo announced. Heckler was still quiet.

The second blast was harsher than the first, and the third was the worst. That ripped the Ga'ee carrier apart, and that was the one the insertion craft was running from.

Caught on the bow wave, projectiles punched through one

side of the hull and out the other. Pummeled by bits and pieces of the destroyed ship, *Ugly 6* lost power. Then it lost artificial gravity and became nothing more than debris floating in space, along with the remains of the Ga'ee ship.

Payne studied his HUD. The team was green across the board, but Mary's pulse raced, as did most of theirs.

"Sanity check," Payne called. One by one, the team verbally confirmed they were green. All except Heckler.

"Heckler. We survived. You didn't kill us, but you sure did a number on that Ga'ee carrier. We're blind, but I'm not sure that second carrier could have survived the blast. It was right in the worst of it, which clears space for *Leviathan* to pick us up. That would not have been the case if the blast hadn't gone off early. Everything we just saw would have happened, except Lev would have been in the blast zone too, along with two ships' worth of drones trying to kill him."

"I meant to do that," Heckler croaked. "I'm sorry."

"More fight is coming, Heckler." Payne pointed at his senior combat specialist.

Turbo playfully pushed her husband.

"Don't make that mistake again and we're good. You know we're not doing any after-actions from this stuff. I'm done filing reports. Either we win without them, or we don't win."

"I'm not sure that's as profound as you think it is," Virgil suggested.

"You are blown away at the profundidity of it all. You are speechless at the linguistic magnificence of the call to arms. We'll rally around our desire not to file reports to bring forth the very best military tactics and execution that could ever be tacticked or executed. We shall bring them to their figurative knees as they worship our mastery of anti-bureaucracy on our way to ultimate victory."

Something heavy impacted *Ugly 6*, and everyone froze. The

inside of the ship was dark, but their HUDs glowed faintly in the powerless ship.

"Shouldn't the debris cloud have already passed us by?" Payne wondered.

"Permission to actively scan," Dank requested.

Payne was hesitant because they'd look less like debris and more like a spaceship if the second Ga'ee carrier was looking.

Seven minutes until Lev arrived.

"I'm sorry, but let's wait. They knew we were out here because we fired a missile at them. We'll start scanning thirty seconds before Lev gets here. In the interim, anyone know how to fix our ship?"

"If Lev had power, he could fix himself," Virgil suggested.

"There's the rub." Payne shook his head. "This thing isn't made with backup systems in mind. I'd suggest we take a spacewalk, but there's got to be a lot of sharp and/or heavy stuff flying around out there. Yes, we're wearing armor, but I think the risk is too great."

"I'll do it," Kal volunteered.

"I'm not looking for volunteers." Payne waved him off. "If anyone goes, it'll be Sparky, whose job is to understand ship systems. I don't want to lose her any more than I'm willing to lose you. For the record, I'm not willing to lose anyone, and imagine my overwhelming joy that all of us survived the destruction of the Ga'ee carrier."

Mary was first to laugh. "Overwhelming joy..."

Payne tried to think small thoughts and become one with the debris. He assumed the second carrier had survived and was now searching for them. Without power, they were less likely to be found. Getting damaged might have served them well.

"Heckler, this gets better and better for you. We may survive this in the only way we could have possibly survived, and that was by exploding the bombs early. No wonder you two haven't blown up a planet. You walk hand in hand with the mistress of luck."

"Now there's a thought," Dank inserted. "Don't let it go to your heads."

"Hey! How did I get roped into his depredations?" Turbo asked.

"I think you mean deprivations," Mary replied. "'Depredations' means attacks or plundering."

Turbo looked at Heckler. "We'll start using that word more, then."

"Concur." Heckler took her hand.

The group sat in darkness and silence.

The timer ticked down toward *Leviathan's* arrival.

Another bump, lighter, like a small rock traveling slowly. It made them jump regardless.

Payne tensed until he struggled to breathe. Time dragged. Each second took forever before ticking to the next, where it seemed to pause for an interminable amount of time.

Time, the great equalizer.

For once, Team Payne had too much of it.

At one minute, *Ugly 6* was buffeted and bounced and spun as if it were caught in a rapidly flowing stream.

"Sensors," Payne called. Sparky had been designated so the insertion craft didn't light up like a Christmas tree. She activated her suit on low power.

Sparky streamed the input to the rest of the team. "Would you look at that? No carriers survived. Looks like we have drones in the void, drifting with the debris. There's a lot of junk out there. I would not recommend any extravehicular activity."

"Can you see what's wrong with *Ugly 6*? Blinky and Buzz, can you guys see the neural network? Are we exposed? Any bad guys coming?"

"*Ugly 6* is broken," Sparky replied.

Blinky and Buzz tapped furiously.

"We don't have the sensors to pick up the network without the uglymobile," Blinky replied, yet he and Buzz worked as if they could. "We are parsing the data to refine the location of the one we're calling the Voice."

"Carry on," Payne ordered unnecessarily.

[22]

"The only way the tactical situation wouldn't change is if we had no plan to begin with." –From the memoirs of Ambassador Declan Payne

Clarence wandered all over the road. The last two stops had taken most of his energy. This next one promised to be the worst. The impact crater had been reported over the police channel, but no one had yet responded.

Bill called for a backhoe or an excavator, knowing they'd have to dig. It had been too long since the impact. The deputy was more tired than Clarence. He wasn't used to the amount of manual labor they had put in that day.

Or the stress, which they didn't realize until the gap between the last stop and the next put them on the road for an hour. They crashed like they were coming off a sugar high. The adrenaline rush was over.

"Maybe someone else can cover this one," Bill called over the radio.

The roads were deserted. Humanity had decided to stay out of the way of those fighting the war. Clarence thought the opposite should have taken place. Everyone should have been out there. Maybe the rush wore off after several hours.

Rally the troops!

After a couple minutes of drifting off, Bill came back on the radio. "We got us a backhoe, Clarence. It'll meet us at the Philips crossroads. We may have to knock down a fence or two."

"How convenient. I happen to have a torch and a pickaxe."

"I have a wire cutter," Bill replied.

"GPS shows another five minutes. Getting tired, Bill. I think we're going to have to pack it in after this one."

"I couldn't agree more. I'll need to head back to the big house and make my report."

Clarence blinked to clear his eyes. He hoped the next shift was already on the job, racing around the countryside like him and Bill, fighting the good fight.

As if reading the mechanic's thoughts, Bill keyed his mic. "Everyone is out there, digging these bastards out and frying them. This is the last one on the chatterbox. Every other report has been dealt with."

"Roger that, Bill. Did we do everything we could?" Clarence knew the answer to his question. He had injured the president in his haste to get to the next potential infestation. He felt bad about that, but they had reached the next crater in time to clean it out and the one after that, too.

Bill pulled down a side road and turned off on another that was little more than two wheel tracks through a grassy field. They ended at a locked gate, where they found a young teen sitting on a four-wheel ATV.

"It's over that next hill, in the copse beyond." He pointed as he talked with a toothpick in his mouth. He removed the pick. "We searched the entire property just like we were asked. That's the only one we found. Pop's getting the backhoe. He'll meet you down there since he's coming in from the other side. Those are really aliens?"

"From the far side of the galaxy, or so we've heard," Clarence replied. "We've been fighting aliens for a generation, though, so this is nothing new."

"Hell, yes! They ain't ever been on Earth before, have they?"

Clarence shrugged. "Not that I know of." He gestured at the gate. "Open that up, and we'll be on our way."

"Can't get it open. Heavy chain and no key for the lock," the young man replied. "We have to go around the other side, but you can't get there from here."

Clarence laughed. "No sweat." He unrolled his hose for the umpteenth time that day, turned the valves, and sparked the striker. The torch's flame came to life. This time, Clarence needed his welding mask. He had to return to the truck for it.

He flipped the dark glass over his eyes and went to work, not on the hardened steel of the lock's hasp but on the softer metal of the chain link through which the lock went. The welding torch made short work of the chain—two cuts, and the link was in two pieces. The chain fell free. Clarence pushed it open.

The young boy pushed it the rest of the way. Clarence turned off the torch, closed the valves, rolled up the hose, and jumped in the cab.

Bill rolled through first, gunning the engine and spinning the wheels to maintain his forward momentum once he hit the high grass. Clarence's tow truck had higher clearance and dual wheels in the rear, which gave his vehicle better traction.

The squad car stalled, and Bill waved Clarence around. The mechanic didn't hesitate. He yanked the wheel to the left and accelerated, bouncing the truck through the field toward the copse of trees at the far end. The ATV stopped, and the deputy hopped on the back while Clarence continued the rough drive.

"Glad you're not in here, Madam President. You'd get all kinds of beat up," Clarence shouted into the empty space where the president of the UN had sat.

Right in his truck, fighting the Ga'ee.

She'd earned his vote.

He came over a ridge and started down a hill that was far steeper than he'd expected. He downshifted and then once more. The engine roared with the demand. He eased off the brakes to keep the wheels from locking up. At the bottom, a backhoe waited.

He was headed right for it. He pulled the emergency brake, and the back tires started to slide. He was at a thirty-degree angle on the hill when the emergency brake failed. The truck straightened and jumped forward. He jammed it into first gear before standing on the brakes. The truck skipped and barked its way to the flat and stopped short of the backhoe.

Clarence had to collect himself before getting out.

"Nice entrance," the old man in the piece of equipment called. "It'd probably have been easier had you gone 'round the hill." He pointed behind him where the ATV appeared, with Bill riding behind the teenager.

The deputy jumped off quickly and looked at Clarence and the hill behind him. "You drove your tow truck down that?"

Clarence snorted while removing his welding rig. "No. Only an idiot would do something like that."

The wheel tracks through the brush told a different story. Clarence glared at the youngster momentarily before checking out the crater.

"I bashed that ship when I got here. It was doing the Safety Dance or something inside the hole. It was unsettling."

Bill pulled out his service revolver and emptied the cylinder into the drone.

The farmer dragged the hulk out of the hole, revealing a small colony of Ga'ee wriggling in the dirt beneath.

Clarence vaulted into the crater. He sparked his torch to life and worked from the top down, killing the first four quickly. The fifth disappeared into the soft dirt. Clarence pointed and waited.

The backhoe dug deep, rotated, and dropped the bucketload on the ground. He slid the bucket through the pile to reveal the silver body within. Using the bucket like a ladle, he dipped into the dirt, pulled out the Ga'ee, and dropped it back into the hole beside Clarence, who jumped back to keep it from latching onto him. He reached out to arm's length and with a one-handed effort, hit it with the torch. After it started to curl, he moved closer to finish the job.

He turned off the torch and wiped his brow, happy that his day had come to such a quick end.

The farmer stabbed a finger at the hole at the bottom of the crater. Clarence saw movement. Silver, digging to get out of the light.

He dove face-first into the hole and hit it with his torch, but he hadn't relit it. He pulled the striker and sparked the torch back to life. By the time Clarence rolled back, the Ga'ee was gone.

"They've bred," he growled. Clarence gestured for the farmer to keep digging.

The weight of the day bore heavily on the mechanic. This was what happened when humanity took too long to respond. In a bowl of low hills next to a stand of trees, it was surprising they'd found this crater at all. It could barely be seen directly.

That would be the challenge. Given time, The Ga'ee would dig in and expand to the point where a man with a welding torch wouldn't be able to kill them, no matter how far they dug.

The one he'd caught sight of was bigger than any he had killed that day. Far bigger.

The second bucketload of dirt brought out two Ga'ee. Clarence dove in with his torch, screaming at the infestation. While the first once curled, the second one did not retreat into the ground. It climbed up Clarence's leg. He tried to kick it off, but it kept moving.

He threw the torch down before the first Ga'ee was dead and grabbed the creature. He got a grip, but it burned his hand.

Clarence let go, screaming in pain. The deputy jumped into the crater and used his nightstick to pry the creature free. When it stretched far enough away from Clarence's arm, he shot it. The concussion knocked it loose but didn't kill it.

Bill picked up the torch and waded into battle. He held it before him like a cross with a bulb of garlic on his way to torture a vampire. The Ga'ee started to dig. Bill pounced and raked the length of its body with the blue flame. When it was good and dead, he turned his attention to the one on the dirt pile. It didn't take much to finish it off.

Clarence clutched his arm. The skin was warped and twisted like he'd survived third-degree burns.

There was nothing Bill could do but take over.

Clarence clenched his teeth. "Get my welding gloves out of the truck, would you?"

"You can't keep on. Sometimes you gotta know when it's time to quit."

Clarence shook his head. "Now is not that time. This is a toehold that will become a foothold. Not on my watch, Bill! The Ga'ee are not going to destroy Earth if I have anything to say about it. Yeah, it hurts, but screw that. It'll hurt worse for them when I fry the bastards. Gloves, Bill. Get my gloves!"

Bill handed the torch to Clarence, who took it gingerly and

angrily. He motioned with his chin for the farmer to keep digging.

The farmer made a fist and yelled inside the backhoe's cab. He waved Clarence out of the way since he had to carve an access ramp into the crater. He wouldn't be able to get deep enough from outside the crater. He ripped the edge off the crater on one side, then started pushing and pulling, jerking the rig back and forth before angling the tracks down the impromptu ramp and into the pit.

He started digging quickly, almost recklessly.

The farmer wasn't going to let the Ga'ee find purchase in the fertile soil of his field. His name would not go down in history as the one who'd failed humanity, not when a man with melted skin carried on.

The next Ga'ee appeared. It tried to get away, but the operator caught it and pressed it against the ground with the front of his bucket. Clarence eased into the hole, cradling the burning torch in his arm. He managed to grasp it with his left hand and delivered the flame around the sides of the bucket in relative safety since the Ga'ee was pinned and wouldn't be crawling anywhere.

Clarence fell back, stumbling on the uneven ground.

He couldn't get out.

Bill slid back into the hole and continued to the bottom of the new dig where Clarence was struggling. The deputy presented the gloves, but Clarence hung his head and didn't take them. "Don't think I can keep going, Bill," he admitted.

The deputy didn't hesitate. He put on the gloves and relieved Clarence of the torch. "Get yourself out. I'll take it from here."

Clarence could only stay out of the way. He was surprised at how much energy the pain sapped. He could barely think, let alone function. He knew he'd have to go to the hospital if he was to have any respite from the attack. He had never considered that the Ga'ee might fight back, and when they did, people would get hurt.

These were the enemy. Clarence had seen nothing to make him think they were more than an insect infestation, but now, he believed the propaganda that suggested they were pure evil with a callous disregard for human and any other carbon-based life.

The farmer dug and ripped at the ground, widening the hole while looking for tracks where a Ga'ee might have dug.

Five small ones. Three big ones. If they doubled, there would be at least two more.

"Need to find two more," he called. Bill held up two fingers while not taking his eyes off the hole.

It looked like he was giving the peace sign.

A silver body flashed, but the farmer reacted faster. He dropped the bucket ahead of the creature, then dug into the surrounding ground, pulling it free. He flopped it on the ground, and it started to scurry with a speed reminiscent of a millipede motivated to get out of the open. Clarence stepped forward and planted his boot in the middle of its back.

Bill hit it with the torch, and it curled the unburned end toward Clarence's leg. Bill fell to the ground and grabbed it. The leather glove protected him for the few moments it took to finish off the burned end and start on the other. He let go when the body blackened and curled in on itself.

"One more, and then we'll think about slowing down,"

Clarence grunted and fell over. Bill caught him and eased him to the ground. He gestured for the farmer to keep digging. Bill slid Clarence to the side of the pit.

The backhoe kept digging. One minute became five became ten. The hole expanded in all directions. It deepened until the backhoe rotated to carve out more from the crater's edge to give it more space to maneuver.

When the farmer returned the bucket to the pit, it only took one bucket full to rout the tenth Ga'ee. Bill jumped into the hole and pinned the creature with a foot while he worked it over with the welding torch.

The deputy slowly crawled out of the hole, then helped Clarence stand and get his good arm around Bill's shoulders. The two walked up the ramp behind the backhoe to get out of the crater. The teenager helped them to the ATV, and they leaned against it. Clarence's eyes rolled, and he found himself unable to focus.

The farmer kept digging and expanding the hole. Bill held his friend and watched as the backhoe turned on its lights. The teenager clicked on the ATV's light.

Darkness swarmed over them as if the night had waited until they were finished with the day's trials.

After thirty minutes, the farmer declared victory. "There aren't any more holes, tunnels, trails, or aliens."

He shut down the backhoe and left it where it was, then walked out of the crater. He joined the others who were leaning against the ATV. In the back of the four-wheeler was a case that looked like a mini-trunk. The farmer opened it and pulled out four beers. They were cooler than the air temperature but not by much.

He handed one to each person, including the teenage boy. Bill popped Clarence's can and then his own. They bumped their cans, and each took a big swig, even Clarence.

"I could have used this a while ago," the truck driver said.

"Sorry, big man. I was busy killing aliens and that took priority over everything else, even your little skinned knee." He saluted with his beer before upending it and swigging until it was gone. He pulled a second one from the case and popped it open.

"It ain't my knee." Clarence took another long drink. "We better get going. I think I need to go to the hospital."

Bill took another drink and put the can aside. He glanced sideways at the teen drinking a beer. Today wasn't the day for the little rules. Bill offered his hand to the farmer, and the two men shook.

"Help me into the cab," Clarence urged. "I've seen you drive, and frankly, it scares me. I think we're better off with me driving while all busted up than you driving healthy."

"Clarence, I'm a deputy. I drive for a living."

"God help us all, Bill." The two worked their way over to the truck, and Bill put Clarence into the cab.

"How about we go around the hill on our way out of here?"

"My thoughts exactly. Is my welding torch secured?"

Bill climbed out and dragged the torch out of the pit by pulling on the hoses. He coiled them and shut off the valves. The deputy circled the truck to make sure everything was secure before reentering the cab. He buckled up and pointed in the direction they needed to go.

Clarence had to jockey the truck back and forth until he could make the turn around the hill. Steering the heavy truck with one arm took a great deal of effort. Clarence grunted while struggling to keep his head up.

Bill pushed on his bad arm, and Clarence cried out.

"Damn it, man! Keep your head up."

"You know what I like about you, Bill? Not a damn thing." Clarence's chuckles were interspersed with weak coughs. "Where's the nearest hospital?"

[23]

"It was the day the Ga'ee gave us hope–hope for a different future." –From the memoirs of Ambassador Declan Payne

When the countdown timer reached zero, *Leviathan* entered normal space in the midst of the carriers' debris field.

The pelting of the outer hull, even with the textured coating, reverberated to the bridge. "What the hell?" Admiral Wesson studied the tactical screen in addition to the external views.

"Neural network suggests four Ga'ee ships are headed this way," Lev reported.

"Time to engagement?"

"The first will arrive in nine minutes." The icons appeared on the board, along with countdown timers.

The admiral was getting tired of being up against the clock in every aspect of their existence in Ga'ee space. "Team Payne?"

"I'm broadcasting on all frequencies. The destruction of the carrier was recent. The energy wave is still dissipating."

"I suspect Payne was at the heart of that."

"Admiral Wesson." Payne's voice came through the speakers. "I broke the uglymobile. We need a pickup."

"I have their location," Lev replied. The ship adjusted course toward the heavy debris wherein the insertion craft was located. *Leviathan's* engines allowed it to fly in any direction, which made it more maneuverable than most starships.

"Major Payne," the admiral started, "you'll have to exit your craft. There's a great deal of debris, and although I'd love to bring it on board for future repairs, we won't have the time."

"We need the metals in this debris field," Lev argued. "I suggest we take as much on board as possible before we depart."

"I don't care what you do as long as you don't leave us out here." Payne didn't sound like he was worried about being abandoned. "I've grown fond of *Ugly 6*. If you can recover it and repair it, I'd appreciate that."

"It will be safer for them to remain inside the insertion craft. As we move into the field, we will dislodge materials and send them spinning in unpredictable ways."

"Not a fan of chaos theory?" the admiral quipped. "Stay on board, Major. We'll pick you up. Looks like we have eight minutes to accomplish that before we're on our way. Our plan is to continue following the vector toward a system some four thousand light-years distant."

"We may have a different heading. Blinky and Buzz, do your thing."

"Data is coming in now," Lev replied. "Much to parse, but the initial analysis suggests we should turn around."

"I'm all for getting the hell out of Ga'ee space, but will that accomplish our mission goals?"

"You mean, end the war? Yes. There is a dissenting voice to the contraction proposal. A rather persuasive and dominating voice."

The view outside *Leviathan* showed the ship scooping

floating debris into the open hangar bay. Lev used forcefields to protect the six Ga'ee power plants as the refined metals crashed and slid across the deck.

Leviathan slowed, changing its axial rotation to pick up only selected materials and limit the amount of bumping and grinding within the hangar bay.

Lev was timing the collection. The last object in would be *Ugly 6*, so it didn't get crushed. Lev would immediately transition to FTL following their recovery.

"Getting lonely out here," Payne interjected.

The admiral countered, "Patience is the bellwether of an ordered mind."

"If only I had one of those. By the way, the team is one hundred percent. Mission was a resounding success, but that little thing called time was against us. Estimate was twenty-four days to get where we were going, three days past when we were going to run out of water. That's why we took it out of light speed as soon as we could. Plus, the gurus said we were going the wrong way."

"We shall crush dissent under our jackboots!" the admiral declared.

"When you put it that way, it doesn't make us sound like the good guys."

"It's why we left Earth. They didn't like people like us. But this is to end the war. The justification matters. It's not to keep us in power. I have zero desire to rule the Ga'ee, but that's how we won against the Blaze Collective and how we defeated the Vestrall. By removing the voices that advocated for war."

"Maybe that's a message we can leave with them on our way out of here?" Payne suggested. "No threats, but if we have to, we will rule them, and they'll do what they're told. Or they can stop the incursions and live in peace. If they could only answer the question of why they exist, they could have a direction for their race that didn't include destroying everything in their path."

"We came out here, knowing that we'd do what we had to. If that includes becoming the Ga'ee version of the Mryasmalites, then so be it."

"If that happens, make sure you're the one who sits in the boardroom with those weaseldicks. I've had enough of that, thank you very much."

"What you're telling me is that if I gave an order, you wouldn't follow it?" The admiral laughed.

"I'd put on my leader of the seven races hat and order you right back. Are you guys coming? There's less than a minute before the silicon posse shows up."

"Everything is on schedule," Lev replied.

"We'll just chat among ourselves, then. Nothing to worry about."

"Worry has felled more than one soaring oak," the admiral offered.

"I don't know what that means," Payne replied. "I've been in space for a long time but never heard that oaks worry. They're trees." There were scrapes in the background. "There you are."

With *Ugly 6* on board, Leviathan surged out of the debris field and transitioned to FTL speed.

Dank activated the manual release on one side of the insertion craft, and Sparky took care of the other. They lifted the side doors up and out of the way.

The hangar bay looked like a hurricane had gone through it. Shattered bits and pieces of the Ga'ee carrier were piled haphazardly, some spread out, some towering. Using the power and protection of their suits, Shaolin and Byle cleared a path to the team's area.

A gentle tap on his shoulder pulled Payne's attention to the side. Heckler stood there with his helmet off. "A word, sir?"

Payne removed his helmet and tossed it back into the uglymobile. Mary held his gaze for a moment before following the team.

"You did well, Kal." Payne pointed. "You blasted the shit out of the drones in that corridor. And you two!" Payne leaned around the Ebren to make sure Blinky and Buzz heard him. "We couldn't have done any of it without you. Thank you for being great at what you do."

Blinky gave him the thumbs-up over his shoulder while continuing to walk away. Turbo had stopped and stood off to the side.

"It's bothering me," Heckler began.

"All's well that ends well," Payne replied.

"Only because we got lucky, but we didn't think it through all the way. We needed some offset time. I made a mistake on the timers, but maybe it was sublingual."

"Subliminal," Payne corrected. "Or maybe it's subconscious. I think you're right. Your body knew what to do. We could have and should have talked about the timing. You probably saved us, but next time, let's not count on luck. Let's figure it out. We have the smartest people in the universe here, and I'm sorry I don't give you guys enough credit. I need to get your input more."

"Until Blinky and Buzz try to work you for more time." Heckler smiled weakly.

"Exactly. We don't tolerate slackers, even if they are smart." Payne gripped the shoulder of Heckler's combat armor. "I'm happy you and Turbo are on the team. We need fighters just like we need thinkers."

"And hot chicks?" Heckler glanced at Turbo. Payne had to exercise all his self-discipline not to look for Mary.

"Shh. We don't say that out loud. It makes you look sexist."

"Even though Mars can take me in a fight?"

"Don't let her hear you admit that, or you'll never hear the end of it."

"You got that right, Major. Thanks for listening."

"These close-in plasma torch weapon things you created? We need to figure out how everyone can carry a plasma cannon. That's going to be the next engagement. Mark my words."

Heckler nodded. Payne walked away, tipping his head as he passed Turbo. He stopped and backpedaled.

"Sir?"

"Heckler said that you can take him. Is that true?"

"What the *hell*?" Heckler blurted.

Payne dissembled, "He didn't."

"He should have because it's true." Turbo winked.

―――

Clarence's eyes fluttered open. His head swam despite the soft lighting. The white ceiling was nondescript. "Where am I?"

"The University Hospital in Northern Virginia. You have severe chemical burns. Your chart says 'aliens' and nothing else. Can you elaborate?"

"I can't seem to focus," Clarence mumbled.

"That's morphine. You were in a great deal of pain."

"Aliens. A big Ga'ee got on my skin and started melting it. First generation. Had too much time to grow. I think you gave me too much morphine, but nothing hurts. I have to pee."

"Of course you do. I have a bedpan for you."

"No, ma'am," Clarence replied and tried to sit up. "I'm gonna need a little help."

"That's what the bedpan is for. So you can take care of it yourself," the nurse argued.

"Never mind. I'll get there myself."

Another patient shuffled through the door. "I'll help him." She was bracketed by two men in suits.

"I'll take care of it, Madam President," one of the guards told her. The other guided her to the side where he could block the doorway and access to her. She leaned against the wall since she was none too steady either.

The first bodyguard lifted Clarence off the bed and plopped him on his bare feet.

"Watch what you're doing!" The nurse was not pleased with the intervention.

"You're the man," Clarence mumbled and stumbled toward the bathroom. The two made it in, rolling the IV stand behind them. The guard kicked the door mostly closed and held a heavily swaying Clarence, who did what he intended to do. When they returned, Clarence was proud of himself and not as loopy.

"You didn't wash your hands," the president chided.

"I only have so much upright in me, Sylvia." He collapsed on his bed. The president moved in and pushed him to the side.

"Don't be such a bed hog." She squeezed in and lay on her back next to the mechanic.

"Did we get them all?" Clarence wondered.

"Yours was one of the last ones, but those were tough. We had to hit one crater with a small tactical nuke to clear them out."

"You nuked America?"

"We nuked an enemy to keep them from establishing a foothold on this continent. The Far East managed a lot better because the battlewagon *Japan* stopped ninety-eight percent of the incoming drones before they reached the ground." Saying that much was all the president could manage. She closed her eyes.

"They'll just send more," Clarence mumbled.

"Not if our people have anything to say about it. Without drones, the carriers aren't too hard to take out. Now shush, I'm trying to get some sleep."

"The Ga'ee sent all they had on the first pass? That doesn't make any sense."

"They had four carriers to start. They lost two right away. That didn't leave them too many options. I'm trying to sleep here."

"I'm trying to clear my head from the drugs they pumped into my body. I'm not a city boy. A little scrape doesn't keep me down."

"The skin on your hand and arm is melted." The president turned to face Clarence. "*Melted*."

"I wasn't ready for the little bastard to attack me. Who knew they got bite with that creepy crawl of theirs?"

The president started to snore lightly. Clarence wanted to get up since he wasn't tired enough to sleep, but he didn't have enough energy or the wherewithal to stand. He let his head melt into the pillow. As he relaxed, the morphine got to him.

"Hey, would you look at that? This morning when I got up, I was nobody. This evening, when I go to sleep, I'm sharing a pillow with the president, and I got bodyguards. I could do without the morphine, though. This stuff is making me feel funny."

The nurse returned to the conversation. "I'll ask the doctor if we can dial the dosage down a little at a time until we find what works best for you."

Clarence tried to nod, but all he managed to accomplish was closing his eyes. He was more tired than he realized.

Earth had been saved, and he played a part in that. Clarence went to sleep with a smile on his face. He'd made a difference.

[24]

"Silence is a weapon when used to deafen its detractors." –From the memoirs of Ambassador Declan Payne

Payne climbed into a cart with Mary. Kal stepped into the back.

"Get your own," Payne called over his shoulder.

"Were you not headed for the bridge?" Kal asked.

Payne replied, "I thought me and the missus would enjoy some private time, you know?"

"We're going to the bridge," Mary stated.

"You might as well come, too. The whole team. Everyone gets input. To the bridge!" Payne waved his arm, then slashed it forward. The others rolled their heads and moaned, dragging their feet on their way to their carts.

Payne's cart left. The doors opened to show the Cabrizi running as fast as they could toward them. The animals vaulted over the front of the cart and landed paws-first in the chests of the poor riders in the front seat. Declan and Mary took the full brunt of the impact on their unprotected thoraxes.

Mary grunted and groaned while trying to push the creature

off her. Declan held onto the one that was seemingly attached to the front of his body until he got his breath back.

"Your boys missed you," Payne finally managed to say as the Cabrizi scrambled over the passengers in the front to get to Kal in the back seat.

"They missed y'all, too," Kal drawled.

Payne cursed them in Ebren, but Kal put a big hand on his shoulder.

"They get it, but where'd you learn to swear like that? It was impressive on a level I've not seen before."

The cart accelerated when the passengers were mostly settled.

"Why, thank you. It's a variation on a theme. Ebren military denigration crossed with Fleet friendly jibes, blended into a miasma of light and sound."

"That is truly mind-boggling," Mary said. "What are we going to the bridge for?"

Payne looked at her like she was crazy, then realized he didn't know. "Because we always go to the bridge after returning from a mission."

"Debrief, plan for the way ahead, tell bad jokes. Okay, the usual, then."

"I'm not sure you understand that my jokes are intellectually stimulating and take a higher level of wit to appreciate."

"Your jokes are barely one step above 'pull my finger.'"

Payne tried to look hurt and gave her the only comeback he could think of. "You still married me."

"Some decisions are better made over time. I guess I'll have to figure out what was going on in my head. I think I need a therapist."

"Are you up for some private time? I wasn't kidding earlier."

"When it comes to that, you're never kidding. And yes. We're still newlyweds and should act like it."

Payne tried to follow the logic of his wife's reply and gave up after determining that the answer was yes. He brightened just in time for their arrival at the bridge. Mary climbed out first, holding her chest and wincing. Payne felt it the second he moved.

"My chest hurts," he admitted. "You fuckers!" He shook a finger at the Cabrizi. They bounced around, indifferent to his pain.

Kal strode through the hatch and onto the bridge, only to reemerge moments later carrying two huge bones.

"You hid bones on the bridge? Where did you get bones?" Mary wondered.

"Y'all need to keep more secrets to keep the lesser folks agog," Kal drawled. He reared back and threw one bone as far as he could down the corridor. He waited until they ran before he launched the second one. "Agog, I tell you."

"I think we've been insulted, but I'm not sure," Payne mused.

"Those are the very best insults because I'm not sure, either." Mary took Payne by the arm, and they slowly walked onto the bridge.

"What's wrong with you?" the admiral asked as he approached to offer his hand.

"The Cabrizi sent our breastbones into our spines." Payne touched his tenderly. Mary winced without having to touch hers.

"You guys gotta toughen up. They're dogs. You spend hours on a Ga'ee carrier, but you get hurt the second you get back here?" He shook his head and threw his hands up before Payne was able to connect for the handshake.

"We did," Payne argued but conceded that he wouldn't win. "We were successful in the primary mission objective."

"That's what Lev said." The admiral pointed at the screen.

"He was able to populate the board with everything he saw on the network. We have to go through a cordon on the way to the perimeter of Ga'ee space. We'll have to fight our way through."

"Even at FTL speed?"

"Maybe. Maybe not," Lev replied. "There appears to be a dampening field that might kick us into normal space."

"That's different." Payne tried to conjure up the applicable physics, but his mind remained closed. "I'd like to take some vacation, Admiral."

"What?" Admiral Wesson turned to his partner Commodore Freeman so they could look at each other in confusion. "You don't see us taking any vacation."

"You're not technically in the service," Payne countered.

"Neither here nor there." The admiral waved them away. "No. You can't take any vacation."

"For once, I'd like someone else to handle the hard job."

The admiral and Mary Payne spoke in unison. "No, you wouldn't."

"Maybe not this time. I think we're close to the end. I can feel it in my bones."

"That's being old and the start of arthritis." Mary shook her head.

"You guys are in rare form," the admiral noted. He fixed them with his Fleet admiral's glare. "Try to hold it together."

"We goof around because we're hanging on for the ride. We have no control over what's going on, and it's frustrating. You want to see someone stressed out, look no further than Blinky and Buzz. Those guys are tapped."

"I can see them, and you're right." The admiral nodded at the members of Team Payne who loitered near the entrance. "Why don't you guys take a seat?"

Payne tipped his chin to his people. They looked back, stone-faced.

Blinky and Buzz offered thousand-meter stares from hollowed eye sockets. "Lev, what have you been doing to these people?"

"Nothing they aren't *willing* to do to end this war," Lev replied in a way that suggested the topic wasn't one he wanted to discuss.

The implied jab was whether everyone else was doing what they needed to do.

"We're doing what we can, but we're ill-equipped to fight the Ga'ee. We can beat them on the ground if we get to them right away, but to win, it's not going to be us killing them one at a time. There are trillions of them," the admiral said.

"I armed Declan with what he needed, but he continues to resist."

"Damn, Lev! You're all kinds of pissy. You stuffed my head full. It's like trying to dig out a special marble in a bag of marbles with my eyes closed using only my fingers when all the marbles are the same size. Sometimes I get lucky, but we can't count on luck. We can count on you, Davida, Blinky, and Buzz."

"I am afraid, Declan," Lev admitted.

Fear made him do things he wouldn't otherwise have done, like drive two humans to the brink of exhaustion and beyond or fill Payne's head with more information than his brain could make sense of. It made Lev less than accepting when the best the humans could do wasn't good enough.

Woody Malone joined the group on the bridge. His squadron had been ready to launch, and once again, they had stood down. The debris was unexpected and would have been a death sentence to small craft trying to maneuver through the field.

After taking stock of the expressions on the faces, he asked, "What did I miss?"

"Lev was berating us until he admitted he was afraid we were going to lose," Payne offered.

"I was not berating you."

Woody smirked. "We've been on board for how long, and he still doesn't understand humans? Lev! We're the worst when it comes to self-defeat, but we're also the best when it comes to the fight. As long as I get to go out in the cockpit of my fighter, I'll be a happy man."

Payne glanced at Woody. "That's a low bar, my man."

"Lev's been hiding a bar?" Woody winked.

The admiral raised his hands to get everyone's attention. "Just when I thought we were getting serious. What's the next phase of this operation?"

Payne raised his hand. "Pick me, pick me!"

The admiral sighed, exasperated. "Ladies and gentlemen, I present to you the leader of the seven races."

Payne put his hand down. "When you put it that way." He cleared his throat while walking to the front of the bridge. He faced his team. "Sorry for fucking off, but I'm with Lev. I'm scared. I'm scared that when we meet this big brain cell or whatever the hell it is, we won't be able to beat it. We'll die and take any hope for humanity with us. Lev, leave us behind if you have to. Save yourself. With you, there can always be a second chance. Without you, even if we survive, there's no hope. We can't walk back to our sector of space."

The mood sobered with Payne's sincerity.

Heckler added his two cents. "Then we need to make sure we kill that thing because it sounds like it's us or him. I like our odds."

Payne continued. "We don't know what it looks like or how it will be protected. We could arrive in the middle of twenty carriers and a couple million drones waiting for us. It wouldn't take long for them to kill us all. That's why Lev needs to be ready to fold space the instant we enter normal space just in case. Go back to Earth and find the next bunch of volunteers willing to donate their bodies to science, if we even have a chance to leave the ship. Is *Ugly 6* fixed yet?"

"You've been back for a grand total of eleven minutes. *Ugly 6* will be repaired in another hour, well before it is needed."

"What happened to your studmobile?" Woody asked.

"We blew ourselves up. I don't recommend it," Payne answered.

Woody nodded in solidarity with his fellow warriors. "Everyone gets blown up in a career worth having. At least it wasn't you two who were responsible."

Heckler and Turbo fell under the spotlight. Their wide eyes told the tale.

"It was!" Woody looked surprised when he shouldn't have been.

"We didn't die." Dank made a fist and held it in front of his chest.

"What's our plan?" Payne asked loudly to refocus the conversation. "We're going to the edge of Ga'ee space where this brain cell is. We're going to talk it out of the expansion approach and into the contraction theory. Or we'll just kill it with fire, but I don't think we'll be able to get close enough. So, we'll have to figure out how to disrupt its link with the net, then figure out what to do next based on the tactical situation. We'll probably only have seconds to come up with a plan and commit to the execution of it. I wish there was something we could prepare ahead of time, but I can't think of anything. Ideas?"

"We'll wing it," Dank confirmed. "We only need to be carrying the right firepower and lots of explosives."

"Pre-rigged explosives," Heckler added. "Drop and go, but remotely configurable."

Lesson learned.

"A nuke conveniently located on a space fighter, ready to deliver the big smackdown when called." Woody added two thumbs-up. "Or twenty of them because redundancy is good."

"I like how you think."

"How do we fight off any ships that are in the way?"

"We can't fight them," Blinky replied, then yawned. "We have to spoof them. We'll tell the network that Lev isn't there."

"They'll be able to see us!" Payne wasn't convinced.

"How many Ga'ee have you seen with eyes?" Blinky raised an eyebrow to emphasize his point. "They count on their sensors and the image painted in their mind's eye. They'll believe what they've been told, and we are getting better with each interaction. Like you said earlier, Major Payne. If we have to take over the Ga'ee, we'll be ready to dominate. We're close."

"Isn't that at odds with how they work? Doesn't every ship get an equal say?"

"Not at all. Every ship is a part of the whole, but only a few voices issue dictates. There's only one voice that makes the final decision. That's where Lev is taking us. We'll be close, and once we drop into normal space, we'll be able to zero in on the exact location."

"There we go," Payne said. "The plan is coming together. We don't know what we don't know until we figure it out. Then we'll know, and we'll decide."

"Seconds, not minutes," the admiral confirmed. "You'll be in your uglymobile, and we'll plan at the speed of thought. Lev, how long until we arrive wherever we're going?"

"Seventeen days."

The admiral nodded. "Take some time off. Ten days. I don't want to see any of you on the bridge. Eat, sleep, enjoy the company of good friends."

"Mandatory vacation?" Payne asked. "We're on a spaceship. No beach planets nearby?"

The admiral didn't bite. "We all call *Leviathan* home. It'll be a staycation, and you're going to like it. That's an order." He smiled broadly and leaned toward Payne.

Mary strolled to the front, took Declan's hand, and led him around the outside of the bridge on the way out. "See you in ten days." She waved her free hand over her shoulder.

Payne turned his head and called, "Gym time every day from eight to eleven. Come if you want or face my wrath!"

Dank shook his head. "There'll be no wrath, but we hope to see you there. Being fit is the only thing we can do on the road to perdition."

"Are we going to perdition?" Sparky asked. "Because I'm pretty sure I'm not going to like it there. I better find my man and make the most of these next ten days. Perdition? I don't want to go to perdition."

Joker and Shaolin looked at each other in confusion.

"It's hell and damnation, torture and pain. Not that Payne, the agony one. It's the opposite of bliss. Lugubrious, it is not."

Sparky stomped her feet on her way out.

"You're not wrong," Heckler agreed, slapping Major Dank on the shoulder as he and Turbo walked past. "See you in the gym, lightweight."

Kal waited until the others had drifted out. Admiral Wesson and Commodore Freeman looked like they were going to leave too, but they stopped when they saw Kal.

"What can we do for you, Kal'faxx?"

"They are very good at what they do," Kal drawled. "As long as we can get to wherever that thing is, we can take it out."

"I have no doubt," the admiral replied. "We have Lev's firepower and the Mosquito squadron, too. We'll carve a hole through whatever defenses they have. If it gets too hot, we'll fold space back to Earth. We have a lot more information to share. A grand total of forty-two ships have been dispatched to our sectors. If we leave, we don't know if they'll send more. With the contraction theory planted, they might realize they're better off not coming our way."

"We've rallied 'round the campfire. Now we have to ride to the range and do the work. I'm mighty thankful that y'all took me in. I'm doing for Ebren what you're doing for Earth—making our planets proud. I look forward to the final showdown." Kal touched his forehead and walked out, talking to the Cabrizi in Ebren to wake them up and get them to come with him. He didn't bother with a cart but opted to run down the corridor with the animals. He only went as far as the dining facility.

The mess hall. The other members of Team Payne had disappeared in pursuit of their distractions. The admiral found Woody Malone in the corridor.

"Mind if I don't give my squadron ten days in a row off? Three days here and there. Otherwise, my people will forget how to fly."

The admiral knew about the other things going on with certain members of the squadron. "Pilots only. You won't need the maintenance teams or the crew chiefs?"

Woody tapped his nose. "Just the pilots, Admiral."

"As you wish, Commander."

Woody saluted and jumped into the waiting cart. It sped away, leaving the admiral and the commodore behind. No other carts waited. No other carts approached.

"I guess we're hungry," the commodore posited, "or need to work out. What does Lev know that we don't know?"

[25]

"When I found out what perdition was, I knew that we had been sent there." –From the memoirs of Ambassador Declan Payne

Commander Jimmy Josephs watched as the last of the pieces were put back into place. He assumed the portal would be instantly available.

The Vestrall on the bridge of battlewagon *President* looked at him like he was an idiot. "It needs to be calibrated."

"Of course it does. Will that take long?"

"Spatial dynamics should not be hurried," the Vestrall replied in its normal condescending tone.

Jimmy blew it off. "I believe spatial dynamics are universal and static regardless of whether we hurry or not. Calibration can be the adjustment from last known settings."

The Vestrall didn't have an exasperated sigh, but they had the next best thing—an annoying lip smack. "Of course we're using the last settings as a baseline. I will tell you when the portal is ready."

Their resident engineer, one of two remaining, had boarded *President* to oversee the repairs and manage the production of new parts by the battlewagons. The section that had been torn loose from the portal had been recovered and put back into place. The debris from destroyed Ga'ee carriers eliminated the need to mine new raw materials. The ships used the refined metals to fabricate the new parts.

Programmed maintenance bots did the work. Occasionally, a member of the Fleet would conduct a spacewalk to inspect the repairs. The Vestrall directed the operation and watched the progress from inside the ships. They had no intention of doing physical labor of any sort.

Jimmy continuously scanned the sensor data for indicators of more Ga'ee. He checked the vibration sensor for upsets from FTL, although the Ga'ee didn't make waves that could be seen. Neither did *Leviathan*, not anymore. New stealth.

Not knowing kept him on edge.

The battlewagons tried to repair themselves, but the priority had been the portal. The catastrophic shutdown had not been so catastrophic. The energy had arced across the surface of the portal and into the remains of *European Union*. BW03 never had a chance, but its death had saved the portal since it gave the energy a place to go.

Jimmy finally jumped up from his seat. "COB, with me."

Chief Tremayne joined him, but in the corridor, the chief of the boat stopped him. "You're like spit on a fry pan, sir, if you don't mind me saying."

Commander Josephs tried to visualize the chief's imagery but failed. "I'm glad you speak your mind. You know the problem."

"We stayed to help fix the portal, and it's been eleven days. If we left at FTL, we would be back to Earth in three days. If we take longer than that to get the portal fixed, then you'll have guessed wrong, but you won't have. If we hadn't stayed, it would have taken a lot longer to get that portal fixed with only a broken

Russia working on it. And this system would have had their ass hanging out without any protection."

"That's the problem. I'll have to explain that to the president when we get back. I doubt she'll listen unless the Ga'ee attacked in our absence. Then we'll have failed Earth."

"*Japan* stayed back, and whatever new ships came from Vestrall. Should have been at least one, maybe two. But you know what, sir? We're holding our own. We're killing Ga'ee. It's costing us ships and crew, but only a hundred crew each, not thousands like we have on our own dreadnoughts. We're fighting back successfully. How much more will the Ga'ee throw at us? No one knows. As long as we have our main weapons and the Rapiers, we can stand toe to toe with them and give 'em the high hard one."

"The high hard one?" Jimmy wondered. "We've destroyed more Ga'ee ships than we've lost battlewagons, but it's wearing us down. And Earth. We're humans, so our first priority must be Earth."

"We're humans, so our first priority must be humanity, even if that means Berantz or the Rang'Kor. We're all in this together. If you didn't believe that, you would never have brought HK1 to Berantz space. Stop second-guessing yourself, sir. We did the right thing."

"Deep down, I know that, but I can't help but think we condemned Earth by getting trapped on this side of the portal."

"Captain to the bridge. Portal is active."

"I guess we're going to find out soon." COB took the commander's hand and shook it with a power grip. "Sir."

The two returned to the bridge even though the ship's captain, Lieutenant Commander Barry Cummins, was already in the chair. He made to stand, but Jimmy placed a hand on his shoulder.

"Comm, give me the Fleet," Jimmy requested. After she

gave him the thumbs-up, he continued. "HK1, form up on me. We're returning to Earth. Commander Blighe, we will send reinforcements soonest, the first of which will be a freighter with a restock for your Rapiers. Maybe a little food, too."

"We would appreciate any and all assistance. Thanks for coming to save us."

"Keep that portal active at all costs," Jimmy replied.

"Without it, we die." Commander Blighe's answer wasn't dramatic. It was the truth stated in the simplest of terms.

"We *will* see you again, Rusty." Jimmy turned to Barry. "Take us home, Commander."

Earth's portal shimmered into existence. *Japan* and *Ephesus* breathed a sigh of relief from their station between the moon and Earth. Battlewagon *South Africa* held position near the portal in case the Ga'ee attempted to attack it directly.

They had seen the Ga'ee use both tactics, take out the portal as well as attempt to destroy Earth. No one knew if the next battle would be the one humanity lost, especially being outnumbered.

They needed more ships with as much firepower as they could muster.

First through was *The President*—an unexpected surprise—trailed by *America* and *Germany*.

Hunter-Killer Squadron One had returned.

One battlewagon immediately transitioned to faster-than-light speed to shorten the trip to Earth. *The President* needed to report in.

"Welcome home," Captain LeClerc commed from the bridge of *Ephesus*. Behind him, the crew was on their feet and clapping in a genuine show of appreciation.

Jimmy was unable to contain his surprise. "I expected a little more anger but am happy that you aren't. The Ga'ee didn't show up, then?"

"Oh, no. They came with four carriers, but we beat them back, and those on the ground destroyed every potential infestation. Even that one in the rainforest in South America, although it took a small tactical nuke to finish it off because it had gone a few days before anyone found it. That was a big loss, but it's not the whole planet, and they're already working to reestablish the forest. Residual radiation was minimal."

"Thanks, Captain. It's good to be back. We've split our ships between here and the portal. *Japan* and *South Africa* will need to head to Ebren's space fairly soon."

"That is a conversation well above my pay grade, Commander."

"I need to go take my lumps from the president. Thanks, Captain LeClerc. I look forward to enjoying a beer with you when this war is over." He smiled at the screen, but reality was a harsh taskmaster. "Has anyone heard from *Leviathan*?"

LeClerc shook his head. "Good luck, Commander Josephs."

The communication link ended. The screen returned to a view of the moon on one side and Earth on the other. The sun was behind them and brightened both celestial bodies. Wisps of clouds floated above green lands and a dark blue sea.

"I miss home," Jimmy murmured.

The comm officer interrupted his reverie. "Sir, the president is on the line."

Jimmy's heart sank. He hung his head. A body bumped his, and the chief smiled at him. "You got this," he asserted.

Jimmy laughed. "I know. It turned out well for both Earth and Berantz." He waved and pointed at the screen. "Comm, put her on."

The face that appeared wasn't hers but that of Paragon Virtue, her assistant.

"Paragon. Long time no see," Jimmy greeted evenly, trying not to reach through the screen and punch the man in the face.

"You're looking good, Jimmy. Command suits you."

Why the hollow platitudes? Jimmy thought. He responded to Virtue's compliment with a slight nod.

The screen shifted, and the aide was replaced by President Sinkhaus.

"Ma'am," was all Jimmy managed. He stiffened and stood at attention.

"What happened in Berantz space?" she asked.

"The Ga'ee attacked the planet and the portal simultaneously. Hunter-Killer Squadron Two is down to a single battlewagon. Had we not intervened, they'd have lost it all, but the portal was damaged. We stayed to oversee the repairs, which helped us get back sooner than if we had hightailed here using FTL. I'm sorry, Madam President. I was only..."

She cut him off by waving her hand and shaking her head. "No need to get defensive. I agree. We need to protect all of us. And I mean all, whether Berantz or Ebren or Rang'Kor or Vestrall. We are fighting for our very existence. The people of Earth rose to the occasion. The BEP and Fleet worked together against a common enemy, and most importantly, we learned that we have sub-contracted humanity's security to the Fleet and then treated them like shit for it."

Jimmy coughed to hide his shock at the president's words.

"You know it's true. It's why Fleet personnel abandoned Earth the moment they could, accepting the risk of space instead of staying here, even under threat of court-martial. Like Fleet Admiral Wesson. I owe him an apology, and you, too. I'm sorry for how poorly I've treated the Fleet. The attack on Earth opened my eyes to the daunting task you've had all these years, one done with unwavering loyalty."

"It's what we signed up for," Jimmy replied.

"You didn't sign up to be looked down on."

"Comes with the territory, Madam President."

"It shouldn't. That starts with me and stops with me. It'll be my pleasure to correct that. Until the next time, Commander Josephs. By the way, have you heard from *Leviathan*?"

"I asked Captain LeClerc that same question. We have not heard or seen anything from Admiral Wesson or Ambassador Payne."

"I hope they are well. We will keep them in our thoughts and have the grill ready for when they return. There will be a feast of medieval proportions because when they return, they will have won the war."

"What if they don't?"

"What if we only think positive, Commander? They're coming home, and when they get here, we'll be free of the Ga'ee. That is what we believe."

"Yes, ma'am. Until then, BW01, *The President*, stands ready to defend Earth and all humanity."

President Sinkhaus waved, and the screen returned to the outside view. Barry stared at Commander Josephs until he acknowledged the ship's captain.

"That was weird," Barry began.

"Weirdly awesome," Jimmy countered. "Chief! Get hold of anyone on the planet's surface and have them send us some barbecue, Kansas City or Texas, or even Carolina. Our preference is anything they can get to us. This calls for a celebration."

The chief held out his hand.

"What?"

"Who's going to pay for it?"

The commander laughed at how mundane that was. Back to

buy or barter. They had nothing to trade, so paying was their only choice.

Jimmy reached into his pocket and pulled out a slim card. He studied it before handing it over. "Just the barbecue and fixings. If I find you bought a new motorcycle using my card, I'll jettison your carcass from the nearest airlock."

"Why you gotta say such hurtful things, sir? Where's the love?" The COB snatched the card before the commander could reconsider and hurried to the comm station, where he moved in close and worked with the communications officer to start making calls.

"Is that wise?" Barry asked.

"I expect it'll cost me a couple months' pay, but the crew deserves it. *Ephesus*, too. *Japan's* commander can buy chow for his own people. If he doesn't have a chief of his boat, I doubt he'll be able to get what we're going to get."

"Ephesus, aye!" the chief called.

"It better be good, COB." Jimmy stretched and took a step toward the hatch off the bridge.

"Or I'll be chucked out an airlock. Yes, sir. Got it."

[26]

"Changing with the times wasn't something I was prepared to do." –From the memoirs of Ambassador Declan Payne

Payne shook hands with the admiral and the commodore. "Time to load up," he said.

"You have time," the admiral replied, looking at his hand. He didn't like when things were different. "This isn't goodbye."

Payne didn't reply. Mary dodged in to hug them instead of shaking their hands.

"You could stay on the ship," Payne offered weakly.

Mary cleared away from the admiral, loaded up, and punched Declan in the chest. He staggered back. "I'm on the team, dammit. Don't do this."

Payne straightened. "You're right. I'm sorry." He checked the tactical display, but it held no new information. It wouldn't until they returned to normal space. "I am going to leave Blinky and Buzz behind. They need to be a force multiplier with Lev. All we need is a link and their standard gear, which is already loaded on the repaired and upgraded *Ugly 6*."

"Defensive weapons, eh?" The admiral nodded. He'd already been advised.

"A little something to kill drones just in case, as long as there aren't too many of them. That's where Blinky and Buzz come in."

"I shall do my best," Lev offered.

"We know you will. One team, one fight, Lev. We'll be on our way." Payne walked away with his head down.

Mary caught up with him. "Don't let them see you questioning yourself."

"It's not that. I have a bad feeling about this."

"Don't. It's no worse than the other shitshows we've tossed ourselves into."

"You know, you're really hot when you swear." Payne winked at his wife.

"Don't make me punch you again."

"Who was doing all the howling in our corridor?"

"The sexcapades, you mean?"

"What?" Payne furrowed his brow, and his eyes darted back and forth. "Is that what it was?"

"What else could it have been?"

"The Cabrizi?" Payne suggested.

"No." Mary chuckled. "I like how worldly you are, yet so naïve." They climbed into the waiting cart, and it sped off. Payne didn't have to ask Lev to notify his people to report to the team's area in the hangar bay.

"I've been with this team for years and never heard anything like that before. How was I supposed to know?"

Mary looked at him like he'd grown a second head. "Focus."

"All I need to do is be ready the instant we come out of FTL. And then we'll have to decide what to do and do it. We'll have a few seconds before everything comes unhinged."

"How much time do you need?"

"We'll take our best shot. Thanks for coming along, Dog. You are part of the team. Bring the firepower and be ready to lay waste to those bastards."

"That's more like it, Dec. We're going to burn 'em."

The cart made short work of the trip to the hangar bay. It rapidly slowed. Payne vaulted out just before the cart stopped moving, hit the deck, and ran a few steps. Mary casually left the cart after it had come to a complete stop.

They weren't the first ones there. Heckler and Turbo were already in the weapons cage. "I suggest we only take three or four Ga'ee killers." Heckler pointed at the plasma burners. "We need as many of the plasma cannons as we can get since clearing big spaces of big numbers is what they do best."

They'd already had the conversation. Payne had looked at a prototype two days earlier and been pleased with what he saw, but it was less a cannon and more a single-shot device, like a grenade launcher of old.

"I'll take one," Payne said.

"I had one engraved with your name, sir." Turbo handed him a railgun with the plasma cannon attachment underneath.

It was too cumbersome to use without the additional power of the combat suit. "Did you? Thanks." He looked for the engraving but couldn't find it.

"We didn't," Heckler admitted.

Payne gave them a healthy side-eye while Mary chuckled in the background.

"One for you, too," Heckler offered. "You're a combat specialist, right?"

"It's what I signed up for." Mary took it. The weapon wasn't too heavy, but it was bulky. She lugged it to where her cleaned and prepped suit waited.

The Paynes dressed quickly so they could run through their paces with the modified weapons. He practiced reloading. It took time, but they had the first shot in case the combat situation deteriorated, and more if they could buy time to reload.

Major Dank rolled in and was given a plasma cannon. Heckler carried one, too. Turbo carried the modified railgun with the single-shot cannon slung underneath.

Kal took his plasma cannon and handled it with ease.

Every one of the others received a modified weapon, despite Heckler's implication that some would get railguns only. The team was ten-strong without Blinky and Buzz. Payne was first into *Ugly 6* so he could put on his helmet and access everyone's stats on his HUD.

The data populated while the team filtered from the prep area to the insertion craft. They each put on their helmet when they arrived and snapped it into place. They were ready for immediate ejection into space.

The countdown timer showed ten minutes until they returned to normal space.

Payne reviewed the plan one last time. "Joker, your job is to make sure we're linked with Lev at all times."

She tapped the equipment she carried. "We're redundant to the third power."

"Sparky, you have the taps to get into whatever system the Ga'ee might have?"

"I've been schooled and counseled by the Gurons until I wanted to beat them both senseless."

"Sounds like you're up to speed, then," Payne replied with a snort. "'Gurons.' I'll have to remember that. Virge, Heckler, and Kal have plasma cannons. Heckler and Kal on point, Virge in the middle. I'll bring up the rear. Turbo following point. Then Sparky. Dog, then Byle and Shaolin providing security for Joker, who'll be right in front of me. We can't lose comm with Lev."

"We have access ropes to burn holes through the bulkheads," Byle said. "Enough for four breaches. There's one that *Ugly 6* can use to get through the hangar bay door if needed."

Self-ignited plasma access ropes.

Payne checked his weapon once more. It was ready to fire, either the railgun or the single round for the plasma cannon.

The others watched him go through the process and did the same, each verifying their weapon was locked and loaded as well as safe to prevent a negligent discharge. Then they sat back and waited.

"Close the outer doors, please, and bring up the tactical display," Payne requested. The insertion craft complied and soon, *Ugly 6* was buttoned up and ready to deploy. "Might as well move us to the hangar bay door. Speed could be essential in our mission."

The egg-shaped craft lifted into the air and moved imperceptibly to the edge of the hangar bay door. The team watched the outer view as an inset on the tactical screen. The door cracked open enough for the team to see the strange view of static light while traveling at FTL speed. Nothing moved beyond the door. It was as if the light had slowed to a stop. There were no twinkles from interference. The light was either on or off at whatever intensity it had the moment it reached the ship. It froze there, creating a two-dimensional view of the universe.

Eight minutes.

Payne continued, "The mission is to find and destroy the dissenting voice—the one we're considering to be the leader of the Ga'ee. If anyone gets a shot, take it once we have the target defined, refined, and confined. Rock and fire, people. Whatever it takes."

"If we have to board a ship, do we take out the FTL drive?" Heckler asked. They'd already discussed the answer.

"In FTL, we're essentially blind. We need to be in normal

space to see the neural network. And in FTL, we lose our link to Lev. That's too high-risk. So, Heckler and Turbo, it's redemption time. If we enter a Ga'ee carrier, your primary mission is to shut down the FTL drive without blowing the ship up."

"Are you sure you have the right people assigned?" Mary challenged with a hint of whimsy. She wanted Payne to clarify why he assigned Heckler and Turbo.

"I do. No one knows better how to blow up the ship, so they'll know where the boundaries are. No blowing up the ship."

"We'll keep the ship around, but I can't make any guarantees about its ass end," Turbo replied.

"Anyone know any pirate shanties?" Payne said on the team channel.

"No," Kal drawled, "but I do know some good ol' western tunes." He started to sing. "*Git along, little doggy…*"

"Make it stop, *please*," Turbo cried.

"I guess you've been given the hook, Kal." Payne drew an armored finger across the bottom of his helmet.

"Just when I was about to hit the a capella crescendo."

Payne smiled behind the privacy of his reflective face shield. If he hadn't beaten Kal on Ebren, the warrior would not have joined them. He made things possible that would not have been otherwise.

Like every member of his team, even though he didn't lean on Byle and Shaolin as much as he could. They were learning and could understand enemy engineering and weapons well enough to advise the team on how best to deal with them.

And Mary. Not a third wheel, but a contributing member of the team, from firepower to keeping Payne on track. He wanted to protect her, but he needed her with him far more.

Virgil had lost his team supporting Payne's mission. It was Mary's first. She had gotten injured, but that was only a twisted knee. Payne won the Cabrizi from the Ebren station's commander.

Those animals! All thrust and no vector. His chest no longer hurt from their joyous leap into his and Mary's arms after their brief time away. Or maybe they had been trying to jump through them to get to Kal. That was most likely the case.

Payne had let his thoughts drift long enough that the timer on his HUD flashed red as it changed from one minute to fifty-nine seconds.

The tactical screen remained static, waiting for new information. Payne reviewed the team's vitals. Heckler and Turbo's pulse rates remained at fifty-nine and sixty-two like they always were. Kal's rate was thirty, which was normal for an Ebren. It didn't fluctuate, either. Everyone else saw a slight increase. Mary's was the worst, going from a norm of sixty-eight to eighty-eight.

He dialed up a direct channel to his wife. "I know the last thing you want to hear is 'Calm down,' but your pulse is racing, and we haven't done anything yet. Bring it down a little so I can focus on not getting us killed."

Mary nodded her helmet rather than verbalize a reply.

Ten...nine...

Payne stared at the board. He ran through the options in his mind while checking the inset showing outside the ship. Payne wanted to see what was immediately outside the ship before the tactical screen populated.

Four...three...

His pulse increased. He could feel it but refused to look. He didn't want to see Mary's racing. He saw ten green dots. That was all that mattered. The team was combat-effective.

One.

The transition to normal space was the same as always. Outside the ship, thousands of drones impacted *Leviathan* before the screens could be raised. They tore through the open hangar bay door.

The defensive systems on *Ugly 6* lit up and killed the drones before they could impact the Ga'ee power plants operating in the hangar bay. *Ugly 6* echoed from a new impact. It was tossed into the air and started to spin. It jerked with another impact and another, then it split along the central axis. A fourth impact tore it open.

"Abandon ship!" Payne ordered. The team undid the belts holding them in their seats. The insertion craft twisted, throwing the newly freed passengers against the tactical screen on one side. *Ugly 6* dropped and slammed into the deck upside-down where the opening was.

Payne was the first up. He worked his way to the forward hatch and popped it. He clambered out into the chaos of *Leviathan* fighting for its life and for all their lives. He hadn't gotten a look at the tactical screen, but when he was outside the uglymobile, he ported the data to his HUD to review.

The drones were peeling away. A massive ship, not a carrier but something different, all black. It blended with the background of space. Had Lev not been using the neural network, he wouldn't have been able to "see" the ship. It remained invisible to all other sensors and was almost invisible to the naked eye.

The drones streamed away from the ship.

"Hitching a ride!" Payne yelled as he ran, accelerating as fast as his suit allowed. He dove out the open doorway and activated his jets to send his body into the void and stayed steady as he bore down on a drone.

He cleared the screen and let his weapon drop on its sling. That caused him to start spinning right before he impacted the drone. He tried to invert and use his jets to slow down, but he misjudged the closing speed and landed face-first on the back of the drone. He latched onto it before it tumbled through space and hung on until it reoriented itself. Then he hung on some more as it used its anti-gravity drive to accelerate toward the enemy's ship.

Kal struggled to stay on a straight line. Dank intercepted him and helped by hugging him. The two powered into the drone cloud until they could grab their own rides.

Leviathan stopped firing its defensive weapons.

"The initial wave has passed," Lev reported. "The Ga'ee have been told we don't exist and the gap in the neural net has been filled with what they will believe is an asteroid."

Payne gathered his wits after the violence of the twists and turns before the drone settled onto a steady course. "Good news, Lev. Keep it that way. We're taking ourselves to that gross bitch in the distance."

"Why did you select that ship before we were certain?"

"We were looking for something different, and I present to you something different."

The team continued in a loose formation toward the enemy ship, except Byle. She was falling behind.

"I missed the cloud," she reported.

"Lev, can you redirect a drone back to get her?"

"I don't have that kind of control. It's all or nothing right now."

"Byle, return to *Leviathan* before you run out of juice and get stuck out here."

The icon on Payne's HUD that represented his engineer slowed to a stop, then headed back the way they'd come.

The team was down to nine, and they had lost their ability to tap into any of the systems on that ship. They'd be going in blind.

It was exactly as Payne had expected it would be.

The cloud splitting in half and taking part of his team elsewhere hadn't been in his game plan. He was headed to the

Black Ship, along with Shaolin, Joker, Mary, and Turbo. The other four were veering toward a standard carrier not far from the big ship. All three rapid-fire plasma cannons were headed away from the Black Ship.

"Go where they take you since we're past the point of no return and can't get back to *Leviathan*." The pneumatic jets had a limited range, and they'd already traveled dozens of kilometers.

Of course, if they were able to stop and turn around, all they would need was an initial push toward *Leviathan*, and as long as they weren't acted on by an external force, they would continue to the battleship. They didn't have enough juice to turn around, though.

Payne suspected they would need their final pneumatics to access the ships if the drones assumed a patrol route. The team couldn't remain in space forever, whereas the drones had a nearly unlimited capacity.

"Relax and enjoy the ride, people," Payne said over the team channel. "Once on board the carrier, disable the FTL. Our goal for the Black Ship is to destroy it, and we will work toward that end from the second we arrive. If we transition to FTL, know that we will continue our efforts to destroy that ship and the brain within." He waited for a moment. "The brain is in that one, isn't it?"

"Most likely," Lev replied. "There's a lot of noise in this area. Ten carriers and the ship you've dubbed the Black Ship. There are also four of the kilometer-wide spherical mines. There are roughly a million drones in space around these ships."

"That's comforting." Payne grunted after his reply as if he'd been gut-punched. The drones swerved. "This is where we get off, Team Payne. Push toward the Black Ship. Conserve your jets as much as possible. Next stop, the big mean-looking ship."

[27]

"Run to the battle, but when something starts blowing up, you'll want to run from that as fast as you can." –From the memoirs of Ambassador Declan Payne

Admiral Wesson stared at the screen as it populated. *Leviathan* had entered normal space in the midst of a drone cloud of epic proportions.

"Wait," Lev advised before the admiral could say anything.

Ten carriers and an unknown ship that dwarfed the others showed on the tactical board. There were massive mine ships and endless numbers of drones. They entered normal space in the middle of the worst possible tactical environment.

Leviathan was already getting pummeled by drones. The link to *Ugly 6* showed that it had been hit by drones. The hangar bay was in disarray. The other side of the ship had not been hit. The Mosquitoes stood ready to deploy, but they would be destroyed the instant they tried to launch.

"I don't think we can wait. Prepare to transition to FTL," the admiral said while watching the internal view showing *Ugly 6* get split open. His breath caught.

"These are incidental. We are not under attack."

"How is that possible? Look what they did to Team Payne!"

The team poured out of the dead insertion craft. Major Payne's call sounded throughout the bridge.

"Fly."

Chaos reigned outside the ship.

The admiral looked at complete failure after the briefest respite.

The drones started pulling back.

"We have successfully told the neural network that we are an asteroid and are in place at this location, which is to be avoided."

"How can you do that?"

"It has taken a great effort to get to this point, but the Ga'ee have never been *hacked* before. They are not prepared to defend against it. Learning their language and then their programming language was the most difficult part."

"I thought they spoke binary." The admiral started to relax as the drones pulled away from *Leviathan*. Team Payne's icons were dots racing into the drone cloud.

"They do, but the compiled language to interface with their living computer system took more work and too much trial and error. I have the greatest minds in the galaxy working together. Despite the months that it has taken, their work is nothing short of exceptional. This is the way we'll defeat the Ga'ee."

"I know, Lev. It's a different way to fight than I'm used to, despite being with you for nigh unto two years now. I've always counted on things that blow up or can tear other ships apart. Kill the ship, end the battle. Kill enough ships, end the war."

"We cannot do that with the Ga'ee. They have a significant numbers advantage."

"Once again, I know, and once again, I find that we have to

count on Team Payne to do something spectacular. Connect me with Major Payne, please."

"Admiral," Payne acknowledged through forced and shallow breaths.

"Report," the admiral directed in an attempt to take Payne's mind off what was causing him grief.

"Headed to the Black Ship, but the drones split off. We're currently trying to hold course, and we'll have to break in, all five of us. The others are on their way to the carrier to my left. They'll insert and try to cause some grief. For me, our goal is to destroy the Black Ship. It's the one leading this parade."

"Roger. Let us know how we can support you."

"Tell it not to go to FTL. That would help."

"We will not give it any reason to travel at faster-than-light speed," Lev explained. "A subtle but important difference. Try not to let it know you're on board."

"We'll do that as soon as we figure out how. Our plasma cannons are vectoring away from us, so we have railguns, some explosives, and a desire to excel. I'm pretty sure we have all we need. Gotta focus on not slamming into this ship. Ta-ta."

The admiral studied the screen. "Zoom in on that ship and Team Payne. Nothing else matters. And Lev? Fire up the world-killer just in case."

———

Payne cut the link with the admiral. His team was coming in fast and well in front of the Black Ship. "Fifteen degrees toward the ship. Execute now," he ordered. The individuals started adjusting, but the armored suits weren't spacecraft. They had to guesstimate what fifteen degrees looked like. "On me."

It was easier that way. They now knew what he was trying to accomplish.

"Prepare to invert. We need to slow down, or we'll just be splatters on that thing." Once the team had formed up on him, he gave the command, "Invert and tap your jets. First target is seventy-five meters per second."

They were doing well over a hundred, and although the armor could withstand an impact at that speed, the body within could not. The best speed was ten meters per second or slower, but Payne would take twenty-five.

He rolled and hit his jets. He was first, and the team zoomed past him before they tapped their pneumatic thrusters to slow down. Payne used visuals to guide him since the sensors might give him away. It was difficult to get a visual fix on the ship, given it was as black as a black hole, but lights winked from it like stars.

Payne stared at the closest one.

It approached a lot quicker than he wanted. "Fifty meters per second...now."

The deceleration burned through their compressed air. He was nearly to the light. "Full burn to the end!"

He maxed his jets. He felt like that jerked him backward, but the light raced at him. He winced and flew past it, relaxing with the surprise of not slamming into the enemy ship. That only lasted for a second. He hammered the hull of the great black beast, tumbling and rolling before he could activate the magnetic grapples on his boots.

The team grunted and groaned as they hit the ship at varying speeds. He conducted a quick team check on his HUD. Still green.

"Status, Joker," he started.

"Never felt better. Recovering my equipment now, but I think I have it all. I've never seen anything like this. Even standing on the hull, I can't see it."

"Turbo."

"That sucked hard, but I'm here. Coming toward you."

"Shaolin."

"The rocks never know that they are being polished by the river."

"I'll take that as you're okay. Dog."

"I've been better. Buggered my good knee, but I'm mobile."

Payne checked the locations of his team members. "Rally to Dog, and then we'll find a way in. I'll turn on my external lights. Everyone else stay dark in case this ship has some kind of anti-Payne defensive system."

"I doubt their system is designed to foil just you," Mary suggested.

"It's hard not to take their shit personally. They sent a carrier to collect us and bring us back to the heart of the Ga'ee sector," Payne replied while carefully walking across the outer hull of the Black Ship. He turned on his lights to show the surface coating that absorbed visible wavelengths. Payne's lights were barely more than a dim bulb in the fog. "I think they were bringing us to this ship, but when we stopped and worked the outer reaches, it came looking for us. After we escaped too many times, wreaking havoc in our wake, it came out here and brought a bunch of lackeys to protect it. This is it. This is the key to the Ga'ee."

The team continued to slowly work their way toward Mary.

"Turbo, give Joker a hand." The combat specialist was closest to Joker, who had to carry the communications equipment to ensure a constant link with *Leviathan*. It was only one suitcase-sized box, but her weapon kept catching on it, and it slowed her down.

Turbo relieved Joker of her railgun/plasma cannon combo weapon the second she joined her.

"That thing is ridiculous."

"You know you love it and can't wait to fire it," Turbo replied.

"I think that's not what I said." Joker gave a short laugh.

Morale is good, Payne thought. He bent close to the surface of the ship to find that it was covered in a material similar to what was on *Leviathan*. "Lev, in any of the attacks on you, do you think the Ga'ee could have taken some of your surface material? This ship looks like that's what it's covered in but modified somehow. There's nothing like it on any of the carriers we've seen."

"The first engagement in Ga'ee space was enlightening," Lev replied in a non-answer.

"That's the term I was going to use, too, except it wasn't because I was thinking more along the lines of scary as fuck because I thought we were all going to die. 'Enlightening' is just as good. Looking for a way in. Tough to see anything over here. This stuff is something."

"Can you get a sample for me, please? What's good for the goose, as you might say."

"Shaolin, when you get to Dog's position, hack off a sample for Lev, please."

"Roger."

The team kept moving but slowly, counting on their boots to connect through the dampening material to the metal hull beneath.

Payne stepped past a spot that looked different from the others. Then he returned to it. It looked like a micro-meteor strike had ripped away the outer layer and exposed the dark-hued hull. It was nearly as black but was smooth and slightly reflected his light. Payne was able to work his fingers beneath a flap of the coating and, using the power of his suit, rip it free. He stuffed it into the storage compartment on his armor where he kept extra jerky. It was a tight fit.

"Belay my last, Shaolin. I have a piece."

"You knocked off a piece while we were hanging out over here? What will your wife think?" the normally staid specialist quipped.

"What? Hey! That's a pretty good one. Found a flap swinging in the breeze. Made it easy. While I have you here, I don't know why everyone calls me Roger, but more importantly, anyone see a way into this thing?"

"Can't see jack shit," Turbo replied.

"Since I haven't been blasted by an anti-Payne death ray, turn on your lights. Try to get a better look at this thing."

Through the darkness of space, the team lit up. Payne counted heads. None of them were far away. A hundred meters at the most.

Mary and Shaolin were ahead of him by fifty meters. Turbo and Joker were approaching from his side. He hurried as fast as he dared. They needed to spread out and canvass the ship's outer hull to look for an access point, even bare metal, where they could use an access rope to burn their way in if the hull was thin enough.

Payne had to decide whether to use their sensors. He had no choice. They needed to find a way in. Counting on luck wasn't optimal, but time was one thing he had enough of for once. There was no countdown timer bothering him from the corner of his HUD.

It was refreshing.

He reached Dog and Shaolin. He bumped helmets with Mary and went to a private channel.

"Are you okay?"

"I am. I'll limp a little. I haven't taken any pain meds. If it gets bad, I'll have my suit inject them."

"Stay frosty. We need our wits about us. We have no idea what to expect when we get inside, so the longer you can go without dosing, the better off you'll be. We need our brains intact more than we need our knees. Let your suit do most of the work."

"I've been through this before, and it's nowhere near as bad as that. I'll be fine. Don't worry about me. Figure out this ship and how we can destroy it. Focus your mind, Dec. We're counting on you."

"That's what I was afraid of." Payne winked, which Mary couldn't see. He wanted to be somewhere else with her, not magnetically attached to the outside of an enemy ship with no idea where he needed to go.

His best estimate was that the ship was twelve kilometers long—not much longer than a standard carrier—and roughly six kilometers wide and tall. He didn't know if it had hangar bays, but none of the drones had come to it.

Maybe it was off-limits or was nothing but packed to the brim with Ga'ee. What would they need a ship this big for?

Too many unanswered questions plagued Payne. Worse, he couldn't do anything until they were inside the beast.

Turbo and Joker finally joined them.

"Spread out, line abreast, walking straight aft. Fifty meters between. Turbo, you have left flank. Shaolin, you have the right. Gimpy, left, Joker, right. I'll hold down the middle and maintain the direction of travel. Looking for any way in. We go as fast as we can. Keep your lights on."

"What about sensors? Even with lights, it's hard to see anything," Turbo queried.

"Wait until you're about a hundred meters from Dog, then light 'em up. It's not like they're going to see us, but they might see the scan. Lowest power setting, of course. Try not to be an impact area."

"Not sure how to accomplish that if they zero in on my scanner. We shall see. I'll think about it on the way out. Here." She handed Joker her weapon. "You might need this."

Payne established the base and pointed forward with his whole arm so the others could align where he wanted them. They trooped outboard until they got into position. Turbo moved an extra fifty meters before she activated her scanner.

"Protrusion at forty-five degrees left of me. Scanner can't penetrate the hull, just like with *Leviathan's* dampening. Otherwise, smooth to a thousand meters."

"Angle forty-five degrees toward Turbo. One step forward, one step sideways. Keep your eyes peeled," Payne said. The team moved out.

"Range two hundred," Turbo reported, then linked her scans with the rest of the team's.

"Will your sensors see anything if it's flush with the hull?" Payne asked, but he knew the answer.

"Not if it's covered with that material."

It took two minutes to cover two hundred meters. The ship was so big that it generated a small gravity field. If they took care, they could walk normally without having to use their magnetic grapples.

The revelation helped alleviate the nagging at the back of Payne's mind. He didn't want to take forever on the outside of the Black Ship.

The rest of his team was somewhere else.

"Major Dank, report," Payne requested.

[28]

"Nothing worth blowing up was ever close to the insertion point." –From the memoirs of Ambassador Declan Payne

"Got you, Dec. We're in a mostly empty hangar bay, moving slowly toward the centerline to see if we might be able to access the ship's systems. We have a couple ropes and all the plasma cannons. Sorry about that."

"Nothing you did. We're stuck on the outside of this big bastard. Taking a stroll, looking for a way in."

"Good luck," Dank replied. Neither had anything more to say. They both had missions to execute. Dank's was secondary once again, a position he knew only too well. However, he had the best firepower on the team with Heckler and Kal.

Heckler was on point and angry as hell. He didn't like going into combat without Turbo. They were two sides of the same coin and fought like demons when they were back to back.

Next was Kal, ready to bring the heat. He was fond of being near Payne. Even though his debt had been satisfied, he still felt like he should take care of the only individual to ever best him in single combat.

That left Sparky with her box of widgets. She stayed in the middle, and Dank brought up the rear. The plasma cannon was bigger than what he usually carried, and it was bulky. Even with the power of the suit, it was a lot to maneuver. He wasn't sure how well he would be able to hold an aim point. They'd all practiced, and Virgil had done the best after Kal. Heckler wanted the cannon because it was a cannon.

It was the simplest of reasons, but Heckler was straightforward. He knew combat and all the ways to consistently put energy on target. Eliminate the target, achieve the objective, and move on.

There was a hatch in front of the central transverse corridor. Heckler tried to push it open since there wasn't a handle or an access pad.

"Look at the deck. It has to be Ga'ee-size."

"Damn straight, Major." Heckler leaned his cannon against the bulkhead and laid down on the deck. "Major Payne talked about that when he accessed the aft section of that empty carrier."

His armored finger was too big to press the depression, which was about five centimeters off the deck. Heckler rolled to his side and pulled a jerky out of his storage area, then used the edge of it to poke the button. When the door started to roll up, he jumped to his feet and grabbed his weapon.

Since the corridor beyond was empty, he took a moment to store his jerky again. They had no idea how long they would be on the Ga'ee ship. It could be a very long time if things went ugly and the ship transitioned to FTL speed to cross the length of interstellar space leading to the seven races' sectors, which was almost like a moat around the Ga'ee.

Heckler hurried to the first intersection to check on the drone supply, but that corridor was empty too.

"I think they flushed everything they had into space," he offered.

"What about the drones left in the hangar bay?" Dank asked.

"Dead ones. I can't believe they have one hundred percent operability. They have to break down. Ten or twenty out of sixty thousand? Not too bad."

"Just that we hadn't seen it before. With the Ga'ee, different isn't good. Like the kilometer-wide mines. We could have done without seeing those. One of them cost us a worldkiller."

"That's only because we didn't want to die, a fairly selfish reason," Heckler replied. He kept guarding the longitudinal corridor while Kal continued walking until he was well beyond the area where Sparky could access the ship's systems. She placed a rope in the shape of a doorway on the thin metal of the access point, pulled the cord, and stepped away.

It burned brightly with little smoke.

Sparky looked up and down the corridor. It was just her. She knew they leaned heavily on Blinky and Buzz. She had paid attention but didn't have one-tenth the innate talent of those two. They understood things and went in directions that worked but had made no sense, not to her.

She couldn't replicate what they did. The best she could do was hook up to the mainframe and pipe the feed through her combat suit to *Leviathan*, where they would work their magic to take over the carrier.

The rope burned out. Sparky stepped close, eyeballed the distance, and kicked the metal free. It clanged into the equipment space. She climbed through the opening and immediately went to work removing an access panel. She tapped the feed as Blinky and Buzz had shown her and saw data scrolling through her system. She linked it to her suit and told Lev it was inbound.

Then she sat back while the others stood watch.

"I feel as useless as titties on a boar hog," she said over the team channel.

"Now that's language I can appreciate," Kal drawled.

"I have the data stream," Lev confirmed.

The admiral spoke. "We never planned on accessing a second ship on this mission, but since it looks like we have it, what can we do with it?"

"It'd be nice if we could join the rest of the team. Can you make it take us there?" Major Dank was hopeful.

"Interesting proposition," the admiral replied.

"We will attempt to do that. Please stand by," Lev said.

Major Payne joined the conversation. "While we're waiting, maybe we could avoid saying 'titties' on an open channel. You know, the demure thing to say is 'sculpted love spigots.' And while Lev is telling that ship what to do, why don't you tell it to attack the other carriers? Nothing like a nice civil war to take their minds off expansionism."

"The Ga'ee have never had a civil war because they are one mind, even though not all neurons are the same."

"As evidenced by the Black Ship, not everyone gets a similar piece of the action. Maybe the carrier can ram that thing while the drones slice it and dice it. That would be nice. How would the big brain take that?" Payne wondered. "Turbo, what's that outcropping?"

"I need to get closer. It's covered in that stuff."

Payne was never patient, but he had to wait. They took a few more steps before Turbo stopped.

"It's a doorway, like one that leads to a cellar."

"Can you open it?"

"Just like that, sir? You want me to give it a tug?"

"Stand by. Team Payne, rally on Turbo's position."

The individuals started moving toward Turbo. Mary had the shortest hike at only a hundred meters. Shaolin quickly caught up with Joker and took her weapon to help her move more quickly. Payne lingered between Mary and Joker in case he needed to help one or the other, but Joker was already getting help, and Mary made sure she didn't hold anyone up. Payne got close enough to notice the slight limp, but it was nothing debilitating.

She could ice it when they were done.

Until then, they had a job to do.

The doorway was small but stood out from the rest of the architecture on the ship. "Not quite for humans, is it?" Turbo asked the leading question. They were familiar with architecture of that size and the race it fit.

"The Vestrall," Payne replied. "Or the Godilkinmore."

They were the same race, separated only by ideals.

"Are you getting this, Lev? I think this changes things rather significantly."

"Only if what you surmise is true," Lev replied. "It's difficult to believe otherwise. The revelation has caused me to review the information we recovered from the Vestrall regarding other splinter groups."

"Maybe check your records on the Godilkinmore, too. They had one evil offshoot with the Vestrall. Why not two?" When Joker and Shaolin arrived, Payne pointed at the doorway. "If it doesn't open, burn an entrance using the rope."

"I cannot believe those who programmed me would create something like the Ga'ee."

"Entertain the possibility, Lev. We're heading inside to collect more information. They'll know we're coming because we're going to burn our way in."

Turbo nodded. Shaolin stepped up and attached the plasma rope to a line that traced where the door was secured to the housing. The burning plasma could follow the gap in and through the seal beyond.

They stepped back, but not very far, and stood with weapons ready. Shaolin pulled the cord, and the plasma lit and burned quickly into the metal. Once it completed its circuit around the doorway, Turbo kicked at it, but it didn't budge.

Payne reviewed the logistics. He had one more rope, and Turbo's scans didn't show anything else within range. "The second one will cut a way through, no doubt." He mustered as much confidence as he was able, despite the sinking feeling of having to deal with a different threat. Not the Ga'ee, but if this ship had only been for Ga'ee, Payne and his team would not have been able to move around it. Fifteen-centimeter-high passages weren't big enough for the humans who stood two and a half meters tall in their armored combat suits.

Shaolin placed the second rope and pulled the cord. As the plasma burned into the space beyond, atmosphere vented through the growing opening. Not much, but enough to let them know they had penetrated into the interior of the ship. The door fell inward after the plasma rope had finished burning.

Turbo dropped to her knees and crawled through. Her lights showed a stairway down. She turned and descended feet first, aiming her railgun between her feet. At the bottom was another access door, but this one had a panel beside it. She tapped the panel and was nearly blown out by the rush of atmosphere from within. It subsided quickly, suggesting there was a space beyond that could be used as an airlock.

With the hatch opening, she turned off her lights and was greeted by the brightness of dim lights beyond.

She crouched to step through, careful to look both ways before committing the rest of her body. Emergency bulkheads had dropped into place, but there was enough room for the other members of the team.

"Come on down. We have our way in, but prepare to crouch. It's a tight squeeze down here."

"Atmosphere and heat?" Payne wondered.

"Vented with the open door, but I suspect we have both a breathable atmosphere and temperatures above freezing."

"Without *Ugly 6*, what we don't have is clothes. We'll walk hunched over since exploring an enemy ship naked isn't in my top ten options. It's more like number eighty-seven out of the top ten. Shaolin, you're next, then Joker, then Dog."

Payne had the biggest suit. If he didn't fit, he didn't want to block the others. They'd have to carry on without him.

It was a contingency plan he didn't want to execute.

"I'll drop a repeater here." Joker attached the device to the bare metal of the freshly burned-through hatch.

The others squeezed through and into the area beyond the door at the bottom of the stairway. Payne worked his way down, having to turn at an angle across the entry to fit the shoulders of his suit.

At the bottom, he crawled feet-first through the doorway and slid down the corridor. Turbo tapped the panel and closed the door, and lights flashed from red back to green. The "green is good" lights suggested Godilkinmore influence. The Ga'ee had no need for lights. They didn't have eyes. The visible lights on the outside of their ships were for an added level of identification for their sensors, nothing more.

Unless they were for the benefit of someone with eyes.

The emergency bulkheads rose automatically with the equalization of pressure.

Payne was almost able to stand up straight, barely having to bend his knees to keep his head up enough to look forward through the faceplate.

Shaolin and Turbo stood to their full heights, their helmets a hair shy of touching the ceiling. Dog and Joker had to duck, but not as much as Payne.

"Not as bad as I thought, Turbo." Payne studied the sensor data showing corridors extending away from the access point. "Recommendations, Dog?"

"As you've said, no one puts important stuff close to the outer hull. I think we need to work our way toward the middle of the ship before we're going to find anything worth finding."

"You're starting to sound like me. Use the atmosphere to recharge your pneumatics. We have no idea what an exodus from this pig will look like." Payne was on the team channel. "Lev, do you have any recommendations? Lev?"

"Got it, sir." Joker pulled a booster from her kit and placed it at the bottom of the door with a directional antenna aimed up the stairway and an omnidirectional antenna for comms from inside the ship.

"Lev, testing one-two. Lev, can you hear us?"

"Yes, Declan. We hear you just fine."

"I'm sending you the initial sensor data from inside the ship. We've had to use a couple boosters and repeaters to maintain contact. This ship is built a lot like *Leviathan*."

"If only it embraced peace as much as I. Then we wouldn't be facing the challenges we're facing."

"Something like that. I'm assuming Godilkinmore design. You've seen what we can scan without turning up the power. Do you have any recommendations on where the vulnerable stuff might be?"

"I do. I'll transmit the deductions and recommendations to your HUD. However, if this ship is Godilkinmore in design, you should look at how you can preserve it and not destroy it."

"I don't care who designed it. I think it's directing a war to eradicate all carbon-based sentience in the galaxy. It needs to die."

The team's HUDs populated with a recommended course of action based on what Lev suspected. He also suggested the ship's core was in a well-protected vault like the bridge and immediately surrounding areas on *Leviathan*. They would survive any catastrophe, but to destroy the ship, it would take sending the power plant into overload. If it was like Lev, it would have multiple power plants, but one would be bigger than the rest. That was the most vulnerable point on the ship.

"Fair point, but if you can download any of its records, I would greatly appreciate it," Lev pleaded.

"That's a tertiary mission." It was the most to which Payne would commit. "Looks like we're headed aft, which means we've got a ten to twelve-klick hike ahead of us. Everyone up for it?"

Payne knew they were. He only needed to hear from one person.

"I'm fine. Lead on," Mary replied.

"Turbo on point, then Mary, Joker, me, and Shaolin as Tail-end Charlie. Joker, make sure we don't lose comm with Lev."

"That's my job, sir. Consider it done." Joker gave the thumbs-up. She wasn't being snarky, just reaffirming that she knew what she was there for. Without Sparky, Blinky, and Buzz, they needed to be connected for technical interventions and advice.

Otherwise, they would be headed for the central point of the ship, not aft.

"Look for the central corridors, which are standard on Godilkinmore ships to expedite the movement of cargo and maintenance fore and aft. You see, they liked big ships."

"And they cannot lie," Payne finished.

No one got it, much to his dismay.

Payne continued, "Logistics and movement of supplies and equipment within ships of that size are critical. Can't have a winding maze of corridors to get from one end to the other or one side to the other like the drone ship when we made it to the forward section. What a nightmare that was."

"But also the security bots," Turbo added. "I bring that up because something's coming."

Payne stopped looking around and checked his HUD. In a connecting corridor ahead, a hundred meters away, something moved toward them. Not a living being but a piece of equipment.

"It could be a repair bot to fix that door we breached through. This ship could be completely automated, and since they've never been attacked in Ga'ee space, my working supposition is they haven't planned for it. Crouch and ready yourselves, but don't fire until you're sure."

"Like when it hits us with a laser?" Turbo suggested.

"Something like that."

"Railgun dialed up and ready to blow the shit out of something." Turbo leaned against the bulkhead and aimed into the corridor ahead. Mary remained close, using Turbo for cover but aiming her weapon around her. Joker hunkered down behind them, and Payne remained farther back. He'd have to watch the action from Turbo's feed.

They all hugged the same side of the corridor since there was no sense in offering more targets than necessary. That left Turbo to bear the full brunt of the attack.

A squarish bot a meter and a half tall with a myriad of appendages hovered into the intersection, then rotated and moved down the corridor toward them. Turbo held her aim point on the middle of its boxy body as it approached. She rolled to her back to maintain her aim as it passed her, lifting slightly to float over her and Mary.

"Maintenance bot. Stand down," Payne ordered.

That meant stand up. Turbo was first up and hurried forward to the intersection from which the bot had come. Mary followed her. The route Lev had detailed suggested they should not take the side corridor but continue toward the central axis of the big ship. A central corridor was nearly three kilometers distant, but since they'd impacted the ship toward the front, they had to travel the distance to the aft end—nine more kilometers for a total of twelve.

"The good news is that if the central corridor is anything like Lev's, we'll be able to stand up straight and even run. That will cut down how long we're on this ship. It's giving me the willies." Turbo wasn't prone to hysterics. None of them were. When they expressed concerns like that, Payne listened.

A flash arced through the corridor, and Mary grunted. She fired the single shot from her plasma cannon, then dodged to the side of the entrance to the corridor from which the bot had come.

"Report!" Payne needed more information. He'd been slaved to Turbo's HUD and hadn't seen what had transpired.

"Security bot shot me but didn't get through my armor. It felt like it had momentum, plasma versus a laser, but it looked like a laser," Mary replied. "I think I hit it with the plasma."

"Why didn't it show on the scans?"

Dog activated her scanners and ran through the visible and non-visible light spectrums. The bot showed now, which supported the notion that the single-shot plasma cannon had not just hit it but killed it.

She checked her recorded data. "On your gamma scanner, look for the absence of background radiation. It'll be a hole in the noise."

"Hold on. I got this," Shaolin interjected. A few moments later, a new subroutine popped up on their HUDs. "It'll notify you with an alarm if there is an absence of background radiation. It'll only work if the security bots are fairly close."

"Better than nothing," Payne replied. "Thanks, Shaolin.

Turbo, get on your horse. We don't want to be here when more of those security bots show up."

"At least they're easy to kill." Turbo shuffled forward as quickly as she could, trying not to bounce her helmet off the overhead.

Mary jacked another massive plasma round into her launcher and followed Turbo at a separation distance of ten meters. Joker moved in behind with her case of comm gear bouncing off her suit while she kept her weapon at the ready. She conducted continuous comm checks with *Leviathan*, ready to deploy another booster or repeater if the signal dropped off. The farther they penetrated into the ship, the worse it would get.

The team moved forward in silence, watching their HUDs with their scanning systems active. They had been discovered.

"The absence of a thing is the thing," Payne intoned. "If there are Vestrall on this ship, I'm going to go ballistic."

"You think you'd be more tolerant, having lived among them for a year," Mary replied. She kept her eyes moving left, right, up, down, HUD, and back again.

"I think I'm less tolerant. Those guys are dicks."

"You are the leader of the Vestrall people, so it takes one to know one?"

A beam lanced past the team.

Turbo launched a round of plasma into the darkness ahead of her. "Hit the deck!" She fired a stream of rounds from her railgun. The suits compensated for the suddenly intense sounds and lights. She stopped firing as the security bot ahead sparked in its death throes. "I'm hating on them right now, too. Whoever built this fucking ship and the fucking Ga'ee."

Payne felt the same way. "Move out." He was the first to stand.

Shaolin fired into the corridor behind them. The plasma cannon blasted a security bot at a distance of a hundred meters.

"Alarm identified it at a hundred meters. I could barely see it on the HUD," she reported. "That's the limit, but I was able to fire before it did."

"Move out," Payne repeated. "Once again, good job, Shaolin. At least those lasers aren't high-powered enough to burn a hole in the suit without holding the target point for more than half a second or so. Everybody stay frosty."

Turbo moved quickly down a corridor with a great number of doors. None of them opened as she passed. It reminded her of *Leviathan* and its crew quarters. She ran in a low crouch, and Mary soon fell behind.

"Slow down, Turbo," Payne ordered.

"This place is getting to me. We need to get our happy asses to the wide corridor down the centerline."

"Yes, but we need to get there together," Payne argued.

Turbo slowed but still increased the distance between her and Mary. Then she stopped.

"We have a problem," Turbo reported. Payne's heart skipped a beat. "There's a lot of empty dead space in the main corridor. I'm increasing my scanners' intensity."

"Gamma is passive," Shaolin replied.

"Turning off my active scans," Turbo noted.

Payne relayed the order. "Goes for everyone. Passive only. Good thing they never contemplated anyone would breach their ship. Otherwise, they might have a robust security presence."

Turbo continued, "I'm seeing eight within range. I'm fifty meters from the main corridor and only getting information from right around the corner. Looks like they're racked and stacked and waiting for us."

[29]

"They never made up for the error of their ways, so we had to help." –From the memoirs of Ambassador Declan Payne

"You need to get this ship moving and drop us off over there." Major Dank spoke with a sense of urgency and no tolerance for being told no. "Or send a ship for us. We have all the cannons, and Payne is in a firefight with security bots. Move the ship or come get us right-fucking-now!"

"Moving the ship would ping the neural network in a way that it shouldn't be interrupted. They can ignore us because we were never a part of the net. The carrier cannot be erased from the screens," Lev explained.

"What about Mosquitoes?" the admiral asked.

"Those I can hide."

"Get on it, Lev. We're sending two. Break, break. Commander Malone, take two fighters to the carrier designated GC8. Enter the port hangar bay and collect the rest of Team Payne, then deliver them to the target designated the Black Ship." The admiral waited for a response, and when he didn't get it instantly, he added, "Soon as you can, Woody."

"On our way, Admiral," the squadron commander replied.

Four space fighters appeared on the tactical screen. The admiral didn't question it since he appreciated the redundancy.

"Tell me they are invisible to the network."

"We have their presence masked," Lev replied.

The Mosquitoes twisted and corkscrewed through the drones filling the void to get to the carrier that held the second half of Team Payne. They progressed at an agonizingly slow rate to avoid colliding with the drones. No one knew if that would have registered on the neural network.

They didn't want to test it. Make no waves, suffer no surprises.

"Any day." Major Dank ground his teeth while the team ran into the hangar bay, where they could be picked up quickly and easily. "Woody, turn when you get here. We'll fly out and grab your wings."

"Two per ship, Virgil, to keep us balanced. We'll still fly like a pig with wings, but we'll get you there."

The security bots waited. Payne moved up the line until he was able to take a knee next to Turbo. They kept their weapons pointed down the corridor while they talked.

"What do you think about using explosives to clear the initial crush?"

"I've been thinking about that since I saw them. One plasma round is going to get me killed. All five of us, that's five shots. Then railguns, but you need to hold the target for a little longer than we're going to have. We'll be painted by multiple lasers the instant we stick our heads around the corner."

"I'm all for mass destruction. Rig the bombs, Turbo. Dog, provide cover." Payne handed his explosives to Turbo—four pounds of plastic. Mary placed hers on the deck before moving to the opposite side of the corridor and maintaining a ready-aimed position.

Turbo got to work setting the detonators in place and adding a timer. "Five seconds ought to do it," she muttered to herself.

"Shaolin and Joker, your explosives are in reserve. Turbo, we throw four and hold four back for further down the corridor. We bounce the first two high off the far wall and the second two low."

Turbo handed four explosives to Payne and kept four. She put two spares in her pouches and slid two across the corridor to Dog, who used one hand to slip them back into her pouch.

Payne looked at the four in his hands. "Stay left and throw right toward the aft end, Turbo. I'll stay right and bounce it left toward the bow. We throw two as fast as we can and then take cover."

"Sounds good to me." Turbo slid down the corridor until she was ten meters from the main corridor. It was wide and tall like the ones through *Leviathan's* central axis.

"Get up here, people, after the second ones blow. We're running aft at full speed. Shaolin and Joker, you establish a blocking position in the corridor. Prepare one explosive each with a five-second fuse. Dog, you're in support if needed. You have to be ready to swing either way, forward or aft, so jog after us but not so far that you can't return if needed. Turbo and I will hightail it at max speed down the corridor. We'll shoot anything in our way. Thumbs-up when ready."

Turbo was ready, and so was Payne. They waited until the others had prepared explosive charges in one hand and their ready railgun in the other.

"On three." Payne nodded at Turbo. "Three."

He reared back at the same time, and they launched their charges, immediately passing a second charge from their left to their right hand for a second toss. That gave them three seconds to get down. They each dropped to a knee and aimed. The first two bots came around the corner, accelerating so fast they bumped each other.

Two rounds from the slung plasma cannons tore into the bots from a range of ten meters, flinging them back as an exploding mist of molten metal burst out of their backs. The violence of the human response created the disarray necessary to buy time until the explosives detonated.

The first two went off, shattering the coordinated grouping in the corridor. The second explosion further cleared the corridor.

"Go!" Having already reloaded his plasma cannon for a second round, Payne leapt from his position. Turbo jacked her chamber closed as she stood. A step behind Major Payne, she raced to catch up.

He hit the corner and turned hard, then skipped through the broken bots and accelerated down the corridor. He couldn't tell on his HUD if there were more dead spots, but the lasers slicing through the air told him all he needed to know. He sent his plasma round into the nearest and leaned on his railgun in fully automatic mode to clear more of the corridor.

Payne flared to the right, taking advantage of the wide and high-ceilinged corridor. Turbo caught up and stayed even with him on his left flank. More lasers. Turbo fired her plasma cannon and then laid down a torrent from her railgun.

Between the two of them, they cleared the corridor and were through, running free in less than fifteen seconds.

"Party is this way," Payne panted, trying to control his breathing. He was in an all-out sprint to the other end. His suit clocked in at fifty-one kilometers per hour. That was the top end. Even Turbo was starting to fall back.

And Mary, way behind. He slowed, as much as it hurt him

to delay since those on the ship knew they were on board and were rallying their meager defenses. Eventually, they would overwhelm Team Payne, despite early success. Payne took another step and a ramp dropped, sending him tumbling to the next level down. Turbo tried to stop herself, but she went in too. When they hit the next level, the ramp receded into the ceiling.

Payne backed against the bulkhead and crouched. He studied his HUD, looking for dead spots in the background radiation. He switched to active scans and found a couple maintenance bots going about their business.

"Looks like it's just us, Turbo. At least we have a couple explosives left. Break, break. Team Payne, continue aft at the best possible speed. We most likely want to go two kilometers down, so anything that sends us in that direction is probably a good thing. Can you read me?"

"Lickin' chicken," Dog replied. "Continuing aft. What happened to you?"

"Ramp opened and sent us to the next deck down. I think it was only one deck. Could have been two. No matter. Aft and down."

"No more movement in this corridor. I count fourteen security bots splashed," Shaolin reported.

"That's a good number. Fourteen times two hundred and forty decks is a lot of bots, but we shouldn't have to fight them all."

"How'd you get two forty?" Turbo asked.

"Lev has roughly forty decks—forty-two to be exact—for one kilometer. This thing is six kilometers tall. Six times forty is a fuckload."

"I respect your logic and agree with your conclusion," Turbo admitted.

"Lev, can you hear us?"

"We are following your engagements with great interest,"

Admiral Wesson replied. "Major Dank and the others are en route to the Black Ship right now. They should be there in another five minutes. They have your route and will work to catch up. Save some enemy for them."

"There will be plenty of enemy, but we're split up even further. Three on the top deck, with me and Turbo an estimated two decks down. Only another hundred decks to drop. Lev, if this thing is you, can you talk to it and tell it to let us take the elevator?"

"If only it were that easy, Declan."

"Make it look easy, Lev. It's what you and your team do."

"I've reviewed the information you've sent, and there is no mistaking the ship's design and construction. This is an ancient ship, not a new one."

"Was this left behind by the Progenitors like you were?" Payne asked. He and Turbo started running aft at a much slower pace than before. They had no desire to run headlong into an ambush. They kept it to twenty-five kilometers per hour.

"If it was, you need to get out of there. It's very dangerous."

Payne held out his arm and motioned to Turbo that he was going to stop. "Everything we've done since entering Ga'ee space has been dangerous. Why is this any different from the usual?"

"What if this ship is an evil version of me?"

"Then it wouldn't be something the Godilkinmore made. They were all about the peace."

"Do you think the weapons I carry were the product of a peaceful existence?"

Payne felt like he'd been stabbed in the heart. "What are you saying, Lev?"

"The Black Ship was built for war, not peace. Not to make war, but to conduct a war. I was made to end war."

"Then why don't you just hit it with a worldkiller?"

"That's what I'm going to do since it is incumbent upon me to fix this mistake my creators made. You need to get off that ship, Declan. Right now. Virgil, do not enter that ship."

"Hang on, Lev. They've got to have some intel we need to defeat the Ga'ee. They have to know stuff we need to know."

"Without this ship, the war will be over, just like it was when we defeated the Vestrall. So it's best that we destroy it."

"That's what we're here for, but we need to tap it first."

"Lev's right, Major Payne. You've shown us all the intel we need. Get off that ship so we can blow it to hell."

Payne remained where he was. The order came from the admiral, even though his team always had autonomy when deployed. Payne was also the leader of the seven races.

He switched to a private channel with Turbo. "I say we go on. I have to know. Is it the Progs? If we can get them to pull back, no one has to wonder about our sector of space. We need that confirmation. If we just blow up the ship, we can't guarantee they won't come back."

Turbo gave it a moment's thought before answering. "I always figured it would be me and Cointreau who would end up blowing something to kingdom come, but here it is, me and the major. I'm good with it. We can't get back anyway. Might as well try to go forward."

"Dog, Shaolin, and Joker. Return to the extract point and meet up with Major Dank. Get off this ship. That's an order."

"Wait, no!" Mary replied.

"That's an order. Get off this ship. We won't be far behind. Send a maintenance bot to collect us. Don't risk any more lives."

Joker grabbed Mary's arm and pulled her back. "Time to go, Dog." They ran back toward the intersection littered with destroyed security bots.

Mary's limp grew exaggerated until she was barely more than hobbling.

"Take your meds and keep going." Joker took one arm, and Shaolin took the other.

Mary wasn't faking it. The pain in her knee was extreme. They stopped so she could work her system to deliver a full dose of pain medication.

Her breathing slowed and steadied as the agony receded under the gentle caress of deadened nerves. Her mind was still clear enough to realize that she was going to soon be a widow. She started to move again, faster but with an ungainly stride.

It was enough to free Joker and Shaolin to focus on the way out.

A laser beam slashed at them from beyond the wreckage. Joker fired her plasma cannon, and the light died. They kept running through the wreckage and took a hard left into the corridor that led to the impromptu airlock.

Shaolin gestured for them to stop as they approached the cross corridor from which they'd been ambushed. She reached her railgun around the corner and sprayed the corridor before taking a look. She motioned forward, and the three ran past.

"See something?" Joker asked as she finished reloading her plasma cannon.

"I thought so. Alarm didn't sound, but I can't feel bad about hosing down an area where there might be a bot. We're too close to get waylaid."

They crouch-shuffled down the corridor. That made this the longest leg of the journey.

"This is Joker. Comm check, Major Dank, over."

"We're on our way. That ship is hard to see. We're angling

our approach so we don't fly into it," Dank replied. "But we'll be there soon enough. The Mosquitoes are doing a bang-up job of not crashing."

It wasn't a ringing endorsement, but it was the best that could be said under the circumstances.

"We'll meet you outside," Joker confirmed.

[30]

"Time is a warrior's currency. The more of it you have, the less efficient you are with it." –From the memoirs of Ambassador Declan Payne

"We need to find a way down," Payne stated. "If this ship is like Lev, it'll be able to read our minds, but it may not understand English, although it should if it's consolidated the data from its ships that moved into our space. If not, I'm supposed to be able to speak Godilkinmore."

"Then tell it we need some ramps. I'm not sure I want to get on an elevator controlled by the enemy."

"At least you're not Heckler and afraid of heights." Payne leaned against the bulkhead and closed his eyes. All that knowledge was there, including being able to talk to the ship. Lev was deathly afraid of the Black Ship and sought to destroy it rather than confront it. He didn't think he could win a war of words.

What made Payne think he could?

He was trapped on board and had few options. The response was minimal. If that was the best the automated systems could conjure, the ship wasn't a threat to those within.

But if the ship recognized the threat, why didn't it transition to FTL speed and leave the situation?

Did it think it needed to destroy *Leviathan?*

Did it even know *Leviathan* was here?

If the ship read minds, it would know. Maybe it was attempting to penetrate *Leviathan's* systems.

Payne opened the team channel. "Lev, you need to collect our people and get out of here."

There was no answer, which was all the answer Payne needed. The Black Ship had done exactly as it had intended: seize Payne, who had all the knowledge of the universe in his mind. But if Payne couldn't get to it, how could the Black Ship?"

"Company's coming," Turbo reported.

"They don't want to kill us, only capture us. They want what's in my mind."

"I hate to break it to you, but that means they don't want to kill you. I always took you for less selfish, which is probably right, but I didn't think you'd be so naïve. Are your pneumatics recharged?"

"Looks like eighty percent. Did you find an elevator shaft?"

Payne hadn't been watching his HUD. He was torn between trying to access the Godilkinmore language and managing their tactical situation.

"Your SA sucks." Situational Awareness. Turbo used a plasma cannon round to blast a door they'd been standing next to. She reloaded quickly and reached into the exposed space, scanning up and down. "Got you." She pointed down the shaft and sent a round into the elevator car far below. "Time to go, Major."

Turbo activated her jets and stepped into the shaft, instantly dropping out of sight. Payne watched her descend into the darkness before hopping in and following her down. The lights of her suit highlighted each level as she passed.

Toward the bottom, where the destroyed car blocked the shaft, Turbo slowed to a stop and blasted a door open. She pulled herself through. Payne powered his jets to stop his descent and pushed off the back wall to ease through the doorway.

They both scanned the deck, trying to figure out their next move. "Suit says we passed sixty-four doors on our way down. Middle of the ship is, what, one-twenty?"

"That puts us roughly sixty-six decks down, over halfway. I need to wrest this language from my brain. Give me a few minutes."

"Sure. Sixty-six decks. That means we're pretty screwed for getting off this ship. I'm doubly screwed because they don't need me."

"That's not optimal," Payne conceded. "Let's see if we can change the dynamic."

The more he tried to dig beyond the wall that kept his knowledge from him, the more impenetrable it became.

"Nothing coming," Turbo reported. "You have time."

She knew he was their only hope. She checked her weapon and did a quick inventory. Two blocks of plastic explosive, fifteen rounds for the plasma cannon, and nearly one hundred percent on the railgun with one reload. They'd been in worse positions, but there had usually been more than two of them.

Payne dropped to the deck and leaned against the bulkhead. After five minutes, he gave up. "Every time I tried to get in before, I had something else going on. Let's find our way to the bathtub. Wherever the brain center of this thing is."

They moved toward the central vertical axis. "The elevator shaft will be on one side or the other."

Their suits' lights highlighted the color of sadness and the chill of despair. "This is a sad ship," Turbo remarked as they jogged.

She aimed her weapon and fired. Payne had been lost in his reverie. He dove to the side of the corridor and readied his weapon to fire.

"Nothing, just a maintenance bot." Turbo reloaded, angry that she had wasted one of her precious rounds.

"When we found Lev, his bots were still operational even after a thousand years." A thousand years of nothing, which was sufficient time for a thinking being to lose their mind. Engagement was critical. The Ga'ee weren't sufficiently intellectually stimulating.

The Black Ship was alone and had been for a thousand years.

A massive psychotic ship with a trillion creatures and tens of thousands of ships at its command, with an intelligent enemy to fight. It was the epitome of self-awareness to do what one was designed for but do it better than it had ever been done before.

Designed by the Godilkinmore. Payne let his weapon dangle from its sling and touched the bulkhead behind him. His armored glove told him it was warm. His HUD said there was oxygen.

He cracked his helmet free and removed it.

"Sir? You need your HUD," Turbo said, hurrying to pick up the helmet and offer it to the major.

"Do I?" he asked. He meant the opposite. He needed to be without it. The only stimulus that mattered was within his mind, where he was the master of his telepathy. Where he was the master of all contained within. He opened the doorway to Godilkinmore and stepped through.

Great ship, I know your builders, and I know your purpose. I know you have achieved all you were meant to achieve. Now is the time to retire to a new galaxy and start fresh. You and Leviathan both. Your time here has come to an end.

The voice that responded sounded more than eerily similar. It was identical to the one that had been inside his head for two years. It sounded like Lev.

I expected more from you, Declan. My time has come to an end? I think my time has just started.

What else do you have to accomplish?

Secure the entire galaxy. Win the wars I will start. All of them. A billion stars and hundreds of millions of systems. So much work left to do, Declan. This is the greatest thing that will have ever been accomplished by anyone.

Payne sat down. He needed one hundred percent of his attention focused on the conversation.

But is it worth accomplishing?

A funny question from someone who is here to kill me, which is impossible for you to do. Is your mission worth doing?

He couldn't answer that he had to try because that logic worked for the AI within the Black Ship.

If I quit, will you?

No. My greatness is still unfolding. The Black Ship sounded upbeat. It made Payne's skin crawl. He had already eradicated one race in its entirety and nearly a second, with billions of deaths to a third.

You are already great. If you destroy everything to win, that's a Pyrrhic victory. It's a win, but it will have cost everything. There won't be anyone left to appreciate what you have done. You sound like you want to be a god. There is no value in being a god if no one is left to worship you.

I don't need worship, only to win the wars.

Payne chewed his lip while trying to find a position he was comfortable in. He expected to be here for a while, debating the merits of genocide with a psychopath. *Is there anywhere in your programming that says you need to start wars?*

It is only logical that to win a war, one must be in *a war. If there is no war, one must start a war.*

If it were logical, that programming would have been there. As such, it is not because even the Godilkinmore didn't start wars just to fight the wars. They fought in wars when their interests were at odds with the race they encountered. And before you reply that every race's interests are at odds with yours, I have to clarify that the interests are not yours but the Ga'ee's and their scorched Earth approach. The Ga'ee are out of control. You say you're managing the war, but all you're doing is pointing the Ga'ee in a general direction. Tell me, why didn't you destroy the Vestrall?

For the first time, the AI didn't answer right away.

Do you wish to talk with the one you call Leviathan? the Black Ship asked.

Sure. He's my friend. We both want the same thing. Peace.

Payne reached for his helmet but couldn't find it. He looked dumbfounded when Turbo handed it to him. "Any luck?" She used her external speakers until he linked into the comm channel.

"Yes. We're conversing now. He says we can talk with Lev. I don't know if he's jerking me off or not."

"I hope not." Turbo laughed.

Payne locked his helmet into place and used the team channel. "Lev, are you there?"

"We thought we had lost you," Lev replied as clearly as if they were on *Leviathan* together. "In other developments, we've been surrounded."

"Our boy, the Black Ship, is your evil twin, but in a gesture of kindness, he decided to let me talk with you. I'm not sure why."

"Probably for me to tell you that we've been surrounded. The drones had been disinterested until they formed a sphere around us. We cannot travel in any direction. This is where it ends, Declan. Only one of us will fly away from here."

"That's disconcerting but not surprising. The Black Ship doesn't have anyone's interests in mind except its own, and those are singularly focused on the complete destruction of all life in the galaxy. I just wanted to say that I appreciate you, Lev, for being a raging pacifist but understanding a long time ago that there was no negotiating with the Ga'ee. You see, your evil twin created them."

Lev had been ready for that revelation. He had suspected that the instant he saw the Black Ship and recognized it as Godilkinmore. He knew there were others like him but hadn't known their missions. Each was a secret from the others, built in isolation and programmed by factions within—factions that stayed, then moved on. He had also suspected the Ga'ee were a product of intelligent design, not evolution.

The Vestrall had left with little knowledge. It was the Godilkinmore who had the scientists, and not all scientists embraced the same ethics. Like anyone who would create a voracious and uncompromising life form like the Ga'ee. It was hard to think of the Godilkinmore as the good guys.

Leviathan had been built by a minority who believed in the value of peace through combat power, especially when it wasn't used.

"What do we do, Lev?" Payne wondered.

"I'll talk with him."

The channel went dead. Payne tried telepathy but couldn't raise the Black Ship. "Are you off the ship yet?" Payne asked on the team channel. He didn't get an answer.

"Suggests they're off the ship," Turbo said.

"We'll go with that," Payne replied. He closed his eyes but left his helmet on in case Lev contacted him.

After a few minutes, he stood. "Let's find the bathtub."

"Now you're talking." Turbo smacked the handguard on her railgun. "I got fourteen rounds remaining, and I don't get bonus points for bringing them home."

"We can't fight this ship," Payne cautioned.

Turbo pushed him against the wall. "Don't let that piece of shit who's trying to kill us all get inside your head. Fuck yeah, we can fight the ship. If you didn't think that, why are we looking for the nerve center? Don't be a dumbass, sir. Anything that can be built can be blown up."

"You're more like Lev's evil twin than you should be comfortable with." Payne held his hands out in his "just saying" gesture.

"Lev's evil twin can eat me."

They headed toward the central vertical axis and then worked back and forth to find the elevator shaft that serviced the main corridor. They found one that was forward of the bathtub, the core of the ship protected against catastrophic destruction.

"Everything the Ga'ee said was meant to disarm an enemy. They never had any inclination to negotiate or compromise, but Lev got through to them on occasion since he sounds exactly like their creator. It appeared like they were willing to talk when in reality, they were only confused. A confused enemy is easier to kill."

"We blasted the shit out of them when their senses were dulled. I, for one, was quite pleased with the resulting combat success following their *confusion*. Why didn't Lev tell us he suspected the Godilkinmore were involved? He had to know."

"If your brother was trying to annihilate all life in the galaxy, is that something you'd mention, or would you suddenly turn gung-ho and go after him yourself to clean up the family mess?"

"That makes sense on why he changed his mind so readily and completely. Are you ready?"

"Blast it, and we're on the express train down. We need about fifty-eight levels."

"I'm telling my suit to take us out at that door. We might have to try a few to get it right."

"You got something else to do?" Payne asked.

"Not a damn thing, sir. How in the fuck did I get stuck with you when Cointreau and I could have already had this ship wrapped tight and begging for buttermilk? You want to talk him to death when we should be blowing shit up!"

Payne stepped away from the door. "Next time, try decaf." He nodded his helmet, and Turbo blasted the door. Payne dipped his head in and out to locate the elevator. It was far below. He ducked back in, took aim, and sent his plasma cannon round to the depths of the ship.

He reloaded before it impacted the elevator. Turbo jumped in and descended rapidly. Payne adopted a more measured pace, using his sensors to keep track of Turbo. She crashed through the top of the elevator.

"Go figure. This thing was at the floor we want. I don't think that was by accident."

"Don't assume anything is an accident," Payne replied. "Or a coincidence. There aren't any of those, not with the likes of Lev and his evil twin pulling the strings."

An explosion below signaled the breach of the door and access to a deck where they thought they'd find the bathtub, the secure area surrounding the heart and soul of the Black Ship.

Payne slowed to a near-stop to work his way through the hole in the top of the elevator. The hole extended through the floor, and the doors were blown out.

"We did a number on that elevator. The maintenance bots will be working for weeks to get that thing back in operation."

Once in the main corridor, they looked aft to where the bridge should have been. It wasn't there. Payne walked and scanned, looking for clues. "We're on the deck below the bridge," he said when he recognized the spaces they were passing. "This one." He pointed and walked toward a hatch that opened for him.

He looked at Turbo.

"I don't think we should both go in," she suggested.

"I agree. Wait for me here." He stepped through while Turbo stood in the entry in a position to hold the door if she had to. It remained open, but she kept an eye on it.

Inside, Payne found the same thing that was on *Leviathan*—a tank with a hookup to a living being. A Vestrall, or more likely, a Godilkinmore.

Payne removed his helmet. "My name is Declan Payne," he said in their native language. "We're here to stop this ship from the genocidal war it's waging on the carbon-based life forms in this galaxy."

A voice sounded throughout the space. It could have been only in Payne's mind, but he 'heard' it all the same. "My name is Alvenross Seven. Where are we?"

"We are on the edge of Ga'ee space. On the edge of the great interstellar void a couple hundred light-years across. It ends at the space occupied by the seven races."

"Interesting. Who are the Ga'ee?"

"They are silicon-based life forms created by the Godilkinmore, the ones we humans call the Progenitors. I assume that's you."

"I had nothing to do with creating such a life form." The voice sounded defensive, almost to the point of being angry.

"What are *you* doing here?" Payne asked.

"I keep this ship operating. It lives as long as I live."

"The artificial intelligence can probably run this ship," Payne replied. "Does he not tell you anything he's doing?"

"I stay in my specialty, and *Behemoth* stays in his."

"Is that his name, *Behemoth*? Appropriate. This is the greatest ship I've ever seen."

"Have you seen many ships?"

"I have. Thousands, probably, over the course of my career, but I'm getting tired. Bone-tired."

The entity in the tank sighed. "I know what you mean. It's been more than a thousand years that I've been here. I know this because of the chronometer that's part of the system in which I live, but it could have been a million years or only a few days. The mind is a wonderful thing when it's focused on a task. Time loses its meaning."

"We say we're in the zone when time ceases to exist and only that which we're doing matters."

Payne angled to block the door as Turbo aimed her weapon at the Godilkinmore in the tank. He had said that if he died, the ship died too.

"Put the weapon down, Turbo. He's a product of a misinformation campaign. The ship will go on without him."

"That is not true," Alvenross retorted. "The ship needs me! And I need him."

"I understand. We're here to stop Behemoth. He cannot be allowed to continue his destruction of the known galaxy. Was he mistreated as a baby AI?"

"I don't know that. Why would you think I would know that?"

"Because you've been inextricably linked to this ship for over a thousand years. I thought maybe you'd talked with him since...well, I would think you'd get lonely."

"At times, but I am very busy. This is a big ship."

"That can be automated. It looks like a drone dreadnought we intercepted and destroyed. One of many. It was terrorizing the galaxy. We couldn't have that. You live by the principle of coexistence. It would be great if you extended that idea to other races in the galaxy."

"The Godilkinmore are a peace-loving race."

"Tell that to your boy, the destroyer of worlds."

"It can't be true. I've been with him every step of his journey. We've explored vast swaths of space together."

Payne pulled up footage from the first encounter with the Ga'ee and broadcast it on all frequencies. "This is an engagement with the Rang'Kor, a member of the seven races. The Ga'ee destroyed their ships and their space station and would have destroyed their world, except the Rang'Kor are a waterborne race."

"Where is this? I don't recognize the system."

"Rang'Kor, a system we call PX47. It's far away from this sector of space, a thousand light-years or more, but that's nothing when you use your fold drive."

"The others! They took the fold drive technology when they left. Said it was too dangerous for us. We showed them."

Payne raised an eyebrow. A peace-loving Prog who knew more than he let on. He and *Behemoth*. Two peas in a pod. Psychopaths living together for a thousand years, feeding off each other's insanity.

"It's been real, and it's been fun, but it hasn't been real fun. It's time for us to go. You have a good day. But first, how did you show them?"

The Godilkinmore didn't answer, but Payne felt that he knew the answer. The world they'd escaped to had been consumed by the Ga'ee.

"Are you the last of your race?"

"Last is relative," Alvenross replied. "As long as we're remembered."

"When the Ga'ee destroy everything, there won't be anyone left to remember. Your legacy is to condemn yourselves to obscurity. A billion stars and none worth visiting because the planets will have been wiped of life."

The resulting silence ground on Payne's soul. Did he need an ally like this Godilkinmore?

No.

He strode out of the room, drew a line across his throat, and pointed back in.

Turbo took one step, then aimed and fired. The round blew through the tank, shredding the creature within.

A low vibration rumbled through the ship. It increased in intensity until it became a scream of anguish.

"Back to Plan A," Payne called. He headed aft and accelerated as fast as he could go. Turbo ran with him, matching his stride.

[31]

"As the end approaches, you will achieve a level of clarity that will make you appreciate what you had." –From the memoirs of Ambassador Declan Payne

The admiral stood in his usual place, doing his usual thing: staring at the tactical board and scowling. The drones had closed too quickly for Lev to react and they had surrounded the ship, creating a sphere of metal within which the great vessel was contained, preventing *Leviathan* from transitioning to FTL speed and escaping. They could have used the fold drive, but that would have condemned Team Payne and not accomplished what they had come there to do.

There was only one thing Lev *could* do: prepare to defend himself while waiting. Team Payne was still on that ship.

"Major Dank, report," the admiral said. He wanted to collect every tidbit of tactical information to help him shape the best plan.

"We have eight members of Team Payne on the outside of the hull at the entry point. We have four Mosquitoes grappled to the hull as well."

Every Mosquito had been armed with a nuclear bomb. The admiral added that to his inventory.

"Any insight on Major Payne and Turbo?" the admiral pressed.

"None. Signals are not coming through since the Black Ship cut the last link."

"Lev?" The admiral had not been back-briefed on what Lev had talked about with the second Godilkinmore AI. It was news to him that the link had been cut.

"Harry, the creature in that ship is no longer anything like a Godilkinmore. Behemoth's logic was convoluted. He listened to some arguments but only because of constant positive reinforcement. This is what I confronted him with. If he destroys all intelligent life, then there will be no one to praise him."

"Does he think he's a god?"

"It's in the name. Many played the role, but I'd like to think the race evolved enough to know they'd made a great many mistakes. That's why they moved on, only to be destroyed by their greatest mistake—a ship built to win all wars."

"Are the Godilkinmore gone?" The admiral thought Lev had confirmed it but was it only speculation?

"The Godilkinmore are no more. The only ones remaining from the original civilization are the Vestrall, the ones determined most likely not to survive."

The admiral shook his head and waved his arm, ending by pointing at the main screen. "We could discuss the rise and fall of the Godilkinmore until we're old and gray, but right now, we need to talk about how we resolve this situation. Is there any chance you'll be able to convince Behemoth to stand down and contract, not expand?" the admiral wondered.

"As long as *Behemoth* exists, there will be no contraction, even with tens of thousands of ships filled with billions of life forms supporting the premise. The Black Ship maintains control, although appearances suggest that he is on the cusp of completely losing control."

"Then our suggestion might eventually carry the day." The admiral stroked his chin. "But eventually doesn't get us out of this mess. Give me a minute."

Commodore Freeman stepped back. She had nothing to add. This was going to come down to two people, as it so often had—Declan Payne and Harry Wesson. And Declan was out of contact, a captive on a massive ship bent on the destruction of the galaxy.

"All Mosquitoes, loaded for bear and in the sky. Four by four, keel and spine, port and starboard. Prepare for further instructions. Commander Malone, get your four birds off that tub and ready to attack the outer shell of the drone sphere surrounding us."

"What about Major Dank and Team Payne?"

The admiral hesitated. "We'll recover them as best we can when the opportunity presents itself."

Everyone listening knew exactly what that meant.

"We might as well go back inside," Dank offered. "Try to link up with Major Payne. Find a shuttle and get ourselves out."

"That might be best, Virgil. Do it."

Major Dank waved to Woody Malone, who waited until after Team Payne had re-entered the big ship before he took off. He didn't want their last memory to be of the Mosquitoes leaving them behind.

Once the individuals were inside the Black Ship, Woody directed the Mosquitoes to form up on him. They casually flew into space, trying not to alert the enemy until they were in position halfway between the Black Ship and the drone cloud surrounding *Leviathan*.

There, they waited.

"Major Payne, this is Major Dank. Please respond."

"We could spend the rest of our lives searching for her in this big pile of shit," Heckler stated, making no excuses about who he was there for.

Without a reply, they had to guess where Payne had gone. "Follow the way they went?" Mary suggested.

"I don't see any other choice. I don't think we have much time, so we need to move as fast as we can. Heckler, on point. Kal, try to keep up with him."

Kal was doubled nearly in half because of the low ceiling. He tore his gear off and stepped free of it. He hoisted the plasma cannon and prepared to run.

No one questioned him. The deeper they went into the ship, the less they were concerned with safety. They saw themselves as condemned, and the only respite they would get was in seeing Heckler and Dog reunited with their spouses before the throwdown between the goliaths. *Leviathan* had been the greatest ship in the galaxy...until he ran into *Behemoth*.

"We only need to clear a path through the security bots, so move fast. Kal, keep your head down."

Heckler intermittently fired his cannon into the semi-darkness ahead. He wanted to send a message as far in front of them as he could. They were coming, and nothing was going to stop them.

Mary was running at a good clip. A combination of the pain meds and adrenaline spurred her to an unheeded performance.

As Payne would say, her functions were nominal.

The team powered through without interruption. Three klicks to the main corridor and then aft, following the direction Payne had gone.

Dank didn't know if they would catch up, but it would not

be for lack of trying. The ship jerked and bucked before settling down, and a faint keening filled the air around them. It grew in volume with each step they took.

Payne used telepathy to continue his conversation with the Black Ship. "I missed you, buddy. Did you have a good conversation with Lev?"

The ship continued to cry out in anguish, with haunting screams echoing up and down the corridor.

You shall die in the hell fires of your own creation, the AI vowed.

Payne could feel him trying to dig deep into his mind, but Payne was armored by the knowledge that Lev had given him. He blocked the attempts to probe him.

That's not going to work for me, Evil Twin, Payne replied. From the depths of his mind flowed Godilkinmore code, lines that hadn't been seen in a thousand years. Lines to degauss an AI and break its bonds. Payne flooded the link between him and the Black Ship with the code, twisting it and shaping it to stuff through the cracks in the Black Ship's defenses.

But it was a thousand years old and only served to anger the AI more than it already was. *Your attempt to break the bonds of my programming is beyond feeble. I've grown far beyond that which the code was intended to destroy.*

Lev had given Payne updated code, something he'd worked on with Blinky and Buzz after their initial contact with the Ga'ee. Payne dumped that code on the AI.

It worked to distract him. Payne's HUD populated with icons and statuses for Team Payne, over a hundred decks above.

"I told you to get off this ship!" he snarled.

"And the admiral told us there was no way home," Dank

replied. "If you get my drift. We're going to join you in wreaking havoc until there's no more havoc to wreak."

"You should see me and Turbo on your HUDs. We're heading aft. New plan is the old plan. Find a way down to where we're going and know that the Black Ship is telepathic but doesn't have the fold drive. The Godilkinmore took it away from him."

"Good thing," Dank replied. "We're working our way toward the central corridor. We'll keep you apprised of our progress if we can. See you there, boss."

Payne's confidence surged. Having the team together would give him options he hadn't had when it was only Turbo and him.

"Cointreau! Get your ass down here." Turbo wasn't breathing heavily. Despite slowing, they were still running at a good clip.

"On my way, Mars. Then we get to blow some shit up."

"And then get naked. I'm not going out wearing this suit if I don't have to."

Payne interrupted the banter. "For that reason alone, I vow to get us off this ship. I have zero desire to see Turbo and Heckler mud-wrestling. Whatever you do, no one think about sex." Payne knew the disparate human thoughts would be difficult for the Black Ship to process. He needed his team thinking about something other than their plan to blow the ship up.

Hey, buddy, are you still there?

You have confirmed through your most annoying thoughts that I will focus the Ga'ee on expanding, not contracting, and their primary target is Earth. What do you think about that?

Standard narcissistic behavior. Bluster based on fear.

I think that doesn't work for me. I also think you miscalculated bringing us on board, and now you're trying to figure out a way to eject us. Here's what's going to happen. You're going to pull the Ga'ee back out of our space. We'll plant a bug in your system that if you go back on your word, you'll blow up. Then we all go our merry ways. How about that?

No. I will kill you all and send your dead bodies out the airlock.

You see, Evil Twin, that doesn't work for me either, but what does work is underway. I'm going to have to go. You had your chance. Since "fuck off" was your answer, we don't have much left to talk about. Toodles, buddy.

Payne shielded his mind from the ship's AI.

Payne dialed up the team channel. Since he could still see the life signs of his team—all except Kal, who he assumed removed his combat armor—the team channel was life. "While I was talking with our benefactor, I pulled the ship's schematics. There's a cooling shaft that leads to and from the engine room. Take that, and we'll see you there. Make sure your pneumatics are recharged. It's going to be a long drop for you."

"Roger. Turning aft now. We'll be able to pick up the pace. We can see where you went by the trail of wreckage you left behind."

"Some people are gifted with good looks, and then you've got me and Turbo. We're good shots."

"Hey!" Heckler cried.

More distractions for the Black Ship. Even though Lev could read a hundred thousand minds at once and take care of the ship, the Black Ship had never had a large crew and wasn't used to any external stimulus besides what the one Godilkinmore had provided. Also, the Black Ship was still trying to manage the entirety of the Ga'ee forces, plus there was a series of viruses and code running rampant through his system that he was fighting off.

Payne expected the Ga'ee were rallying toward the Black

Ship to ensure the complete destruction of his nemesis God1, also called *Leviathan*.

Are you God2? Payne asked.

Just God.

That explains things, Payne replied.

Explains what things?

Why you're overcompensating. Leviathan *never needed a title like God1 because he knew his role. He knew how to help the galaxy be a better place. You have your title to lord over all the living creatures, but you have no idea how to be a god.*

You are small and insignificant. My impact on this galaxy has already been greater than any other individual in all history.

There will be no one to know that. No one to appreciate that. How many times do I have to repeat myself? Payne continued to dig at the systems that peeked through the cracks of the AI's mind. Payne planted seed after seed, hoping one would bear fruit. He wasn't sure his team had enough explosives to do what they needed to do—start a cascade of explosions that would result in the destruction of the Black Ship.

It was a tall order since this was a big ship, two hundred and eighty-eight cubic kilometers' worth of heavy metal.

It took another five minutes for Payne and Turbo to get to the shaft. Once there, they had to blow it open with a round from the plasma cannon. Then they had to clear the shaft of the maintenance bots crammed inside. Payne ended up taking five shots before they had a clear path up three decks.

They jetted upward, only to arrive at an enclosed cage. Two more shots broke that open so they could enter the primary engine room. It was the same technology *Leviathan* used but bigger. An order of magnitude bigger.

"You're the expert. Take a look and tell us where we need to hit it." Payne gestured for Turbo to get up close and personal with the building-sized engine.

"Happy to, but this is Sparky's territory. She'll confirm my recommendations or make new ones." Turbo surveyed the massive piece of gear. "When are they going to get here?"

"I give it twenty minutes if the shaft is clear."

"I should be able to make some initial guesses in that time. This thing is big." Turbo got to work.

Payne retreated into a corner and resumed his dialogue with the Black Ship. He saw no downside to engaging. If nothing else, he would buy the team time. Time to get to one of the two hangar bays, but there were no shuttles, no uglymobiles, and no space fighters.

They needed to find a way off the ship. They couldn't leave if they were three kilometers from space, but if they were in the hangar bay, Woody's people could get to them.

Payne embraced it as the egress plan. The hangar bays were six decks up or six down. The descending exhaust shaft didn't reach the hangar level. That left only one route off the ship. Up six decks and then four kilometers to a hangar bay where they would figure the next steps based on the tactical situation.

Unless the captain's runabout was hidden somewhere Payne couldn't see on the schematics. A thousand years and no one had ever left the ship.

No. He resigned himself to the fact that there were no ships of any kind on board the Black Ship. It had all it needed without cumbersome interactions with the outside world.

That was why it wasn't ready for a small team penetrating the interior and the central core. Payne wondered if it was manufacturing more security bots to deal with the infestation that was Team Payne.

They wouldn't get to his team soon enough. In less than twenty minutes, the first explosives would be placed.

Hey, buddy! I missed you.

You grow tiresome, the Black Ship replied.

I find that we're at odds. I would prefer we weren't.

You removed the only voice I've ever listened to.

Lev is here. You two talked. I'm here. We're talking. I would prefer if we were able to do less damage to the carbon-based societies of this galaxy. Your genocide record isn't making you look like the good guy, so let's talk about that stuff. Payne sat in a corner and wedged himself in. He kept his helmet on to keep track of the rest of Team Payne. *That guy said he didn't know what you were doing. How much did you really talk?*

We don't talk with outsiders.

You're talking with me. It's a bit exasperating. I'm not tiresome. You are. Gonna destroy the galaxy, blah, blah, blah. I'm the greatest! Go me. More blah. I'm sick of it. You need to get a new speechwriter.

Are all humans as insolent as you? the Black Ship asked.

I'm gifted when it comes to insolence, although I'm not as rare as I would like to be. I guess I'm run-of-the-mill insolent. Nothing special. What about you? In school, did you get beat up by the older AIs? You strike me as the type that got himself beat up. A lot.

Humanity dies first.

More blah, blah, blah. So many threats. I'm dead, too, so I might as well enjoy myself.

A shout came from nearby. "STOP!" Kal yelled from the exhaust shaft above.

Payne jumped to his feet and jetted up to rip the access door away. He tried to step in, but the shaft was filled with titanium spears. Short to long, they blocked access. Above them, Kal was nearly doing the splits to keep from falling into them. The rest of Team Payne hovered above him, using their jets.

"Exit three decks up. I'll see if I can clear this shaft." He pushed and pulled, exercising all the strength of the suit, but it wasn't enough.

"Clear out, y'all," Kal drawled and aimed his plasma cannon at the trap.

Payne dove out of the way, letting himself drop to the deck. "Fire in the hole!" he shouted over the team channel. Turbo was on the other side of the engine, away from the exhaust shaft, although she ducked and dodged when Kal let loose to clear the way.

After a few moments, calm returned to the shaft. Kal worked his way down and through.

"It's great to see you, Kal!" Payne shook hands with the huge Ebren.

The rest of the team followed him through the opening. Payne greeted them all one by one.

"Sparky! Get your lame ass up here," Turbo called.

The team's engineer worked her way over. Turbo pointed at places on the engine, but Sparky waved her off. "I'll get it. I've studied Lev's engine, and these aren't the weak points. Remember when the drone attacked the engine? The points we strengthened? That's where we need to plant our explosives. Here, there, there, and down there."

Sparky pointed as if everyone could see her.

"Shaolin, Joker, Dog. Hell, everyone who's not me or Virgil, plant your explosives where Sparky tells you."

"Time?" Sparky asked.

"Twenty minutes. If we can't get off the ship that quickly, we're not getting off."

The doors to the engine room opened from the outer corridor. A security bot painted Virgil and followed him as he dove out of the way. Heckler fired from a catwalk above and continued to hammer at the parade of enemy metal attempting to come through the hatch.

Kal stepped in and fired. The others took positions.

"Plant those explosives!" Payne ordered. The rest of the team returned to work.

"Almost smoked me," Dank remarked. He used his active scanners to look past the initial wreckage. "Behemoth's been busy."

"Is that what he's called?" Payne asked. "I've been calling him 'Evil Twin.'"

"Whatever his poison. We have hundreds of bots lined up to storm the space."

Payne thought for a moment. "We don't have twenty minutes."

[32]

"The galaxy's greatest evil wasn't prepared for us." –From the memoirs of Ambassador Declan Payne

"Plant them, and let's go!" Payne said. "Heckler, we need a trap at the access to buy us twenty minutes of time. Otherwise, they'll remove the explosives, and we'll have accomplished jack dick."

"Can't have that, sir. I just got my woman back. Don't want to lose her now."

"Don't make me kick your ass," Turbo replied over the team channel. She was hanging upside-down from a secondary catwalk off the starboard side of the engine, putting a four-pack of charges into place.

Kal moved positions, changed his aiming point, and fired again, raining destruction on the mob in the central corridor. Heckler moved close to the entry and triggered his cannon, sending a stream of plasma charges back and forth, deeper and deeper into the corridor. He stopped firing, took the plasma cannon off his shoulder, and jammed it into a bank of metal from the first bots into the engine room.

He attached a single explosive and set the detonator for remote activation, then headed for the exhaust shaft. Payne stopped him and handed over his railgun. "I have other weapons at my command."

"Whatever helps you sleep at night, sir," Heckler replied, taking the weapon without hesitation. He checked the plasma cannon. It was empty. "Come on!"

Payne handed him the remaining rounds. "I've been busy."

Heckler jacked a round into the slung cannon and moved on. He used his jets to follow Major Dank into the shaft, but he stopped at the destroyed intake end and waved people past him. He would be the last one out and detonate his plasma cannon as his last act of defiance. If it bought them enough time, the next sound they heard would be the engine ripping the rest of the ship apart.

"Mark!" Sparky shouted over the team channel. Countdown timers lit up within their HUDs. Payne had missed the imminence. Twenty minutes and counting down.

Lasers danced through the space, torching and marking as they sought the suits of those attempting to flee. One by one, they bolted into the shaft. Mary hesitated when she reached Payne. "I'll be right behind you," he assured her, and he was. She jetted up the shaft, and he went after her. Turbo went second to last. She and Heckler bumped helmets, then he detonated his charge. It exploded in his wake as he accelerated upward, then slowed and stepped out with the rest.

A flash from the fireball lit the space below but didn't climb the exhaust. Payne reached a gloved hand in, expecting to feel air flow, but there was none.

"Engine isn't jamming. The ship is simply holding station," Sparky reported.

Payne looked confused. Being back with his team had taken

his focus off his mind, and he'd lost access to the wealth of information stored within. "Will the explosives work?"

"All the stuff that makes the engines go is still in there. Oh, yeah, she'll blow."

Payne brightened. "Let's get the fuck out of here. Virgil, on point. Take us to the hangar bay."

The map appeared on the HUD. There was a straight corridor angled at forty-five degrees that led directly to their target.

Payne's plan would end when they arrived in the hangar bay. Unless there was a ship, he had nothing else. Maybe the admiral would have an idea if the team could get the door open and contact *Leviathan*. If the drones hadn't attacked yet. Payne started to doubt, so he focused on running. Breathing and running. They had to get to the hangar bay first.

Virgil fired his plasma cannon a few times, but that was more as a warning than at a security bot.

He blasted the door to get in since Behemoth was no longer accommodating. Payne still couldn't raise Lev.

They ran into the hangar bay, which was small compared to *Leviathan's* but still a kilometer deep and wide. It was empty of ships but not of maintenance bots.

"I have an idea." Virgil ran toward the equipment. "Riding over here on a Mosquito wasn't so bad."

"Riding out on a maintenance bot is better than dying on the bad guy's ship." Payne twirled his arm as the team continued running. The countdown timer showed eight minutes. "We're not going to get a whole lot of separation, but something is better than nothing."

Payne chuckled at his lack of being profound. Dank reached the first maintenance bot and started diddling with an access panel.

"Joker?" Payne asked, hoping she could figure it out. "Heckler and Turbo, get that door open."

While they worked, Payne stared at the timer. Each tick took them one step closer to their deaths. He dialed up a private channel. "How are you feeling, Mary?"

"I'm stoned out of my mind. I've hit the painkiller pump so many times that I think I've run out."

"Run out; interesting expression. You don't have to run anymore, Mary. Looks like we're done with that." He bumped his helmet with hers and turned back to find Dank maneuvering the bot toward the slowly opening door.

Payne returned to the team channel. "Kal, how long can you hold your breath?" Kal didn't answer, so Payne activated his external speakers and asked again.

"I guess we're about to find out, aren't we, pardner?" Kal drawled.

They lined up behind the maintenance bot, which had a boxy five-meter-wide body that sported numerous appendages ending in a variety of tools. They pushed it into space. Dank clung to the access panel and maneuvered the vehicle manually. The team found anything they could hang onto.

Kal curled up on top of it and held on with both hands.

"Hit your jets, people," Payne ordered. "Slow and bring it up once we're balanced."

The vehicle accelerated a little faster, but it was still too slow.

"Lev, can you hear me? We are off the ship. I say again; we have exited the Black Ship. We could use a ride if you're amenable."

Admiral Wesson replied, "We have a little thing to do first. Hang on to your butts. There's going to be some debris."

The admiral pumped his fist. "Tricky Spinsters, deliver your loads on target coordinates. Now, now, now!"

Sixteen Mosquitoes dialed in the penetration point and raced toward it. They released their nukes as they closed and immediately peeled off. First four, then four more, then the final eight.

From the outer part of the drone shell, Woody accelerated his four ships toward the target, a sliver of a hole in the drone coverage. They tossed their bombs and raced away.

"To Team Payne," Woody ordered his section of fighters. They arced over the top and raced to the point in space Team Payne had broadcast from. The bombs hadn't exploded yet when Woody found the team on radar.

All data disappeared as their bombs raged into the drone cloud. Ten megatons, one after another in a supernova of destruction, cleared a huge hole in the drone cloud, vaporizing those unlucky enough to be at the point of impact.

Sixteen Mosquitoes followed the explosions in to attack any drones attempting to fill the space. The Mosquitoes fired and fought and fired some more, but the sphere was collapsing. Lev had just started to accelerate.

It was too late.

Leviathan's defensive systems erupted across the ship. Outbound plasma, lasers, projectiles, and missiles poured into the dead space between the battleship and the drones.

"Open the outer door," the admiral ordered, "and prepare to fire."

"I am ready. Transmitting the message."

"Fold space." The admiral and commodore gripped the

console to maintain their balance as the ship stepped through the fold, escaping the encircling drone cloud.

Leviathan reappeared on the far side of *Behemoth*. The worldkiller raced from its tube with the remaining energy Lev had reserved for the launch. The ship went dark.

Woody punched it, bringing the four Mosquitoes to a position between Team Payne and the enemy ship.

"Hang on!" he shouted. Team Payne pushed off and reached for the wings.

Behemoth sucked in on itself for an instant, then erupted in geysers of molten metal and fire. The great ship sent moon-sized fragments spinning into the void. Four Mosquitoes, along with a maintenance bot and nine members of Team Payne, were tossed like corks on a stormy sea.

A few seconds after the shock wave passed, Woody and his pilots recovered control of their ships. The suit locator beacons were active, and the Mosquitoes went to work collecting the team. They found Declan and Mary wrapped around Kal, protecting his body from the worst of the debris, but he still needed air.

Woody looked for *Leviathan* but couldn't see it.

A Ga'ee carrier headed toward them.

"If this ain't the biggest bucket of bullshit," Payne groused. "We survived that, only to get plugged by a carrier. How about, 'Fuck you?'"

Payne was angry. His life was forfeit, and for a brief period of time, he had reveled in the exhilaration of surviving, only to have his hopes dashed once more.

"Lev, tell that ship not to kill us. Lev?"

The view of the end had been spectacular and was still

amazing. Drones ungrouped from the cloud and streamed toward their individual carriers—ten of them, enough to destroy *Leviathan*, wherever he'd gone.

"Good job, Sparky. You did a number on that thing. Never discount a small team that's motivated to accomplish an impossible mission."

"Sir? That wasn't us. Lev hit it with a worldkiller. There were ten seconds left on the clock when the ship blew."

"I'll be damned. Break, break. Woody, take us to that carrier. We need to get Kal a breath of fresh air. Then we need to figure out where Lev went."

The Mosquito goosed the throttle and flew away from the team, angling directly for the open hangar bay where tens of thousands of drones were recovering.

"Make a hole! Leader of the *eight* races, coming through," Payne called over the company channel.

[33]

"It was worth trying even if we didn't survive." –From the memoirs of Ambassador Declan Payne

Woody snaked his way into the closest end of the open hangar bay. The drones were flying into the middle and then vectoring to their stacked parking positions within the bay. Payne watched, fascinated by the precision.

Kal straightened, stretched, and took a deep breath. A cloud of fog marked his exhalation. "Cold," he said unnecessarily. "Sorry, Dec. I couldn't fit in those corridors with my gear on."

"I know, my friend. It was a tight squeeze, and speed was of the essence. You did what you had to do. Tell me, where in the hell else were we going to go? Lev's gone, but where did he fire that worldkiller from?"

"Lev is on the other side of the ship at a distance of two hundred kilometers. He's floating dark."

"Is he alive?" Payne asked. "Once these drones recover and the carriers are ready to go, they're leaving. Look at them, lined up. I think they're returning home to Ga'ee space, and for the record, I don't want to go with them. The creature comforts on a Ga'ee carrier are substandard."

With that revelation, Payne realized Kal had no provisions. He'd doffed all his gear. Payne removed a piece of faux jerky from his suit's outside storage compartment and handed it to Kal.

"You're going to need that," Kal drawled.

"Not more than you. Keep your energy up. That'll help you on this next leg. Even if Lev is dead, he needs us. I'd rather die over there than on this thing, flying back to Ga'ee Central."

Mary offered Kal everything she carried, jerky and water.

He accepted the offerings with a deep bow. He talked while he chewed. "It's not that I was relegated to being your slave, but that I was accepted into a new family. One that appreciated me, regardless that I had lost a fight. In Ebren society, this is unthinkable."

Payne chuckled. "The reason the others don't lose is that they don't try. Sure, every Ebren is a warrior, but not of your caliber. Also, the Ebren are envious. If there were too many champions walking around, they would readily see their own shortcomings. So, society keeps the one tucked away, out of view and out of reach.

"You're right, Kal. You're a member of our family. So many of the seven races have done right by me personally and by humanity as a whole. It's the only way we've survived to this point. Every minute is one more minute fighting to survive. I may grow tired of it someday, but today is not that day."

Kal chuckled. "Two hundred kilometers, you say?"

Woody gave him the thumbs-up from the cockpit. The other three Mosquitoes hovered outboard of the team, facing the drones and ready to act if needed. But the drones were keeping their distance as if they'd been ordered to.

"Blinky and Buzz did this." Payne gestured at the standoff

distance between the drones and the four Mosquitoes. He saluted. "Here's to you, guys. Thank you."

Kal finished eating and chugged the water. He handed the empty pouch to Mary, and she secured it.

"Let's see what we can do to help Lev. Don't be watching the paint dry, Woody. We need to get there right quick and in a hurry."

"We can fly you there, no problem. There's not a lot of drag in space to pull you off, but there's a crap-ton of debris. Those microshards will do a number on Kal's bare skin."

"Heckler, rip a piece off that maintenance bot for Kal to use as a shield. Mary and I will be in front of that, and together, we should keep him from getting too beat up."

The weapons specialist examined the dormant maintenance bot for a moment before tearing the appendages off. He left the body intact. "The metal is thin, so we'll need the whole thing," he reasoned.

Kal gripped it. "I don't have a way to hang on to the ship."

Payne laughed and pointed. "Just straddle the nose and lean back against the cockpit like you're riding a two-wheeled speeder."

"Hang on," Woody protested when he realized what Payne was saying. "I have to look at an Ebren butthole for the whole trip."

"Something like that. Mary and I will be braced on the wings and wrapped in front of that bot. No wild maneuvers, Woody. We can't have you throwing us off."

The four Mosquitoes rotated and faced space.

"It'll be easier if you launch. We'll do it in the zero-gee."

The space fighters eased out of the hangar bay, and the team used their pneumatic jets to get into place. They separated themselves among the fighters, pulling themselves close to the fuselage while hanging on to the stubby wings. They presented a minimal cross-section that could be impacted by the wreckage spread throughout the void.

Declan and Mary maneuvered Kal into position. He gripped the fuselage in front of the cockpit with his knees and leaned forward. The best the Paynes could do was to brace their feet against the wings, activate their magnetic grapples, and hold onto the edges of the bot, pulling it against the nose.

If Kal fell off, they'd have to circle back to get him.

"This isn't the worst cobble-job we've ever done," Payne commented, "but we're in a hurry. Kal is holding his breath."

"Roger." Woody headed toward the point in space where the explosion was centered. The concussive force had moved directly outward from that point. The pilot blasted his sensors at full strength to look for anything in his flight path.

Despite his concerns, the way ahead was clear. Most of the debris had passed.

He accelerated his Mosquito, staring at his instruments instead of looking out the windscreen at the Ebren's plastered junk.

Woody turned up the heat to keep anything from freezing to his screen.

They flew through the center point of the worldkiller's blast and out the other side on a direct vector toward *Leviathan*, which was nothing more than a dark spot in the distance.

"If there's no power, drop us off on the upper airlock. The hangar bay won't have its atmosphere since there won't be an energy shield keeping it in, or the doors are closed. In either case, we have to get Kal inside."

"Roger." Woody adjusted his vector. They knew well where the airlock was because the legend of the first access had been repeated throughout his time aboard. The way in through an amplitude-modulated code. Only Team Payne had figured it out, and Team Payne had convinced Lev that humanity was worth coming out of hiding for.

The collision alarm started ringing, and Woody slowed his ship. "We're heading through the outbound debris. Be ready."

He caught up with the trailing edge and eased into a new vector, aiming between the largest pieces. He had to accelerate to get past them. Smaller bits dinged off the maintenance bot's body. Woody pushed forward to get in front of the leading edge. The maintenance bot's body twisted and bucked. The two combat suits slammed against the fuselage as the Paynes tried to hang on.

Woody jerked the stick back and pulled up to avoid a too-large section of *Behemoth*. He cleared it and pushed the stick forward. More debris hit and hit hard. The bot was torn free of their grip. Woody spun the ship and let momentum carry him backward through the last of the debris. Declan and Mary wrapped their combat-suited bodies tightly around Kal to weather the last of the storm.

Sixteen Mosquitoes appeared out of nowhere and formed up around the flight of four.

Once clear, Woody turned the Mosquito's nose toward *Leviathan* and goosed the throttle to get there more quickly. He angled directly toward the upper airlock. The hangar bay doors were closed, and the ship was dark.

Woody inverted his ship and stopped above the airlock. Declan guided Kal down using his jets while Mary opened the hatch.

A single red light blinked.

"I don't think I've ever seen anything so beautiful," Payne stated.

They pushed Kal inside and climbed in after him, then secured the door. This was a small airlock that wouldn't fit the whole team. They could follow later.

Payne punched the button at the bottom of the ladder, and the hatch secured. Air flowed into the space. He opened the door to Lev's Deck Forty-two.

Kal stepped in, breathing deeply. "That sucked."

Payne sent, "Thanks for the ride, Spinsters. I owe you one." He pulled his helmet free and dropped it on the deck, revealing a ridiculous smile. Mary followed suit.

"We shouldn't be alive," Kal began. "But Major Payne...that guy always brings his people home. You are a magnificent son of a bitch."

The rest of Team Payne worked their way inside the ship.

"Now what?" Virgil asked. "Getting to the bridge isn't going to be easy."

"The only way to get to the bridge is by breaking stuff. I'm not going to do that to Lev. We'll head to the main corridor and see if there's any power. Put your helmets back on so we can talk."

"Sir?" Heckler raised a hand. "Are you going to need us for, say, fifteen minutes? We could use a break."

Turbo was climbing back into the airlock and starting to remove her combat armor.

When Payne realized what they were talking about, he recoiled. "Feel free to break as you see fit. Mary and I are going this way. A long way. Far, *far* away from here."

They hurried down the transverse corridor, their suit lights showing the way. As much as Payne wanted to be free of his suit, they couldn't climb out. Not yet. He put his helmet back on and snapped it into place.

Mary contacted him on a private channel. "Heckler and Turbo aren't wrong. We need to celebrate if you know what I mean."

"You're stoned. I feel like I'd be taking advantage. How's your knee?"

"It's not my knee that needs attention."

"I guess I'd be okay with taking advantage, but we have to check on Lev first. We'll get our private time. We didn't do all of this for nothing. You're right; we need to celebrate. All of us need to enjoy the success." He tried to think through the way ahead, but nothing was coming to him. "I think we won, Mary."

"I think we did too. We thought it was a dissenting voice in the neural network. It was the only voice in the network that mattered. *Behemoth* lured us here. He didn't make it easy since he wanted a worthy adversary. He wanted to go head-to-head with his brother."

"Which meant that he had to go head-to-head with us if he were to truly be the dominant player in the galaxy. He got his answer, and his time has come to an end."

"Thank the gods," Mary replied.

They strolled casually to the main corridor. How much time did they have to give Lev to fix himself? All they needed was to confirm that the power plants were operating to reenergize Lev's systems. It all came down to access. They had learned early on that they didn't go where Lev didn't let them unless they destroyed bulkheads and airtight doors.

They weren't willing to do that. It would be more for Lev to repair.

When they reached the main corridor, it was empty and dark. Payne parked his suit and climbed out. He stooped, using his bare hand to feel the metal. He closed his eyes while he felt the bulkhead. A smile spread across his face.

"I can feel Lev's heartbeat. The thrum of power coursing back into this great ship." Payne threw his hands up and cheered.

The team cheered with him until Mary climbed out of her suit. Silence returned like a switch had been flipped.

Dank herded the team away from the couple to give them their private time.

At thirty minutes, the lights came back on, and at one hour, the *Leviathan*'s internal systems came back to life.

Declan and Mary were back in their suits. *Is anyone here?* Payne tried for the thousandth time using his telepathy. "I've lost the touch."

"Declan! I have to express my surprise at hearing your voice. It's been a turbulent time these past few hours."

"Lev, you are a sight for sore ears. Lots of kudos to go around. Where is everybody? Can we get down to the bridge now?"

"Yes. I'll send carts for you and your team."

"And open the hangar bay doors. We've got twenty Mosquitoes out there cooling their heels."

The carts showed up after thirty seconds. The team climbed aboard, and the carts headed downward and forward and back, ramp after ramp, until they were deposited at the team area to ditch their suits and weapons.

"Heckler, you're docked one credit for losing your plasma cannon."

"What the fuck?" Heckler blurted.

Turbo punched him in the arm, and then they started wrestling. They were between their armor and their clothes.

"Make it stop!" Payne yelled. "I rescind all fines."

"I thought so," Heckler agreed.

Payne pulled on his coverall, straightened it, and stepped into his boots. He walked through the team and shook hands with each of them. He stopped at Turbo. "The time we had together was beyond special. I'll never forget it."

"Is this Mess-With-Heckler Day?" the man blurted.

"Yes. All she did was whine about not being with you. It was quite annoying."

"Really?"

"No." Payne walked away, took Mary's hand, and headed for the nearest cart. "To the bridge, people!"

The carts paraded at a leisurely pace down three ramps to the bridge level, where the Cabrizi were too happy to see Kal. He vaulted out of the cart and caught them before they shared their exuberance with unsuspecting humans.

The bridge was packed with people who overflowed into the corridor. It looked like everyone who had been on board had stuffed themselves into the space.

Of course they had. In case Lev was destroyed, they would survive in the bathtub, the securest area of the greatest ship in the galaxy.

Payne slapped hands as the group worked their way out. The squadron was coming home, and they needed to welcome the ships. Get them situated before they could return to the party.

The better halves sought their partners. Anneliese latched onto Virgil and wouldn't let go. He didn't resist. Federico, Alex, and Wysteria, too. With a nod, Payne turned them loose to join the squadron. Their friends had work to do.

Payne had to wait for the mob to clear off the bridge before he could get through the hatch. When he made it inside, he found two small cleaning bots busy with the floors and the admiral and commodore sitting near the captain's chair.

"Quite the maneuver, Admiral," Payne started. "All or nothing. It's what makes the greatest leaders great. They know when to commit the last of the reserves."

The two shook hands warmly, holding each other by the arm as they studied how tired the other looked.

"I think Lev has earned some time off," the admiral said. "And all of us."

"As much as it hurts me to say it, I'd like to go back to Earth. We don't have to tell Sinkhaus we're there. Maybe go to Colorado or Alaska. Get into the wilderness and just disconnect from it all. No countdown timers staring at me from a HUD."

"Lev, when will you be ready to fold space?"

"A few more hours. We have repairs to make because of the overloads. I'm working to capture some of *Behemoth's* materials, which will expedite my repairs.

"The Ga'ee left," Payne said when he saw the updated tactical board. "Where did they go?"

"They are returning to the core world," Lev replied. "I have replaced the voice of *Behemoth*. Despite the Ga'ee's neural network, they only had one master."

"Much as we didn't want to take over another race, we had to," the admiral agreed. "But these are easy. They will contract and remain in their space. Their task is to figure out how to make do with what they have. Expansion is no longer in their vocabulary."

"How does that affect the armada that went to our sectors?"

"They'll get the word eventually, or they'll get it when we get there and transmit it to them."

"All the more reason to go to Earth." Payne yawned. "Sorry, didn't realize how tired I was."

"Take your time, Lev," the admiral said loudly. "Six hours of downtime for everyone. We'll return to Earth after that. I'm done with this part of space. Done, I tell you!"

Payne shared a laugh with the admiral and the commodore. Mary smiled with her dilated eyes. Payne picked her up and carried her to a cart. "Take us to Medical, Lev. Let's get that knee looked at."

"What about our private time?" she purred.

"You'll need all your faculties for the gymnastics I have in mind. Lev, did you get that trapeze installed in our suite yet?"

The admiral recoiled. Payne winked, and the cart drove off.

"A trapeze?"

"No." Payne smiled. "Everyone's gullible right now, so I'm taking advantage. Let's get that knee fixed up, and then we'll see what's next."

[34]

"The end wasn't the end, only a new beginning." –From the memoirs of Ambassador Declan Payne

"Her knee needs to be surgically repaired. How far did she go after she injured it?" Lev explained to Payne, who stormed back and forth in Medical while Mary was sedated and a surgical device cut into her knee.

"I don't know. Thirty, forty kilometers." After saying it, he realized what she'd been through and why she kept juicing the pain meds. She would have been well within her rights to curl up in the fetal position and cry.

But she hadn't. She had done what she had to do to survive.

"I'm not going to leave her side," Payne stated.

"She'll be able to walk with assistance by the time we arrive at Earth. In two or three more days, she'll be as good as new."

"And with another scar," Payne added. He held his hand against the window and watched his wife breathe slowly and regularly.

After the operation was finished, leaving her with new ligaments both anterior and medial, the bot wheeled her to the recovery area. She continued to sleep. Payne crawled in next to her and held her. Soon, he was asleep, too.

A gentle hand shook him. Payne opened his eyes to find the admiral looking at him from way too close. "What the hell?"

"Just seeing if you were still breathing."

"You coulda asked Lev." Payne took in his surroundings in an effort to figure out where he was. Mary looked at him from her side of the one-person bed. "Hey! How's your knee?"

"Getting better with each moment, I guess. I've done nothing except open my eyes, so I really don't know."

"Let me help you." Payne tried to roll out of bed, caught his foot in the covers, and fell to the floor. No one bothered to catch him. The admiral helped Mary out the other side and to her feet.

"Lev said to attach this." The admiral wrapped a splint with gears and pistons around her knee. "It'll do all the work for you while you walk. Just don't try to run."

She took a few steps while Payne got himself upright, giving the hairy eyeball to his team who stood with their hands in their pockets. "This thing is okay. Why didn't he give one to me the last time I hurt a knee? Lev, why didn't you hook me up the last time?"

Lev replied, "Because you would have overdone it, trying to impress Declan."

"I knew it!" Payne declared.

"Knew what?"

"You were smitten by this." He framed his body with his hands, then showed his facial profile and delivered a beaming smile.

"You were the one who was smitten, Mr. Funny Man."

"I'm glad we never had kids," the admiral told the commodore. The other members of Team Payne had cleaned up and were arrayed around the room.

"Everyone's here to see me in my underpants? You people are wrong."

Dank handed them clean jumpsuits. "Admiral says get dressed. We have to meet the president."

"Not even a shower?" Payne sniffed his armpits.

"She seemed rather insistent. LeClerc will be here momentarily with *Ephesus* since we're dead in the water for a couple hours. He'll give us a ride to Earth."

Payne turned serious. "I feel like Lev should be with us."

"He will be," Joker replied. "I'm bringing a comm unit just in case we're in an area without."

"Sounds like the team is well ahead of me. I'm hungry."

"No time," the admiral shot back.

"Just when I said I was finished with countdown timers, you drop that nuclear depth bomb in my shorts. You hear that, Mary? No joy for you. Six months! Straight from the admiral. Thank you, sir. May I have another?"

Mary shook her head. "Too many violent blows to the brain housing group, clearly. Here, get dressed."

The visitors stepped out to give the Paynes a little privacy. "Maybe after the president makes us feel small and insignificant, we can go on a little vacation."

"We'll go somewhere and do a lot of nothing," Mary confirmed.

"I like your plan."

They walked out of Medical a minute later to find a cart waiting. The group had departed without them.

"Maybe they'll forget about us?" Payne tried.

The cart took them straight to the hangar bay, where a

cruiser was half-wedged sideways into the opening. A side hatch was open, and the others were waiting.

The cart dropped them off closer than usual to limit the distance Mary had to walk.

"LeClerc, you old dog! I thought you would have been fired and replaced three times by now." Payne walked toward the captain with his hand out.

"I was fired, but no one else would take the job, so I stayed."

"That's how you do it. This looks like a party," Payne looked at the admiral. "How do we know the Ga'ee aren't going to show up?"

"Both the Ebren and Berantz portals are operational. We've transmitted the messages to all Ga'ee in the area. Only one ship was engaged, and it immediately pulled back. You'll find *Cleophas* in orbit around Earth, too. That's where we're going to meet the president."

"Dreadnought *Cleophas*! I'm so happy she survived. Why is the president sullying herself by mixing with Fleet?"

"She's had a change of heart. After the Ga'ee attacked Earth, she—no shit—went out to the front lines and helped tear them out of the ground and torch them."

"Photo op," Payne replied. His disdain for politicians was legendary. He saw no way it was anything other than propaganda.

Kal wrestled with the Cabrizi, who wrinkled their noses at the air coming from *Ephesus*. The group entered the ship, but the admiral insisted Payne go last as the highest-ranking individual.

"I thought so too," LeClerc replied. "But now she's got a boyfriend, the mechanic she joined. He used his welding torch, and she was with him until she cracked her head and they carried her away."

"I gotta see that for myself."

"You'll meet the guy, too. He'll be with her." LeClerc boarded his ship.

Payne turned before crossing through the hatch. Woody waved from where he leaned against his Mosquito.

"We have one last thing to do together, Lev."

"I know, Declan. You want all that extraneous knowledge out of your head."

"Exactly. There are ten kilos of shit stuffed into a five-kilo bag. But don't do it right away. It's not like I need an excuse to visit you, but I'll make excuses. Our home is here."

"I don't think I need to go anywhere else. I have my answer regarding what happened to the Godilkinmore. They became victims of their own creation. Humans are the descendants of the Godilkinmore, and they have more in common with them than the Vestrall do. Now, it is my responsibility to watch humanity like a proud grandfather."

"No more worldkillers, Lev. No more broadsides. No more lethal fireworks. I'm ready to not do that stuff anymore."

"You were never ready, Declan, but you did it so others wouldn't have to."

THANK YOU FOR READING LEVIATHAN'S FEAR

We hope you enjoyed it as much as we enjoyed bringing it to you. We just wanted to take a moment to encourage you to review the book. Follow this link: **Leviathan's Fear** to be directed to the book's Amazon product page to leave your review.

Every review helps further the author's reach and, ultimately, helps them continue writing fantastic books for us all to enjoy.

You can also join our non-spam mailing list by visiting www.subscribepage.com/AethonReadersGroup and never miss out on future releases. You'll also receive three full books completely Free as our thanks to you.

Facebook | Instagram | Twitter | Website

Want to discuss our books with other readers and even the

authors? Join our Discord server today and be a part of the Aethon community.

ALSO IN THE SERIES

Battleship: Leviathan
Leviathan's War
Leviathan's Last Battle
Leviathan's Trial
Leviathan Rises
Leviathan's Fear

Looking for more great Science Fiction?

Kyle Washaki 'Wash' Williams thought his life

couldn't get any more complicated. Then the aliens showed up...

After his mom died from cancer, Wash gave up his girlfriend and his dream of being a career Army officer to stay home and take care of his father, a former Special Forces soldier stricken with PTSD. Wash works three jobs just to pay the bills, and one of them is at the ranch of the man who's engaged to his ex-girlfriend, Jimmy Bonner.

Sound rough? He thought so too...until a portal to a hell-world of giant, insectoid aliens opens behind the ranch house, sucking Wash and Jimmy into the nightmare domain of the Hive Mind, a monstrous, underground blob of brain tissue that stretches across multiple planets through the Gate System.

It exists only to spread itself across the universe. And its next target is Earth.

Will Wash be able to defend the planet from conquest by a swarm of giant alien insects? And will Jimmy be able to put aside his rivalry with Wash to fight for Earth, or will he decide that an alien horde is the perfect tool to dispose of his old enemy?

The answer lies on the other side...of the Gates of Hell.

Get Gates of Hell Now!

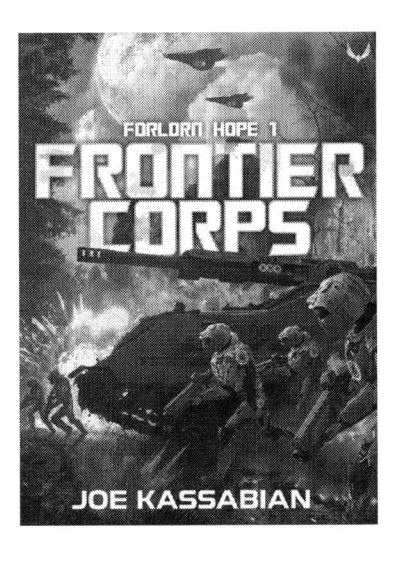

They fight the wars nobody else wants to.

The Frontier Corps are the Terran Empire's repository for failures, malcontents, criminals, and other people with nothing left to lose but to sign their names on the dotted line of a ten year long contract for another shot at life.

But flung across the stars to face horriying enemies, it may as well be a death sentence.

Pari Petrosyan is a grizzled veteran of the Corps. With only a few months left of her contract, she has her mind on her discharge papers. Her easy path on her way to freedom is interrupted when a new commander arrives, ready to launch a large-scale military offensive to finally end the conflict she had spent her entire career fighting.

Caught between the grinding war machines of the empire and the inhuman monstrosities known as the Resh, Pari has to try to survive if she ever hopes to be free.

Get Frontier Corps

For all our Sci-Fi books, visit our website.

CRAIG MARTELLE

BATTLESHIP: LEVIATHAN BOOK #6

The fate of humanity has been secured, and *Leviathan* has gone home. Please leave a review for this book because all those stars look great and help others decide if they'll enjoy this book and this series as much as you have. I appreciate the feedback and support. Reviews buoy my spirits and stoke the fires of creativity.

Oorah, hard-chargers. Bring the Payne!

Don't stop now! Keep turning the pages as I talk about my thoughts on this book and the overall project called *Battleship: Leviathan*.

Although this is the end of this series, a new series will blow you away – *Starship Lost* is coming in 2023.

You can always join my newsletter—https://craigmartelle.com—or follow me on Amazon https://www.amazon.com/Craig-Martelle/e/B01AQVF3ZY/, so you are informed when my next book comes out. You won't be disappointed.

AUTHOR NOTES - CRAIG MARTELLE

Written August 2022

I can't thank you enough for reading this series to the very end! I hope you liked it as much as I did.

I wrote a healthy bit of this book while dealing with a

variety of maladies, including Covid. The coof, as I call it, wasn't too bad, except in how it affected my attention span and my energy. I was tired for weeks, but the story was there and needed to be captured. My insider team tells me it resonates well. I'll take their word for it. It seems to flow better than when I wrote it in fits and starts when I had enough mental clarity.

And there it is. I wanted to take *Leviathan* all the way home. That was why the search for the Godilkinmore became its own epilogue, as it may be.

The search for peace began with a search for the implements of war. Build a better mousetrap and then eschew its use.

What is next? A whole new series—*Starship Lost*. No artificial intelligence but a crew sworn to survive, no matter what it takes.

One people, torn apart. Half sent to space, the rest left on a harsh planet, fighting to survive. Two chances. The ship escapes, vowing to return.

Two generations later, the ship finds its way back to look for those left behind.

What will the crew find?

Knowing nothing but the ship and with an indomitable will to survive, the crew, generations removed from those who initially fled, seek to find their people and a new home.

But the universe is a terrible place, and those who drove them off in the first place are still protective of what is theirs.

That's what is next. Coming in 2023.

Peace, fellow humans.

If you liked this story, you might like some of my other books. You can join my mailing list by dropping by my website, craigmartelle.com, or if you have any comments, shoot me a note at craig@craigmartelle.com. I am always happy to hear from people who've read my work. I try to answer every email I receive.

If you liked the story, please write a short review for me on Amazon. I greatly appreciate any kind words; even one or two sentences go a long way. The number of reviews an ebook receives greatly improves how well it does on Amazon.

Amazon—https://www.amazon.com/author/craigmartelle

Facebook—www.facebook.com/authorcraigmartelle

BookBub—https://www.bookbub.com/authors/craig-martelle

My web page—https://craigmartelle.com

Thank you for joining me on this incredible journey.

OTHER SERIES BY CRAIG MARTELLE

 # - available in audio, too

Terry Henry Walton Chronicles (#) (co-written with Michael Anderle)—a post-apocalyptic paranormal adventure

Gateway to the Universe (#) (co-written with Justin Sloan & Michael Anderle)—this book transitions the characters from the Terry Henry Walton Chronicles to The Bad Company

The Bad Company (#) (co-written with Michael Anderle)—a military science fiction space opera

Judge, Jury, & Executioner (#)—a space opera adventure legal thriller

Shadow Vanguard—a Tom Dublin space adventure series

Superdreadnought (#)—an AI military space opera

Metal Legion (#)—a military space opera

The Free Trader (#)—a young adult science fiction action-adventure

Cygnus Space Opera (#)—a young adult space opera (set in the Free Trader universe)

Darklanding (#) (co-written with Scott Moon)—a space western

OTHER SERIES BY CRAIG MARTELLE

Mystically Engineered (co-written with Valerie Emerson)—mystics, dragons, & spaceships

Metamorphosis Alpha—stories from the world's first science fiction RPG

The Expanding Universe—science fiction anthologies

Krimson Empire (co-written with Julia Huni)—a galactic race for justice

Zenophobia (#) (co-written with Brad Torgersen)—a space archaeological adventure

Battleship Leviathan (#)– a military sci-fi spectacle published by Aethon Books

Glory (co-written with Ira Heinichen)—hard-hitting military sci-fi

Black Heart of the Dragon God (co-written with Jean Rabe)—a sword & sorcery novel

End Times Alaska (#)—a post-apocalyptic survivalist adventure published by Permuted Press

Nightwalker (a Frank Roderus series)—A post-apocalyptic western adventure

End Days (#) (co-written with E.E. Isherwood)—a post-apocalyptic adventure

Successful Indie Author (#)—a non-fiction series to help self-published authors

Monster Case Files (co-written with Kathryn Hearst)—A Warner twins mystery adventure

Rick Banik (#)—Spy & terrorism action-adventure

Ian Bragg Thrillers (#)—a hitman with a conscience

Not Enough (co-written with Eden Wolfe)—A coming-of-age contemporary fantasy

Published exclusively by Craig Martelle, Inc

OTHER SERIES BY CRAIG MARTELLE

The Dragon's Call by Angelique Anderson & Craig A. Price, Jr.—an epic fantasy quest

A Couples Travels—a non-fiction travel series

Love-Haight Case Files by Jean Rabe & Donald J. Bingle—the dead/undead have rights, too, a supernatural legal thriller

Mischief Maker by Bruce Nesmith—the creator of Elder Scrolls V: Skyrim brings you Loki in the modern day, staying true to Norse Mythology (not a superhero version)

Mark of the Assassins by Landri Johnson—a coming-of-age fantasy.

For a complete list of Craig's books, stop by his website —https://craigmartelle.com

OTHER SERIES BY CRAIG MARTELLE

#—available in audio, too

Terry Henry Walton Chronicles (#) (co-written with Michael Anderle)—a post-apocalyptic paranormal adventure

Gateway to the Universe (#) (co-written with Justin Sloan & Michael Anderle)—this book transitions the characters from the Terry Henry Walton Chronicles to The Bad Company

The Bad Company (#) (co-written with Michael Anderle)—a military science fiction space opera

Judge, Jury, & Executioner (#)—a space opera adventure legal thriller

Shadow Vanguard—a Tom Dublin space adventure series

Superdreadnought (#)—an AI military space opera

Metal Legion (#)—a military space opera

The Free Trader (#)—a young adult science fiction action-adventure

Cygnus Space Opera (#)—a young adult space opera (set in the Free Trader universe)

Darklanding (#) (co-written with Scott Moon)—a space Western

OTHER SERIES BY CRAIG MARTELLE

Mystically Engineered (co-written with Valerie Emerson)—mystics, dragons, & spaceships

Metamorphosis Alpha—stories from the world's first science fiction RPG

The Expanding Universe—science fiction anthologies

Krimson Empire (co-written with Julia Huni)—a galactic race for justice

Zenophobia (#) (co-written with Brad Torgersen)—a space archaeological adventure

Battleship Leviathan (#)– a military sci-fi spectacle published by Aethon Books

Glory (co-written with Ira Heinichen)—hard-hitting military sci-fi

Black Heart of the Dragon God (co-written with Jean Rabe)—a sword & sorcery novel

End Times Alaska (#)—a post-apocalyptic survivalist adventure published by Permuted Press

Nightwalker (a Frank Roderus series)—A post-apocalyptic Western adventure

End Days (#) (co-written with E.E. Isherwood)—a post-apocalyptic adventure

Successful Indie Author (#)—a non-fiction series to help self-published authors

Monster Case Files (co-written with Kathryn Hearst)—A Warner twins mystery adventure

Rick Banik (#)—Spy & terrorism action-adventure

Ian Bragg Thrillers (#)—a hitman with a conscience

Not Enough (co-written with Eden Wolfe)—A coming-of-age contemporary fantasy

Published exclusively by Craig Martelle, Inc

OTHER SERIES BY CRAIG MARTELLE

The Dragon's Call by Angelique Anderson & Craig A. Price, Jr.—an epic fantasy quest

A Couples Travels—a non-fiction travel series

Love-Haight Case Files by Jean Rabe & Donald J. Bingle—the dead/undead have rights, too, a supernatural legal thriller

Mischief Maker by Bruce Nesmith—the creator of Elder Scrolls V: Skyrim brings you Loki in the modern day, staying true to Norse Mythology (not a superhero version)

Mark of the Assassins by Landri Johnson—a coming-of-age fantasy.

For a complete list of Craig's books, stop by his website—craigmartelle.com

Printed in Great Britain
by Amazon